It was familiar, it
since Allison had he

She was listening to her father's voice. "Don't you under—Damn it, tell her! You owe me nothing, but you owe *her*."

"Don't tell me how to treat my daughter."

"If they're looking, *they* can find out about the doctor's appointments."

Allison could hear tears and near panic in her mother's voice. "Those were nothing, *nothing*! It was the stress of school. The doctor said that himself. It didn't mean anything. It cleared up right after the visit—"

"Did the doctor know the other possibility?"

There was silence on the line.

"Carol, there's always been the chance."

Allison's mother made a noise. It sounded like a sob.

"If she's a teek, they'll—"

"LEAVE US ALONE!" The yell made Allison drop the phone in shock. Even so, she could still hear her mother yelling. "These people are crazy. Stone's crazy. You're insane, John. They're insane. I'll go to court this time, publicly, if you call me again. I don't care who gets pulled in. And if you come near my daughter, I swear to God, I'll kill you!"

TEEK

STEVEN KRANE

DAW BOOKS, INC.

DONALD A. WOLLHEIM, FOUNDER

375 Hudson Street, New York, NY 10014

ELIZABETH R. WOLLHEIM
SHEILA E. GILBERT
PUBLISHERS

First Printing, August 1999
1   2   3   4   5   6   7   8   9

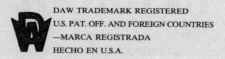

This book is dedicated to Abby, Carrie, Duke, Flynn, Jessica, Key, Tim, Tony and the rest of Rod's fellow alumni

PROLOGUE

TWELVE YEARS AGO   DALLAS, TEXAS

"Please, Carol, let me explain." John's voice took on a pleading tone. Carol knew that tone all too well. John had lost track of other people's feelings again. He was using his "why me" voice.

Carolyn Ann Boyle, for once, felt no twinge of sympathy for him.

"You've had over six years to explain." To avoid looking at him, she grabbed another box from the closet and tossed it on their bed. It nested in a mass of clothing Carol hadn't thought worth packing. She shoved more clothes in the new box. She tore part of a nail as she forced a handful of her underwear in with her old college textbooks. Her hands shook.

"It isn't what you think," he said.

God save us from clichés in moments of crisis, Carol thought.

She glanced at John and felt the familiar sympathy trying to make itself felt. She was supposed to love this man, wasn't she?

John stood at the door of the bedroom, hands spread, framed by the chaos Carol had wrought of their clothing. John didn't belong here, not with his Marine haircut, creased pants, and polished boots. He was too neat, too organized, for a world that was falling apart around her. For too long, it had been easy to look at him and pretend that he could make everything right.

A flare of anger knotted her gut, now as much for herself as for John.

Carol stood there, bra and panties in one hand, lab coat in the other. She couldn't believe that he didn't understand. It was inconceivable that he could be that blind.

Not just blind to the risk he had placed her and Allie into, but blind to the fact that his lies *mattered*. How could he have lied about his connection to Prometheus? How could he have continued that lie for all the years she knew him? How could he do that and claim this was a misunderstanding?

She shoved more underwear in with the textbooks, emptying the pockets of her lab coat after it. "You told me you had no connection to their research." A torn sheet of manila computer paper fell out of one of the coat's pockets amidst scattering pens and paper clips.

Seeing the paper again made Carol's breath catch. That sheet of paper had driven her from the Prometheus Research Institute this afternoon. Her flight had been so panicked that she had left her street clothes and had fled wearing the lab coat. . . .

If John wasn't head of security, Carol supposed PRI would already be looking for their wayward PhD.

"Exactly what am I *supposed* to think?"

"What could I say—"

"You could have said *something*!" Carol shouted as she shoved the paper deep in the box with the clothes and textbooks. She yanked the last item of importance from the lab coat, a flat gray film canister. It sat cold and heavy in her hand. She felt the embossed plastic text on the label. It read "Case #867."

She'd grabbed the film in the rush to get away. She had some idea that she could threaten Prometheus with it if they came after her. Right now the idea seemed small, silly, and useless.

She shoved the film canister into the box so that John couldn't see what it was. She still clutched the lab coat. She'd been carrying it ever since she had begun packing. It was bunched up, but she could still see PRI's eternal flame logo on the right breast. Her ID tag was still clipped to it:

"Prometheus Research Institute: Dr. Carolyn Ann Boyle," next to an incongruously smiling picture.

The tag was green. If it wasn't for Dr. Colson treating her like a delivery girl rather than a researcher, then she wouldn't have been anywhere near a yellow area: if only she wasn't a speed reader; if only Cobb and Charvat weren't names close together in alphabetical order; if only John hadn't lied to her . . .

Carol dropped the lab coat; neither it nor the ID mattered much anymore.

"Something," Carol repeated. "You could have said *something* about this! My God, you knew how I felt."

"But—" John began, but he was interrupted by a cry from behind him.

"Mommy?"

Carol stormed out of the room, shouldering John out of the way. Allie was standing in the doorway, looking as lost as her father did. Carol picked up her daughter and said, "Shh, Mommy's sorry for waking you up."

"Scared me," Allie said into Carol's shoulder. Guilt started clawing into Carol's heart, and she glared at John over Allie's head. "Shh, Mommy's here." She carried Allie back into her bedroom and placed her in bed. *God, can I do this? To both of us? She needs a father.*

Carol kissed Allie on the forehead.

"Can I have a drink of water?" Allie asked.

Carol gave a smile that hurt deep in her chest. "Sure, honey."

As Carol left the bedroom, John was there. Carol ducked around him, heading toward the kitchen. "You can't just leave," John said.

Her hand shook as she filled Allie's glass. "Why not? Why not, John?"

"I love you," John said.

Carol looked into the sink and whispered, "Bullshit."

She heard his voice, but she was seeing the moment when her world had fallen apart.

Dr. Colson had sent her to pick up a video cassette from the lab where they were doing film to video transfers. She had been given a temporary pass into the secure part of the PRI lab complex, just so she could run errands for Colson. They hadn't even allowed her to enter the transfer lab.

She'd waited, alone in an anteroom with all the obsolete junk the PRI complex was in the process of disposing of— acoustic modems, old VTR terminals, a row of teletype machines.

Two cardboard boxes sat by the door. One overflowed with yellowing manila computer paper, the other was filled with old film canisters, both violently marked, "to be destroyed."

It had been a long wait, and curiosity got the better of her. She had glanced in the box of paper to be shredded. Most of the box had been a list of names, a list that she had never expected John Charvat's name to be on.

When she had seen Carol Cobb's name on the same list, she had panicked. She had taken that page from the print-out, and a random film canister. She hadn't known exactly what she'd been doing then, and she still didn't.

All she knew was that John ran security at PRI, and had a red clearance.

"Carol?" John's plea brought her back to the present.

"I said, 'bullshit,' John. If you cared for me and Allie like you cared for your job, you would have told me."

John started to say something, but he just stood there, looking lost again.

"You were just about to tell me how you might lose your job for telling me, right?"

John remained silent.

"I make my point," Carol said. She walked to the door, stopping in front of John. "Would you please step out of my way?"

"You couldn't expect me to—"

Carol backed up a step. "Expect? *Expect!*" Carol threw the glass of water at John's feet. It shattered on the linoleum. "I gave up the idea of marriage so that you could keep your position. You expected me to *defraud* them. I went six months without pay so that you could keep Allie a secret. *I expect too much from* you?"

John limped backward. Some of the damp on his trousers was blood. "Please—" he began.

"Mommy!"

"Mommy's coming, honey," Carol said, shouldering past

John. As she did, John grabbed her elbow. "Let go of me," she said.

"I didn't plan things like this."

"Did *they*?"

"What?"

" 'Did *they*?' I asked. Did Stone and his cronies at Prometheus encourage our relationship?"

John dropped her elbow and looked stunned. "God, is *that* what you think?"

"It's what they do, isn't it? Don't they have a standing bounty for names on their list?"

"Yes, but that's—"

"Your name's on the list, John. You didn't tell me about that."

"I'm sorry, I really am sorry. I didn't think you'd understand. You've never liked that part of PRI. I thought you'd see me as some sort of botched experiment."

"All this time I thought you cared about company policy."

"If we got married, one of us would have to quit—" John said plaintively.

"And what you cared about was the bounty."

"That's not it. You know that's not it."

Carol sighed. "I know, because my name's on the list, too."

John stared at her, disbelieving.

"Mommy," Allie cried in the distance.

"If you don't mind, John. My daughter needs me." Carol walked to Allie's bedroom.

"You can't be . . . ." John whispered behind her.

Allie was sitting up and sobbing in bed, and Carol went and hugged her. *You don't like Mommy angry, I know. I don't like me angry either, kid.*

Carol rocked with Allie cradled in her arms. John appeared in the doorway and said in a whispery voice, "I checked."

"I have more than one name, John. I'm listed under one of my foster families."

"Oh, God," John whispered.

"You honestly didn't know, did you?" Carol looked at him with more pity than anger. He wasn't part of the scientific establishment of Prometheus, he was security. Carol doubted he understood the implications of what she was saying, for either of them, or their daughter. In certain ways, on a genetic level, she and John had been a perfect match.

For her, for John, and especially for Allie, that was very bad.

"I didn't know," John repeated.

Allie seemed to have calmed down, now that the adults had stopped shouting. Carol picked up Allie's favorite stuffed animal from the floor. It was a ratty old Cat-in-the-Hat doll that had come from a garage sale. Allie's four-year-old face broke into a grin the moment Carol produced it. Carol wiped the tears from Allie's cheeks with the back of her hand.

"It's not just you, John. You have to see that."

John nodded.

"You know what's happened with kids at Prometheus. You don't want that for Allie."

"I can't stop you?" John's voice held a resigned tone.

Carol hugged her daughter. "No."

SIX YEARS AGO,   GRAND RAPIDS, MICHIGAN

Jessica Mason watched her house burn. The sight rooted her to the spot even though she knew she should run. She had only moved when pushed aside by firemen and gawking spectators. The crowd had gradually pushed her away from her house until she stood in the snow and could barely feel the heat from the blaze.

She felt invisible. No one recognized her. No one connected her to the burning house. If her neighbors knew her or cared about her at all, it was only as a hysterical voice they heard in the night. They probably knew her father, but not her.

No one knew her, no one cared for her, and her father was the first part of the house to burn. That was probably why she felt safe standing here. That, and the fire had its own power, power to hold her.

She faced a scene of terrifying, potent beauty. The house formed the center of an invisible sphere that had folded in from another world. Inside the circle of spectators and fire trucks, the world upended. The blue-gray of snow and moonlight changed into the red-yellow of mirrors and flame. Water coated every surface with ice. Neighboring clapboards, the sidewalk, a telephone pole, all had turned into refracting mirrors. Every icicle held a flame in its heart.

By the time her head had ceased throbbing enough for her to understand what she was seeing, her house was unrecognizable. The walls, where they were still visible through the flames, were black. In less than ten minutes, the house where she had lived for all thirteen years of her life had faded to nothing more than a shadow. A shadow that was the only barrier between the real world and a force from another universe. A force that Jessica had unleashed.

I did that, she thought.

Her memories were still confused, hazed by the pain in her skull. Too much had happened. All she could clearly remember was the fire embracing her father. She remembered him falling to the couch, igniting it. She remembered him calling desperately for help before the fire sucked the air out of his lungs and turned his skin black.

She remembered the same fire burning inside of her brain.

Jessica remembered thinking of all the times in this house that she had called for help, and no one answered. Then the peeling walls had erupted with sheets of fire, and she ran.

As her mental fires receded, the house began to dissolve. The windows on the top floor were first, folding into the rolling fire with a majestic slowness. The collapse released a million embers to spiral into the sky like negative snowflakes, like something finally set free. . . .

That's me, Jessica thought. *Free.*

Jessica kept watching the fire. She watched well past the point of the fire's death. By the time the flames were gone, and the crowd was reduced to firefighters and police, she was left hugging herself in the cold, waiting to be arrested.

She was paralyzed. Even more so than when her father

had come home and the pain had begun in her skull. It was ridiculous. She was finally free of her father, and she couldn't move. She couldn't even decide between turning herself in to the cops, or just running away into the night.

Now that the crowd was gone, it shouldn't take long for them to figure out that the redheaded teenager with no jacket had something to do with the fire. Jessica hugged herself and shivered.

I don't regret it, she thought. *If the cops pick me up, I'll tell them exactly what I did . . .*

If I can remember what I did.

After her house had become little more than a heaped pile of smoking ash, rejoining the night-gray world, she felt a hand on her shoulder.

"Miss Jessica Mason?"

She turned around, expecting to see a uniform—police, paramedic, or firefighter. But the man talking to her wasn't any of those, at least not to look at him. He was stocky, in his late forties, or early fifties. Older than her father. He was balding, and what hair he had was slate gray. The expensive suit he wore was marred by standing in the snow too long. Abstract salt stains rippled across the legs of his trousers and the lower edge of the black trench coat he wore. His tiepin was a golden bald eagle.

To Jessica, the eagle looked as if it had been caught in the midst of diving after some small mammal.

"Miss Mason?"

"Who are you?" Jessica asked. They were the first words she'd spoken since her father's clothes had ignited. It made her realize that her mouth tasted like smoke.

The man flipped out his wallet to show her an official-looking ID. "Special Agent Fred Jackson, ASI."

The initials meant nothing to Jessica, and Agent Jackson only held out the ID long enough for her to see his picture and catch the fact that ASI stood for "Agency for . . ." something or other.

As far as Jessica was concerned, that meant this guy was a cop. She felt an urge to run, but there were cops and firemen all over the place. There was really no place to run to. She began to realize that she wanted to be caught. She had freed herself from her father, permanently, but she had also destroyed her home, and her life, in the process. Her mother was dead, and she had no relatives to turn to.

She looked up at Agent Jackson. He was smiling, trying to project a reassuring manner. In it she thought she saw a hint of the same false sincerity that her dad projected when he wanted something from her.

It took Jessica a few moments to remind herself that her father was dead. She nodded at Agent Jackson because she didn't trust herself to talk.

Agent Jackson nodded. He obviously knew who she was. He'd probably been watching her watch the fire for a long time. "I'm sorry to come to you at a time like this," Agent Jackson said.

For some reason, that struck Jessica as funny. As if there was any other reason to talk to her. She wasn't anyone. The only thing that made her partway noticeable was the fact she'd torched her only parent and the house she'd lived in. Barely enough to make the news.

Jessica shivered and felt her eyes watering.

"I'm here to help you," he said.

"Yeah, right," Jessica responded, sniffing. She was long past anyone's help. If anyone had ever bothered to help her, her father might still be alive. She didn't want any help.

"We want to help you understand what happened here."

Not a cop, a damn social worker. She tried to fix him with a withering glare. The effect was ruined by the tears streaming down her cheeks. "I know why. I just think of Daddy, and I know why."

Jessica realized, belatedly, that she had just made an indirect admission of arson. She also realized that she didn't care.

Agent Jackson, however, looked unsurprised at her outburst. Either he was too dense to read between the lines, or he already knew what Jessica had done. Jessica looked at him and suspected the latter, even though there was no possible way he could have known.

"You know why," Agent Jackson said. "Do you know how?"

Jessica opened her mouth, but no words came out. It wasn't the question she expected. It was also a question to which she had no answer. She remembered her anger, she remembered Daddy's clothing sprouting a dozen jets of flame, she could remember that she had done it—

But she didn't remember what she had done, or the memory didn't make any sense. She knew she had set him on fire, but she didn't remember touching him, or even so much as lighting a match.

The fact that this stranger saw so deeply into her own confusion was terrifying.

"We want to help you, Jessica. We know what you're going through."

Jessica was frightened, but she also had an intense desire to understand what this man was offering. The fact he knew so much scared her. But it also meant he probably knew more.

She had done something to her father. She was just beginning to understand that it might not have been anything simple or mundane. She had watched her house explode into an inferno in a matter of minutes. She had watched the walls of the living room spontaneously erupt into rippling sheets of flame.

Maybe understanding exactly what happened was the only way she could prevent it in the future. She looked at the smoking ruin of the house, remembering the power of the flames that had reduced everything to ash.

Maybe understanding exactly what happened would be the only way she could do it again.

Jessica looked up at Agent Jackson. "What do you want?" she asked.

CHAPTER ONE

"Please, David. Do something about him." Allison Boyle spoke in a harsh whisper. She hated the pleading sound in her own voice. It had been nearly an hour since Chuck Wilson had crashed the party, and it had taken that long for Allison to work up the courage to talk to David.

"Allie," David's voice had a nasal whine to it which was only made worse by the art-deco Darth Vader mask he wore. "I really don't want to start a scene with the guy."

"It's *your* party," Allison lowered her voice even further, because she saw Chuck weaving in from the kitchen. He was hard to miss. He was at least a year older than everyone else, and wasn't wearing even an attempt at a costume. "You didn't even invite him."

"People show up." David lowered his own voice to a point that was barely audible. "Allie, my folks don't know about the party. If I just ask him to leave . . ." David glanced over his shoulder. Chuck stood by the rear wall of the dining room. He had an arm up to the elbow in the cooler sitting there. He fished out a can of beer, grimaced at the label, and opened it anyway.

". . . he hasn't disrupted anything." David finished.

"He's disrupting *me*."

"Has he done anything—" David made a helpless gesture with his hand, rustling the black cape he wore. "Anything?" he repeated uncertainly.

Allison wrung the tail of her costume in her hands. "No," she said. *Nothing real.* "But he scares me."

David exhaled. He sounded relieved. "At times he scares me, too. But he's behaving himself. If I start something with him—" David shook his head. "I know the police would get involved. If he didn't kill me, my parents would."

Allison nodded and backed away. "I understand," she said.

As usual, David's chivalrous instants hit him a little belatedly. "Allie, if you really want me to—"

She shook her head, "Never mind."

"If he does start up—"

"Yeah, sure. Thanks, David." Allison backed into the living room, still wringing her tail.

Why did Chuck have to show up?

She found a safe corner to back into so she could watch everyone else enjoy themselves. She'd been looking forward to this party for weeks. However, right now, she wanted to be anywhere else. Another house, another city, another planet. All because of Chuck Wilson.

She hugged herself and shivered.

The way she felt made her disgusted with herself. Chuck had never even done anything to her. Nothing *real*. Nothing anyone would understand. He had a perfect right to hang around the school yard, right? If she saw him in the corner of McDonald's or at a movie theater, that was just coincidence, right? There was no rule that said he had to use a different mall.

But when she caught him staring at her, she felt hideously naked.

And she couldn't get someone arrested for *staring* at her.

Calm down, Allie, she thought to herself. *You're going to freak out and give yourself a migraine. If it bothers you that much, you can just leave.*

She shook her head. That would be giving in, and she didn't like giving in. She hadn't given in to the headaches, and she wasn't going to give in to Chuck. Besides, she had spent too much time on her tiger costume—even though the leotard that made up most of it helped her feel even more naked around Chuck.

Someone tapped her shoulder and she jumped, knocking her fake nose and whiskers askew.

A tall, black Princess Leia looked down on her and asked, "Cat got your tongue?"

"Very funny, Macy." Allison dropped the tail of her costume to straighten her nose. She looked up at Macy, a fair distance since Macy was probably the tallest girl in the entire sophomore class of Euclid Heights High School. "You nearly scared the fur off of me."

"That'd be a show."

"Ha. Ha."

"So why're you wedged in a corner instead of joining the party? You missed Ben putting some candy corn and a can of beer through his nose—"

"I'm not in the mood, Macy."

"Chuck?"

Allison nodded.

"He didn't do—"

Allison put her hand to her forehead and tried to push back the throbbing she felt there. "No. He didn't *do* anything."

Macy stepped back at Allison's tone. "Sorry."

Allison shook her head. "It isn't your fault." She sighed. "I just got through talking to David."

"Ah-ha."

Allison looked up. "Ah-ha, what?"

"Nothing—"

"You meant something by that."

"Chill, girl." Macy backed away, holding up her hands and smiling.

"Yeah," Allison nodded violently. "You should talk. You go with a guy who puts *corn* through his nose. Why I—" Allison's voice trailed off with a strangled gurgle.

"Allie?"

Allison felt her breath knocked out by the headache even before the pain hit her. She managed to whisper, "All . . . right," before the first wave of agony ground into her temples. Then her eyes watered, and colored rings began sprouting from every light source in her field of vision.

"Like hell," Macy said.

Allison could feel an arm groping for her and she grabbed it. "Bathroom," she managed to whisper.

The headache was a hot iron band strapped over her skull, squeezing in time to her pulse. Even as the fire in her skull made her cry, she thanked God that it wasn't one of the bad ones.

Dimly, she heard Macy yelling, "Make way, make way—the lady's going to hurl. Move it. Move it."

Macy maneuvered her up the stairs, through a crowd of costumed teenagers. Witches, vampires, spacemen, and soldiers blurred into an amorphous mass of sound and color. Allison still had enough mind left to be embarrassed at the scene she was making. Then the pain flared again and all she could concentrate on was not falling over.

She barely noticed the crashing sounds behind her.

Macy got her to the bathroom and knelt her over the toilet. Allison blinked at the blue water in the bowl. It rippled into colors that made her eyes hurt as badly as her head. "Alone," she managed to say.

Her nose—whiskers and all—fell into the toilet, splashing blue drops on her face.

"Girl, I don't think—"

"Please. Leave." It took all of Allison's breath to say those two words.

After an eternal pause she heard Macy back up and the door close.

She started hyperventilating into the toilet—deep gasping breaths. She tried to clamp down on the pain by force of will. The effort screwed her eyes shut.

She pulled herself upright, one hand clamped on the sink. She swayed and almost fell over. With a shaking hand she pulled open the medicine cabinet, spilling a bag of cotton balls, an open box of Q-tips, and a plastic cup filled with Band-Aids.

She cursed David's parents as she knocked aside antacids, prescription bottles, bunion pads, cough medicine—

Aspirin, Advil, Tylenol, Motrin—please, something.

She managed to find a bottle of generic headache medicine behind a bottle of Peptol Bismol. The Peptol Bismol fell into the sink as she tried to fumble open the childproof cap on the aspirin.

She accidentally ate part of the cotton batting as she dry-swallowed a handful of pills.

She gagged and sat down on the tile floor. The pain made her dizzy. She leaned her back against the door and closed her eyes. Red flashes shot across the inside of her eyelids in time to her pulse. After a while, she heard a knock on the door and, "How you doing, girl?"

"Fine, Macy." Allison spoke while moving as little as possible.

"No 911?"

"No. Go watch Ben put something through his nose."

"You'll be all right?"

"I'll survive. Join the party."

It was a few moments before she heard Macy's steps recede down the stairs. The pain was becoming bearable. That's how she'd learned to deal with the headaches, sit still, breathe, wait for the painkiller to kick in.

At least their frequency was diminishing.

She didn't know which was worse, the headaches or Chuck. Both were responsible for her godawful attendance during the start of the school year. Both were something that she wouldn't be able to make anyone understand. She'd been to the doctor twice for these headaches and—supposedly—nothing was wrong.

Her mother thought that the headaches had been psychosomatic, some sort of stress. Something that showed that Allison couldn't deal with school.

Allison wouldn't admit that.

That was why she couldn't talk to her mom about Chuck. It would be an admission to her mother that she couldn't handle herself. She never again wanted to hear the condescending tone she'd heard from her mother after the second visit to the doctor, "What's the *real* problem?"

The question made Allison want to scream.

Since then, Allison had kept her headaches to herself, spending too much of her allowance on Tylenol, Advil, Motrin, even Midol. Unfortunately, that meant she now had over a dozen unexcused absences on her record that Mom didn't know about. All in less than two months. Her teachers, according to school policy, had the right to flunk her for that alone.

Allison still didn't know what she was going to do when report cards came out. Her mother would freak.

"The doctor didn't find anything *wrong*," Allison said, tears streaming down her cheeks.

Allison sat in David's bathroom long enough to tell four people to go away. None of them was David. Allison didn't know whether or not she was grateful for that. She didn't want to admit that her feelings toward David were changing. They'd been together since they'd started high school. But in the last two years she'd changed, and David had stayed David.

I don't need to be thinking about this.

Allison opened her eyes and found that the light in the bathroom wasn't painful any more. As she pulled herself upright, she saw the mess she'd made of David's parents' bathroom. She felt deeply guilty. Band-Aids and Q-tips had scattered all over the floor. Bottles filled the sink and spilled on the ground. Worst was the Peptol Bismol, which had come open, slashing thick pink liquid over the sink, mirror, and wall. She looked down on herself and was surprised to find that her costume was unviolated.

She pushed the fading headache from her mind as she did her best to repair the damage she'd wrought. Cleaning the mess ended up being easier than figuring out how all this stuff had fit in the medicine cabinet in the first place. She ended up tossing out the Q-tips and the nearly-empty Peptol Bismol bottle to make room for everything else.

She hoped David's parents wouldn't notice.

She finished by cleaning herself up.

Between losing the nose, blue water stains, and smudging from the palm of her hand, she had to wash off the makeup on her face. It took a while to remove the black-and-yellow stripes. In the end, all that was left of her costume above the neck was a pair of black ears peaking out from her blonde hair.

There were red rims around her eyes, but it didn't look like she'd been crying.

She grimaced and fished her nose out of the toilet. She wrapped it in toilet paper and promised herself that she'd disinfect the thing before Halloween came around.

She opened the door and peeked outside. The party was still going on downstairs. She could hear it. It sounded like a lot fewer people though. She caught a glimpse of a clock through a bedroom door. It read eleven-thirty.

I was in there two hours?

"Time flies when you're having fun," she muttered.

Someone had posted a note on the bathroom door. It read "Do not disturb," and had a crude cartoon of a cat with its head in a toilet. Allison ripped it off the door and crumpled it up. She was never going to hear the end of this. She never should have come to this party.

She hoped Macy hadn't left without her. She didn't want to walk home the way she was dressed.

Allison caught up with Macy, next to the nachos in the living room. Most of the party seemed to have gone, the food mostly untouched. "Where's everybody?" she asked.

Macy turned around, looking surprised. "Allie, where've you—"

"Bathroom."

"I thought you left. What'd you do, fall in?"

Allison sighed.

"How you feel?" Macy asked.

"Better, I think. I want to go home and lie down."

"Sure thing. Let me get my coat— "

Allison looked at the uneaten food. "What happened to the party?"

Macy shrugged. "I'm not quite sure. Apparently a table full of food upended about the time I was helping you upstairs—"

Allison nodded. She could picture David's reaction, especially now that she saw all the stains on the carpet. The whole costume party was beginning to seem like a less than great idea all around. "Where's David? I should say good-bye."

"I think he's sulking in the kitchen. Is your coat in the bedroom?"

She tossed Macy her nose. "Yeah, and would you put this in my purse?"

"Ah—sure." Macy wrinkled her nose at the blue-stained toilet paper and said, "I ain't even going to ask."

Allison shook her head and started for the kitchen. There

were still some people left, chatting quietly. Presumably they were uninvolved with the table incident.

Poor David.

He didn't deserve to have his party collapse around him, even if he could be, at times, what Macy unkindly referred to as a "prime-quality wuss." Allison sighed. She didn't like thinking badly about David.

She was weaving past a sheeted ghost, toward the kitchen, when an arm appeared to block her way. She was brought up short and turned to see Chuck Wilson grinning at her.

Oh, God.

"Hiya, sweetcakes. Wondering where you went to."

Instinctively, she backed away and hugged her arms to herself. Chuck had managed to slip between her and everyone else. His jeans were rolled up over combat boots. He wore a wide leather belt with a brass Marlboro buckle. Hanging off the belt was a chain for his wallet and a sheath for a buck knife. He wore a red flannel lumberjack shirt that was rolled up to the elbows. He chugged the can he held in the hand that wasn't blocking her way.

"Don't want to miss you without a hello."

"Sure," she said. She tried not to appear frightened, even though she knew it was futile. The best she could do was look him in the eyes, and even *that* felt as if she had to fight invisible weights chained to her neck. "You've said hello."

He was only a foot away from her. She could smell beer and sweat. No one else seemed to notice them. There could have been half a dozen people in the dining room, but she still felt terribly alone.

Don't let him touch me. Please, don't let him touch me.

Chuck had her cornered by the cooler. She could've ducked under his arm, but that would have meant brushing by him, in a leotard that felt more and more like it was only painted on.

"Come on, sweetcakes. You gotta know I like you."

Please go away.

Chuck bent to get another can out of the cooler. He had to reach across her, backing her into the corner. Allison was on the verge of panicking. Chuck's right hand was on the doorframe in front of her, his other was reaching around behind her. Her back was pressed to the wall, and she felt a light switch digging between her shoulder blades. His face couldn't be more than three or four inches from her own. His breath smelled of alcohol.

"You don't know how special you are, sweetcakes."

She could feel his hand rummaging in the cooler. The plastic jostled against her thigh and she felt drops of water splashing on her leg.

"We should get to know each other—"

Chuck was moving his right hand, away from the doorframe. She didn't know if he was going to use it to touch her hair, grab her shoulder, or help him fish for beer—but it gave her an opening.

As she ducked around Chuck, her back brushed the light switch and the lights in the dining room went out. Someone on the far side of the room distinctly said, "Shit," as he tripped over something.

"Where you going?" Chuck said.

Allison felt a tug on the tail of her costume. It felt like the fabric was tied directly to her heart. For a moment she couldn't breathe. She stood there, frozen, until she felt something brush the lower curve of her behind.

The feeling, knowing it was Chuck's hand, made her want to vomit. Pain flowered behind her eyes again, and she could almost see his hand. She screwed her eyes shut and tried to pull away, and this time it felt like the tail was tied directly to the middle of her brain. When she heard it tear, it almost felt as if it was her spinal cord, and not the fabric, that gave way.

However, the fabric was what ripped, and suddenly she was free and in a stumbling run toward the living room.

She turned to face the dining room in time to see someone turn on the lights. Chuck was on the floor. The cooler had upended, drenching him with gallons' worth of melted ice and broken beer bottles. In his left hand he held the remains of her costume's tail, as well as about two square feet of her leotard.

She felt a breeze behind her, and her face began to heat up.

She backed away from the scene, grateful that Chuck

was the center of attention. She kept backing until she bumped into Macy descending the stairs.

"What the hell happened?" Macy asked.

They were out of sight of the dining room now, but she could hear Chuck yelling, David yelling, everyone else laughing. Her cheeks burned hotter, and she realized that she was crying uncontrollably.

Allison took her jacket from Macy and wrapped it around her waist to cover the hole in the rear of her leotard.

"Allie?"

Allison wiped her eyes and said, "I want to go home."

CHAPTER
TWO

Chuck Wilson felt like shit. He was drunk, damp, and clutching a paper bag containing a forty-ounce bottle of Colt 45 whose origins were lost in the fog of his memory. Worst of all, his head was throbbing again and the beer was barely able to keep the pain at bay.

He'd been wandering the empty streets of Euclid Heights since he'd left that geek David Greenbaum's party. *David-fucking-Greenbaum.* The guy was a high-pitched squealing twerp who wouldn't be worth the effort to grind into the pavement—

If it wasn't for the fact he was Allison Boyle's boyfriend. "What a match."

Chuck shook his head, and the gesture ignited the pain behind his temples. He raised the bottle to his lips and found it empty.

"Fuck!"

He threw the bottle, paper bag and all, at a stop sign. The bottle shattered. Foamy glass flew everywhere, one splinter biting his cheek.

Belatedly, as the sign's gong echoed into the darkness, he looked around for cops. Fortunately, now that the bars were closed, the streets were vacant. No witnesses except for an idling van far down the street from him.

He exhaled in relief and wiped his cheek. His fingers came away beaded with blood.

No cops was good. A tangle with the Euclid Heights

Gestapo was something he didn't need. He already had one
DUI this year, and had managed to get his car impounded
and his license suspended. The cops in this town were really
into harassing him.

Now that he was eighteen, once one of the local Nazis
got a hold of him, he'd be in serious trouble.

"Ah, never happen."

He took a step and bumped into the stop sign.

"Boy am I fucked up," he said to no one in particular.

He staggered back, holding on to the pole. A sliver of
glass ground into his middle finger.

"Shit."

He got back on to the sidewalk, sucking the wound.

As he stumbled down the darkened street, he wondered
when, exactly, his life started going to shit. It was a drunk
question, and it didn't really have an answer. Life and shit
had been equivalent terms for as long as he could
remember. . . .

The headaches and what they brought had only confirmed Chuck's opinion of the universe.

In fact, if there was a God, the only break He'd given
Chuck was a girl named Allison Boyle. And, like usual,
that had gone balls-up with everything else. He knew four
girls who'd go down on him if he just said the word—or at
least bought enough beer—and *the one* turned out to be
some uptight ice-bitch.

Chuck thought about the cooler upending and it was almost funny.

Why her?

Chuck stumbled out into the middle of the empty street
and yelled at the sky, *"Why her, you bastard! Haven't you
fucked enough with my head?"* His words drifted skyward
on a wisp of fog. Above him, a single stoplight flashed on
and off, rocking gently on the wind.

I'm asking to get busted, ain't I?

Chuck looked around for cops again. All he saw was
empty houses and empty streets. No cars were left on the
curb. Euclid Heights ticketed them after three in the
morning.

As he glanced around, one of the streetlights fractured

into concentric rainbows. He felt a spike drive into his forebrain—

<<**breathing, heavy rapid breathing.**>>

Chuck grabbed his temples to try and force the thoughts back.

<<**warmth. sheets damp with sweat and fresh semen.**>>

"I don't want to know," he whispered.

<<**gut hanging over milk-white thighs. slack penis in a bony hand. sense of exhaustion. magazine slipping from left hand. the picture is of two young men giving each other blow jobs.**>>

Chuck wanted to throw up.

The beer was a refuge, but sometimes it played traitor, making it hard to push such alien thoughts back. Even as he managed to push the other mind out of his own, he knew where it came from. It was a lit window, shades drawn, across the street from him.

Before he'd gathered the pieces of his brain back together, a pickup, the back filled with kids, blared its horn and swerved around him, barely slowing. Chuck jumped back as someone tossed an empty can at him.

He gave the finger to its shrinking taillights. "Shit-eating fuckheads!"

Chuck wanted to gut one of the motherfuckers. Cut one of those fuckheads bad—

He realized that the middle-aged fag was out of his head. Chuck breathed a sigh of relief. That had been a bad one. So bad that it left a sour taste in his mouth. He found himself rubbing his hands on his pants, as if he could wipe away the memory of . . .

"Ignore it," he mumbled. "Forget it. Sleep it off."

Chuck stumbled off, down the street. He had long ago figured he had gone a little nuts. Voices in your head, that was a sure sign you were psycho. The voices had been in Chuck's skull ever since he was thirteen—nasty, ugly voices.

Worse than the voices was the fact that Chuck had to believe them. They were always right. And anyone who thought he could see into someone else's melon was a candidate for the nut factory. He'd been trying to shut out the images for years now, and the effort was turning him into a drunk and a half-assed junkie.

In all the time since other minds had begun forcing their
way into his own, he had found only one reliable way to
shut them out. Somehow, for some reason, when he hung
around Allison Boyle, the voices shut up.

And she had to be a stuck-up bitch—

Well, she wasn't going to be rid of him that easily.

Chuck staggered home. He was too drunk to notice the
van following him.

17 OCTOBER   EUCLID HEIGHTS, OHIO

04:17 AM   SUNDAY

Allison raced to get to school. She was late for Mr.
Counter's class and she desperately needed to deliver this
history paper. She was horrendously late. When she got
there, she discovered that somehow she had missed the rest
of the semester and it was time for finals. She pushed into
the classroom and took her seat in the front of the class.

Behind the desk sat Chuck Wilson. He wore Counter's
white sideburns and tweed coat, but the stare was Chuck's.
Allison felt panic when she began to realize that she had
been so rushed to get to school that she was only wearing
a bra and panties.

"No talking during the exam," Chuck said, gaze fixed on
her chest. "If I see anyone peeking, I'll kick you out. Turn
your paper over when I tell you, not before."

Allison realized she was the only other person in the
room. Even though the voice was Mr. Counter's, the leer
was all Chuck's.

"Begin," Chuck/Counter said.

The phone rang.

Allison stirred at the sound, thankful for being drawn
out of the dream. She'd reached over and grabbed the
phone off the nightstand before she was fully awake.

She raised the handset to her ear and said a muffled,
"Hello?" She was talking into her pillow. She rubbed her
eyes and untangled herself from her comforter. In the pro-

cess she dropped the phone. She had to hunt down the handset in the dark.

Who's calling at this hour?

All she could think of was that it had to be for Mom, and after dropping the handset she'd probably made them hang up.

She saw a green glow peeking out of a wrinkle in her comforter and she fished under it until she uncovered the handset with its glowing buttons.

What'd you expect? she thought at the caller as she looked at her alarm clock. *It's four in the morning in bright red glowing numbers.*

Allison expected a dial tone by now, but instead, as she raised the phone to her ear she heard her mother saying, *"—dare you call me here!"*

It *was* for Mom.

There was a man on the other end. He was saying something like, "They're looking for a teak out there—"

Allison was torn between a desire for sleep and a morbid curiosity.

"I don't care what they're doing at the Institute. That's been over for a long time. You have no right calling me here."

"Damn it. You mentioned headaches. Don't you think—"

"Good-bye." Allison heard the phone click, and she could hear the phone slam downstairs. After a pause, a dial tone began to sound through her phone. She unfroze and scrambled to get it back on the cradle before the line began beeping.

When she heard her mother pound up the steps, she pulled the comforter over herself. She shouldn't be listening in on other people's phone calls. Especially her mother's.

However, with the mention of headaches, she had a sneaking suspicion that she had eavesdropped on a conversation about her. Allison couldn't make heads or tails of the possibility—other than that it had ticked off her mother—and eventually she fell back to sleep.

CHAPTER
THREE

"Cheer up, girl," Macy grabbed Allison by the shoulder, causing her to raise her head. She had been staring at a Butterfinger Blizzard that was slowly turning into soup. "You aren't still upset about the party? Are you?"

Allison shook her head and tried to put a good face on it by eating some of her Blizzard. After a few bites, a subliminal throbbing behind her temples told her that Dairy Queen hadn't been the best of ideas. "Sorry I'm such a lump, Macy. I've been in a rotten mood all week."

Macy nodded. "Why do you think I dragged you out to the mall on a Tuesday?"

Allison set down the melting ice cream and looked around the food court. It wasn't filled like it'd be on the weekend, but there were the obligatory groups staking out their territory. Here a collection of jocks after football practice, there a collection of black-clad Goth types trying to look like something out of an Anne Rice movie . . .

No one she knew from Heights High, which was something of a relief. If she'd had her way, she'd be moping all by herself, without Macy.

"Thanks for trying." Allison's voice was distant as she stared past Macy toward the entrance where the sky was purpling beyond the glass doors into the food court. If she tried, she could just make out the neon reflected in the parked cars outside.

I don't want to be here, she thought to herself—and "here" meant more than the mall. It meant Euclid Heights, Heights High, home, everything. . . .

Macy was saying something.

"What?" Allison asked. Her gaze remained fixed on the shadows of the parking lot.

"Would it be too much to ask you to stay on this planet?"

"I was thinking," Allison said. "What was it?"

"I asked you, what's up with you and David?"

Allison looked down at the floor. "Nothing . . ." She turned around and stirred the Blizzard with her spoon. It was two thirds full and almost completely melted now. "Why do you think there's something up?"

"The fact that he spends more time with me and Ben than he does with you now?"

"I haven't been feeling all that great, okay?" Allison made a face at her Blizzard and stood up and walked over to the trash cans.

Macy got up and followed her. When Allison chucked the melted mess into the garbage, Macy frowned and folded her arms. "Well that's a news flash— The Allie I know wouldn't throw away two bucks' worth of Dairy Queen if things were okay—"

Allison sighed. "What's between me and David isn't your business."

Macy walked up and put an arm around her. "Get real, when'd we start keeping secrets from each other?"

Allison looked up into Macy's face with the intention of telling her to bug off, but the look of concern on her face was too genuine for Allie to do it.

A boy in a pair of shredded jeans pushed his way to the trash can behind Allison. There were half a dozen unoccupied trash receptacles, but for some reason—probably the proximity of two girls—he'd decided to use this one to dump his tray of Taco Bell wrappings.

The tray followed the wrappings into the garbage and the guy turned around and made it obvious. He looked at the two of them, smiled, and said, "Hey."

Macy made a disgusted sound.

Allison couldn't bring herself to say anything. He was

barely a year older, and he had his nose, left eyebrow, and his lower lip pierced. They were just small silver rings, but the thought of it made her shudder.

"You wanna party?"

The guy said it with such deadpan earnestness that Allison could hear Macy snicker. Allison sucked in a breath but couldn't stop it. She started laughing. It started as a small giggle, but before she'd raised her hand to cover her mouth her entire body was shaking. The giggle fit was contagious, and in a moment Macy was laughing as loud as she was. Allison tried to control herself, and she could feel her face flushing with embarrassment. But she couldn't stop, especially when the guy's expression showed that this wasn't anywhere near the reaction he was aiming for.

Macy steered her away, toward the entrance, and Allison caught sight of what had to be this guy's friends by the Taco Bell. They all wore abused jeans and black T-shirts advertising metal bands. They were also in the midst of their own laughing jag, which made Allison laugh even harder.

As they pushed through the glass doors to the food court. Allison heard the guy's voice behind them. "What're you? A couple of lesbos?"

Macy shouted back, "One look at that face makes me seriously consider it!"

The door closed behind them, and Allison stumbled out into the parking lot. She was actually gasping now, no longer laughing. She had begun hyperventilating, and she was in the light-headed throes of an oncoming migraine.

Macy was still laughing until she had caught up with Allison where she stood, doubled over, hands on her knees.

"Allie?"

"I'll be fine," Allison said between gasps. "I just have to catch my breath."

"Can you believe that guy?" Macy asked, rubbing Allison's shoulder.

Allison shook her head.

"His face could set off a metal detector."

Allison nodded.

"Are you sure you're all right?"

Allison pushed herself upright. The wind felt as if it was

biting into her temples, but she told Macy, "I'm fine." She turned to look back toward the mall entrance. "I kind of feel bad about laughing like that—"

"Sometimes I don't believe you." Macy shook her head in disgust, grabbed Allison's arm and started dragging her toward where her sister's car was parked. "You can't feel sorry for that guy. He copped the clumsiest feel of the millennium and hit us with a line so moldy I don't know if he was offering a joint or tickets to a Grateful Dead concert."

Macy stopped next to the car and looked at Allison.

Allison's head throbbed a little, enough to let her know that later on tonight she would be clutching her head and trying to smother herself with her pillow. Still she forced a smile.

"You look like hell, girl."

The smile collapsed. "Thanks."

"Just worried about you."

Allison nodded and patted Macy's arm. "Thanks, really. But I don't know what you can do."

Macy grabbed her hand and said. "So what *is* up with you and David?"

"Nothing," Allison said.

After Macy let go, Allison continued. "Totally, completely and absolutely— Nothing." She shook her head. "I don't know, but when I talk to him, it's like, sometimes, I'm talking straight through him. As if nothing sinks through, takes hold. It's like he doesn't hear the same words I do." She shook her head. "Sometimes I think he's afraid of me."

"That's rough."

"I mean, I can't tell him what's going on in my life, because every time he thinks something's wrong he goes into paralysis mode—" Allison looked back at the mall. "Can you picture him back there just now, with metal head?"

"I see what you mean—"

"Let's get out of here." Allison walked carefully around the car and let herself in the passenger side. She rubbed her temples.

"So is that it?" Macy asked as she got in the car. "You and David. Is that what's got you in the dumpster?"

Allison shook her head. "He doesn't have anything to do with the way I feel."

Not for a long time now, she thought.

"Is it the party?" Macy asked.

Allison nodded slightly but said, "No."

"I thought that once you got a little distance from it, you'd realize how silly Chuck looked."

"I don't want to talk about it right now."

"Come on, you don't think the guy will mess with you after—"

"Not. Now." Allison spoke through gritted teeth. Macy must have heard the seriousness in her voice, since they didn't say anything more until the car pulled up in front of Allison's house.

As Allison got out, Macy asked, "Are you really going to be all right?"

Allison nodded.

"No problems, like between you and your mom?"

The question startled her, and Allison looked back at Macy. "What makes you ask—of course not."

Macy looked relieved. "I didn't think so. But I know, that's the kind of problem that gets you. Hard to escape from . . ."

"Well don't worry about *that.*"

"If you ever do need to get away from that kind of problem—you got my help." Macy reached across the seat and pulled shut the passenger door. "Got to get the car back before *my* family thinks I ran away with it. See you tomorrow?"

"Sure."

Allison watched as Macy drove away.

Problems between her and Mom. That was ridiculous. . . .

CHAPTER
FOUR

By the end of the week Allison had, for the most part, recovered from the party. All the whispering she'd overheard had been about Chuck's header into the beer cooler. No one seemed to be talking about her part in the episode.

Even so, her gaze kept scanning the school yard as she walked home with Macy. It was a paranoid reaction, but she couldn't help it.

And—in response to her paranoia—there he was, leaning against the wall of the South Gym. As she and Macy rounded the football field, Allison couldn't take her attention off of him. Chuck's eyes held hers like a magnet.

"Stop looking," Macy said with a resigned tone. "You'll only encourage him."

Allison yanked her gaze away from the side of the gym and hugged the backpack in her arms closer to her chest.

"He still scares me," she said. She whispered the words as if Chuck could hear her from across the football field.

She *knew* that Chuck Wilson had been watching her— no, he'd been *staring* at her—since she'd walked outside. *Had he been loitering there, all last period?* She wondered. *Just for me?*

"Allie, look out!"

Allison turned toward Macy just in time to realize she'd strayed off the sidewalk. She pulled herself up short just too late to avoid colliding with a tree. She didn't fall, but she dropped her backpack and her books went everywhere.

She staggered back and looked at her history textbook. It had spilled from her backpack and was spread open before her, flapping its pages in the wind.

Allison looked from the textbook to Macy's face. The concerned look in her best friend's eyes made Allison mutter, "I'm fine." She bent to retrieve her backpack and her history textbook. The book closed against the wind as she reached for it, but a twinge behind her temples kept her from noticing.

"No, you're not, girl." Macy looked back, over her shoulder. Their view of the gym was now hidden by the bleachers flanking the football field. No Chuck in sight. "He still hasn't done nothing. Has he?"

She shook her head and tried to let go of the paranoia that clutched at her. "No, not since the party," Allison said, slipping most of her books back into her backpack and slinging the pack over her shoulder. Her history text she hugged to her chest.

"Then he's off of it, right?"

Allison nodded vigorously and started down the sidewalk, forcing herself to watch ahead of her feet. "I'm just being paranoid."

Macy matched her stride easily. "This is really freaking you. Maybe you should tell someone—"

"No."

"You could talk to your mother—"

"No!" Allison winced at the sound of her own voice. "I just have a morbid imagination, that's all. Can we change the subject?"

Macy made a dissatisfied grunt. "Okay." After a few moments she asked, "You have the paper for Mr. Counter yet?"

"Ugh!" Allison said. "Don't remind me."

"What? You trying to flunk history, girl? He don't like your attendance already—"

"I'll get it done."

"Ten pages by Monday? He'll dock you a letter just for your attitude."

Allison sighed. "So what?"

They crossed the intersection behind the high school and walked down Grant.

Euclid Heights High was mired in a suburban commercial district like a fly in amber. A few houses congregated in the gaps between the intersections, but the areas around the major streets were hives of commerce. Some—mostly fast food places—served the high school students. Others—mostly the bars—served the college students who overran the eastern suburbs this close to John Caroll and Case Western Reserve University. The rest of the shops—like the BMW dealership and the Thai restaurant Allison and Macy were passing—served the middle class population that lived farther east of the city.

For some reason it all depressed Allison.

As they passed the BMW lot, the sun gleamed so intensely off the accumulated windshields that Allison thought she should see circling buzzards in the reflection.

"Ahem," said Macy.

Allison turned around and saw Macy standing a few steps behind her, tapping her foot. Allison felt guilty again. "I'm sorry. What did you say?"

Macy turned her head up at the sky as if to say, "What am I going to do with you, girl?" Instead she asked, "Have you at least done the reading?"

"Ah . . ."

"Counter's going to spaz." Macy stepped up and gripped Allison's shoulder. "You've got guts if you even show up on Monday."

Allison shrugged. What was done was done. "I'll do what I can over the weekend."

"That's half the class. I'd forget about it and sneak an extra lunch period the rest of the semester."

As they walked down Grant, Allison shook her head. "It hasn't been my fault. I won't give up like that."

"Counter'll look at the attendance sheet and flunk you anyway."

"I don't care."

Macy shrugged. "I don't understand you."

They walked a block and a half in silence, passing a convenience store. Sometimes Allison didn't understand herself. What Macy said was tempting. With her godawful attendance, it would seem a lot simpler to give up and count the semester a loss.

She was running flat out, and she was still losing ground. What was the point of it? She knew, already, that she'd be lucky to pull a passing GPA this semester. For sure she'd be going to summer school. She'd be lucky to graduate on time the way things were going.

If she relaxed and stopped pushing, the picture would only be slightly worse.

But it would be giving in.

Fortunately, her headaches were diminishing. Since the party she hadn't had any bad ones. This had been her first week of perfect attendance this year.

The fact that her skull was ceasing its unexplained throbbing should have buoyed her through anything. But she found herself depressed, under siege from a load of neglected homework and eviscerated academic prospects.

Not to mention Chuck.

"Hey," Macy said. "Cheer up."

Allison looked her friend in the eye and asked, "Why?"

"I tell you they left me back in sixth grade?"

"Huh?"

"End of the world, girl! They pinned a note to my sweater, big red letters. Mama cried. Dad creamed me. Six kids and none of them, not even Russell, had been left back in grade school."

Macy spread her hands and looked down at Allison. "Today, does it matter? See my point?"

"Yeah, I suppose I do."

"Good." They'd reached the intersection where they usually parted ways. Macy squeezed Allison's shoulder and started down her own street. "Don't kill yourself," she called back.

"I don't plan to," Allison said.

As Allison walked home, her morbid introspection began to diminish.

It was Friday, she was free of Euclid High for the rest of the weekend, and that thought helped her get over her funk. It was a beautiful day, the sky blue, the sun shining, and the air so cool and clean that it crinkled at the edges. After a while she was kicking her way through mounds of raked leaves, humming an Indigo Girls tune and surprising herself with exactly how good she did feel the farther she walked from school.

She still couldn't help thinking about her history project as she walked down the hill. Ten pages comparing the French and American Revolutions. Ten pages in a single weekend.

Once she thought past the oppressiveness of Counter's history class, she admitted she could do it. Half the job was making the paper literate, and no matter how many classes she'd missed, she had her classmates beat in that area. Over the summer she had managed to write ten chapters of a romance novel. It was a horrible romance novel that embarrassed her deeply, but against those hundred pages or so, ten seemed no big obstacle, especially when half the grade was spelling and punctuation.

It was close to four when she got home. By now she was smiling and had almost convinced herself to dig the novel out of the closet and make an attempt to finish it. She had decided against it because there was no way she could do anything on top of Counter's paper this weekend, and— more important—she had stopped writing in the middle of a steamy sex scene that she had never finished.

She blushed slightly whenever she thought about it. *Restless Nights* would wait a little longer.

Instead, she planned out the paper. She could probably get by on common knowledge and common sense. Counter's class was bonehead history, and if she got the grammar and the dates right, he'd have to pass it.

She *would* have to fudge the bibliography a bit—

Rhett and Scarlett, two thirds of the feline population of the house, attacked Allison as soon as she let herself in. Scarlett butted her ankles and purred while Rhett jumped on a chair by the door, the better to nose into Allison's backpack as she unshouldered it. When Allison put the pack down, Rhett's black form managed to disappear entirely into it, spilling books and notebook paper.

Allison didn't put down the history text that she'd clutched to her chest all the way home. The muse was upon her and, if she struck now, she might be able to crank out at least a rough draft of her paper before sunset. She might manage to have some of her weekend free.

After a side trip to the kitchen to grab a box of Low Salt Wheat Thins, she went upstairs to the study.

The study was half hers, half Mom's. Allison had no idea what her mom used it for. There was a bookshelf and a filing cabinet on Mom's side of the room, all of it a little too neat. Allison's mom was an accountant, a profession that Allison found so boring that she rarely asked for any specifics. The bookshelf was filled with books as dry and impenetrable as Allison could imagine. Economics, Business Accounting, Taxes, Ugh.

Opposing Mom's neat half, was Allison's part of the room. There was a tiny desk from Allison's kindergarten days, still bearing multicolored Crayola scars. Piled on top of it were cardboard boxes of dog-eared paperbacks; westerns, romances, mysteries. Piled on top of them was a riot of lined paper and spiral-bound notebooks. Piled on top of *that* was Meowrie Antoinette—Allison had been six when she'd named her—the matriarch the felines. Old tufts of white cat hair coated all of Allison's homework.

Allison gently petted Meowrie to let the cat know that she was there. Meowrie was older than Allison, nearly deaf, and blinded by milky cataracts. Meowrie made a half-purr, a sort of catlike sigh, licked Allison's thumb, and went back to sleep. Allison liberated her history notebook from the pile while trying to disturb the old cat as little as possible.

Her mom's souped-up HP sat alone on an austere table with only its peripherals for company. She cracked the notebook to the page where she had copied the assignment and set it down next to the keyboard. Allison flicked on the PC and began typing with one hand, digging in the Wheat Thins box with the other.

By seven-thirty Allison had managed to print out ten pages of airy but well-written essay that only needed a few footnotes and a bibliography to get past Mr. Counter's requirements. It was the kind of thing that Allison suspected drove Mr. Counter nuts—a technically perfect vacuum of an essay.

She shouldn't have been so pleased with herself, but she smiled anyway. The way Mr. Counter graded, the paper rated a C as it was. With a little polish, anything less than an A would mark an obvious personal vendetta on Mr. Counter's part. It would count, in some twisted way, as a moral victory.

Allison lay on her bed. Red-marked computer-draft essay surrounded her. An unfinished Gothic paperback lay open, facedown next to her pillow. Across from the foot of the bed, a crotchety black-and-white TV nattered on, half-buried in stuffed animals. It was tuned to PBS and Lehrer was going on about the latest difficulty around Taiwan. Allison wasn't paying much attention to it.

Instead, she was looking at the shoebox she had fished out of the closet. It rested on her lap, and inside it nestled a small stack of gaudy paperbacks that her mother would never approve of. Their covers bore no titles, only blurry photos of naked models in Victorian settings. The women were well endowed, and lounged amidst red velvet and white lace. Some models wore white gloves, some black. A few wore spiked heels. On two of the covers men were present, backs to the camera, muscular and equally nude. The titles on the spine were all *The Passion of* . . . something-or-other. Allison had read every one several times, and usually just the sight of the covers could bring a catch to her throat.

The books were a secret embarrassment. Mostly because Allison didn't want to admit that a rather tame sextet of mid-seventies drugstore erotica could get her legs rubbing together like that.

However, at the moment, she was concentrating on another embarrassment she kept in that shoebox. In her hands were the last of the hundred and two pages of *Restless Nights*, her novel.

It had been calling to her all afternoon, and she'd finally given in. She was a fast reader, and she had managed to read through the draft—cry at the really awful parts—and reach the end all in half an hour. And here, the last five pages, she had slowed her reading to a crawl.

Mr. Lehrer droned in the background.

She felt her face flush as she closed on the scene where Randolph and Melissa finally met, after their years of separation. Randolph had managed to escape the Nazi prison camp, but not the false rumors of his treason. Meslissa had survived the deaths of her father and her brother to become the chaste caretaker of the family home.

Allison might hate parts of the story, parts that were wooden and clumsy now, but every page, every single word, had been an arrow pointing to this reunion. She had written these last five pages in a white heat. A heat that wasn't entirely literary.

In one way it was so wrong, the book was supposed to be a dance, weaving Melissa and Randolph together. Melissa was chaste and virginal. Randolph was gruff and still had to prove himself not to be the traitor he was believed to be. It was 1944, and premarital sex was a naughty thing.

However, the second that Allison had written them into the same room, the two of them had slammed together like opposing poles of a magnet. Allison had written through nearly to the end of the scene, and it was so hot and explicit that it scared her.

Every time she reached the end, she found her pulse racing and wondered at herself. *I wrote that?*

She was still frozen to the page, picturing Randolph's hands exploring Melissa's body, when she heard her mother's car arrive in the driveway.

Allison dove, stuffing her manuscript back into the shoebox. She slipped on a throw rug and had to catch herself on the dresser opposite the foot of her bed. An avalanche of stuffed animals buried the *News Hour* as she bent and stuffed the box under the debris cluttering the bottom of her closet.

The closet was shut before she heard the door open downstairs. Allison slumped, her back holding the closet door closed, as if her manuscript might escape. She was still flushed and a little warm.

Realizing that, and how silly she must've looked, made her flush that much hotter.

A smiling Babs Bunny sat on top of the mound of animals Allison dislodged, winner of king of the mountain. "Stop laughing at me," Allison said to the stuffed pink rabbit.

Allison started to replace the dislodged multitudes as, below her, she heard her mom say, "Allie?"

"In my room, Mom."

She heard her mother start up the steps and willed herself calm. She was certain that her lascivious thoughts were visible on the surface of her skin.

Her mom peeked in the door, and upon seeing Allison, pushed the door the rest of the way open. "What happened?" she asked, waving a hand at the scattered animals.

Allison gaped for a moment, frozen at the question. Then she managed to regain her bearings. Pasting on a smile, she waved her stuffed Bunny toward the dresser, "A revolt. Babs went over the wall, and suddenly I had a mass escape on my hands."

Mom smiled. The contrast made Allison realize just how tired Mom looked. She took Babs from Allison and gave the stuffed rabbit a mock-serious look. "A troublemaker, eh? Perhaps she should be put in solitary." The humor sounded forced.

"You okay, Mom?"

"Oh?" She looked a little surprised at the question. "No, I'm fine, just a tough day at work, that's all. What're you doing home so early on a Friday? Not feeling under the weather again, are you?"

Allison hated the phrase "under the weather." As far as she was concerned, anyone who wasn't in a plane flying above cloud cover was "under the weather."

"No, Mom." Allison tried to keep the sigh out of her voice. "I just wanted to get some homework out of the way before the weekend." She waved absently at the bed where her history essay was laid out like a reenactment of the battle of Gettysburg in computer paper.

Mom stepped over to the bed, as if Allison's wave was an invitation.

Mom seemed to try to involve herself with Allison's schoolwork. However, lately, Allison had come to the cynical realization that her mother really didn't pay all that much attention. She thought her mom really did try, but the details seemed to slip her attention. Otherwise Mom would've realized just how many days Allison had cut to sit in the bathroom and down Midol and Advil like M&Ms.

Allison watched her mother leaf through pages of her history report, when she was struck by a horrid realization. The page Mom was currently reading was not part of her history report. It was a page from *Restless Nights*. It must have fallen out of the shoebox in her dive for the closet.

Mom arched an eyebrow and asked, "What's this? Not your homework?"

Oh, God, oh, God, oh, God. Allison just couldn't get her mouth to work. What could she say? Some bandit broke in and planted blatant pornography in her history report?

Mom was smiling at her, and Allison felt her face turn beet-red.

"Come on, tell me."

"It's—ah—something I wrote."

"That's obvious."

"A—a—novel I worked on over the summer. The page—it—ah—got mixed in by accident."

"A whole novel?" Mom was looking at the page again. Allison wished she could see what her mother was reading. *Oh, please don't let it be Melissa's trembling breasts or Randolph's manhood, anything but that.*

"Ab–b–bout a hundred pages."

She set the page down and looked at Allison. "Why didn't you tell me?"

"I was embarrassed."

"Well, don't be." Mom seemed to finally recognize Allison's discomfort. She bent down and kissed Allison's forehead.

"Wha?"

"I'm sorry. I shouldn't be reading unfinished work, should I?"

"I—uh—well—"

"I won't stifle you. I don't want to see any more of it. Not until you finish it, of course."

Allison just nodded, lamely.

"Good. I'm going down to fix myself some dinner. Want anything?"

"No."

When her mother nodded and left, Allison rushed to the bed and grabbed the paper.

It was page number seven.

Allison sighed in relief and was choked short when a small jab of pain lanced her forehead. Just then, the animals she'd replaced on the bureau collapsed on to the floor again, Babs in the lead.

The pain vanished as quickly as it had come.

CHAPTER
FIVE

The phone woke Allison from another nightmare. Mr. Counter had been passing out papers. When she turned over her paper, it was the love scene from *Restless Nights*. Mr. Counter had covered the scene with illegible red corrections. Across the top he'd scrawled a great big "F" and the comment "do over."

The phone rang again.

She turned, half-asleep, and startled a cat. Rhett jumped out of bed right across the front of her face, waking her fully.

The phone stopped ringing.

It's nearly three in the morning, she thought, simultaneously irritated at the caller and remembering the last call that'd roused her in the middle of the night.

From downstairs she faintly heard Mom yelling, "—dare you call here again!"

Something in Mom's voice frightened Allison. It was the same tone she'd heard in the previous call. The call that might have been about her.

Hating herself for doing it, Allison gently lifted the received on her extension so she could hear both ends of the conversation. As she held it away from the sound of her breathing she heard a strained, slightly familiar, male voice say, "I deserve the chance to talk to her, Carol." The sound came through a lot of interference, as if the man was speaking on a cheap cordless phone or from a really long distance.

"You have the nerve to say you deserve anything? After all this? Good-bye, John."

Allison had never heard her mother sound like this, and a tiny voice was screaming at her to hang up, that she didn't want to hear any more. . . .

However, the male voice was beginning to register. It was familiar, it had just been such a long time since she'd heard it. But the voice, in connection with the name, froze her so that she couldn't even breathe.

Her father's name had been John.

She was listening to her father's voice. "Don't you under— Damn it, tell her! You owe me nothing, but you owe *her*."

"Don't tell me how to treat my daughter."

"If they're looking, *they* can find out about the doctor's appointments."

Allison could hear tears and near panic in her mother's voice. "Those were nothing, *nothing*! It was the stress of school. The doctor said that himself. It didn't mean anything. It cleared up right after the visit—"

"Did the doctor know the other possibility?"

There was silence on the line.

"Carol, there's always been the chance."

Allison's mother made a noise. It sounded like a sob.

"If she's a teek, they'll—"

"*LEAVE US ALONE!*" The yell made Allison drop the phone in shock. It bounced off the bed and landed on the floor. Even so, Allison could still hear her mother yelling. It came through the tinny speaker of the phone, and it also came, muffled, through the floor of her room. "Those people are crazy. Stone's crazy. I don't believe in any of this, none of it. And I won't have my daughter believing it. You're insane, John. They're insane. I'll go to court this time, publicly, if you call me again. I don't care who gets pulled in. And if you come near my daughter, I swear to God I'll kill you!"

She could hear the phone slam downstairs. She tried to get the receiver before her dad hung up, but by the time she'd gotten to the phone, there was only a dial tone.

Allison gently replaced the receiver. She felt dirty for listening in, but the feeling of confusion was worse. She had just heard an argument about *her,* and she didn't understand any of it.

Worst was the awful thing that ate at Allison's heart as she tried to sleep—

Mom had told her that her father was dead.

23 OCTOBER   EUCLID HEIGHTS, OHIO

08:05 AM   SATURDAY

It was a rotten Saturday morning.

The temperature had dipped below freezing during the night and was now straining to get over forty. The sky was an ugly uneven slate gray, and all the tree colors had faded into a uniform mud-brown that fit Allison's mood perfectly.

Allison couldn't remember the last time she'd been awake this early on a Saturday. It had probably been back when she spent her mornings watching cartoons.

It wasn't that she'd woken early. She'd never managed to get back to sleep. By the time she glanced at the clock and it read six-thirty, she'd given up, showered, and gotten herself breakfast. All along, Allison felt on the verge of a migraine, but the headache had never materialized.

At least the fresh air helped push away that prospect.

Now she was kicking her way through the leaves in the gutter, past mostly silent houses. She was winding her way toward the library. It would open at nine, so she was doing her best to take a twisted route to eat up time. She'd left at seven-thirty, as soon as she got her hair dry. She wanted to slip out of the house before her mother woke up.

Allison still didn't know what she would say when she finally talked to Mom. Would she mention the overheard conversation at all? Would she simply ask about her father.

Would she tell her mother the fact that the headaches had not ended with the doctor's visit, and, in fact, had persisted nearly six weeks beyond and were only now fading?

"Tell her!" her father had said to Mom.

Tell me what? Allison thought. Tell me that my father

was still alive? That was an obvious interpretation, but the way her father—

She amazed herself by how calmly she was taking that. Her *father*. She was thinking about him as if he'd only been gone for the weekend.

But the way *John* had spoken made Allison doubt that he simply wanted to divulge the fact of his existence.

When Allison turned back onto a main street, she sat down in a bus shelter across from a closed deli and opened up her backpack. A sheet of frost on the seat chilled a strip of flesh through the material of her jeans. She ignored it.

She pulled out a spiral notebook—her trigonometry homework, notably sparse—and flipped open a blank page. She fished out a pencil and tried to transcribe the conversation from memory:

Mom: "How dare you call me here."

She erased that. It irritated her that she was already confusing the two calls. She rethought what she'd heard last night. What was the first thing she'd heard?

Allison replaced her first line with:

Mom: "Calling here again."

Allison decided she should have done this immediately after she had heard the phone call. It was very hard to get the words down from memory. Mom's first line was close enough. She wrote:

Dad:

Allison erased that as soon as she wrote it. She didn't *know* that yet. Until she had some sort of confirmation it was probably saner to assume that Mom's late-night caller was some other person named John. It was a common name.

John: "I deserve the chance to talk to her."

She thought for a while and couldn't remember Mom's next words exactly. She wrote down:

Mom: "You have some nerve. Good-bye, John."

The good-bye, *that* she was sure of. Now, what did he say?

John: "Tell her. You owe her that."

That was close enough.

Mom: "Don't tell me how to treat my daughter."

Allison nodded to herself. It was an odd sensation she

had. It felt like she was trying to discover the plot of an entire novel from a stray page she'd found.

She felt her eyes watering and thought, *Why are you keeping things from me, Mom?* Her breath was fogging in front of her, and she felt frozen to the seat.

The next line was the strange one:

John: "If they look, they'll find out about the doctor's appointments."

Allison stared at what she wrote. Slowly, with a trembling hand, she underlined *"they." "They"* would be interested in her doctor's appointments over the headaches. John, or someone—*they*—thought her headaches meant something.

"Maybe I misheard it," Allison mumbled. "I was half asleep."

She thought about Mom's next line. It was impossible to remember the tirade exactly. She decided just to write down the gist of what she'd heard:

Mom: (goes off on the fact my headaches weren't anything to worry about.)

As she thought about it, she added the line:

"They cleared up after the visit."

Allison was sure Mom had said that. But the headaches *hadn't* cleared up after the visit. Allison simply had stopped telling Mom about them. She had managed to hide the six weeks of intermittent agony, and Allison began to think she had some unconscious complicity from her mother. Mom didn't want to believe Allison was having these migraines. On the phone she'd been psycho about it. Mom had broken down telling this John that Allison's headaches were nothing.

Allison added the words, *"nothing, nothing, nothing!"* to that line.

Now that it was daylight and she was beginning to think clearly, Allison was scaring herself. When Allison had returned from the doctor, what Mom had shown her wasn't condescension, insensitivity, or disbelief. It had been screaming denial.

I've contracted a rare genetic disorder, and it's going to kill me because Mom can't deal with it.

Allison got a grip on herself. If it was a disease, those

endless examinations would have shown *something*. Even
if the doctor didn't understand what. If there was *anything*
medically wrong, they would have ordered even *more* tests,
not sent mother and daughter home with the all-clear and
a speech about tension headaches.

Allison's hand shook as she wrote the next line:

*John: "Did the doctor know the other possibility . . . ? If
she's a*

Allison paused.

That word again. It was the only word she remembered
from the first phone call, because its use was so odd.

"Teak?" she said to herself. *Am I a piece of wood?* Was
it some other homonym? How many ways could you spell
that? Teke? Teec? Teake? Were any of those words? Allison wrote, *"teak(teek?)"*

"If I'm a teak, they will what?" Allison asked the paper
in front of her. "Thanks, Mom."

She underlined *"they"* again and finished the last two
lines so they read:

John: "If she's a teak(teek?), they'll—"

*Mom: "Leave us alone. I don't believe any of this. They're
stone insane. You're insane. Call and I drag you into court.
Touch my daughter and I'll kill you."*

Allison wondered about the third sentence. The phrase
"stone insane" sounded more like her romance heroine,
Melissa, than it did Mom. However, Allison was certain
that her mother had said *"stone insane"* or words to that
effect.

Allison sighed.

Would someone please tell me who "they" are?

And what in the world did "teak" mean? It sounded
vaguely like some obscure ethnic slur. "What?" Allison
said out loud. "I'm not a WASP?"

She decided she'd killed enough time and packed up her
backpack again. Whatever was going on in her family's life,
she doubted it would be an adequate excuse for Mr.
Counter. She still had to flesh out that bibliography.

She checked her watch and saw that it was past nine.
Good, the library was open. She crossed the street and
resumed her journey.

*   *   *

She spent the morning roaming the stacks, and by noon she had amassed an impressive bibliography for her paper. She'd scanned books on revolution, American, French, and otherwise, and had found herself involved despite herself. One of the books had a distinctly Marxist flavor to it that she knew would absolutely infuriate Mr. Counter if she included it as a reference.

She sat behind a desk in a reading room that at one time had been a master bedroom. *Mission accomplished,* she thought. All she had to do now was type up the bibliography and slip in a few of the supporting quotes that she had picked out while scanning the books.

Her sense of victory was muted.

She wished she'd never listened in on that phone call. It wasn't as if she didn't have enough on her mind already. She pulled the notebook out of her backpack and looked at the transcribed conversation again.

She wished she'd had the sense to write the thing down when it was fresh in her mind. She knew the conversation had eroded in her memory. The gaps in it might contain something important. Something that would explain everything.

You could ask her. Confront Mom directly . . .

Allison sniffed and realized her eyes were watering. She sucked in a shuddering breath and wiped her face with the back of her hand. A small damp spot now marred the notebook paper. She smeared it with her thumb. She felt pathetic.

Problems between me and Mom? How'd you know, Macy?

Allison needed a tissue badly now. She gathered her papers and headed for a bathroom.

On the way she walked right into David Greenbaum. He'd been carrying a stack of books nearly three feet high, and the collision caused books to fly everywhere. Allison raised her arms to ward off the falling literature, but the books hooked to the left at the last second to career off a defenseless marble drinking fountain.

The impact left her head throbbing.

David stood there, gaping, for half a beat, before he realized who she was. "Allie! Oh, gee, I'm sorry—"

Allison shook her had. The throbbing subsided below the pain threshold. "My fault. I wasn't looking where I was going."

"The books just got away from me." David stared at the pile of books at their feet. He looked as if he couldn't quite believe the mess they'd caused. Allison had once found his befuddled looks cute. Nowadays she just found David's perpetual confusion irritating.

What did *he* have to be confused about?

She bent and began handing books up to him, rebuilding the stack he'd been carrying. He flinched when she handed him the first one, and Allison couldn't figure out why.

It's last weekend, she thought, *the scene between me and Chuck. Now David probably blames me for ruining his party.*

Great, that thought made her feel even worse. About herself. About David. About the whole awful world. She rushed through stacking the rest of David's books.

"Are you all right?" David asked as she began stacking books past his face.

"No damage." Allison balanced the last book in place, half-obscuring David's nose.

"That's not what I mean. You look like you've been crying."

She resisted an urge to wipe her face. *Do you really care, David? Or are you just asking because you think you're supposed to?* "I took a long swim and decided to peel some onions afterward."

"Ah. Okay." David's voice sounded resigned.

Allison picked up her backpack and stepped around him toward the lady's room. As she retreated down the hall, she heard David say, belatedly as usual, "I'm really sorry about the party."

She didn't respond because she didn't know what to say.

In the bathroom she blew her nose into a wad of coarse toilet paper. Then she managed to reclaim some of her face from the ravages of her emotions. She wished she was more into makeup right now. If she had some with her, she could cover some of the effects of her near-sleepless night. But all the makeup she had in the world was in the top left drawer of her bureau. It amounted to some eye shadow and two tubes of lipstick. One tube to go with each of her really good dresses.

When she thought about it, the natural look was better. If she wore mascara, she'd look like a raccoon right now.

What she did look like was a rather plain-looking blonde who'd spent too much time watching the late movie. She stepped back and smiled. At least her hair made up for her face. It was full and fell to just beyond her shoulder blades. The hair was what kept her from looking like a clone of Marcia Brady.

She grabbed some more toilet paper and wiped her nose.

As she left the bathroom, she still wanted to go down to the reference section and find a dictionary. She wanted to know any meanings for the word "teak" that she wasn't aware of.

She left the bathroom, turned to descend the stairs, and froze.

The stairs descended in a marble sweep toward the main entrance. The entrance fronted a lobby, all glass and pillars. Ahead were the doors outside, to the right was the main adult fiction area, to the left was the children's room.

Right in front of her, standing in the lobby next to the checkout desk, was Chuck Wilson.

The sight of him, here, crushed her insides into jelly. She couldn't move, and all she could think of was the phrase, *Don't see me, don't see me, don't see me . . .*

Her temples began to throb with her pulse.

Chuck looked around the lobby, seeming out of place in the library. His head turned in her direction, and Allison felt her heart shrivel in her chest. But Chuck's head kept moving until, seeming to find what he was looking for, he stepped out of her view into the adult area.

Allison made a made dash for the front door. She stopped only when she saw the white sentries of the anti-theft detectors flanking the exit. She was carrying books in her backpack that she'd wanted to check out.

She backed to the checkout desk, yanking the books out of her bag and fumbling out her library card, wishing the whole process would *hurry*.

As they ran the books over the demagnetizer, Allison

looked around nervously. Chuck stood there, right in the center of the magazine section, *staring straight at her.*

Allison wanted to collapse.

She could barely take her eyes away from him as she scooped up her books. She shoved her books into her bag and dashed for the exit, not bothering to zip the bag closed.

She made it to the sidewalk. She started to cross the street, but it was against the light and she was almost hit by a van. In the passenger window she saw a twelve-or thirteen-year-old boy with sandy hair. The kid's face was pressed to the glass, and he seemed to be staring right at her. Then the van was across the intersection and Allison was stumbling back onto the sidewalk. She turned away from the street and the library and began walking away, fast.

She had hardly gotten half a block before she heard a terrifyingly familiar voice say, "Allison! Allison Boyle!"

She turned, slowly, as if she was in a dream.

Chuck was there, on the top steps of the library, looking down at her. He was tall and thin, graced with unruly black hair. There was too much shadow on his face for an eighteen-year-old. He wore the same type of clothes he'd worn at the costume party—wide belt, jeans, boots, flannel shirt rolled to the elbows. The cold didn't seem to bother him. In his right hand he held up a red-covered spiral-bound notebook that Allison recognized.

The sight of it made the walls of her stomach fall away, leaving an empty void.

It was her trigonometry notebook. The same notebook she'd written Mom's conversation down in.

"You dropped this," Chuck called down to her, smiling.

Allison wanted to run away as fast as she could. Instead, she found herself walking back toward the library steps. The walk was endless. Chuck made no move to meet her halfway. He stood at the top of the steps waving her notebook as if it was a treat, and he was enticing a trained animal to do a trick.

Allison loathed herself as she climbed the stairs. She loathed herself for being so afraid, and for being so blatantly manipulated despite her fear.

She reached the top step and grabbed the notebook. She forced herself to say, "Thank you."

"No prob, sweetcakes. Anytime." He didn't let go of the book. "I wanted to apologize for the costume party."

"Don't bother," Allison said.

Her head was flaring now, the pain distorting her vision. Her view was fracturing and wrapping itself around the notebook.

Please, not a bad one, not here. Not now.

She pulled frantically, but Chuck was a lot stronger than she was. Macy might have been able to pull the book away, but Allison couldn't do more than tug futilely.

"No, really. Too many beers, and I don't know what I'm doing. No hard feelings?"

You've got to be kidding? Allison thought through a blood-red haze that gripped her head like a punch press linked to her pulse. *As if that drunken grope was accidental?*

She realized the only way she'd get her notebook back was to accept this creep's apology.

No!

The pain hit some sort of breaking point, lancing through her skull and vanishing.

As it did, she tried one last heroic tug.

To her surprise, with a tearing sound, the notebook actually came free. Chuck's smile evaporated into a look of shocked surprise. He stared at his hand.

His hand now had a narrow red cut, diagonally across the palm, where the wire of the spiral binding had caught. The spiral wire had unwound for two inches and now bobbed out the top of the notebook like an antenna. As Allison watched, a piece of the notebook's red cover, the exact size and shape of Chuck's thumb, drifted gently to the ground.

"Hell, yes, there are hard feelings," Allison said. She turned and walked away, trying her best not to run.

After half a block she passed the van that had almost hit her. The young kid in the passenger window was still staring at her. She ignored the kid and the van as she walked back past Euclid High.

23 October   Euclid Heights, Ohio

12:11 pm   Saturday

Chuck froze for a few long seconds before he registered
what had happened. He had actually gotten to apologizing
to the bitch, and he had never apologized to anyone in his
fucking life—

And—goddamn it all—it wasn't enough.

He stood at the top of the library stairs, looking at her,
thinking he might actually get to talk to her at least. And,
suddenly, she yanked the notebook out of his hand. The
shock of that immobilized him.

The notebook tore out of his grasp as if it was welded
to the back of an accelerating semi. It was so fast that he
barely felt the spiral binding catch in the meat of his hand.
It left a thin, ragged gash across his palm.

A piece of the notebook's red cover floated to the
ground.

Chuck looked up from his hand.

"Hell, yes, there are hard feelings," she said. Then she
turned her back on him and walked away.

Little Miss Perfect said "Hell," Chuck managed to think.

"Hey—" he began to say.

Then he felt his hand.

"Oh, shit!" Awareness of the injury slammed into him
like an out-of-control bus. The pain vibrated through his
arm and he had to grab his wrist with his other hand to
stop the shaking. In the brief time he had looked away
from the wound, his hand had pooled with enough blood
to spill through his fingers and splatter on the ground.

Chuck staggered back from the sight, slamming backward
through the doors to the library. The pain was triggering a
headache, a bad one. As bad as the pain in his hand. Rain-
bowed auras wrapped around the library's fluorescent
lights, and sounds rang with reverberating echoes that
shook apart the back of his skull.

Blood from his hand was going everywhere. His arm,
pants, the floor of the library.

"The bitch *cut* me!" he yelled. "The *bitch* cut my fucking hand!"

Dozens of people were surrounding him yelling, talking . . .

Thinking.

One of the interns at the checkout desk said, "Oh, God! Diane, call 911 <<**view of himself from across the checkout desk, mental voice,** *please, jesus let him be all right. our Father who art in*>>"

An old librarian held back a tide of children in the kid's section. "No, everyone back. <<**view from inside the kid's section. frantic glances behind at twenty or so storytime kids. six to eight years old. storytime forgotten.** *don't let the children see this. that boy has got to be on drugs. what are their parents going to think*>>"

"Oh, gross. <<**view from behind the skirts of the librarian worried about parents. old lady smell and eyes are close to the ground. everything seems much too large, hallucinogenicly large.** *man's hurt. that real blood. will they let us see the am-blance. i wanna see. maybe he's in a gang. police too? i wanna see police too*>>"

People began running toward him. Chuck felt almost fully disconnected from his body now. Prismatic colors washed out his vision when he was seeing through his own eyes, and his own ears were hearing voices as if he was in the bottom of a well. His throbbing hand was distant, like his own heartbeat, and he was only dimly away of the fact he was on his knees cradling it. A pool of blood had formed below him.

A man in a suit ran up to him. He was the first to reach him. He tore off his tie. <<*blood, oh fuck. too much blood. is it venous or arterial—oh damn. just get pressure on the thing. where is that damn ambulance. hope this kid ain't doped on anything. should have stuck with med school. forgotten everything by now. no, too tight. stop the bleeding, not lose the hand. god his color sucks. how much has he lost? where're the fucking paramedics?*>> The man's tie clamped on to his hand with a fiery grip.

Chuck realized that he was yelling at everyone.

"Get out of my fucking head!"

<<gee, that is chuck wilson. oh wait till I tell kelly about>>

<<that guy is hopped to the gills. probably did it to himself>>

<<I hate blood>>

<<where's the fucking ambulance>>

<<and deliver us from evil>>

Chuck rocked back and forth on his knees, looking at the crowd around him. None of them really gave a shit about him. He was some sort of goddamned spectacle for them. He felt his vision giving out, turning dim at the edges. As he swayed, he saw David Greenbaum at the top of the stairs at the end of the lobby.

<<allie did that?>>

"Damn straight she did, you fucking geek."

Chuck fell over, losing consciousness.

23 OCTOBER   EUCLID HEIGHTS, OHIO

12:16 PM   SATURDAY

A twelve-year-old child stood next to an unmarked gray van, watching the paramedics take Chuck Wilson away. The boy had sandy red hair cut in short bangs. He was in jeans and wore a black T-shirt with Marvin the Martian on it. He wore a Walkman headset, and the wires fed into the case clipped to his belt.

The people who passed him on the street and met the boy's gaze would quickly look away, as if by reflex. If asked, those people might have said that the boy's eyes looked a little too deeply for comfort. At the moment, there was only room in those intense green eyes for the ambulance, and Chuck Wilson.

"Why didn't we follow the girl, Mr. Jackson?" The boy's voice was a barely audible whisper, but it was picked up by a microphone embedded in the Walkman headphones he wore. The case on his belt wasn't a Walkman, it was an altogether different kind of radio.

"Our instructions are to monitor and take in Mr. Wilson,

Elroy." The voice in the headset was slightly distorted by a mass of digital scrambling equipment. The boy called Elroy thought the radio made everyone sound like Darth Vader.

"But she's *loads* better than Charlie."

The doors to the ambulance closed and the voice on his headphones told Elroy, "Come back to the van, we're following him to the hospital."

"Loads better," Elroy repeated.

"We have time. You got a good look at her, right?"

"Uh-huh."

"Then get in the van. You can look through yearbooks for her while we're at the hospital."

Elroy turned around, and the sliding door in the side of the van opened for him. Inside was a bank of surveillance equipment and a balding, gray-haired man who wore a bald eagle clip on his tie.

The door slid shut, and after allowing the ambulance a respectable lead, the van pulled out and followed.

23 OCTOBER   EUCLID HEIGHTS, OHIO

07:55 PM   SATURDAY

As far as *Webster's NewWorld* was concerned, "teak" was a kind of wood and "teek," "teke," "teake," and "teec" didn't exist. That exhausted Allison's research material at home. She was running that, and the overheard telephone conversation through her head, as she sat down with Mom for dinner. The question kept gnawing at her, and Allison kept trying to think of a way to broach the subject without admitting she'd been eavesdropping.

They were halfway through dinner, and a long, uncomfortable silence, before Alison got up the nerve to ask, "How come you never talk about Dad?"

Mom's fork screeched on the plate. The sound startled Rhett, who dashed out from under the table and up the stairs. "Why do you ask?" Mom looked away from Allison, her distress lined in her face. It wasn't just the overwork that Mom always complained about. She looked worried.

She looked *old.*

"You don't talk about him. About why you left, or what he was like . . ."

Mom nodded slowly, still looking away. The light carved out harsh shadows on her cheeks, and her eyes were too shiny. "I'm sorry. Maybe I haven't been fair to you. But—" Her eyes closed. "It's hard for me."

Seeing Mom like this was beginning to upset Allison, but she tried to keep it out of her voice. "I'd just like to know what he was like."

"He was stubborn. He was persistent . . ." Mom's voice lowered until it was barely audible. "He was better than I gave him credit for."

"Mom, why . . ." Allison's voice trailed off. Mom was on the verge of tears and she was about to hit her with something like: *"Why did you say he was dead?"* or *"Why are you hiding things from me?"* But Allison couldn't do it.

Mom stood up and grabbed the plates. Allison could see her hands shaking. "I love him," she was whispering. She was talking more through Allison than to her. She hurried to the kitchen with the plates, and Allison could barely make out the rest of her words, ". . . but I loved you more, Allie." The sentence ended with what could have been a sob.

Mom.

Allison could feel her own eyes burning with the start of tears. After a moment she got up from the table and walked to the kitchen door. Mom was there, leaning on the edge of the sink, staring down, her body shaking with crying too soft to hear.

"I'm sorry," Allison said. She stood in the doorway, paralyzed, unsure of what to do.

Mom shook her head and did a shallow imitation of laughter. "I'm just a bit tired, Allie. I'm overreacting."

Are you? What was that call about? The question went unasked.

"Mom, I heard—"

The phone rang. Mom seemed almost to wince as Allison reached for it and picked it up.

It was Macy. "Hi. Allie?"

"Uh-huh?"

"Me, Ben, and David are going to the Cinemark to see a movie. Can we swing by and pick you up?"

"Uh—I really got to work on that history paper—"

"I know, David's been talking about your 'research' at the library—"

"Talk to you later."

"Wait a minute, girl. You got to tell me—"

"Bye."

Allison hung up the phone. She looked at Mom who still seemed to be tensed from the phone call. "It was Macy," Allison said. "The guys wanted to take me to a movie."

Mom nodded and said, "Maybe you should get going on that paper, huh?" She gave Allison a weak smile, wiped her cheek with the back of her hand, and started running water in the sink.

"But . . ." Allison shook her head, she was almost as stressed out as Mom looked. *Not now.* She would wait until she was a little calmer, that'd be the only way she could deal with Mom breaking down on her.

She sighed and climbed the stairs back to her room.

She spent her evening slogging through the bibliography and whatever other homework she could think of. Anything to keep her mind busy. By nine, she'd reached the point where sleep was a dull ache pulsing just behind her forehead. She knew she'd reached her limit when she'd read the same paragraph five times and had to look at the cover to see what textbook she was reading.

Is it me, or is it a prerequisite for textbook authors to be unable to write an interesting word?

She let the textbook slide from her hand and over the edge of the bed. She was surrounded by a rat's nest of homework paper and notes, all of which seemed terribly obscure at the moment.

She looked at her alarm clock and saw that it was nine-oh-one. It seemed longer since the last time she'd looked.

At the foot of her bed her TV blabbed on at low volume. She turned off the light on her bed stand, and the room filled with the blue phosphor glow from the picture. On the TV was some PBS nature documentary. She yawned and told herself that she'd get it in a sec.

She just wanted to close her eyes for a moment.

CHAPTER
SIX

24 OCTOBER   **CLEVELAND, OHIO**

12:03 AM   **SUNDAY**

Chuck Wilson's first conscious thoughts weren't his own.
*<<fucking doctor should be here by now. fuck they
want me to bleed to death? fuck.>>*

<<"It'll be all right honey. *God let her be all right.* The
doctor will give you something to make it all better. *is it
strep, please don't let it be strep.* Shh, Mommy's here. *can
a baby die from strep?*">>

*<<should have known better than to come here on a Sun-
day night. too many people.>>*
The thoughts were accompanied by a fractured view of
a crowded waiting room. The scene came from a dozen
different viewpoints, some overlapping, none lasting long
enough to make any sense of. There was a black woman
holding a squealing baby as if it were a life preserver. There
was a scruffy-looking man in an army jacket holding a
bloody bandanna to his thigh. A dozen others, all of whom
tried to grab space in Chuck's semiconscious mind.

*<<when are they going to get to me? I think my arm's
broke.>>*

*<<so much easier when they're a minor. just lean on the
parents a little.* feelings of fatigue. fingers come to rub eyes.
a glance down at the papers in his lap.>>*
What the fuck? was Chuck Wilson's first lucid thought
that he could call his own. He could feel the contact slipping, even as Chuck realized that on that paper was the
name Charles W. Wilson. For the first time in a long while,
Chuck tried to hold onto the voices in his head.

<<*should have been here a year earlier. no question the mother wants to be rid of him.* **another glance downward. glimpse of a tie graced by a gold bald eagle. papers in lap with Chuck's picture on them. dates, ages, police record.** *shouldn't have used him to bait the girl. now we got all this hospital red tape.* **glance up at a clock on the wall of the waiting room. clock reads 12:09.** *yeah, a year earlier, before the asshole turned eighteen. mom would've caved in five minutes, and then nobody would miss the creep.* **glance down at the papers.** *especially the euclid heights police.*>>

Chuck Wilson was fully awake now. He was dimly aware of straps holding him down on some sort of table.

<<**a tap on the shoulder. right hand experiences an almost subliminal jerk toward left armpit. awareness of pressure of holster, and of the dozen civilians. surprise over in an instant, hand doesn't move. turn to look over. sandy-haired kid with a black cartoon T-shirt. "What is it Elroy?** *don't like that look of his. never did. what the hell does the kid really see?*" **the kid looks up and says, "Charlie's awake, I can feel him here—"**>>

Chuck's eyes snapped open, and he lost contact. *Shit boy, you in trouble.*

The voices in his head might mean he was nuts, but some hard experiences made him trust them. Hell, if the voices weren't right all the time, they wouldn't have fucked up his life so much. Chuck tried to sit up and found that he really was strapped down.

"Fuck," he whispered.

The stellar medical staff of wherever-the-hell-he-was had parked him on a rolling stretcher off in a corridor somewhere. A chart lay on his stomach, and was slowly sliding off, knocked askew by his attempt to sit up.

He was held fast by thick leather straps across his chest and arms just above the elbow, by large cuffs on his wrists and ankles, and another belt across his legs just above the knee. None was tight enough to be painful, but any real movement was impossible.

God, why didn't they just get a straitjacket and get it over with?

Chuck had been questioning his sanity for so long that there was little doubt in his mind that they were bottling him up for the nut factory. That was probably what the man with the eagle on his tie was all about. Either that or he was some sort of cop. Either way, Chuck didn't want to deal with the man. But, strapped down here, he didn't have much choice.

The chart kept sliding until it fell into the crook of his arm.

"What the fuck I'm going to do?" Chuck muttered. He tossed his head around, to get an idea of where he was. It didn't help much. He was in an empty corridor flooded with fluorescent light. The corridor was a short one ending with a T-intersection at each end. All the doors around him were closed, no signs of any doctors, nurses, or anyone else.

He suspected he was close to the emergency room.

Midnight? I've been here twelve hours?

At least they hadn't taken his clothes, such as they were. His jeans were splattered with blood, and the sleeves of his shirt had been slit up to the shoulder. A bag suspended over him was dripping into a needle in his left arm, and his right hand was swathed in bandages.

Fuck that bitch, this is all her fault.

Chuck froze as he saw a uniformed cop cross past the intersection in front of him. He didn't breathe until the cop had passed. Then he had to catch his breath again as a barely audible conversation started up around the corner.

"Hey, Doc, how's the patient?"

"Fine, still sleeping," said a mumbled voice.

"Any more word from those feds?"

A grunt.

"Yeah, I know. Never heard of the ASI either. But I'm just here to take a statement from the kid."

Chuck's eyes finally focused on the chair by the foot of his stretcher. It was surrounded by several paper cups, and hanging off of the chair's arm was a cop's hat.

Fuck and double fuck.

Whoever the eagle dude was, the bastard had to be the fed the cop was talking about. And if he didn't want to meet up with the guy, he had to get off this stretcher before the cop came back.

Quietly, Chuck tried all the restraints. For a few seconds it seemed hopeless. Then he realized that the cuff holding his right hand was looser than the one on his left, to accommodate the bandages and his injury.

Listening to the cop's voice, just down the corridor, made Chuck desperate. He folded his right thumb over the palm to make his hand as small as possible. The effort reminded Chuck that it was his hand that had put him in the hospital. His thumb barely moved before he felt the cut in his palm. As he kept closing it across his palm, his hand burned. It felt like he was splitting his hand in half along the seams of his wound.

Somehow he managed to touch his thumb to the base of his pinkie with only a grunt. He held his hand like that for a few moments, letting the pain recede to a dull ache. To his surprise, the white bandages didn't erupt into a blossom of arterial blood.

The cop was still talking to the doctor.

Now comes the hard part.

This was where he had a chance to undo everything the doctors had done. He took a deep breath, and moved his arm back, pulling his hand through the cuff. It felt as if he was trying to tear his hand off. First the bandages caught on the edge of the cuff, then they began to rip and peel off his hand. The tape holding the gauze felt as if it was made of tiny metal hooks embedded in his skin. He clenched his teeth and stopped breathing to keep from crying out. His eyes watered, and tears streamed down his cheeks.

He didn't stop pulling. The worst thing that could happen was to get his injured hand caught inside the cuff.

The half minute he pulled his hand felt like half an hour. Pain shot up his arm so bad that it caused his bicep to vibrate. Sweat broke out on his arm and forehead, and blood began seeping through the folds in his palm. Between the blood and the sweat, his hand finally slipped free of the cuff, the bandages were left on the other side like shed skin.

For a few long seconds, all Chuck could do was lie back and breathe. But the cop was still talking, and any second he could turn the corner. There was no way he could afford to stop now.

What he saw of his hand was an ugly mass of black bruising and stitches. He didn't look too closely. He lay back, breathing heavily, as he fumbled with the strap on his chest. Every movement hurt his hand, but nothing like what he'd just gone through. The main problem was the fact that he had to work with only his last two fingers and his thumb. He couldn't move his index or middle finger at all.

The strap fell away, and Chuck sat up. When he did, he had to make a panicked grab for the chart, which had escaped to slide to the ground. Chuck grabbed it, leaning so far over that he thought the stretcher would tip over. He clasped the chart between his thumb and little finger. The pressure he exerted felt as if it was dislocating his pinkie. It wasn't enough. The chart slowly slipped though his fingers, sliding on the blood and sweat covering his hand.

The chart slid out of his grasp and fell the remaining foot to the ground. Chuck's heart stopped as the chart landed, the sound seemed to echo in the corridor forever. He waited for the cop to come running around the corridor.

He waited.

Around the corridor he heard the cop say, "So, you going to catch the play-offs?"

"Eh?"

"Somehow one of my friends got hold of some Indians' tickets and I haven't heard the end of it."

Chuck could breathe again. They hadn't heard, or hadn't noticed. Once he was relaxed a bit he felt the tension of the tube pulled taut in his arm. He leaned back into a sitting position and realized that the place where the needle fed his arm hurt like hell now. Nothing like his hand, but pretty nasty.

He pulled the needle out of his arm, gripped between his thumb and pinkie. After slipping three times, on the fourth it came out with a sickening, sliding pressure.

Then Chuck began freeing himself in earnest. Once he got his other wrist free, the remaining straps were loosed in short order. He had just taken his first unsteady step off of the stretcher when he heard a gasp and a crash from behind him. He turned to see a nurse. She had dropped a tray full of test tubes on the floor, and blood samples went everywhere.

She took a step back, more from the blood than from him. He heard her say, *"Shit"* just before the cop came around the corner. Unlike Chuck's chart, the shattering of a dozen test tubes wasn't a sound to be overlooked in the midst of conversation.

Chuck turned to see the cop at the other end of the corridor, a cup of machine coffee in his hand, arms held wide. "It's all right, Charlie," said the cop in what was supposed to be a reassuring voice.

Chuck looked back, and saw the nurse looking at the cop. No voices played in his mind—thank God—but Chuck could see in her face the event change from a mess on the floor to a psycho on the loose.

He was trapped. He knew if he ran toward the nurse, the cop would shoot him. That was the way cops thought. Chuck was frozen, his hands out in a parody of the cop, trying to think of what to do. Fear was rearing through him like a pack of dogs gnawing at his gut.

"Look, you had a scare. That's all right. You had a bad time at the library, but everything's all right now."

Chuck knew that voice, it was how cops talked to crazy people. The bastard was going to grab him and someone would shoot a needle in his arm, and he'd wake up in a little cell, padded or unpadded, with no way to escape the voices in his head.

His temple began to throb and . . .

<<view of himself, standing befuddled. "Everything's all right Chuck *just a little bit closer and I can grab him.***">>**

Chuck turned to face the cop. The cop was almost up to him now. Behind the cop, he saw a nervous-looking doctor inching toward the intercom. *Fuck, what did I ever do to deserve this?*

"Look, man, I just want to go home." Chuck could hear the note of hysteria in his own voice.

"We'll talk about it, but why don't you sit back down." The cop was within six feet of him now.

Chuck glanced at the stretcher where he'd been strapped down. He saw the cop's feet move. Chuck didn't know if the cop was grabbing for him, but that was what he was expecting, so he lashed out. His hand was useless, but the doctors had left his steel-toed boots on, so he kicked as hard as he could.

Chuck caught the cop in the stomach. Coffee sprayed the

wall as the cop's hand clutched on the cup he was holding.
The cop's eyes widened in a single moment of lucid fury,
and his other hand started moving to his belt. Chuck never
knew if it was for the baton or the gun. Chuck kicked
again, near the kidney.

The cop folded as if he had taken a bullet.

The next kick took the cop in the side of the head, and
the cop dropped. Before the bastard had time to recover,
Chuck wrestled the gun out of the cop's holster. Chuck
looked to either end of the corridor and neither the doctor
nor the nurse had moved.

Boy, are we in trouble now.

He pointed the gun, left-handed, at the cop on the floor.
*I'm not going to jail or a nuthouse, period and excla-fuck-
ing-mation point.*

"You two," he said to the nurse and the doctor. "Get
over here, or I waste the fucking pig."

After a brief hesitation, both came. For the first time
Chuck thought he might actually get out of this hospital.

24 OCTOBER   EUCLID HEIGHTS, OHIO

02:16 AM   SUNDAY

Allison was ripped from sleep by the worst pain she had
ever experienced. She was curled in her bed, drenched with
sweat in a room that felt like a freezer. She was transfixed
by the pain in her skull, unable to move, unable to say
anything but a low moan that sounded like a car unable
to start.

Talons ripped at her brain. Something buried deep in her
skull was hatching, tearing its way out. Every beat of her
heart sent razor claws to rip at the back of her eyes. She
tried to cry, but every throb caught her breath short.

Her arms, legs, and back knotted into cramps that felt
as if she was being peeled apart from the inside. Her abdomen felt like it was being clutched by a giant fist in an
endless squeeze.

She tried to scream, but she could only get breath for a

whimper. She couldn't move. The pain wouldn't even let her think.

All she knew was she was dying.

24 OCTOBER   CLEVELAND, OHIO

05:52 AM   SUNDAY

The sky was just lightening by the time Chuck walked out onto the streets of Little Italy. He had gotten himself thoroughly lost within the boundaries of University Hospitals and Case Western Reserve University. In a way, that was good, since three minutes after he'd found his way out of the University Hospital, ER building, cops were everywhere, looking for him. If he didn't know where he was going, the cops certainly didn't.

The only real touchy part was avoiding all the damn security cameras. That had meant no well-lighted thoroughfares, and, consequently, no visibility on an overcast night. He'd nearly broken his ankle twice, running where he couldn't see. Eventually, after dodging cop cars with spotlights, and hiding in dumpsters, he had stumbled down to a set of train tracks and had followed them up to Little Italy.

Through the night, he had managed to ditch the lab coat that he'd stolen from the doctor, as well as everything from the doctor's, the nurse's, and the cop's wallets, except for the cash. Chuck felt he was owed that much, since the hospital had taken his wallet, his knife, and his keys—everything but the loose change in his pockets.

Everything else from the hospital was stashed in a plastic bag he'd found fluttering by the Food Co-op when he'd climbed down from the tracks. Even the gun was in the bag. With his shirt as it was, a gun in the belt or a pocket would be an invitation saying, "shoot me!"

All the shops down here were dark and closed at this time of night, except for a doughnut shop he passed. A doughnut shop with, fortunately, no cops.

Chuck kept an eye out for cop cars, but he didn't see any. But he was worried about going up into the Heights area. The place was crawling with police, especially at night. All he had to do was walk in front of the wrong speed trap.

It was time to drop a dime on a friend.

Chuck stopped at a pay phone, and called up one of the more available girls he knew. He bent over the phone and nodded a lot, "Yeah, I know . . . sounds like a party, Gigi . . . I know, always a party there . . . yeah, was wondering if I could come crash . . . uh huh I got something for you . . . yeah, you'll like it . . . no, the couch is fine, just if anyone's looking for me . . . you got it—could you send someone down here to pick me up? . . . Little Italy, in front of Presti's Doughnuts . . . don't ask . . . yes, I have some for him, too . . . and if anyone asks for me . . . yep . . see you."

Chuck hung up the phone and picked up his little plastic bag of contraband. He faded into a shadowy part of an alley, where he could watch for his ride without being observed, and he fished through all the stuff he'd liberated from the hospital.

The bag held the cop's gun, gauze for his hand, and what had amounted to impulse theft on Chuck's part. He'd swiped a half-dozen hypodermic needles and syringes, rubber hoses, a scalpel that was still wrapped in plastic, and a dozen small vials filled with various medications.

He was glad he'd thought of it while he had a doctor at gunpoint. Gigi was about to have quite a party.

CHAPTER
SEVEN

Allison woke with the hazy memory of agony and the dull ache of faded cramps in her arms. She didn't try to move, or open her eyes—she barely breathed, for fear of triggering the pain again.

Eventually the need to be clean won over the fear.

The sheets were drenched with sweat. The clothes she'd slept in had adhered to her body in the most grotesque way. She could smell the fact that her bladder—and worse—had given way while her mind had abdicated.

She was sick with embarrassment. The last time she had wet the bed was when she was six. Upon opening her eyes, she saw a puddle of vomit next to her head. She bolted upright—

Bad idea.

The sudden movement overwhelmed her with a tidal wave of dizziness. She clamped her eyes shut until she was certain that she wasn't going to throw up again. She took several deep shuddering breaths, trying not to gag on the sour taste in her mouth.

When her brain stopped spinning, she opened her eyes. When she finally saw her room, she almost threw up anyway.

"Oh, my . . ."

First she thought that she was in the wrong place, but the feeling passed.

It *was* her room, but it was a godawful mess. Her bedding, and some of the clothes she'd slept in, had been thrown to the walls. Her bed stand had been upended, spilling lamp, phone, and alarm clock. Something must have hit her bureau because stuffed animals were everywhere and the TV was blind, silent, and facedown on the throw rug between the bed and the dresser. Frozen in shafts of dawn light, her homework lay in drifts like an academic blizzard.

At the foot of her bed, on top of the naked mattress, Babs Bunny sat a little cockeyed on top of Allison's history textbook, as if the rabbit had planned all this.

I must have been delirious, Allison thought. *Delirious and violent.* She was frightened by the fact that she remembered none of it. She couldn't remember moving at all.

Where was Mom?

There had to have been a hell of a racket, at least when the TV upended. Why didn't her mother come to check her out?

Scared in more ways than she could name, Allison got out of bed and walked the length of the hall to her mother's bedroom. She had to hold on to the wall to stay upright. Her perception felt off in odd directions that she couldn't fathom. Her arms and legs didn't occupy the right spaces. She had to think about simple motions like walking.

It reminded her of the one time she'd been drunk. Except her vision was so oddly sharp. She felt she actually saw more of the world than she should. When she thought about it, her eyes hurt.

Allison reached her mom's bedroom door, the last one at the end of the hallway, and knocked on it softly. "Mom?"

She heard breathing beyond, and pushed gently on the door.

Scarlett's striped-orange form bolted out of the room, between Allison's legs. She had to hold on to the doorframe to keep from falling over.

The first thing Allison saw was the empty bed. Her breath caught in her throat. But when she turned away from the bed, she saw Mom, asleep on a recliner in the corner.

Across Mom's lap was a photo album Allison had never seen before. Yellowed newsprint stuck out the edges of the book, and it was open to a picture of a uniformed man posing in front of the American flag. The pose was familiar. Macy's oldest brother, Jason, had sent home a picture just like that when he joined the Marines.

On the floor, by Mom's dangling right hand, was a half-full tumbler of amber liquid, and a nearly empty bottle of Jim Beam.

"Mom?" Allison repeated, softly.

A grumble and a slight stirring, but no other reaction. Allison looked at the tumbler, and the scrapbook, and knew that this was a scene she wasn't supposed to see. She closed her mother's door and walked back to her room, trying not to think of how far away the floor seemed, or the thought that her questions about Dad had driven Mom so deep into a bottle that she couldn't hear it when Allison was tearing her room apart in some sort of delirium.

She grabbed all the bedding that had scattered to the points of the compass, pulled her white fluffy bathrobe out of the closet, and went to the bathroom. The bedding, and her clothes, went into the laundry hamper, filling it. She managed to confirm, to her disgust, that all her bodily functions had let go in the night.

She let her underwear soak in the sink while she tried to shower off the filth. The hot shower was the best thing she'd felt in quite a long while.

As she put her room back in order, she thought, *Maybe that was it. The worst for last.* She hoped that was right. The headaches, up to last night, had been growing less frequent. Maybe they would finally come to a stop.

You're kidding yourself, Allison thought. *Things are* not *going to be all right. Not the way this is going.* She had to break it to Mom that she'd been hiding the headaches, no matter what kind of weirdness it would cause. She wasn't ready to go through another night like this, even if she had to get someone to sedate her to the gills to stop it. Another night like this would probably kill her. . . .

Fortunately, the only fatality of this evening was the light bulb in her table lamp.

Her crotchety TV seemed to have even improved its reception somewhat. Though now it was missing both the contrast and brightness knobs.

As she put Babs up next to the TV's antenna, she heard Mom wake up. Allison froze, as if she was doing something wrong and was about to be caught. *Is it now? Do I just run out and spill everything while Mom's still hungover?*

She'll just say it's nothing, it's stress, it'll go away . . . and she's keeping things from me . . . and . . . and . . .

"I don't want to find out something's wrong with me." Allison whispered, trying not to cry.

"Allie, you awake?" Mom's voice came from the hall, sounding half asleep. The sound made Allison feel watery inside. Mom never drank heavily, never alone.

"Yes, Mom." Allison could hear the catch in her own voice.

She heard her mother fussing in the bathroom. "We're going to have to do the laundry. Whose turn is it?"

Allison thought of the stained sheets in the hamper and lied, "My turn." *Tell her.*

There was a pause, and Allison thought her mother was going to correct her. "Okay, hon. Do it sometime today." Then Allison heard the bathroom door close.

"Yeah," Allison said.

The shower started.

You can't bring yourself to tell your mother that something's seriously wrong inside your head.

Allison stayed there, staring at Babs in her hand. Babs stared back with a goofy fabric smile. "What if I'm dying?" she asked Babs in a whisper. "Is that what Mom is afraid of? Is everyone just lying because it's hopeless, inoperable, or what?"

She clutched the stuffed animal to her chest and whispered, "The doctor said there was nothing wrong with me. Nothing. Nothing." Allison repeated the word until she realized how much like her mother she sounded.

Mom: "Calling here again."
John: "I deserve the chance to talk to her."
Mom: "You have some nerve. Good-bye, John."
John: "Tell her. You owe her that."
Mom: "Don't tell me how to treat my daughter."
John: "If they look, they'll find out about the doctor's appointments."

Mom: (goes off on the fact my headaches weren't anything to worry about.) "They cleared up after the visit. Nothing, nothing, nothing!"

John: "Did the doctor know the other possibility . . . ? If she's a teak(teek?), they'll—"

Mom: "Leave us alone. I don't believe any of this. They're stone insane. You're insane. Call and I drag you into court. Touch my daughter, and I'll kill you."

The page sat there, on top of all her homework, christened by a few drops of Chuck's blood. Allison stared at it, knowing that it meant her headaches were something evil.

If it wasn't for that third person plural pronoun. They. *Them.* Allison was beginning to hate that word. If it wasn't for that reference to "they," then all of it would make sense. If not for these unnamed third parties, and their implied activity bearing on her, the conversation was simple.

John thought she was imperiled by these migraines, and Mom didn't. Or at least Mom very much didn't want to see things that way. Allison couldn't blame her mother for acting as she did. Allison managed to hold up more than half of the fiction that she felt all right.

Allison wondered who "they" were. Could they be relatives she didn't know about? Maybe someone on her father's side would want to fight for custody, declaring her mother unfit for ignoring her daughter's medical problems—

"But she hasn't. I was at a doctor the same day I mentioned the first headache. Two visits, scads of tests . . ."

No, that didn't seem likely.

She sat cross-legged on her bed, hugging Babs Bunny, her homework stacked in front of her. She was surrounded by cats offering their feline brand of comfort. Scarlett was draped over her left leg, purring into the crook of her knee, while Rhett was intermittently stalking her hair. Meowrie had even come in, to curl up next to the radiator.

Right now Allison wished she was a cat. Cats managed to understand things without having a too complex existence.

Maybe "they" were some foreign government whose exiled royalty had a genetic predisposition for adolescent migraines.

Maybe she'd been half asleep and misunderstood the entire conversation.

As she mused, the doorbell rang. Mom had left after her shower with a, "love you, be back soon," so Allison was the only one in the house—except for the cats, who stubbornly refused to go answer the door. The doorbell rang again.

Allison sighed and closed the cover of her notebook, marveling again at the straightened wire binding and the thumb-shaped tear. She got up, scattering cats, and went downstairs. Some latent paranoia made her keep the chain on when she opened the door.

Standing on the porch, waving at her, was Macy Washington. "Hi, girl, let me in? Or are you too busy reverting to infancy?"

Allison looked down and saw that she was still carrying Babs.

"I was discussing my career opportunities with Babs here. She thinks I might have a future as a cartoon." Allison unchained the door and let Macy in. "Enjoy the movie?"

Macy shrugged. "Just another of Ben's action flicks."

Allison sat on the sofa and perched Babs on the coffee table on top of an issue of *The Economist*. "Why do you let him drag you to movies you don't like?"

"Free popcorn? Milk Duds? Sitting up front to crick my neck?" Macy sat down and leaned forward. "You look better."

"Huh?" Allison's mind seemed to slip a gear. "I do?"

"The color's back in your cheeks, and you lost that crease." Macy tapped Allison's forehead with a long ebony finger.

"I can't think why . . ." Allison's befuddlement allowed it to dawn on her that she *was* feeling better. She'd been too preoccupied to notice that, after that horror last night, a weight had lifted from her body. It wasn't until then she realized that, for weeks, the headaches had never quite left. She had been living with a constant low-level pain that she had learned not to notice. It was as if, for two months, she'd been on the verge of a sneeze—and then she went "achoo" when she wasn't looking.

"Hey," Macy said, "you're smiling."

Allison supposed she was.

"What happened to the old grump?"

Allison shrugged and said, "Ask Babs."

Macy picked up the stuffed pink rabbit and threw it at her.

Allison ducked and sat down, "Sorry I couldn't join you guys."

"It's all right," Macy took up a position on the couch. "But I did want to talk to you, and you hung up rather abruptly last night."

Allison felt a wave of embarrassment, "Sorry about that."

"Like I said, no problem—" Macy leaned over and looked seriously at Allison, "But I hear you pulled a number on Chuck yesterday."

Allison, who had been feeling free of her personal problems for the first time in weeks, came crashing to earth. "What do you mean?"

"David went on about Chuck in the library, hollering and bleeding, cussing you to high heaven. What happened, girl?"

Allison tried to think of a snappy comment to deflect the issue, but for once she couldn't find one. "I let him scare me too much."

"How?"

"I saw him in the library, and I ran." Allison waved her hands toward the ceiling. "I rushed, dropped one of my notebooks. And there Chuck was, holding it out. And he. Wouldn't. Let. Go." She had to stop because tears were welling up. She grabbed a tissue from the box on the table and blew her nose. "He wanted to apologize for what he did at David's party. No hard feelings, he said. *No hard feelings!*"

She was breaking down now, trying to pull herself into a ball. Macy came over and sat next to her. Macy stroked her back and said. "I'm sorry. I just wanted to know what happened. Shh."

It took Allison a few minutes to pull herself together. She kept thinking about David's costume party. About her ruined costume. She couldn't even remember what he had said. All she remembered was the crowding presence, the hands, and the alcohol smell of his breath.

"I want my tail back." Allison muttered.

Macy chuckled. "He does have a talent for slapstick. Now tell me, girl. What'd you do that pissed him so much at the library?"

Allison snuffled and sat up, getting another tissue to wipe her nose. "He was baiting me with the notebook, and I ripped it out of his hand."

"Huh?"

Allison shrugged. "I must have been even angrier than I thought. I tugged a few times, and then it just—well—came loose."

"He let go?"

Allison shook her head. "No, he was holding on for dear life. Let me show you." She ran up and got her trigonometry notebook and came downstairs with it. She placed it in Macy's hand.

"No, palm up. Now the binding is here." She aligned the cover so the straightened wire was parallel with Macy's outstretched arm. "You see that hole? That's where the thumb goes."

"He was holding tight enough to tear the cover?"

"And the pages underneath. Now see?" Allison slowly drew the book over Macy's palm. The wire drew across slowly. "The corner of the binding hooked in his palm, cut him a little."

Macy sighed.

"What?" Allison asked.

"Wasn't a *little*." Macy took the notebook and looked at the wire. The end of it was hooked and it bobbed like a sheaf of metallic wheat. "David told us Chuck sprayed blood all over. Called an ambulance. David thought you knifed him."

"Me? A knife?"

"All David heard was Chuck screaming, 'The bitch slashed me.' What would you think?"

Allison looked at her trigonometry notebook with a little more respect. "I didn't mean to do anything like that . . ."

Macy smiled and shook her head. "I know, girl. Chuck's such trash that no one'd care if you *did* knife him—'cept maybe the cops and his folks. Then only because they have to."

"How badly did I hurt him?"

"David overheard one of the medics say something like two dozen stitches an' a lot of blood loss. He also said that Chuck keeled over before the medics showed."

Allison winced even though she thought Chuck deserved it.

"Hey," Macy said. "David's probably just exaggerating to make a good story. You know how he is."

"Too well."

"Want some advice?" Macy asked.

"What?"

"Go to the kitchen, right now." Macy tapped the cover of the notebook. "Put this here thing in a baggie and keep it safe."

"Huh, why?"

Macy sighed. "Think, girl. Chuck's pissed. He might be too he-man to call the cops on a girl who bit him. But he might not be. He might figure the embarrassment's worth it."

"But . . ."

"This proves your story. Don't lose it. Especially his bloodstains."

"Okay, okay." Allison felt really silly, but she went in the kitchen to package the "evidence." She couldn't find a Ziplock bag that'd fit her notebook, so she put it in a Hefty trash bag and put it up in her room.

Allison came downstairs, and Macy assured her that she'd done the right thing.

24 OCTOBER   CLEVELAND, OHIO

11:23 AM   SUNDAY

Three vehicles were parked, facing each other inside one of the dozen parking garages that dotted University Circle. They were a gray van, an old green Oldsmobile, and a blue, late-model Dodge sedan that stopped just short of looking like an unmarked police car.

A blond man in jeans and cowboy boots sat on the hood of the Olds. The sandy-haired teenager called Elroy leaned against the rear bumper of the Dodge. Today his T-shirt was white and had a picture of Foghorn Leghorn on it.

A thin man, white-haired and in his sixties, paced in front of all three cars.

"Calm down, George," said the man in the cowboy boots. His voice had a southwestern flavor to it.

"Oh, 'calm down,' he says," said the white-haired man. "Great, Barney, I'll remember that advice when *you're* in charge of a kid that blows up and starts threatening the local cops."

"You ain't in charge of them till we *have* them, George. Now if Elroy started waving a gun, then I'd worry." The cowboy cocked a head in the direction of the kid leaning on the Dodge.

"I'm sure Elroy appreciates that," George said and resumed pacing.

"Do you, Elroy?"

"Sure," Elroy said without turning around.

"Y'all know what'd happen if you waved a gun around?" asked the cowboy.

"You'd shoot me in the head, and Mr. Jackson would dump the body in a storm sewer."

"Smart kid—"

George stopped pacing. "His IQ is twice yours, Barney, and I'd like you to shut the fuck up."

"Touchy," said Barney, but he shut up.

"God," George muttered, "of all the teams to be saddled with. The boy was eighteen. We should have snagged him the moment we found him."

"The girl is better," Elroy said.

"I know, and that's what you're here for." George couldn't see the small smile cross Elroy's face. "*But*—" George stared at Barney, "using someone as unstable as Charles Wilson to draw her out again was not the right way to do things."

"Fuck you very much," Barney said politely.

At that, the sliding door on the van shot open, and the

woman inside said, "Would you children stop bickering."
She was pointedly looking at George and Barney, "Some
people are trying to sleep."

"Sorry, Jane," George said.

"He started it," said Barney.

Jane ignored him. "Is Jackson back yet?"

Three heads shook in unison. George said, "He's off with
some local cops, but I don't see the federal bit lasting much
longer—" George stopped in mid-sentence because a gray-
haired man was walking toward them.

"Speak of the devil," Jane said.

Fred Jackson walked up to the trio of vehicles. He nodded toward George and Jane, "Doctors—"

"What's the good word, boss?" Barney said from the
hood of the Olds.

"The word is, Charlie Woodrow Wilson is no longer a
concern of ours."

"You're kidding," George said.

Fred shook his head. "No. We're supposed to avoid local
involvement, and waving firearms at policemen is pretty
involved. For what he is, Mr. Wilson isn't worth the trouble
of extracting from the criminal tangle he's put himself in."

"What a waste," Jane said.

"It's his own fault, Doctor."

"What now?" George asked.

"Now we shift our attention to the powerful focus that
Elroy drew our attention to."

"The girl?" Barney asked.

"The girl."

"I told you she was better," Elroy said.

CHAPTER
EIGHT

Allison felt better than usual when the last bell rang on Monday. Despite her preoccupation over the weekend, her obsessive streak had managed to pull some of her classes out of the gutter. Even Mr. Franklin, her physics teacher, smiled at her as she filed out of his class.

She had thought physics was a lost cause.

Physics was the last class of the day. Afterward, she went straight from the science wing to the school courtyard.

The original high school was an H-shaped building. The science wing had been built across the top of the H, turning it into a squared-off A. Flanking the science wing were the south pool and the new gym, giving the top of the A much broader shoulders than the rest of the building.

The courtyard filled the top of the A and now that school was over it, in turn, was filled with students.

Allison came out into the courtyard as usual. And, as usual, she walked past bike racks and started along one of two short tunnels that led through the first floor of the science wing. After school she always met Macy at the McDonald's across the street.

She swung her backpack, whistling something to herself. Even the ominous echoes the tunnel threw back at her didn't depress her. She hadn't seen Chuck around all day, and that lifted her spirits more than anything. After what she'd heard about the scene at the library, it was a good thing not to run into Chuck.

She walked along the left wall of the tunnel, whistles echoing around her, running her hand along the brick. Bright sunlight filled both ends of the tunnel, cloaking the interior with shadow. The noise from the courtyard behind, and the traffic-filled street beyond, seemed far away.

She stopped halfway to the street. A kid with a Walkman was standing at the head of the tunnel, and seemed to be staring at her. The kid was too young to be in high school. But there was something about the kid's stare that was familiar—

Oh, jeez, the library.

The kid had been in the gray van that had nearly run over her. It was the same sandy hair, and the same merciless gaze. Allison almost said something but, just then, someone from behind sped past her on a skateboard.

She nearly dropped her backpack as she flattened herself against the wall.

"Sorry," said the skateboarder without slowing down.

Allison clutched her backpack to her chest and exhaled. Her heart was racing. *Little high-strung today, aren't we?*

As she calmed down, she suddenly became aware of two things; the kid with the Walkman had vanished, leaving her alone in this dark tunnel; and she was leaning next to a brown-painted fire door.

The door was open, slightly.

She'd barely had time to notice the door was ajar before Chuck reached out of it and grabbed her. She was so shocked that she didn't even think to scream. Her backpack spilled on the ground as he pulled her inside the door. She was frozen up until the time she heard the door chunk shut behind them.

Then she screamed.

Chuck slammed her against the cinder-block wall and covered her mouth.

The echoes of her aborted cry for help continued forever.

Chuck had pulled her into the fire stairs. The door next to them was thick steel, tagged with the sign, "Emergency Exit Only." The walls were dirty, whitewashed cinderblock, the floor damp, gray concrete. The stairs went down to the tunnels that connected the basement locker rooms to the

pool and the gym. The light was from a flickering, un-
adorned fluorescent tube set high in the ceiling.

Chuck looked bad. His eyes were wide and bloodshot.
He wore a sleeveless flannel shirt, and his jeans were spotted with blood.

Chuck held her pinned to the wall with his left hand. It
wrapped around half of her face, crushing her lips to her
teeth. Salty blood was leaking into her mouth. He leaned
against her face with all his weight, pinning her and igniting
the embers of another headache.

She felt as if her heart had stopped beating. Her insides
had fallen away, leaving a vacuum.

"Hi, sweetcakes," Chuck said. His breath stank. His
hand stank.

"Remember this?" Chuck held up his right hand. Allison
felt her eyes widen even as hysterical tears began filling
them. Half his right hand was covered with dirty white
gauze. His index and middle finger were discolored.

"You did this, you little bitch—here, lemme give you a
better view."

Chuck grabbed part of the dressing in his teeth and
pulled.

He's crazy, Allison thought. Her lungs burned, and her
limbs seemed to have receded away from the rest of her
body. A fire burned behind her temples, flaring with every
attempt to breathe.

The white gauze spiraled away from Chuck's hand, revealing a purple bruise covering most of the palm. The
bruise darkened to black where a line of puckered flesh
ran diagonally from the heel of the palm to the web between Chuck's first two fingers. The slice was knitted together by a line of black stitches. Chuck flexed the hand
and viscous black blood seeped between a few of the
stitches.

Allison wanted to throw up. She felt as if she was on a
roller coaster, but there was no upward turn, just the downward curve, down, and down, and down . . .

"This *hurt.*" Chuck balled his injured hand into a fist.
Allison could see his neck strain with the effort, and Allison
was afraid he was going to punch her with it.

She pulled at the arm holding her, kicked at him, but

Chuck barely noticed. He held a trembling fist closed until beads of fresh red blood began to appear between his fingers.

"I should hurt you, sweetcakes," he said. The way he said it made Allison stop struggling for a moment.

He reached into his pocket, smearing more blood on his jeans with his bad hand. He withdrew something thin and glittering. At first it looked like a pen, but then Allison saw the blade on the tip.

When Allison saw the scalpel, she redoubled her efforts at kicking and pulling herself free. But it wasn't just Chuck's strength holding her captive. He was leaning in, all his weight crushing against the hand on her face.

It was so damn hard to breathe.

Oh, God, why doesn't anyone hear this? Didn't anyone hear me?

The pain in her skull was beginning to fracture her vision. Rainbows grew from the fluorescent tube above them. The exit sign burned like a hot coal in the corner of her vision.

"I should cut you, like you did me." Allison tried to claw his face, but her nails were blunt. She had always thought long nails got in the way.

Chuck laughed at her.

Laughed at her.

The sound made Allison curl up within herself. As if all her fear meant nothing.

Allison felt the blade of the knife against her throat. "Calm down, or I *will* cut you."

Allison felt her arms drop. She wasn't getting enough air, and her vision was turning red around the edges. Her head was on fire and she could feel her consciousness slipping.

It would be so easy just to stop fighting.

The hand fell away from her face, and for a moment she gasped for breath. She had a few breaths as Chuck reached around behind him. It took her a second to realize what he was pointing at her.

Her eyes widened as she realized that Chuck held a gun.

He's going to kill me.

The blade in Chuck's right hand traveled down the front of her blouse, taking buttons as it went. "I don't want to hurt you, sweetcakes. I like you—really I do."

The blade severed the front of her bra.

It wasn't until Chuck had dropped the knife and was reaching for his own pants that Allison's panic-fogged mind registered what Chuck wanted to do.

Oh, God, no! I never—and with him—

The thought ignited such a pain within her skull that she thought she was going to die right there.

"NO!"

Anger and pain balled up within her and erupted outward, toward Chuck.

"NO!"

All her panic and rage fed into that one word. All she could think of was pushing him away. She threw up her arms to defend herself and stared at Chuck's right hand, still at his pants. At that moment she felt the ball of pain shoot away.

She heard something.

It was a loud snap, something like a muffled rifleshot, or someone flicking God's own wet towel.

As her vision cleared, she watched Chuck's cheeks puff out as he violently exhaled. His eyes widened. He wheezed, as if he couldn't catch his breath.

The gun fired into the wall, deafening Allison and spraying her with concrete shrapnel. It fired again, into the floor, filling her nose with acrid gun smoke. Then it clattered to the ground.

Both of his hands shot to his groin as he doubled over.

He collapsed to the ground, next to the gun.

She was frozen to the wall as she watched bright red blood begin to leak from between his fingers.

Something had happened to his jeans. It looked as if all the seams had given way. Blood pooled under him.

Chuck screamed. The sound brought Allison to her knees, knifing her with a pain in the temples that rivaled any headache she'd ever had. She nearly passed out.

She was barely aware of people arriving. From below, where the locker rooms were, a half-naked teenager ran up the stairs, trunks still damp and eyes red with chlorine. His gaze landed on Chuck's prone form and began yelling for help. He whipped a towel from around his shoulders to put pressure on the spurting wound. The swimmer kept crying and cursing because Chuck wouldn't let go and every attempt to staunch the bleeding made Chuck scream even more—

Howling animal screams that tore into Allison's skull like a band saw.

The pain drove her away from everything. She wasn't really there, couldn't really be seeing this.

The swimmer and Chuck screamed at each other, both unintelligibly. The towel turned red.

More people raced up the stairs. The swimmer shouted them back. Mr. Geraldi, the swim coach, carried one of the ubiquitous blue-bottomed first-aid kits. Geraldi saw the blood and a look of hopelessness crossed his face.

Geraldi screamed at the students to call an ambulance. Not a yell, but a scream, as if it was his own flesh torn and bleeding. He dropped the first-aid kit and knelt next to the swimmer. Geraldi's muscles knotted as he pried Chuck's hands away, so he could get pressure on the wound.

Chuck's screams finally died away, and that was the worst sound of all.

Then the door was open and there were police.

One of the cops had to drag her outside, away from the bloody chaos on the concrete landing. Allison realized that her blouse hung open, and she folded her arms.

People—students—were everywhere. Dozens of uniformed cops seemed to have arrived out of nowhere. A cop car, flashers going, had driven into the courtyard. Police kept the students and faculty back, away from the fire door and the path under the science wing.

Someone, it might have been Mr. Franklin, draped a jacket over her shoulders.

Paramedics she didn't remember arriving carried out Chuck on a wheeled cart. Their orange windbreakers were spattered with blood.

She was surrounded by cops when she thought she saw a twelve-year-old kid staring at her from the crowd. The kid's gaze seemed to pierce her, straight through what had just happened. It was as if the kid saw everything, and didn't care at all.

That was when she finally began to cry.

25 OCTOBER   EUCLID HEIGHTS, OHIO

03:30 PM   MONDAY

In a gray van in the McDonald's parking lot, George was yelling, "What the fuck happened? Will someone just tell me what the fuck happened?"

Fred kept watching out the rear windows with a pair of binoculars. The last ambulance had pulled away. "Apparently, our Mr. Wilson wasn't satisfied with threatening policemen."

Jane sat at the consoles lining one side of the van, typing on a computer keyboard and listening through a set of headphones. "Elroy identified the male as Charlie, and I'm picking up police traffic that confirms that. Attempted rape, apparently."

"What's Charlie's condition?" George asked.

"According to Elroy, and the medic's radio, our girl did something fairly drastic. Severe lacerations, both femorals, crushed testicles—" George flinched. "—broken pelvis, severe internal hemorrhaging, pupils fixed and dilated . . ." Jane shrugged. "Can't say I blame her. Remember I said missing out on Charlie was a waste? Forget it. Charlie's the waste. Good riddance."

"Shall we dispense with the editorializing?" Fred Jackson said from the rear of the van, putting away his binoculars. He turned around to face the rest of the occupants. He looked at Jane, "Did Elroy sense anything about what happened?"

"You can ask him yourself," Jane said as the side door of the van slid aside and Elroy stepped in.

"So," Fred looked at the child, "what did you see out there?"

"See *eye,* not much. Lots of cops. Lots of kids. Girl's the same one I picked out of the yearbook, Allison Boyle. The guy bleeding all over the place was Charlie."

"See *head,*" George said, placing a finger on a white-haired temple.

Elroy gave him a humorless smile, flashing machinelike braces. "Getting to that. Both of them did something pretty head-powerful. She's way beyond him, though. Whole different level."

"What did she do?" Jane asked.

Elroy shrugged. "Nothing I ever saw before."

That revelation was enough to silence the whole van for a few long moments. After a while, Barney, who'd been silent in the driver's seat throughout the whole episode, said, "What now, boss?"

Fred sighed. "This complicates things."

"As if they weren't complicated enough," George said. "We should have gone for the mother as soon as we ID'd the girl. We could have pulled her out of school before—"

Fred stared at George, "Doctor, your expertise is not in covert ops, and I am sick of your second-guessing. I'm security. You and Jane are the PhDs and the baby-sitters. Remember that."

"We should have talked to her mo—" George began, but before he could get the words out, Fred had slammed him into the wall of the van.

Fred leaned in, calm demeanor dissolved into an angry scowl and glaring eyes. "I will say this once, *Doctor*. I will not jeopardize the Institute by confronting a subject's parent on the strength of a drive-by sighting and a yearbook photo. Snatching the wrong kid is much worse than losing the right one."

"But losing *this* one—" George managed to croak.

"Is infinitely preferable to what I'll have Barney do to you if you make one more contrary comment during this mission. Understand?"

George nodded, slowly.

He released George, and a visibly calmed Fred turned to Jane. "How're the tails going?"

Jane sighed. "They've followed both of them back to University Hospitals. Everyone feels that we're going around in circles."

"Can't be avoided," Fred said, maneuvering to ride shotgun in the front of the van. "If anyone starts complaining too much, tell them what I told George."

"Great," Jane said.

"Mr. Jackson?"

"What is it, Elroy?"

"It's Charlie," Elroy said. "Don't bother with him, he's gone."

"He's critical," Jane said. "But if they'd lost him, I'd hear—"

"Breathing," Elroy said. "But *gone*." Elroy pointed to his forehead.

Jane watched him for a minute, then shivered and returned to facing the console.

Fred shook his head. "We counted him a loss anyway. To the hospital."

Barney peeled rubber out of the parking lot to belatedly follow the ambulances.

25 OCTOBER   CLEVELAND, OHIO

06:45 PM   MONDAY

Hours later, at the hospital, Allison finally stopped crying. She'd used all of it up.

Everything after Chuck's collapse was a fog that didn't settle into any coherent pattern. She remembered the doctors asking her questions. She remembered the lady volunteer from the rape crisis center giving her a jogging suit after the police had bagged her clothes for evidence.

She remembered looks from some of the uniformed cops, and a few orderlies, that felt nearly as demeaning as having Chuck touch her body.

The cops seemed to be avoiding the questions they must have been wondering about. Allison almost wished that they would ask. Then she could tell someone that she didn't know the answers.

She sat in a room at University Hospitals, wearing a too-large sweat suit. She was slowly crumpling a pamphlet from the rape crisis volunteer. They were leaving her alone, for that she was grateful. She hadn't gotten a chance to shower, to eat, or do anything but sob through a too-slowly diminishing hysteria.

Chuck had tried to rape her.

That rocked her at least as much as what had happened

to Chuck. The simple fact that someone had beaten on her and nearly raped her on the grounds of her own school building—

She could never feel safe anywhere again. She could never pass a closed door without wondering if there was another Chuck there waiting for her. The police didn't help. Some of them, the male ones anyway, looked at her like she was the criminal, as if she had done something wrong.

She hugged herself and tried to see it from their point of view. Surely, from the condition of her face and clothing, Chuck's intent was obvious. They'd even bagged the knife he'd threatened her with.

He had a *gun,* for crying out loud.

However, Chuck had nearly died while she'd only gotten a few cuts and a fat lip.

If *she* couldn't figure out what happened, how could she expect them to?

Mom, she silently prayed, *get here quick. I want to go home.*

Chuck still could die.

The event kept playing through her head and she couldn't get it to make any sense. She couldn't remember how Chuck had been so grievously wounded. There had just been the noise, the gunshots, and Chuck was lying on the ground, bleeding.

Did he shoot himself?

But he was hurt before he fired the gun. At least that was how she remembered it.

The door opened, letting in Detective Teidleman. He was short, well groomed, and wouldn't have looked out of place teaching mathematics at Euclid High. He was one of the nicer policemen, one who didn't make her feel like a criminal. "Allison? Your mother is here."

For the first time since all this had happened, she smiled. "Thank God." She felt like crying again.

"I want to apologize for taking this long to reach her."

Allison nodded. Trying to reach Mom at work was hitting a moving target. She was always traveling all over the city. Suddenly, Allison felt an overwhelming wave of sympathy for her mother—how did Mom hear about this? A call on her pager? Voice mail? "Your daughter's in the hospital."

She hadn't even thought of how her mother might be hit by this—and that opened the floodgates again. She began weeping. She tried to control herself in front of the detective, but she couldn't.

Teidleman gave her his handkerchief.

"I have a patrolman taking her around the back to avoid the press."

Press? Allison thought, and blew her nose. Then she realized she was using someone else's handkerchief. She looked up to apologize, but instead of seeing Teidleman, she saw her mother.

"Oh, my baby." Mom'd been crying almost as much as Allison had. They hugged each other for a long time.

"Tell me he didn't harm you," Mom said, clutching her as if she might run away.

"No, Mom. Just a bloody lip."

"Thank God," Mom said, echoing Allison's earlier words. "The police haven't mistreated you?" she asked, loosening her grip so they could face each other.

"No, Mom. They just did their job."

Mom looked her up and down, as if just realizing what Allison was wearing.

"My clothes were evidence," Allison said. "Bloody, too."

"What happened?" asked her mother, a trembling note in her voice, as if she was afraid of the answer.

Not fear, Allison thought, *terror.* Allison started crying again, more in frustration than anything else. "*I don't know.* He was about to—and then he—there's this sound and he's on the ground, and *I don't know what I did.*"

"Shh." Mom pulled her close again and kissed her on the forehead. "It's all right now. Mommy's going to take you home."

"I hurt him." Allison cried into her mother's shoulder. "I nearly killed him, and I don't know what happened."

"Shh."

They remained quiet for a long time before Mom spoke again. "Allie, make me a promise."

"What?"

"Don't ever let yourself regret what you did."

Allison pulled away, and saw a frightening look on her mother's face.

"Never regret protecting yourself, Allie. Promise me."

Allison nodded.

"Say it. Please."

"I promise, Mom."

"Always, always, protect yourself, Allie."

Allison could feel Mom's hand shaking on her shoulder. Allison nodded and said, "I will, Mom. Promise." *I don't even know if I did anything.*

Mom hugged her and said. "Thank you. Let's go home."

As they left, Mom said, "You know I love you more than anything."

Allison had been left breathless by how quickly events could spin out of control, how a disaster, even if it didn't bodily harm her, could rip the fabric of her life. Chuck had managed to find all the loose threads of her life and tug at them, until nothing was left.

The police had kept saying "attempted rape."

It wasn't "attempted." Chuck had raped her the minute he pulled her through that door. Allison was sitting in numbed shock during the drive home when Mom said, "I'm so sorry about your father, Allie."

After what had happened, the comment seemed to come from out of nowhere. For a moment Allison couldn't make sense of the words, as if Mom was suddenly speaking a foreign language. "What?" she asked, her voice hoarse from crying.

When she turned, she could see tears on her mother's face, too. "I took your father away from you—"

We left, Mom. We left.

"I felt it was too dangerous. I had to try and bring you up in a normal house, with a normal life, please don't hate me for it—"

"I don't hate you, Mom . . ." Allison sucked in a breath. "Is Dad really dead?" She tensed for some sort of explosive reaction, but Mom seemed to be in shock as much as she was.

"I'm sorry, Allie."

"Why?"

There was a long silence before Mom said, "You were too young to understand. I had to give you an explanation you could grasp."

The numbness was leeching away; beneath it was an ugly feeling. "Too young?" The copper taste in the back of Allison's throat was her own anger. "Am I too young to understand now?"

Mom pulled into the driveway and screeched to a halt. "Please let me—"

"No, Mom," Allison shook her head, tears were burning her eyes again. "I *don't* get it. Was I too young *last* year? What were you waiting for, my eighteenth birthday?"

Mom looked down at the steering wheel and shook her head. "Why I had to take you, I didn't have any way to explain why we couldn't see him again. Why we couldn't have any contact—"

"Jesus Christ, Mom—people break up every day!" Some part of her made Allison want to stop. But the part of her that didn't want to hurt her mother was overwhelmed by the part that was enraged by her mother's lie, her headaches, her failings at school, and most of all, Chuck. She wrenched the passenger door open and stepped out.

"Allie—"

"Half the kids at Heights have divorced parents. I bet I'm the only one who's been told her father was *dead* because her Mom didn't like to talk about it."

"It wasn't like that, there was—is—a danger . . ."

"What is it? Did he beat you, Mom? Rape you?" Mom sat there looking stunned. "I don't think you can say I don't understand *that* now."

Allison started walking away from the car, fury still burning within her, mixing with an even more painful brand of shame.

Behind her she heard the car door slam and heard her mother call out. "No, Allie. It wasn't like that. I *loved* him."

"Yeah, right." Allison spoke without turning around. She was half running for the door. She wanted this conversation to end, right now. *Please, God, let's just stop it now . . .*

"Please, stop, you don't understand what—"

"That's what you've been telling me." Allison stormed through the door, slamming it behind her. Once inside, the sobs started, burning her throat, and she ran for the stairs. She stumbled, tearing the knee of her sweatpants on the stairs, but she didn't let it slow her dash for her room. Her door was slamming behind her before Mom had entered the house.

The bedroom seemed much too small. She threw open the closet door grabbing the shoebox she'd shoved there so hastily last Friday.

The shoebox fell to the floor, and in her hands was the one hundred and two pages of *Restless Nights*.

Randolph, Melissa, her perfect fictional couple . . .

Tears streaming down her face, she methodically began to tear every single page into pieces. Mom pounded on the door. Allison told her to go away, leave her alone. Eventually, Mom did, and Allison's shaking hands continued dissecting the pages.

By the time she got to the end, the box was filled with confetti and her throat was raw from silent sobbing. When the last page had been shredded, she curled up on the bed and tried to sleep.

The clock read ten when the phone woke her up. She didn't answer it. The phone had been a nightmare lately. The school had called to inform Mom that Allison had been suspended, "pending further investigation." Police had called to schedule an interview. Some reporter, somewhere, had gotten their number—

She'd barely gotten two hours of dreamless slumber.

The phone stopped ringing as her mom answered it.

"Allie," came her mom's voice at the door. "Do you want to talk to Macy?"

Allison sat up and picked up the phone. "I got it. Hello?"

"Allie? Oh—ah—" The hesitation was totally unlike Macy. Hearing Macy's voice made Allison silently forgive her for waking her up. Macy paused, and finally said, "Damn it, can I do anything?"

Allison smiled sadly. "Thank you."

"For what? Christ, I'm sorry—I didn't know—I saw the cops, but I didn't think—"

"Shh, it's all right."

"No, it ain't. My best friend is—and not a hundred feet from me—it wasn't until—"

"Shh."

Macy took a deep breath. "Saw the cops out front. Someone says some guy got hit in the balls. That's all. Thought I lost you while I was rubbernecking. My sorry ass didn't know you were—" Macy was crying into the phone. "Not till I hear Chuck's name on the *news,* man! I should've been there!"

"You're forgiven, Macy. You didn't know, you couldn't have known."

"If I was there—"

"If you were there, Chuck would've waited until you weren't there anymore. You weren't going to stop him."

Macy sniffed and Allison could picture her nodding into the phone. "Oh, man. *You* stopped him, didn't you—" Macy sucked in a breath. "Look, I'm sorry. You don't want to talk about this, do you?"

"I'm not sure what happened, Macy. I don't even know what hit him."

There was a pause. "Girl, on the news . . ."

"What's on the news?" Allison sat up straighter.

Allison listened to Macy breathe.

"Macy, I was there. Tell me what they're saying on the news."

"They had Geraldi on the tube saying his balls were shredded."

Allison gulped. "Geraldi said *that?*"

"I don't wanna be saying this—can I—"

"What else, Macy?"

"Doctors were talking about hemorrhages and internal injuries and a broken pelvis—and *I should have been there, damn it!*"

She realized that she was putting Macy through the wringer and felt awful for it. Just because she was numbed at the moment . . .

"It's my fault," Allison said. "I should have told somebody about Chuck before this. You tried to get me to. I should have listened to you."

She heard Macy blow her nose. "Damn straight. But, God, don't feel sorry for Chuck. He went over the deep end. He pulled a gun on a cop."

"He what?"

"Yeah, on the news. After you put him in the hospital

the first time— Oh, shit, I'm doing it again. I'm sorry. Me and my mouth—"

"It's all right, calm down."

"Yeah, calm's good."

After a pause, listening to Macy breathe, Allison asked, "Are you all right now?"

"Girl, what sense is it *you* asking *me*?" Macy caught her breath. "I'm unloading on you at the worst time—"

"What're friends for?"

"Can I start this over?"

Allison shook her head and said, "Okay. Hello?"

"Allie, can I do anything for you?"

"No, I'm doing okay for now."

"I could come over—"

"Not right now, okay?"

"Okay, you hurt at all?"

"Not in the body."

"Will you call me after school tomorrow? Tell me how you're doing?"

"Sure."

"Tell me if you need me to bring over anything?"

"Uh huh."

"I guess that's it, sort of. I'm sorry my call's so screwed up."

"We're all screwed up. Ah, Macy?"

"Yes?"

"Thanks for being such a friend."

"Likewise, girl," Macy said. "Likewise."

Allison hung up the phone and felt a little less empty inside. *I'm making the news,* she thought. The idea made her feel queasy.

Macy must have called just after the ten o'clock news report. Allison turned on her little black-and-white TV and waited for eleven, when the three other stations did their news reports. She tuned in channel five, because it had the best reception, and waited for *Eyewitness News* to come on. The promos confirmed her fears, showing an exterior shot of Euclid Heights High School.

"Major violence stains the halls of an East Side high school earlier today, critically wounding one student. More at eleven."

She began to feel more violated than ever.

CHAPTER
NINE

Allison spent the night staring at the ceiling of her room, trying not to think of what had happened. Her rebellious mind used the effort as an excuse to drag up more and more grotesque recollections. Her half-awake mind would drift into slumber, then hit her with something so vile that it would shock her awake.

She couldn't stand the sight of blood, and Chuck's injury had been indelibly marked on the inside of her skull, a surrealist portrait in Day-Glo red and nightmare black.

And when she wasn't thinking of what Chuck had done, or what she had done to Chuck, she was thinking of what she had said to Mom.

Whatever Mom might have lied about, she didn't deserve what Allison had said to her. Thinking about it made her almost feel as if she had deserved what had happened with Chuck.

As if summoned by her thoughts, during the night she heard her mother's voice on the phone downstairs. The words registered blankly in Allison's exhausted mind.

". . . Hello? Yes, yes, it's me. . . . You were right. . . . No, I haven't told her yet . . . I need you there to . . . The phones. If you're right, they're probably listening . . . Yes . . . When I first called you a baby-killer? You have a sick sense of humor. . . . Yes, I remember, send it. . . . See you there. . . ."

Allison drifted into sleep listening to her mother.

26 OCTOBER   EUCLID HEIGHTS, OHIO

07:00 AM   TUESDAY

Allison's alarm woke her at seven, as usual. She sat up
and had a blissful three minutes where everything was normal again. It wasn't until she was fully awake that she
thought, *What am I doing up this early? I'm suspended.*

Allison threw herself back on the bed, muttering. "After
all that homework—"

Thinking of her homework—as if it mattered after what
she'd been through—was so incongruous that it started her
laughing. Once she began, it was hard for her to stop. The
universe was playing some sort of elaborate practical joke
on her so that not only did she get to play the part of a
helpless victim—nearly raped on her way home from
school—she'd been immediately cast into the role of savage
tormentor. It was rich. It was insane. How could anyone
believe she had done *that* to Chuck. It was impossible.

Impossible.

She had tapped such a deep well of hysteria that she
couldn't stop laughing until she saw her mother standing at
her door. Mom had such a look on her face that Allison
managed to come to a choking halt.

"It's okay, Mom. I haven't gone crazy." *Yet.*

She came in and hugged Allison. "I'm so sorry, Allie."

"No, Mom. I was a bitch yesterday. I don't know how
you can forgive me."

Mom sucked in a breath. "Allie, you're the last one here
that needs forgiveness." She let go and stood back, still
holding on to Allison's shoulders. "I thought I was doing
the best thing for you, but—" Mom's voice caught, and
Allison saw that she was on the edge of tears again. "—I
think I might have done more than anyone to hurt you."

"No, Mom. I can understand how it must have been,
things going bad between you and Dad."

Mom shook her head. She looked almost as distressed
as she'd been when Allison had been yelling at her. "No,
honey. That's as far from the truth as you can get. If there's
anyone who cares about you as much as I do, it's your

father. John is a good man, Allison. He would never do anything to hurt you or me."

"But why lie, then? Why haven't I seen him since I was four?"

"Because no one else could know he was your father."

Allison stared at her mother and tried to understand what she meant. "What has that got to do with anything?"

Mom sighed and looked pained. "Oh, God, I wish I had the time . . ." For the first time Allison was beginning to realize that Mom looked as if she had gotten no sleep at all. "Honey, I've got to get to the office as soon as it opens. I *have* to arrange some things—"

Work again. Allison nodded and said lamely, "I understand." She turned away, but Mom reached around and cupped her chin, turning Allison's face to look at her.

"If there was anything else I could do right now instead, I would. Believe me, the last thing I want to do right now is leave you, especially with only half an explanation." She stood up. "But I have to do some things before we leave."

Allison straightened up. "Leave? Where?"

Mom looked as if she debated a moment before she said, "We're going to see your father."

Allison's jaw dropped and she was left speechless. Mom let her go and backed toward the door. "I'm sorry I have to go. I want to stay here, but—"

Allison nodded and whispered, *"Dad?"*

Mom nodded and said, "I know he wants to see you very badly. I'll be home by one, two at the latest. Then we can talk about what's happening."

"Yeah . . ."

Mom wrung her hands a few times. "Please, stay in the house, please?"

"Mom?"

"Promise that you won't go anywhere. I don't want to worry about you."

"I promise, Mom." Allison felt a burning in her chest and before Mom had stepped outside the door she said, quickly, "I've been lying to you, too."

Mom paused in the doorway. "Allie?"

"I lied about the headaches going away. They've been pounding me constantly—"

"Oh, baby," Mom took a step toward her.

The confession kept rushing forward, "It's been eating my brain until last Saturday night. I threw up, Mom. I tore apart my room. I've been so scared—"

Mom rushed up and hugged her. "Oh, honey, shh."

"I thought you wouldn't believe me, after the doctor— am I dying?"

Mom crouched down so she was at Allison's eye level and holding her hands. "No, honey. You aren't dying."

Allison looked into her mom's eyes. For once she didn't see fear there, or denial. What she saw was a fierce determination. "I know," Mom said. "I've known since I heard what happened to Chuck." She squeezed Allison's hands. "You inherited those headaches from me and your father. I'm sorry I was so blind—I was just praying that we hadn't passed on those genes. You are not going to die, understand?"

Allison nodded. What she saw in Mom's eyes now was almost scary. She had been going to admit to listening in on the phone, but she decided not to.

Mom let go of her hands and stood up. "I love you more than anything, honey."

"I love you, too, Mom."

As she left the room she said, "Stay in the house—"

"I will."

"And don't answer the door for anyone you don't know."

"Mom?"

"Promise."

"Yeah, sure . . ."

Allison was left thinking about that until she heard the door close downstairs.

Allison spent the morning trying to catalog memories of her father. The images that came to mind seemed half childhood memory and half romantic fantasy. She remembered a tall, dark-haired man. A giant from a four year-old's perspective. She remembered a one-story house with blue curtains. She remembered a uniform that smelled of mothballs in a bedroom closet. She remembered a station wagon driven by a smiling man with heavy eyes.

Two scenes focused in her memory.

She remembered wearing her Sunday best and going with her father into town. The town wasn't Cleveland. Her daddy wore his uniform, still smelling of mothballs. She remembered thinking. *Something's wrong with Daddy.*

He took her to a city square. All the people had scared her, and she'd hidden behind his legs. She looked up at Daddy, and—for the only time in her life—saw Daddy crying.

"What's wrong, Daddy?" she asked.

"A great man died here," her daddy said. "A long time ago."

"Why'd he die?" Allison looked around and only saw grass, roads, and buildings.

He paused. "Because there are bad men in the world, Allie. Men who like to hurt people."

"Will the bad men get me?"

Her daddy's eyes welled with tears, and he hugged her to him. "No, I won't let the bad men get you."

The other scene was more chaotic, jumbled. She remembered being pulled out of bed. "Where we going, Mommy?"

She was thrust into the back of a waiting taxi, half-asleep, still wearing her Smurf pajamas with the little feet. She clutched her old Cat-in-the-Hat doll as she stumbled into the taxi. Mommy's overcoat was wrapped around her, and she remembered how comfortable it felt. Then Mommy was yelling, up at the house, and that scared Allison. Things were shoved into the taxi, suitcases, a cardboard box—

Somehow that devolved into a memory of a Greyhound bus, and asking Mommy, "Where's Daddy?"

"Daddy had to go away, hon."

That's silly, we're *going away.*

Allison could remember being distracted from everything by the endless scenery out the Greyhound's window. For the first time in a long while Allison could remember being awestruck by the St. Louis arch. Then there were hills, trees, and she was going to school in Euclid Heights, Ohio.

When she finally got out of her bed and dressed, around ten, she did so with a great feeling of emptiness. And a sense of almost surreal anticipation.

"We're going to see your father."

Allison still couldn't quite get her head around her mother's change in attitude. It was as if the woman on the end of the first two phone calls was completely different from the one who'd talked to her this morning. *What does she need to get done at the office?*

She had barely gotten dressed when the doorbell rang.

What? Who?

Irrational fear gripped her gut, and for a moment she was paralyzed. Mom's warning about strangers rang in her head.

The bell rang again, and she told herself that it had to be one of two things—Macy or the police. And even if police had come for her, they didn't rate the gut-wrenching fear that rooted her to the ground. She moved to descend the steps.

What if it's a reporter?

Oh, God, I'll deal with it. I have to deal with it.

She looked through the peephole, scaring herself with her mother's ominous words, and it was none of the above. It was a gentleman in a UPS uniform holding a clipboard gadget and a red-banded cardboard envelope. She opened the front door, chain in place.

"Yes?" Allison asked.

"Package for a Ms. Boyle. Sign for it?"

Allison took the cardboard envelope, through the partly open door. The guy gave her an odd look, but let her sign his clipboard gadget through the gap. Then she stood there watching as he walked away. She didn't stop staring until he had boarded his brown UPS van and had driven down the street.

My life is turning surreal, Allison thought to herself. *Soon Rhett is going to start talking to me.*

Her neighbors in the duplex had a paper on their stoop. The one headline she could see on the folded *Plain Dealer* was, "Alleged Teenage Rapist Victim of Savage Beating."

Allison stared at it, the words lodging in her mind and tumbling over each other. *Okay, is he an alleged teenager who's a rapist's victim? Is he beating up savages? Or was the savage beating up on the teenage rapist's alleged victim?*

I was there and the beating is a lot more alleged than the rape.

She was on the verge of laughing hysterically or bursting into tears.

In front of the house, Allison saw a familiar figure across the street. Standing motionless in a driveway was a twelve- or thirteen-year-old boy wearing a Bugs Bunny T-shirt and Walkman headphones. The kid was staring straight at her, through her. She locked eyes with the kid and felt a brief wave of sickness reminiscent of her headaches. It wasn't that the kid's look was intense, really. It was more the emptiness. The kid's eyes were dead, staring at something that wasn't there—or at least at nothing that Allison could see.

It took all of her willpower not to slam the door. When she closed it, she remained slumped against it, shaking. That kid's stare was nearly as bad as the looks Chuck gave her.

Just a kid, she thought, *he's probably on some sort of drug.* The more she told herself that, the more she felt it had to be the case. Whoever he was, he certainly *looked* spaced-out.

After a while Allison shook her head, dismissing her own paranoia. "He was at the school yard when I got hysterical. If he recognized me at all, of course he'd stare."

She collapsed onto the living room couch and tossed the "UPS Urgent Mail" letter on the coffee table on top of back issues of *The Economist* and *U. S. News and World Report.*

The way she was falling apart was pitiful. She had come near collapse just because someone looked at her funny. She couldn't do that If she ever— *When* she went back to Euclid High, she was going to have more than one boy looking at her funny.

She wondered if David would ever go out with her again.

She wondered if she'd ever feel safe going out with anyone.

Another thing lost, Allison thought. *Along with my past, my school career, nearly my virginity—*

"And Babs?"

Her stuffed rabbit was missing. She had left it down here

yesterday—no, two days ago—right there, on that issue of
The Economist, the one with a constipated-looking Boris
Yeltsin on the cover.

She started looking all over the living room for Babs
Bunny, and found no sign of her. Not under the couch or
the table. She even pulled the cushions from the sofa in
the search for her rabbit.

She was standing there, holding a sofa cushion in each
hand, when she noted Rhett and Scarlett sitting on the
dining room table. The two cats were looking at her a little quizzically.

"Okay, what'd you two do with her?"

Scarlett began to lick an orange paw, and Rhett jumped
off the table to amble into the kitchen. Allison was suddenly struck by how silly she looked, and meekly replaced
the cushions. It was so childish, being upset over a missing
stuffed animal.

"I don't care," Allison said. "I deserve a little childish-
ness. I don't have much left."

She sat down on the couch and her gaze landed on the
UPS letter.

The return address was somewhere in California.

Allison picked it up. She had assumed that this was
something to do with Mom's business, boring accountant
stuff. Now, Allison was beginning to wonder why that'd be
sent here, rather than Mom's office. As she looked at it,
Allison felt a thrill run through her body.

The sender was a John Charvat in Los Angeles.

The same John?

The thin cardboard of the envelope began to feel hot in
her hands. Her pulse raced in her neck. She remembered
last night Mom had said, "Send it."

Here *it* was.

Allison could almost feel the answers in this envelope.
Who "they" were, what had happened to her father,
everything.

Allison looked at the addressee.

"Ms. Boyle."

No initial, no Mrs. Just the last name. Theoretically, this
envelope was addressed to her as much as to Mom.

I'm sorry, Mom. I have to know.

Allison tore open the cardboard envelope and out fell two more envelopes bearing the United Airlines logo.

Of course. She'd overheard the conversation last night, and Mom had said they were seeing her father. Did she expect her mother to *drive* when Dad was probably half a dozen states away. More, if the return address was any indication.

She opened one envelope and lost the certainty she'd had that she knew what was going on. Inside was a pile of tickets from a half-dozen airlines.

"St. Louis," Allison read. "Dallas. Los Angeles. Phoenix. St. Louis *again*? Atlanta. Washington, D.C. New York."

This almost crosses the whole continent, twice.

She kept reading the itinerary with growing incredulity. The layovers stretched from an hour and a half in Atlanta, to nearly seven hours in Dallas. Getting from Cleveland to New York by this cockeyed route was going to take more than three days. The total price on the grand tour was over two thousand dollars.

For each envelope.

Two sets of tickets, leaving Cleveland Hopkins Airport for St. Louis at 11:15 AM tomorrow, arriving in New York at 2:35 PM on *Saturday*.

"You could get there sooner by boat."

Allison held in her hands an expensive hopscotch across the country, for no apparent purpose. They were just flying to see Dad. But why all the layovers?

The more Allison thought about it, the more it worried her. Last night, she was beginning to remember Mom talking about tapped phones. Mom was paranoid about strangers knocking on their door.

If someone tapped your phone, wouldn't they also follow you around?

Maybe Dad was worried about someone following them to him. Maybe any one of these layovers could be the real destination, and the rest just a smoke screen.

But New York?

Allison looked at all the destinations, and only one had any special resonance for her.

Dallas?

"A great man died here. A long time ago." Allison recog-

nized that place from her memory now, and felt foolish for
not recognizing it sooner. She knew where she had been
born, where she lived the first four years of her life. It had
just been buried under other parts of her life. Her memory
hadn't been lost, just misplaced.

Yeah, but if they *know anything about me, wouldn't my
home town be a stupid place to meet?*

Allison nodded to herself. Dallas was probably there just
for that reason, to draw attention away from other destinations. All the tickets were from different airlines, and each
had its own boarding pass, a few were even two-way. Allison would just bet that every one was bought at a separate
travel agent.

I can figure this out.

Logically, New York was out as a destination. It was the
last ticket, and it had to be a smoke screen. Dad lived in
Los Angeles; that was obviously a draw for the baddies.

For a long moment, Allison wondered if they *had* to be
meeting in St. Louis. Otherwise, to go anywhere else they
would have to take lengthy layovers in two cities that were
obvious destinations. She wondered about that just long
enough to feel foolish when she realized that there were
two stops in St. Louis. She and Mom weren't supposed to
go any farther west of the Mississippi. Dallas, LA and—by
extension—Phoenix were all there just to confuse the issue.
They would just lay over a day in St. Louis.

That left Atlanta and Washington, D.C.

She felt that she should know which—but at the moment
it escaped her. She smiled to herself and slid the tickets
back. Maybe, when Mom showed up, she could dazzle her
with her deductions. Narrowing seven destinations to a possible two, that wasn't bad.

The smile lasted up until she thought that *they,* if *they*
had access to John Charvat's itinerary, could make the
same deductions she had.

Allison stood there holding the envelope. After a moment, she threw it to the table, "I don't even know who
they are. I don't even know what I'm being paranoid
about!"

She looked toward the ceiling and shouted, "Whoever
you are! I refuse to do this, hear me? My name is Allison

Boyle. I'm sixteen years old. I was nearly raped yesterday. I've been suspended. I have awful headaches. I HAVE OTHER PROBLEMS!"

No one answered her. *You've lost it,* she thought. Feeling silly, she went off in search of her missing stuffed rabbit.

26 OCTOBER   EUCLID HEIGHTS, OHIO

10:00 AM   TUESDAY

In the back of the van sat Fred Jackson. Behind him stood George and Barney. Jane, Elroy, and the other members of Jackson's field team were keeping watch on the Boyle house.

All three of them in the van watched the bank of consoles, even though the transmission was audio only and there wasn't much to see. The voice through the speakers came through a scrambler and a satellite link. It sounded as if it came from the bottom of a well.

"I apologize for the delay in your orders, Fred. I've been talking with Mr. Stone all night."

Fred nodded. He was the only one in the van who seemed unmoved by the mention of Stone's name. He asked, "What do you have for me, Scoob?"

"On the girl, nothing. That's why you weren't briefed on any other potential subjects in the target area. There weren't supposed to be any."

Fred straightened in his chair. "Your database is supposed to have *all* the project's kids. Even the illegitimate ones."

"That's why security and science are tied in a knot up here. Science thinks we might have a natural—and according to your spotter, a powerful one." The voice paused.

"And security thinks?" Fred asked.

"Who's there with you?"

Fred arched an eyebrow. Barney and George looked at each other. "The two ranking members of my team, Scoob. You know the drill."

"Dismiss them."

"What?"

"This is just for your ears, Fred."

Fred turned in his seat and looked at George and Barney. Without saying a word, Barney slid the door aside and waved George ahead. George looked at Barney, glared at Fred, then stepped outside. Barney followed, sliding the door shut behind him.

When the door shut, Fred said, "Just me now, Scoob." He didn't turn around.

"Fred, what we have here is a massive security breach. Science thinks we have a natural only because they haven't been told about the mother."

"What about the mother?"

"Carolyn Ann Boyle, Doctor Boyle, used to be staff here."

Fred spun around on the seat. "What?"

"She was one of our junior scientists, and she quit without notice over a decade ago. Security did a standard follow-up, shows her settling up there. We even have a record of her change in profession before the surveillance was dropped."

"Okay, I follow you so far. What's tying security in a knot?"

"She quit twelve years ago. Get it? Do the math. We have no record of the kid. None, Fred. The kid had to be at least four years old when she was working here."

Fred put his palms to his temples and pushed his hair back. "Adopted?" he said without much hope in his voice.

"Possible, but we have records of a six-month leave she took, without pay, at about the right time. We doubt that's a coincidence. We've also tried to contact the man who oversaw Institute security when she left, the man who oversaw the follow-up investigation on Boyle. Up until yesterday he was resident in Los Angeles."

"Up until yesterday?"

"Left his apartment around two in the afternoon, LA time, and has yet to turn up."

"Opportune timing."

"Good chance he was on a plane to anywhere an hour before our people arrived at the apartment."

Fred shook his head. "Okay, other than keeping the security boners quiet, what do I do?"

"First off, the kid is still a priority. She still might *be a natural, Elroy says she's hot, and Stone wants to make up for losing Wilson. In fact, the Institute will be willing to absorb some heat to get her."*

Fred nodded, "Considering the police involvement, we have to."

"As long as the heat doesn't reach Dallas, understand?"

"Of course."

"Second, we want the mother."

Fred was quiet for a moment before he said, "Getting parental consent? I know it's better when we do, but with her history—"

"No, Fred. We want the mother. *Security needs to talk to her. We need to know how she slipped through the cracks. We need to know who the father is. The daughter might not be able to tell us. And, most important, we don't want to leave someone out loose who could point anyone toward us after her daughter disappears."*

"Better if both mother and daughter vanish."

"Exactly."

"Consider it done."

CHAPTER
TEN

Allison's quest for her rabbit took her through the entire house. She'd covered almost every inch—including the most improbable areas of the kitchen and attic—and was beginning to worry a little about the obsessive nature of her search, when she caught sight of a flash of pink fuzz through her mother's partially open door.

Mom? What are you doing with Babs?

She pushed her mother's door all the way open.

Mom's room was neat, almost astringent. The bed was neatly made with a white comforter—

She looked at the bed and wondered, really wondered, if her mother had had any relationships since she'd left Dad. It had been twelve years.

Babs Bunny was there, on the bed, sitting on a pile of folded laundry and looking out the door. Allison picked up her rabbit and came to the realization that Babs wasn't the only thing Mom had taken. The folded clothes on the bed were all Allison's. She hadn't recognized them at first because she usually did her own laundry, so she rarely saw any of her casual clothes folded. But here was most of the stuff that had been waiting on a wash. There was her Garfield nightshirt. The jeans she'd slept in. Nearly half of her T-shirts. The red Marines sweater that Macy's brother had given her.

Even as she started to ask herself what Mom was doing with her clothes, she saw, on the other side of Mom's bed, her old Girl Scout duffel bag. She'd never been a Girl Scout, but she had been to a number of summer camps and that bag had seen a lot of use. It was zipped open next to the bed, and half filled with her own underwear. Next to the duffel was a single suitcase and an old cardboard box.

They were going to see Dad, but Allison was beginning to wonder if Mom intended for them to come back. It began to dawn on Allison, the fact that all those separate tickets, some with such a short layover between flights, meant that there might only be a chance to take on-flight baggage.

Mom had to have been doing this all night, no wonder it looked as if she hadn't gotten any sleep.

Mom couldn't be planning to just up and leave. That couldn't be right. There were Scarlett, Rhett, and Meowrie. Not to mention the fact that maybe Detective Teidleman might object to Allison leaving the area. She stared at the bags, and at Babs, and began felling frightened.

Mom planned to leave town, right in the middle of a police investigation. Her uptight, straitlaced mom was acting like a fugitive.

It brought an eerie sense of déjà vu. Allison remembered the hodgepodge of packages that had filled the taxi when Mom had left Dad, dragging them both out of Dallas. Hastily packed cardboard boxes, mostly clothes.

Back then, Mom had remembered to bring her favorite stuffed toy, a raggedy-blue Cat-in-the-Hat. Allison looked at Babs, and imagined Mom remembering the same day last night, as she was packing. Mom was scared of something, and it wasn't Dad.

Allison didn't know why this was happening. But she trusted Mom. So she finished packing the duffel bag, up to and including Babs.

As she zipped the bag shut, she tripped, knocking over the suitcase and the cardboard box. She steadied herself on the bed as she saw a flat, metal canister roll out of the upturned box. The box itself dumped a chaotic pile of books and papers.

Allison sighed and walked out into the hall to catch the wayward object.

It was a flat film canister, the sort of thing that people

used to keep home movies in. When she picked it up, the weight told her that there was a reel of film inside it. It wasn't large, less than five inches in diameter and less than an inch thick—just short of too big to fit in somebody's pocket.

Before she looked closely, she thought it might have been some old home movies of Mom's. But the peeling labels made it look institutional. Who'd label a home movie "Case #867?" There was also a sticker that said "ASI File #" followed by an obscenely long typed sequence of numbers and letters.

Allison was about to give in to the urge to pry open the can, when the doorbell rang downstairs. On the way down, she tried to wedge the can into the rear pocket of her jeans.

She was cautious with the door again, looking through the peephole.

This time it was the police. Detective Teidleman, in fact, accompanied by a statuesque black woman.

Allison opened the door with the chain on, and he looked so shuffling and nervous that she felt some sympathy for the man. "Ah, Miss Boyle? Is your mother here?"

"No." Allison shook her head. "Can I do something for you?"

Teidleman appeared surprised. "Damn she was supposed—" he muttered to himself. Then he caught himself. "Well, that isn't your fault." Teidleman looked up at the black woman and sighed. He fished in a pocket and pulled out a card. "You see, we need to talk to you, but we need your mother's—" He looked at the black woman again. "—*and* your— permission, etc. etc."

He handed her the card. "We'd really like to talk to you. If you could impress that on your mother."

"Sure," Allison nodded. "So you aren't here to arrest me or anything?"

"No, no, no—" Teidleman shook his head repeatedly. "It's just an investigation. And we can't talk to Mister Wilson."

Allison was beginning to wonder who was making Teidleman nervous, her or the black lady. She glanced at the card and said, "I'll tell Mom."

"Thank you."

Before she closed the door, Allison swallowed hard and asked, "How is he?"

Teidleman looked pained and glanced at the black woman, who shrugged.

"Bad," Teidleman said.

"How—uh—bad . . . ?"

Teidleman looked at her appraisingly. "He's still critical. As far as I know, he's still in surgery, undergoing reconstruction. At best he'll be permanently crippled."

Allison put her face in her hands. "At worst?"

The silence she heard was worse than an answer. God, did Chuck deserve being put into surgery for eighteen hours?

"I should go," Teidleman said.

Allison nodded and closed the door. She felt sick.

26 OCTOBER   EUCLID HEIGHTS, OHIO

10:15 AM   TUESDAY

Elroy sat on a rock, just in sight of the ugly blue-gray duplex that Allison Boyle lived in. The Institute's van was up the street, not in direct view of the house. The Oldsmobile was parked on the other side of the block, in sight of the rear of the house.

Elroy sat on his white-painted rock, idly digging in the grass at his feet. The rock was part of the property of the house behind him, part of a sculpted garden, but Elroy knew that there wasn't anyone in the house to chase him away. He could *see* things like that, people's minds were a constant fuzzy smear across his vision. Rainbow wakes trailing everybody.

The colors had always fascinated Elroy. Every time a new image crossed his path, he stared at it as if his eyes were hungry and needed to be fed. Fortunately, the sights were as varied as the people he saw. Even now, on Allison Boyle's side of the street, a stocky blonde woman was jogging. To Elroy, it seemed that she caused a ripple in the air that radiated from a teardrop-shaped area just behind the woman's forehead.

The ripples followed her, waving in a complex pattern that almost made sense to Elroy. Watching it was like trying to remember a word frozen just behind his tongue. Elroy watched the woman jog by him, studying the colors. There were translucent shimmers of every color Elroy could name, and a few he couldn't. As usual, there were parts of it that were unique to this woman. One small part of the pattern was frozen, unmoving—a blazing red ember that the remaining pattern flowed around and tried to avoid.

What's that? Elroy thought to himself. It wasn't the first time he'd seen such a thing. Barney was followed by a swarm of such things, a few not nearly as nice-looking as this woman's defect.

The jogging woman glanced over at Elroy, met his eyes, and, like most people, she lowered her gaze and turned away. *Do they know what I see? Is she ashamed of that little red spot? Does she know it's there?*

Elroy sighed. He was bored, waiting for something to happen. He looked up at the Boyle house, and he still sensed her in there. The patterns around Allison Boyle were the most intricate and mesmerizing that Elroy had seen outside the Institute. Since yesterday, it had grown in complexity, almost as if he was seeing two patterns, one embedded and almost overwhelmed by the other.

The main pattern itself almost hurt to look at, it was so intense. The colors burned. Elroy saw an increasing potential there, straining, like an angry dog chained to a wall.

Elroy thought he'd seen that leash snap once, but there had been too many people around the high school, too many overlapping ripples. All he knew, was that when the medics wheeled Charlie Wilson away, Elroy hadn't seen Charlie's beer-shot pattern. There had been nothing. No pattern. As far as Elroy was concerned, that meant you were dead.

His Walkman headphones spoke to him.

"Elroy—" Mr. Jackson's scrambled Darth Vader voice, "—what's the status on the girl?"

"Still in the house, Mr. Jackson." Elroy spoke without

moving his lips. "Nothing's happening." Nothing. Nothing, *but.* Elroy could sense the buildup, the extension. The dog straining on its leash. He felt the strain, too, because he was *willing* the leash to break. Elroy had the sense that he would see something amazing when that happened.

"Good," said Mr. Jackson. "I'm taking the field team downtown to pick up her mother."

"Uh huh."

"I'm leaving you, Jane, and George here, *only* to keep tabs on the girl. We're not to touch her until we've taken care of her mother."

"Uh-huh."

"Good, if you see anything happening, *especially* something you can't explain, radio George and Jane here in the van."

"Yes, sir."

The Walkman blared static a moment, then faded into silence.

Elroy returned to digging around with his stick. In a few moments, he found what he'd been looking for. Under an overgrown tuft of grass between the garden and the driveway, a small bird was hidden. Its feathers were gray, and its beak was open, panting. One wing was splayed behind it, like a casually tossed blanket.

Unlike people, the ripple surrounding the bird was a simple blue sphere barely larger than its head. Every few moments the body would jerk, and a ripple would cross the sphere, leeching a little more color, a little more brightness.

The bird's small black eyes met Elroy's, and the animal began a manic chirping that racked its tiny body. Elroy watched, motionless and fascinated, as the bird died next to him.

26 OCTOBER   EUCLID HEIGHTS, OHIO

10:25 AM   TUESDAY

Allison returned to Mom's room to clean up the mess she'd made. She uprighted the cardboard box and began replacing the contents, placing her hands on the album she had seen on her mother's lap—

Was that only two days ago?

It was the same album her mother had drunk herself to sleep looking through. Allison picked it up and slowly sat on the recliner her mom had been sitting in that night. She had never seen this scrapbook before.

The first page in that beat-up black scrapbook was a yellowed birth certificate, dated 1952. Carolyn Ann Boyle, born to Franklin James and Francine June Boyle. The first few pages were typical family portraits. Carol as a baby. Franklin—Allison's grandfather— holding Carol in front of the monkey cage at some zoo. The pictures accumulated until 1956, and then they stopped.

Up to 1956, it looked like this had been Francine June Boyle's record of Mom's childhood. The last picture was a color-faded Kodachrome of four-year-old Carol on a swing.

Francine had been quite a photographer, and all the pictures had been taken by her. Allison had wished to see a picture of her grandmother, Francine.

Allison got her wish on the next page, in the worst possible way. On much newer backing paper, was a yellowing newsprint picture of Francine. It fronted her obituary. April 26th, 1956. The sight moved Allison, though she had never known her grandmother—even though Mom had told her that both her own parents had died a long time ago.

The next clipping was from an old copy machine. The copy paper was slick, yellowing, and brittle. The ink was much grayer than Allison would expect from a modern Xerox machine. The copy was of a news article dated three days after the obituary. It announced the arrest of Franklin James Boyle in connection with the death of his wife. Between the lines, Allison could see hints of horrifying abuse. The mere mention of two other children who died before Carol was born . . .

This wasn't anything Mom had told her. Even so, Allison didn't need Mom to tell her what probably happened to her infant aunt and uncle.

Her mother was four years old when these things happened. She must have had to hunt down these clippings years after the fact.

The next pages were on old mounting paper of a different color. Each was a family group shot. In each one Carol Boyle was in it somewhere. The families were all different. Mom had been living with foster families nearly all her childhood.

It became disturbing to see how few of the pictures showed Mom smiling.

One particularly ugly picture didn't look like a family shot. In it were three men whooping it up in front of a TV that had seen better days. What could be seen of the house was a scene of beer bottles and ashtrays. The picture was a blistered black-and-white Polaroid that had been folded in half so the two pieces had fallen apart. It was held together with yellowed cellophane tape.

The next page was another news clipping folded over itself to fit in the book. Allison unfolded it gently, expecting another obituary. What she got was totally unexpected.

The paper was from 1965 and the headline read, "Poltergeist Rampages Trailer Park Home."

"What?" Allison whispered.

From the story, one fine June day, for no apparent reason, miscellaneous objects in the trailer owned by the Cobb family began to be thrown about. Ash trays, beer bottles, brick-a-brac—and in one notable incident the family TV— flew around inexplicably, driving Mr. Cobb and his two sons out of the trailer. The incidents happened repeatedly, and supposedly once in front of the eyes of the reporter.

There had been no injuries, "unless you count the TV, which Mr. Cobb demonstrated as being dead on arrival."

The incidents revolved around the Cobb's foster daughter. " 'Started about the time the wife took ill,' said Mr. Cobb." The Cobbs reluctantly had to give up the child.

The child, of course, was Carolyn Boyle.

Allison flipped back to the damaged Polaroid. That could be the inside of a trailer. She looked at the three men swilling beer in front of the TV. She thought of that TV flying across the room and smashing on the far wall. Probably served them right.

More families, and pictures of Carol as a teenager. Carol with boys. Carol looking somewhat happy. But every few pages would be a new family shot and after that new family,

the high school in the background pictures would change.
The scrapbook was becoming a severely depressing
document.

Then, filling a page, was an acceptance letter to Duke
University.

More pictures. Mom protesting the Vietnam war. Mom
marching in Washington. Mom making some sort of speech
to a congregation of her fellow students. Mom receiving
her degree.

The degree was in the scrapbook, folded in quarters to
fit. Allison unfolded it, read the degree, and said, "Psychology, Mom?" That didn't make much sense; Mom was an
accountant.

People change careers . . .

Then came the picture Allison had seen before, the man
in the uniform, posed before the American flag. Her father.

More pictures. Mom in a lab coat for the Prometheus
Research Institute. Mom in front of a house. Mom
pregnant.

No wedding pictures?

Then it was Allison's baby pictures. Allison kept flipping
through domestic scenes. Then the pictures abruptly ended.

Allison looked around, checked for pages sticking together, falling out, looked in the box. But the last page was
eleven years old, at least. The last picture was Allison, in
her Smurf jammies, Cat-in-the-Hat with ragged tail jammed
in the crook of her arm.

The same things she was wearing when Mom abandoned
Dad in Dallas.

Were Mom and Dad ever married? Allison wondered. It
wasn't a question that had ever occurred to her before.

She didn't know what to make of the album.

Mom had kept a scrapbook cataloging a lifetime of pain.
It made Allison's current problems seem paltry by comparison. Mom *did* know how Allison felt. Mom probably knew
better than *she* did.

She bent to replace the scrapbook in the box. The remainder of the box was filled with books. Allison was so
used to boxes of books in this house that she'd barely noticed the titles.

Now one caught her attention. A textbook.

Parapsychology. 2nd ed.

Para-psychology?

Allison flipped the scrapbook open again, to Mom's degree.

She'd misread the calligraphy. It read *Parapsychology.*

She flipped through Mom's university pictures and now saw that she was celebrating her degree with the Duke University *Parapsychology* Laboratory.

Allison's mouth felt a little dry.

She wondered what the Prometheus Research Institute had researched.

The books in the box were all related to Parapsychology. Poltergeists. Psychokinesis. Telekinesis. *There's a difference?*

One book, a blue-covered seventies paperback with a cracked spine, had the title, *"TK: Mind Over Matter."*

The text-strewn cover made clear that TK was an abbreviation for telekinesis. The cover was a montage of dated photographs. Someone who could do a seventies bad-haircut retrospective was holding a bent spoon, some woman was waving her hands over a compass.

Allison's eyes couldn't stay away from those two letters, "TK."

She could see that, if used often enough, the abbreviation would shorten itself even further. From the two syllable "tee-kay," perhaps, to the one syllable, "teek."

I can't be thinking what I think I'm thinking.

Allison gently put down the scrapbook.

"If I take this idea seriously, I *have* gone crazy."

But what happened to Chuck? I was looking right at him. Who else was there to, to . . .

The phrase that came to Allison's mind was "crack his pants like a whip." That's what happened to him, the popped seams, the towel-snapping sounds. Allison could picture it all too vividly.

"But I didn't touch him."

That's the point, isn't it?

Allison backed away from her mother's box as if it were filled with live snakes. Recent events flew around in her mind, finding patterns to fall into.

The headaches. The sense of something awakening in her skull.

Her room trashed without a memory of her moving. She even remembered, now, back at David's party, she had heard that table upending in time to the worst of her throbbing skull. Dozens of memories of things moving of their own volition around her. Her stuffed animals. The books David had been carrying in the library, the ones that had made a left turn in midair. The fact she could rip her notebook out of Chuck's hand, even . . .

Her father had said, on the phone, "If she's a teek."

Her mother had been a parapsychologist. Mom had been the center of a poltergeist event when she was thirteen.

It made sense.

"Yes, sure, uh huh. It makes loads of sense. It even explains what happened to Chuck. But how come you've never done it consciously?"

Well, I've never tried.

It couldn't be that simple, could it?

Allison unzipped her duffel bag, and pulled out Babs. She placed Babs on the bed, on top of a pillow.

Here's where I get to show myself how silly I'm being.

"Here goes. Babs, *hop!*" Allison, while still feeling half-scared and half-silly, *thought* at Babs as hard as she could.

Something opened inside her head, an invisible hand feeling through space and matter, latching on to her stuffed animal. The effort hurt, but not as badly as her headaches.

The stuffed rabbit flew off the bed and slammed into the ceiling with a thud. And it stuck there.

Allison's jaw dropped. She took a step back, staring at the ceiling and the rabbit now spread-eagled there. She tripped over the box of books and fell with a crash, landing on her backside in a tangle of paranormal literature. The pain of the forgotten film canister digging into her behind broke her concentration.

Babs fell from the ceiling, bounced off the bed, and landed at her feet. The rabbit's frozen smile seemed to say, "What took you so long?"

CHAPTER
ELEVEN

Allison tore through her mother's books, frantically searching for some explanation. She didn't know what she was looking for. All she knew was that the universe was playing games with reality, and if she didn't find her bearings quickly, she'd crawl into a corner and start whimpering.

It would be very reassuring to find something in black and white that told her what had just happened, and why. The books didn't cooperate. In the first place there were just too many of them, ranging from textbooks to pocket paperbacks that shed pages when she cracked their spines. Even when it became obvious that the majority of these books dealt with wholly mental phenomena—telepathy, precognition, clairvoyance, and such, not her problem at all—the mass of text was too much to absorb.

What she did scan was universally unhelpful. The giant parapsychology textbook had whole sections on psychokinesis, but it all seemed to be about dice rolling and probability. What she read was very boring, very statistical, and made it a lot less surprising that her mom had made the peculiar leap from parapsychology to accounting.

From the look of the textbooks, parapsychology *was* accounting.

Nothing in there about levitating rabbits.

Despite her frantic search, she found nothing that matched what she seemed able to do—

Unless she counted the poltergeists. They—at least the case histories Mom had gone through with a highlighter—were the only events Allison could find where it looked like someone was—telekinesing? teeking?—large objects. Only it didn't seem that the people central to the events were in control of the matter.

Allison dropped the last book in disgust and looked at Babs again.

Am I imagining this?

Allison concentrated on the rabbit again. She felt the weird disorientation she'd felt after her last bad headache. She had the sense of seeing too much. She closed her eyes and the feeling, instead of disappearing, grew more intense. It was a nagging sense that, out of the corner of her mind's eye, she could see around, maybe even *within* objects. Her dislocated vision made it seem as if the universe was turned inside out and she was looking inside herself to see—everything.

"Too weird."

She could feel her mind reaching for the stuffed rabbit. The sense of touch from her mental fingers seemed numbed and fuzzy, as if the matter they contacted was semiliquid. When she grabbed the rabbit with her mind, it was like trying to hold a thin pudding. She had to embed the whole object within her mental grasp—like wrapping it with clay—or it would slip through her fingers.

Allison opened her eyes to assure herself that the world hadn't gone semiliquid on her. Seeing the world with her eyes tempered the disorientation, but didn't make it go away.

As she watched, she made Babs rise, slowly.

It felt as if the rabbit was going to slip out of her grasp like a wet watermelon seed and hit the ceiling again. However, she managed to maintain some control—which was hard since she felt as if she was losing her mind.

Babs hovered there, in midair. Allison slowly got to her feet, staring at the stuffed animal.

I'm doing that. I have to be doing that.

"Either that, or Chuck managed to really snap my mind and I'm comfortably sedated in a mental ward somewhere."

Allison made Babs rise to eye level. She spun the rabbit

around, turned it over, made it orbit her head. The rabbit complied with her mental efforts with increasing ease. Soon Allison had Babs jumping and swooping, hopping over the bed, doing pirouettes . . .

After a while Allison discovered that the fear and disorientation had given way to wonder. As Babs flew across her mom's bedroom, Allison began to smile.

Eventually, Rhett poked his black head in to see what was up. His eyes caught sight of Babs, floating in midair. Rhett ran halfway into the room, past Allison's feet, to stare at Babs, transfixed. Allison made Babs swoop down and buzz the cat.

Rhett leaped straight up, mewing, turned in midair, and hit the ground running. He shot past Allison, and she could hear his little cat feet machine-gunning down the stairs.

Allison laughed, a real, honest laugh. The first one in quite a while. It felt good. Allison flew Babs down, into her arms, and hugged the rabbit.

Mom, why didn't you tell me?

26 OCTOBER   CLEVELAND, OHIO

11:38 AM   TUESDAY

Fred Jackson stood in the hall outside the glass-fronted offices of "Levy, Mahyer & Boyle Associates." He stood between a drinking fountain and a potted plant, in the corner of an L-shaped corridor. Down one arm of the L were the offices, down the other were the two elevators serving the building.

Barney had a position on the opposite side of the building from him, where another L mirrored off of the elevators. Between the two of them they had every access to the floor, elevators, and stairs covered. There were two additional men down in the parking garage, waiting for Carolyn Ann Boyle to show.

In the half hour since Fred's field team had taken up position, she hadn't.

The digital clock over the elevators turned from 11:38 to

11:39, and a soft beeping came from Fred's breast pocket. Fred slipped a cellular phone out of his pocket and flipped it open. It wasn't a true cell phone, since it didn't use either the frequencies, or the public cell network—but it was less obvious than a walkie-talkie.

"Yes?" he said into the pseudo-phone while switching his gaze casually from the office to the elevators and back again.

"Elroy says she's doing it again."

Fred shook his head. "Wait for us, George."

"Something's happening—"

"Your job's to keep an eye on the girl. *Just* keep an eye on the girl."

"You should have the mother by now . . ."

"George, don't make me explain things to you again. We do things in order."

"I'm sorry, but the activity here is making me nervous."

"Don't make decisions in times of stress, George. It's not your forte. Wait for us. Good-bye." Fred folded the phone and slipped it back into his pocket.

More minutes passed. Fred took a sip from the fountain. At 11:41 his pseudo-phone beeped again. He flipped it open.

"Yes?"

"She's here, Northwest elevator. Rocky is following, Northeast elevator. I'm in the parking garage."

"Acknowledged," Fred said. Then he hit the button that would activate Barney's beeper, warning him that the target was on her way.

Carol rode the elevator alone up to her office, just as she had every day for years. She knew, however, that it was the last time. Even if nothing happened, even if there was a safe ever after for Allie, Carol had spent the morning committing several felonies in preparation for leaving the state. She had visited five branches of the same bank so she could withdraw nearly twenty-five thousand dollars from her company's escrow accounts without causing any alarm. It was in her purse now, ten bank checks and two thousand in cash.

In the damage of her retreat, her second career would be as finished as the first.

What she had to do now, while the office was empty for lunch, was to doctor a half-dozen spreadsheets and files to cover her tracks. It was a job she didn't relish, but if she left the records untouched, she would find the police after her as early as tomorrow morning.

Can I do this? Abandon everything in my life again? Uproot Allie again, after what she's been through . . . ?

All of the buried wounds were coming to the surface. Not just leaving John, but her own role in an evil that might be coming after her own daughter.

She rubbed sleep from her eyes and thought John's baby-killer comment was well-earned. She'd been such a hypocrite, going from college activism to work at a place like Prometheus. That was something she couldn't blame on John, since she met him *at* PRI.

The doors opened on her floor and she stepped out, barely watching where she was going. She was lost in self-recrimination. She hadn't wanted to believe John's warnings, not just because Allie was such a normal, happy child. That might have been excusable. Carol was afraid the primary reason was that she never wanted to admit the evil she'd once worked for, or that she'd been hiding from that responsibility for twelve years.

She almost ran into the man before he said her name.

"Carolyn Boyle?"

The name brought her up short, and she stood staring at a balding man with slate-gray hair. On his tie was a clip showing an eagle in flight. The man had an easy smile, like a politician. He held out his hand as if he wanted her to shake it.

Carol clutched her case close to her and took a step back. "W–who are you?"

"I'm Special Agent Fred Jackson, ASI. I was hoping that you'd come with me to answer a few questions."

The man kept smiling, kept his hand out, and even began to reach for identification. He wore a secure cloak of authority around himself, and his tone of voice said that everything was going to be fine.

Alarm bells began going off in Carol's head, and she

backed up, nervously, saying, "I–I'm afraid you have the wrong person, Agent Jackson."

"It's just a few questions, Ms. Boyle—"

Carol wasn't listening anymore. She turned and started walking briskly away from the man, toward the elevators. Suddenly a younger man, in cowboy boots and a blond ponytail turned around and grabbed the shoulder of her blouse. "Come on, Miss, the man just wants to *talk* to you." The man spoke with a Texas accent, and that was enough to panic Carol. She had left all her nightmares in Texas.

She slammed her foot down on the man's shin hard enough to half-remove the heel of her right shoe on the edge of his boot. The cowboy said, "Shit!" and let go long enough for her to start a limping run to the elevators.

Just before she reached them, the doors on the right one opened, revealing a man in a dark suit who looked directly at her. The man took a step forward, and Carol threw her case at him as she turned toward the fire stairs.

She slammed the door open, and started running down the concrete steps. She heard the door open again, and she heard two more sets of footsteps echo down toward her.

She had lost her case, but she still had her purse, the money, her keys. If she could just make it to her car.

Please, God, don't let them have Allie. Punish me for my mistakes but not her—

She passed three floors and was rounding a fourth, when the fire door next to her suddenly exploded open, and the cowboy with the pony tail reached for her.

Elevator, he beat me on the elevator.

She tried to dodge around him, and almost made it, He grabbed at her arm and caught the right sleeve of her blouse. It was enough to stop her movement, but her momentum was still forward and her left arm and leg swung out over the stairs.

For just a moment, she was precariously balanced on her right heel, supported by the tension the cowboy had on her sleeve, dangling over a flight of concrete steps. She looked into the man's eyes and felt the knuckles of her left hand brush the steps below her.

At the same time, she brought her free hand up to reach for a guardrail, and the man swung his free hand to grab something more substantial than cloth. Both movements came too late, as cloth tore and the loosened heel gave way under the weight.

Carol cried, "Jesus," as she fell.

Barney said, "Shit."

Carolyn Ann Boyle tumbled backward down the stairs, leaving Barney holding the sleeve of her blouse. She landed, unmoving, facedown at the foot of the stairs.

"Shit," Barney repeated, as two sets of footsteps caught up with him.

26 OCTOBER EUCLID HEIGHTS, OHIO

11:48 AM TUESDAY

It was close to noon when Allison walked out of her mother's bedroom. She had no idea what to make of it all. Everything—Mom, Dad, herself, the rules of the universe—everything had changed on her. Worst of all, she couldn't understand why Mom kept this from her.

If Allison had known what she'd been capable of, would she have hurt Chuck as badly as she had? Could she have done something less destructive if she had *known* what she was doing?

What *could* she do?

Dozens of images came to Allison unbidden, from books and movies. She had seen enough evil portraits of paranormals for her to feel terribly uncomfortable. Exploding heads from *Scanners,* the flying cutlery from *Carrie,* whole houses exploding in *Firestarter* . . . .

David even had a tape of a Japanese film, *Akira,* a cartoon where an adolescent telekinetic had managed to destroy Tokyo.

No. There have to be limits.

She found herself wandering around the house, cradling Babs, her mind a whir of fictional imagery.

There was a Dean Koontz novel where a telekinetic caused earthquakes, manifested otherworldly monsters, and had nearly driven himself insane with his ability.

Could it be that Mom didn't tell her because she was scared of her?

Allison was doing a good job of scaring herself. What if she *could* lay waste to a city?

"Hold it." Allison stopped and looked at herself in the mirror. She stared at herself and tried to force some reality back into her head. She knew she was prone to get romantic and overblown in her fantasy life. That just meant that she had to make an extra effort to retain some sort of control over her speculation.

Just because the rules had changed, didn't mean there weren't any rules at all.

And, movies to the contrary, there was nothing in Mom's parapsychology books that showed anything approaching the destruction of a *house,* much less a city. Allison smiled at herself in the mirror, proud that she could keep some semblance of reason when the world had obviously gone insane.

She winced at that thought, and stuck her tongue out at herself. She shouldn't undercut her own sanity with thoughts like that. When it came down to the nitty-gritty, she had two choices. Either she had gone nuts and literally anything could happen, or she still lived in a rational world with natural laws.

Despite the fact that she seemed to have been misinformed about what those laws were.

"That means," Allison said to her reflection, "that the more reasonably and consistently this teeking behaves, the less chance I'm crazy." She looked down at Babs and said, "That makes sense, doesn't it?"

That logic led to the premise that she had to find out how reasonable and consistent her teek was. After a little thought, Allison went through the house, gathering a number of objects and putting them in a paper bag. The expedition took her through her room, the study, through some boxes of old toys in the basement, and through the kitchen.

When she had filled her bag, she tried to think of where she'd conduct her experiments. It really shouldn't be in the house, some of the stuff she'd gotten was potentially messy—

Especially the kitty litter.

But Mom had made her promise to stay in the house. Allison didn't want to disobey her mother. Mom would be upset, probably too upset to discuss the things they needed to discuss. Allison could too easily see important things, like meeting her father, and the gaps in her family history, being sidetracked for the typical mom-daughter fight, "You promised to stay inside—" "But, Mom, I didn't want to soil the carpet with the power of my mind."

Excessive silliness during grave events is a sign of a disturbed mind.

Allison figured she'd earned the right to be disturbed.

Eventually, Allison compromised. Since the basement was too crowded with boxes, laundry, and furnace, she decided to go and play in the garage. Technically the garage was still "the house."

Allison put on a fleece-lined denim jacket, and remembering Mr. Franklin's rules on lab safety, borrowed a pair of her mother's sunglasses in lieu of safety goggles.

As she walked to the garage, she saw her neighbor, Mr. Luvov, washing one of his three cars. Luvov lived in the other half of Allison's house. He was a recent Russian immigrant, in his late forties, spoke with a thick accent, and was probably one of the most thoroughly American people Allison had ever met. Mr. Luvov would probably *enjoy* her civics class.

He stopped hosing down his Ford pickup—Allison thought he had aspirations to be a redneck—and smiled beamingly at her. "Pleasant day, Miss Allie."

"Good afternoon, Mr. Luvov."

"Should you not be in school? You are home too much for your studies."

Allison sighed. "I'm suspended."

"This is not right. Perhaps I call, make protest?"

Mr. Luvov had a passion for writing letters to the editor, calling radio talk shows, speaking at public meetings—Allison had no question that he was sincere. She shook her head. "Don't bother, it'll work itself out." *I wish.* "Thanks anyway."

"Is nothing. Education is important. This I tell my boys, but—" He shrugged and began to use the hose again. "I want smart children. I get boys who watch cartoons." He turned to Allison as she passed. "You are young, tell me why my boys like *Beavis and Butthead*? I do not understand."

The incongruity of the question made Allison laugh. "I don't know why anyone likes that show, Mr. Luvov."

Mr. Luvov shook his head as if there were some things American that he never would understand. He was probably right.

Allison walked to the garage at the end of the driveway. It was detached from the house, set far enough back in the house's yard so that Mr. Luvov could park all three of his cars in half the driveway and leave enough room for Mom to use her half of the garage.

Allison put her bag down and opened the garage door and walked in, closing the door behind her. It was a two-car garage, one space occupied by Mr. Luvov's Jeep Cherokee.

That man and his cars, Allison thought.

Enough sunlight was filtering in to see by, so she set her bag on the table that ran the length of the rear of the garage. Allison's half of the table was empty except for bottles of car stuff—antifreeze, oil additive, wiper fluid, and such—stacked at the far end. The empty space was a contrast to Mr. Luvov's half which was an ecstatic jumble of tools, rags, and miscellaneous junk.

The first thing Allison pulled out of the paper bag was Babs. Babs was more moral support than part of the experiment, so Allison looked for a clean place to set her down. She finally perched the stuffed rabbit on the hood of the Jeep.

Then she lined up the other things in her bag.

First she took out a sheaf of Dixie cups and lined up six of them. Then she filled them with various materials she'd gotten from the kitchen. Bottled water in the first one. Barely liquid corn syrup in the second. A few glops of grape jelly in the third. Salt in the fourth. Kitty litter in the fifth. A dozen sugar cubes in the last one.

Allison's first idea was to see exactly how slippery things were to her teek sense. Babs, in reality a fairly solid, fluffy creature, had felt like Jello-O when Allison had levitated her.

Once she had the cups lined up, Allison stood back and said to Babs, "Here goes."

She wondered if she should close her eyes. She decided not to at first.

The sugar cubes were first. Again she had the sense of mental fingers running across too-spongy matter. When she finally seemed to get a grip on the cup she was concentrating on, she lifted, gently.

Obligingly, the whole cup lifted off the table.

"That's not what I want at all."

She lowered the cup from its hover and tried to think smaller. The mental sense slipped through the walls of the cup like it was melted wax. The individual cubes of sugar seemed to be cubes of wispy foam rubber. It was very hard for Allison to think herself into surrounding the cubes. Her mind seemed to slide through them. A cube slipped through her grasp and fired itself out of the cup, shattering on the ceiling of the garage.

It made her head ache.

Eventually, after a moderate effort, the cubes seemed embedded in her mental web, and she could raise them out of the cup.

The mass of cubes moved as a group wherever she willed them. However, she found that there was no way she could make individual cubes move independently of one another. She tried to make a single levitating cube rotate, but the whole mass would spin around a common axis, each cube in orbit around a common center.

The best she found she could do was "let go" of individual cubes. That she could do very selectively, to have them bounce off their fellows and land on the table below. On an impulse she let go of all the cubes but one on the top and one on the bottom. The structure of the handful of cubes collapsed like a house of cards, leaving the two floating cubes of sugar, their relative positions intact. Allison frowned and tried to push the cubes closer together. She couldn't. It was like the cubes were embedded in some invisible lump of clay, and all she could do was push the clay around.

She stepped up and took hold of one of the cubes with her hand and yanked. The yank was accompanied by a bizarre sense of a similar, and slightly painful, tug inside her skull.

She expected her mental grip on the rogue cube to be lost. It wasn't. The "clay" seemed forgiving, and when Allison let go of the cube, it still hung there in midair, three feet away from its cousin. Allison tried to teek the cubes again.

As before, they wanted to maintain their relative positions.

Allison tried to grab cubes off the table, and managed to, but once they were in her mental grip they maintained constant separation. She just could not move multiple objects relative to each other unless something else intervened, like her reaching out with her hand and grabbing one.

Allison dropped the cubes to the table, wiped her forehead, and swept the cubes back into the cup.

Her physics teacher would be proud of her.

Allison pulled a small yellow pad out of her pocket and wrote on it, *"Teek Rule #1: You can't teek different objects in different directions."*

How can I word this? she thought. She plagiarized some language from her physics textbook. *"Teek embeds things in its own reference frame, then it moves the frame. Within the frame, the objects remain stationary relative to each other."*

She looked at the note and smiled. She could write a textbook. For completeness' sake she added, *"unless acted on by an outside force."*

Now that sounds *like a law of nature.*

She could see one consequence of that right off. She couldn't bend any spoons. Not unless she was holding one end firmly in her hand.

Next she tried the kitty litter. The effort was much like that with the cubes, but the granules were much harder to get a grip on. It took her twice as long to lift a mass of litter from the cup, and when she tried to let individual granules go, whole sections of the cup-shaped mass would let go and spill on the table. She flicked the mass with her finger, and it collapsed in a heap on the table.

It also caused more of a headache. Endurable, but she was glad when her efforts ceased.

The salt was hopeless. The only way she could move it at all was if she allowed it to stay in the cup. She tried to embed the grains in her "teek reference frame" but they insisted on slipping through the cracks.

She wrote down in the book, *"Teek Rule #2: The smaller it is, the harder it is for me to teek it."*

She expected the jelly to be even worse, but in fact it seemed easier to handle than the kitty litter. It came out of the cup in one easy glop.

But when she tried to let part of it go, it *all* fell on the table with a messy splat. She cut the mound of jelly in half with the edge of the cup and tried levitating both mounds. They rose and she let the left one go. The left glob went splat while the right one remained airborne. She plopped the airborne jelly back into its cup and got the paper towels out of the bag.

After cleaning up the jelly, she tried the last two cups, expecting to make an even bigger mess, but she could barely sense the existence of the corn syrup, and her mind passed through the water as if it was air.

She wrote down her third rule.

"Teek Rule #3: You can't teek liquids." After thinking of the jelly, she wrote down, *"The denser (more viscous?) the better."*

"Well, Babs, we've put paid to spoon bending and exploding heads."

Allison moved the cups out of the way and removed an electronic bathroom scale from the bag. She placed the scale down on a clear spot of table and took out a small brass unicorn figurine she'd taken off her nightstand.

"I guess now we get to find out how much force I can exert."

She put the unicorn on the scale. The red digital display lit up and said "LO."

Allison concentrated on the unicorn, pushing it down, into the scale. She started gently, increasing the force as she went. Numbers began flashing. The "LO" was replaced by the number 15. and the digits began to roll. Twenty pounds. Fifty. One hundred. Two hundred. Three hundred.

Within two seconds the display was maniacally flashing "HI" at her.

Allison let go of the unicorn, but the machine kept flashing "HI" at her.

She rubbed her temples.

Once the effort faded from inside her skull, she tried to pick up the unicorn. The brass was warm to the touch.

It was firmly embedded in a dent in the scale. 'When she finally worried the unicorn loose, there was a hole the size and shape of its base sunk a quarter inch into the top of the scale.

The display still flashed "HI" at her.

"Oops."

Scratch one digital scale, she thought.

There had to be more than one way to measure the force she could exert.

Allison looked around the garage until she saw a stack of red bricks lining the inside wall on the other side of the Jeep. Simple enough. She'd pick up more and more bricks until she reached her limit.

One brick, up and down, no problem.

Two, likewise.

She began multiples of five. Ten bricks, no sweat. Thirty, and she could barely sense some effort involved. When she had the entire stack of available bricks a foot off the ground, she could sense the effort—a dull pressure at the back of her skull—but wasn't near the limit at all. It had to be something like five hundred pounds she was levitating.

She lowered the bricks and thought. She didn't want to abandon this line of questioning yet.

Her eyes lit on the Jeep.

No. It's Mr. Luvov's car. I can't hurt it.

"I won't hurt it. I bet I can't even move it."

Her mental fingers reached out and stretched, enveloping the car. They found solid purchase on the metal, which was good, because trying to move it required a supreme effort. The second she tried to pull the Jeep upward, her brain slammed on the razor edge of a migraine. Her heart began racing, sweat poured from her, and her breath began to burn in her mouth.

The effort forced its way through her head in a burning

wave. It was like trying to lift the car with her own hands. She could almost hear the mental muscles tearing. Then, as she watched, Babs—who'd been sitting, unmoved, on the hood of the Jeep—fell over.

The sight broke Allison's concentration, and the garage filled with the thud of the Jeep falling back on its tires from a height of about a foot.

I did it. Allison thought.

She felt like she was going to throw up.

She staggered over to Babs, wondering if Mr. Luvov had heard the sound of his Jeep testing its shocks. As she picked up her rabbit, Allison heard a car roll up the driveway. Mom must be home.

"Good enough. I can't do much more of this."

Allison walked to the door of the garage and was about to open it, when she looked out one of the windows.

It was Mom's Taurus that had pulled up into the driveway.

It *wasn't* Mom driving it.

CHAPTER
TWELVE

26 OCTOBER   EUCLID HEIGHTS, OHIO

1:03 PM   TUESDAY

"Mom?" Allison whispered, feeling a sickness grow in the pit of her stomach. She clutched Babs closer to herself, and nearly dropped the bag of miscellaneous junk she carried.

Through the dirt-smeared window she watched a man she didn't know get out of Mom's white Ford Taurus. The man wore an expensive-looking suit, and he had a build like a wrestling coach. He wore a reassuring smile that Allison didn't like at all. It was a smile that went with the phrase, "This won't hurt a bit." Beyond the end of the driveway, out on the street, Allison saw a gray van park in front of her house.

She dumped Babs in her bag, reached down, and locked the door of the garage.

A second man got out of Mom's Taurus. He wore jeans and a blond ponytail. She didn't like him at all. He looked everywhere with an expression Allison would make when turning over a slimy rock. It was as if he was hunting for something icky to step on with his snakeskin cowboy boots.

Mr. Luvov had turned off his hose and walked up to the men. Suddenly, Allison was very afraid for her neighbor. She may have managed to disprove the omnipotence of the fictional telekinetics. But what about the other assumption all those stories made? The bad men who wanted to use the paranormal for their own purpose? The government in *Akira*. The corporation in *Scanners*. The Shop in *Firestarter*.

Her heart almost stopped when the man with the boots

looked right at her. She froze and told herself that the sun was streaming right at the window and all he'd be able to see was a glaring reflection.

Even so, she felt their eyes lock together for a moment.

The man's head kept moving, and Allison breathed a silent sigh of relief. A sigh that caught in her throat when the man's denim jacket moved and she saw a gun under his left armpit.

Allison still didn't know who her father referred to when he'd said *"they,"* but she was very afraid that she was looking at *"them"* now.

Mr. Luvov was talking to the gray-haired man, the one in the suit, the one who seemed to be in charge. Allison strained to hear what they were saying. Through the garage door it sounded muffled and far away.

"Please, Mr.—Luvov, is it?—Mr. Luvov. There's no need to be upset."

"You are government agents, you say. Where is your warrant to walk into Mrs. Boyle's house?"

"We have permission from Carolyn Boyle to be here."

He's lying, Allison thought. *Mom'd never—*

"Where is Mrs. Boyle, then? This is her car, but you drive it? This is not right."

Mom, where are you?

They were interrupted by another suited man walking out the back door of Allison's side of the house. He was dark-haired and wore thick glasses. To Allison he looked nervous.

No, don't hold the door open like that—

Allison's heart sank when Rhett shot out past the man's legs. The man was oblivious to Allison's escaping cat. He shook his head, "No" at the two men flanking her mom's Taurus.

"I should perhaps call—" Mr. Luvov began.

The other man interrupted. "Carolyn Boyle is making a statement at our office downtown. Here." He handed Mr. Luvov a card. "This is the number. Call there and everything will be explained."

"I should talk to Mrs. Boyle."

"I'm sure they'll let you. She'd appreciate your concern."

Mr. Luvov looked up from the card and said, "Agent . . . Fred Jackson, I do not ever hear of this Agency for Scientific Investigation."

The leader—Agent Fred Jackson, apparently—fingered his tie clip. "Jurisdiction-wise we're under the auspices of the FDA, though we're administered out of the Treasury Department like the ATF."

Mr. Luvov gave a blank look.

"Bureaucracy," said the man with the ponytail, "go figure." The man spoke with a southwestern accent, and was facing away from Mr. Luvov and toward Allison. She could see the evil smile the man made, an expression harboring some nasty joke at Mr. Luvov's expense.

Even as she watched, he was walking toward the garage. Allison backed away from the door as the man approached; each click of boots on concrete pushed her a step back and tore the breath from her mouth. She had to stop when she'd backed into the table. Her heart nearly stopped beating when her paper bag rustled.

The man's face was almost at the window when she heard Mr. Luvov say, "What are you doing here now?"

The man turned away from the garage, and said with a slight Western twang, "Wanted to park the car."

She couldn't see much out the window from where she was. She couldn't see Mr. Luvov, she could barely see the top of Agent Jackson's head.

She heard Mr. Luvov say, "This is also my garage." Mr. Luvov was trying to protect her, and she was deeply afraid for him. "If you have no papers to enter my garage, you will not. You do not have *my* permission."

"Now look you—" began the man at the garage.

He was interrupted by Agent Jackson, "No reason to antagonize Mr. Luvov, Barney. Leave the car in the driveway." She could barely see the small gesture Agent Jackson made, tilting his head in the direction Allison knew Mr. Luvov was standing. "Why don't you go make that call, Mr. Luvov? We'll wait here for you."

She saw Barney nod at Agent Jackson, and step off in the direction of Allison's house. Allison walked back up to the little square window. She made it to the window just in time to see Mr. Luvov reach for the handle of the back door to his side of the duplex. As he reached for it, she saw Barney step up behind him and wrap his arm around Mr. Luvov's neck.

Allison gasped and stumbled back. *No, my God, Mr. Luvov.*
When she looked out again, she couldn't see Mr. Luvov
any more, only three men approaching the garage. *My God.*
My God. My God.

"Miss Boyle," said Agent Jackson, "Would you please
come out of there? Believe me, it's for your own good . . ."

Allison scrambled back, falling to the ground. She
backed away from the door, clutching her paper bag to her
chest as if it could protect her. She backed away until she
was wedged under the table at the rear of the garage, and
her back was against the wood clapboards forming the rear
wall of the garage.

"Please, Miss Boyle. We know you're in there."

He heard someone try the handle to the garage and
curse. "Locked," Barney said.

"Get the keys off of Luvov," Agent Jackson said.

I'm trapped. Did they kill Mr. Luvov? What about Mom?
Allison's thoughts were screaming around in furious circles, all questions without answers. It was a herculean effort
for her to clamp down on the emotion and focus on one
thought. *Out, I have to get out of the garage. How?*

Agent Jackson continued his reassuring, authoritative
talk at her through the door. She didn't listen. She looked
wildly around the garage for another way out. There was
a window in the wall to her right, but it was blocked by a
stack of red bricks.

Someone tried the door again. She pushed herself back
against the wall. A nail bit into her lower back, and she
turned and looked behind her. All that was between her
and freedom was a quarter inch of wood and dry rot.

She started pushing against the clapboard and found that
it was a little loose. Then she realized that they would see
it from the windows in the door. It might be too dark to
see in the garage, but if she opened a hole in the wall in
their line of sight—

She scrambled, under the table, to the wall in front of
the Jeep Cherokee. Unfortunately, the wall down here was
in much better condition. She pushed at the board and it
didn't budge.

She heard a jingle behind her and Agent Jackson said,

"We have the keys to the garage, Allison, but we'd much prefer if you opened the door yourself."

Oh, God.

They waited a moment, and Allison peeked around the fender of the Jeep. All three were there, Barney holding up a key ring. After a few seconds of waiting for her, Agent Jackson nodded, and she could hear Barney sliding a key into the lock.

Allison panicked and did the only thing she could think of. When the handle on her side of the garage began turning, she grabbed it with her teek and turned it back. It happened so fast that she barely felt what had happened. A great *ker-chunk* echoed through the garage. The garage's handle spun freely for a second, then clattered to the ground.

"Fuck," Barney said from outside. "The key snapped."

For a moment Allison's heart lifted. But then she heard all three men grunt, and the whole door vibrated. She began to hear metal protest, and a thin line of daylight momentarily sprouted at the bottom edge of the door, vanishing as the door fell back.

Another trio of grunts, and this time the light stayed.

Allison ducked back behind the Jeep. She had to break through the wall, somehow. She pushed at it with her feet, but the boards didn't want to move. Her head was throbbing, but the only thing she had left was her teek.

Unlike her instinctive grab at the garage handle, she had to close her eyes and focus herself. The effort caught her head in a vise, and sweat stung her eyes, making her squeeze them even more tightly shut. The sound of the men forcing the garage door faded in her awareness as her world became an odd blending of inner vision and touch. She could sense the structure of the wood, old and fibrous—like rectilinear cotton candy. Nails were crystalline and solid, offering much more of a purchase for her sense. She grabbed all the solid nails she could manage.

Just before she felt the effort might blossom into a crippling migraine, she pushed all the nails away from her. The speed at which they moved broke her contact, and shocked her out of her trance.

Her eyes shot open, even as the bottom three clapboards began to sag to the ground. Behind her she heard the garage door straining, and she only had to see the shadows on the wall in front of her to know that in a second or two the door would be open enough to let them in.

Allison scrambled out of the hole she'd made in the wall, digging through the musty leaves that accumulated behind it. She had to bend the wood to get out, the long boards were only freed along four feet of their length. She was concentrating on moving out as fast as possible, which was why she didn't see the kid until he grabbed at her.

She had just made her way outside, free, when she felt a tug at her jeans. On the ground, behind the garage, a twelve-year-old kid lay in the leaves. One hand was to his thigh, holding a bleeding wound. In fact his right leg was dotted with red holes that almost looked like gunshot wounds. Then Allison saw the pointed end of a rusty nail sticking out of one of the holes, and felt ill.

"They'll get you," the kid whispered, and she turned to look at his face. When she saw that gaze, she finally recognized him. The same kid who'd been in the gray van— the gray van out front, Allison realized. The same kid she'd seen at Heights High. The same kid who'd been out on the street this morning. His Walkman headphones lay in the leaves next to him, and his Bugs Bunny T-shirt had been torn in his fall. Tears streamed down the kid's cheeks, but his expression had an alien detachment. "They always get you," said the kid, the only emotion in the voice was a hint of a sob.

Allison pulled herself away from the kid's weak grasp, and ran off behind her neighbors' garages. She was several blocks away before she realized that the running footsteps pursuing her were her own echoes.

26 OCTOBER   EUCLID HEIGHTS, OHIO

2:13 PM   TUESDAY

Elroy lay on the couch in the Boyle's living room. The leg of his jeans was slit up to his hip, and Jane was busy taping gauze to one of half a dozen wounds on his leg. Elroy stared at the ceiling, oblivious to his surroundings.

George, his white hair frizzed out more than usual, paced

back and forth in the living room, occasionally cursing under his breath. From upstairs, there came the occasional sound as Fred Jackson searched the premises.

Jane looked up at him and said, "Would you calm down, George? Hysterics won't help anything."

"Hysterics?" George asked, the manic lilt to his voice lending a little irony to the word. "What have I got to be hysterical about?"

"Please," Jane hissed in a near whisper. "Lower your voice."

"What? It is like Fred doesn't know how fucked up everything is now?" George threw himself down on an easy chair. "I called him, told him the girl was manifesting something, that Elroy—God, I hate these names."

Jane sighed. "Don't try and pretend you didn't know what you were getting into when you joined the team."

George shook his head. "But killing people?"

Jane mopped Elroy's brow, "Heartwarming, but hypocritical coming from someone who's been kidnapping children for most of his professional career."

"That's different," George said limply.

"Ah, the crutch of conditional morality," Jane said. "Just remember what we're protecting."

George sighed, "I just wanted to work with these kids. How's Elroy doing?"

Jane looked at him, "The leg's fine. But I'm worried about the way he's withdrawn—more than usual." She waved at the coffee table where six bloody nails lay on a paper towel. "None of those penetrated very deeply. I don't think that's the problem."

George leaned over and asked, "How're you doing, kid?"

"There's something cold," Elroy said flatly. "It doesn't like us."

George looked at Jane, and Jane shrugged. "Don't push him right now," she said.

"Damn it, what'd he see?" George shook his head. "This girl could be the most powerful Class I we've found since that pyrotic in Michigan. God knows what she's capable of."

"Don't worry about it. At the moment, she's security's problem."

"Yeah," George said, "and if Barney makes the same 'mistake' he did with her mother?"

"You think he did that on purpose?"

"The man's an assassin, Jane. Or haven't you noticed?"

Just then, Fred Jackson came down from upstairs. In his hand was a ratty-looking red notebook and a photo album. Fred wasn't quite smiling, but his expression said he was pleased about something, which was unusual considering the circumstances.

"Do any of you recognize this?" Fred asked. He went on without waiting for an answer. "This is the notebook that put Charles Wilson in the hospital."

Fred tossed it down on the coffee table and flipped it open. "What do you see?"

George leaned over and said, "A play, dialogue, something—"

"Read it," Fred said.

George did so, his face growing whiter. "Christ, how much do these people know about us?"

"A lot," Fred said, "Carol Boyle was a PRI employee."

"If that's 'Mom,' " Jane said, "who's John?"

George tapped John's first line on the page, where the erasure of the word "Dad" was just visible. "Allison's father?" he said.

"Exactly," Fred Jackson said. "Which was something Mr. Stone was considerably interested in." Fred slapped the side of the album he still held. "This is confirmation. One bright spot in an otherwise dark picture."

26 OCTOBER   EUCLID HEIGHTS, OHIO

3:23 PM   TUESDAY

Allison stood in front of a pay phone across the street from Heights High. At her feet was the paper bag that had come with her from the garage. It was open and Babs lay on top of the junk inside, staring up at her. She was flipping through the phone book, and all she could think of was Rhett. It was bizarre for her mind to fixate on her cat when her mom was missing. But she kept wondering if those men would think to let Rhett back in when he came mewing back to the house.

Will you try to get some priorities straight? Allison thought at herself.

She had already tried to find the Agency for Scientific Investigation in the phone book. There was no such animal listed. She had hesitated about calling information, or the ATF, or the police—

What if they *were* from the government?

What if they traced the call?

Allison told herself that she was at a pay phone, and she'd already hesitated long enough to be surrounded by people streaming out of Heights High. That, and there was a news van parked across the street. No one would try anything in front of *Eyewitness News,* right?

Allison couldn't convince herself she was safe.

But Mom?

Finally she decided to call Mom's office. She pulled out a quarter and dialed the number. *Please, let her be there, or I don't know what I'll do.*

The phone rang a few times before a female voice answered, "Levy, Mahyer & Boyle Associates. Can I help you?"

Allison sucked in a breath and said, "I'm Allison Boyle. Is my mom there?"

"I'll check." There was an agonizingly long pause. As she waited, she heard someone call, "Allie!" from down the street.

Allison looked up from the phone to see Macy in front of the McDonald's. She was waving and coming toward her. "Hey, girl, how you doing?"

Allison waved her hand nervously at Macy and pointed at the phone. Macy nodded and stood mute, waiting for Allison to hang up. The pause seemed to get longer and longer. It made Allison nervous, even though she knew it was mostly in her head.

Then, eventually, the woman came back and said, "I'm sorry, she hasn't been in yet today. Can I take a message?"

With a shaking hand, Allison hung up the phone.

"Allie, what's wrong?"

Allison looked at Macy and broke down in tears.

Macy put an arm around her shaking shoulders and said, "Come on, tell me about it. I'll buy you a shake." She led Allison into the McDonald's.

CHAPTER THIRTEEN

Macy ushered Allison into the restaurant, and Allison didn't resist. She was stunned, numb.

What was she doing?

Where was Mom?

Allison shook, hugging her paper bag. Things were moving too fast for her to handle it. All she wanted to do was go to her room, pull the covers over her head, and forget the rest of the world existed.

But, right now, Agent Fred Jackson was probably *in* her room. She could picture him sifting through her torn-up manuscript, picking up one of the half-dozen paperbacks she had kept in the box with it. She could *see* him glancing at the out-of-focus Victorian nude on the cover, and *laughing*.

She could feel him laughing at her.

Allison began crying again.

Macy hugged her shoulders. "Calm down. You need to sit, girl."

She gently led Allison to a booth and sat her down. Allison sniffed, telling herself that she'd done too much crying already. At this rate she'd die of dehydration before any government nasties caught up with her.

If things like this keep happening, I can't break down at each one. I'll paralyze myself.

It wasn't as if she had the three years for emotional turmoil she'd given Melissa in *Restless Nights*. Melissa only had one problem, her lover-to-be, Randolph, and she'd had all the time in the world for histrionics. Unlike her fictional heroine, it didn't look like events would allow Allison the chance to sit down and blubber—

Much as she wanted to.

Maybe, Allison thought, *if I don't get hysterical, I'll see the next blow coming.*

Macy had put down her backpack and gotten in line at the counter. Allison put her paper bag on the table. And, after trying to get comfortable in the already uncomfortable seat, she pried the film canister out of her back pocket and tossed it on top of the bag.

Macy came back with a tray of food. "Looks like you need this." Macy sat down across from her and placed a large vanilla shake in front of Allison. When Allison sat mute for a moment, Macy peeled a straw and shoved it through the top for her.

Allison tried to remember the last time she'd eaten anything. Not today. She'd played with her food a lot, but eaten it, no.

"Thanks," she told Macy. "You're a good friend."

Macy smiled as if that was self-evident, and watched, quietly, as Allison emptied the shake in less than a minute. Allison realized she was ravenous.

After the shake was gone, Macy said, "Wanted to apologize for the brain-dead call last night."

"You don't—"

"Don't know what I was thinking."

"I understand. I can imagine how you felt."

"I was freaked, girl." Macy looked out the windows. "I'm your friend, and the thing freaked me bad. And today—" she shook her head.

"Today what?" Allison asked.

Macy nodded her head toward the front of the restaurant, and the shadow of Heights High beyond. "Today, Principal Burkel called in the cops to clear the reporters. Think every senior had a mike in their face sometime during lunch period."

"Uh huh?"

"I slugged a reporter."

"What?"

Macy smiled. "Shoved him, really. A little too much on
Chuck's side. Got a bunch of sisters together to shout at
him. Bet that won't make the news—are you all right?"

"Yes. No. I don't know." Allison shook her head. "*No,*
I'm *not* all right. Miles from all right. Farther from all right
every minute." She almost broke down in hysterics again.
She only stopped because she didn't want to do that to
Macy.

Macy shoved the tray at Allison and said, "Have my fries
and tell me about it."

"I don't think—"

Macy reached out and touched her hand. "Please."

"I don't know what to tell you, where to start . . ."

"Start with Chuck?"

Allison shook her head. "It's not that simple." *Nothing's
that simple.*

"Then how's about the phone call that put the fear of
God into you?"

Mom. Allison sniffed and rubbed her nose. God, she had
to tell someone, and she was too scared of the cops. If not
Macy, who? David would wet his pants. "Okay," Allison
whispered. "But don't tell me I'm crazy until I'm done."

Macy held up her hand and said, "Promise."

Allison looked around, but none of the students flooding
McDonald's were paying any attention to them. She sucked
in a breath and began in an even lower whisper.

"It started when this phone call woke me up . . ."

"I should slap you, girl," Macy whispered back across
the table.

"Macy, hold on for a sec—"

"Do I look like a fool, child? You trying to turn this all
into some joke? I don't think it's funny."

Macy had listened patiently through the entire story.
Macy hadn't objected when Allison had polished off her
entire order—Big Mac, fries, apple pie. Now, when she had
gotten to the end, when she began to talk about telekinetics, Macy had finally given in to the inherent unbelievability
of the situation.

I don't blame her, I can barely believe it myself.

"Wait, I can show you." Allison moved the film can and

rummaged in the paper bag she'd been lugging around all this time. Near the bottom was a box with some eggs still left in it. Allison took out an egg.

"What's this," Macy said, glaring at her. "A magic trick?"

Allison looked around, then moved the paper bag to the end of the table to hide her hand. She didn't see anyone else paying attention to them.

She held the egg up in her palm, in front of Macy.

I just bet the fact someone's watching is going to mess me up.

Her mind wrapped around the shell, feeling it as insubstantial as a soap bubble. Once her grip was secure, she very gently raised it slightly off her palm. "Look," she whispered at Macy.

"Lord Jesus," Macy whispered back.

Allison smiled at her friend's reaction. "Push down on it."

Macy did the same look back and forth that Allison had. Looking for people watching her, or maybe a hidden camera. Macy looked back at Allison uncertainly.

Allison nodded.

Macy placed her fingers on top of the egg, and Allison resisted the push.

"Harder," Allison said. She knew Macy could bench press two hundred pounds in gym class—but Allison could teek a Jeep Cherokee a foot off the ground.

Macy pressed, and pressed. Allison's smile hardened into a thin grin as Macy put both hands on top of the egg. Macy's biceps bulged under her windbreaker.

To anyone else in the McDonald's, it would be an odd, but not paranormal, sight; two girls in some weird form of arm-wrestling. The egg itself was fully concealed with Macy's hands on top, and Allison's hand cupped underneath. It would take very close observation to note that the girls weren't touching each other.

Eventually, the predictable happened. The egg cracked, spraying its contents. Macy's hands slapped Allison's messily.

Allison shook her hand off.

As she did, Allison was shocked to see that she still had

a hold on what was left of the egg's shell. What remained of the egg, a number of shell fragments, hovered there, dripping. She let the fragments fall to the tray below and looked frantically around the restaurant to see if anyone had noticed.

Around them, people milled, talked, and ate—oblivious to the fact that something miraculous had happened.

Macy looked at the egg-mess on the tray between them. Egg had slopped over the paper wrappers, and the few remaining fries were dotted with fragments of shell. Macy looked at the mess on her hands. From the expression on her face, Allison could tell that she had to be thinking about Chuck and what had happened to him.

"Dear Lord," Macy said.

Allison reached up and grabbed Macy's shoulder. "Macy?"

"This is scaring me," Macy said quietly.

"How'd you think I feel, huh? Last Friday all I had to worry about was Mr. Counter's stupid history paper."

Macy kept looking at the yolk on her palm.

"Macy!" Allison said, harsher than she intended to be.

Macy looked up.

"I need a friend," Allison said gently.

Macy looked at Allison, and then an expression of self-disgust crossed her face. Macy wiped her hands on the few remaining dry napkins and said, "I'm sorry I yelled at you. Kind of hard to take's all."

"Like I was given a choice?"

"Hell of a friend I'm turning out to be this week." Macy tossed the napkins on the egg-spattered tray. "Your life's turned ass-backward—all *I* think of's how upset it makes *me*."

"That's not true—"

"Don't correct me when I'm apologizing." Macy looked at the tray and said, "Ugh." She got up and dumped the tray.

When she came back, she returned to their original conversation. "Before I shot my mouth off, you were saying what about these feds?"

"I don't know who they are, and I didn't see what happened to Mr. Luvov. And that Agency for Scientific Investigation isn't in the phone book."

"ASI? Sounds like a *Six Million Dollar Man* rerun."

"You watched that?"

"I was nine, we didn't have cable, and nothing was on Sunday mornings—stick to the subject."

"There were at least three of them. Two drove Mom's car, the others rode in a gray van they parked out front. And there was a kid—"

"Let me guess, the others are Betty and Wilma—"

"What?"

"The names you're telling me, Fred, Barney . . ."

"I was a little too upset to notice. Someone has a warped sense of humor."

"You said these ASI guys had a kid with them?" Macy sounded incredulous.

"Yeah, at least I've always seen this boy around that gray van. He was in the wrong place when I broke out." Allison shook her head. "I still feel bad about that."

"Damn it, girl. That ain't your fault. And if the kid's with these guys, he deserves it."

"You didn't see his leg."

"These ASI Flintstones have kidnapped your mom, maybe killed your neighbor, and you're worried about—Hey, I know that look, what you thinking?"

Allison had just remembered something. "God, and I have to be hit over the head three times . . ." Allison rummaged in her bag and fished out the film canister.

"And what the hell's that?"

"The only thing left from Mom's memorabilia box. See?" Allison pointed out the yellowed label with the words "ASI File #" on it.

Macy hefted it.

"I don't believe I didn't see that immediately, the initials, ASI."

"You were busy," Macy looked at the labels on the film can. "Okay," she said. "Let's go."

Allison grabbed her bag and slid out of the booth after Macy. "Where?"

"Where else?" Macy said as she grabbed her backpack with a free hand. "We're going to the movies."

"I don't like being here," Allison said.

It was getting close to five, and the halls of Heights High

were nearly empty. Allison felt like an invader, which was totally irrational. Students were still here, for club meetings, athletics, a few just loitering. The hall monitors didn't give either her or Macy a second look.

Allison still felt she was about to be arrested.

Macy led her up stairs to the third floor, "You know a better place to borrow a movie projector?" Macy stopped her in front of a door. Through chicken-wire glass, Allison could see carts of TVs, VCRs, and a few movie projectors. A monitor sat behind the desk in the room.

"How are you—"

"Shh, I don't have an AV pass for nothing, girl." Macy pressed a button next to the door. "Wait here."

The door buzzed and Macy opened it and went in. Allison was left in the hallway, waiting, feeling alone. It seemed like hours before Macy came back out.

What am I doing here?

Macy came out holding a key ring attached to a foot-long plastic paddle with "AV Room" scrawled on it in permanent marker. When the door shut behind her, she said, "No one ever expects you to BS your way *into* more work."

"What are we doing, Macy?"

"Collecting AV equipment from the classrooms," Macy said. She began walking off down the hall. Allison followed, helplessly.

Macy led Allison up and down the elevator, dragging cartfuls of TVs, slide projectors, and VCRs back to the AV room. Between the two of them, they managed two carts at a time. During the second trip, Allison peeked around the fake wood grain of the third TV and asked, "So when do we get a movie projector?"

Macy was ahead of her, pushing a cart too big for the slide projector sitting on it. "There's only one movie projector signed out," she said. "I'm saving it for last."

"Great," Allison said.

"Hey, I only signed up for an hour. With two of us hauling this stuff, we'll have half that left to play with the projector with no one the wiser."

"Whatever you say," Allison said.

As Macy promised, the last room held a movie projector.

She pulled the door locked behind them and looked at her watch. "Got till six—call it six-fifteen before anyone notices I'm late."

At the rear of the classroom, pushed out of the way, was the metal cart with the projector on it. Allison walked up to it and took the ASI film can out of her paper bag and looked at the complex arrangement of sprockets and gears. "You know how to work this?"

Macy snorted and said, "Get the shades."

Allison pulled the blinds while Macy maneuvered the cart to an aisle between the ranks of desks. Allison turned and watched Macy as she pried open the film can. As she struggled with the can, dented by being repeatedly sat upon, she said, "Pull the screen down."

Allison pulled three maps down over the blackboard before she found the right roll. By the time she was done, Macy had liberated the ASI film and was busy threading it through the projector. Allison watched her and felt dread, as if she really didn't want to know what was on the film.

"Got it," Macy said, turning the pickup reel with her finger to gather up the slack. "No broken sprocket holes, no Scotch tape gumming up the leader. You can tell this didn't come from the Heights High film library." Macy looked up and said, "Get the lights."

Allison hit the light switches, throwing the classroom into a dirty-gray twilight. Dust hung in the air in sunlight fractured through closed venetian blinds. Color had leeched out of everything. The darkness and the emptiness so disturbed her that, for a moment, Allison had to fight an urge to switch the lights back on.

God, I'm not afraid of the dark, Allison told herself. *It's not even dark.* The scariest part of it was the complete irrationality of the emotion. It made no sense.

Allison swallowed, forced herself to ignore the feeling, and sat at a desk in the front of the class. "Roll film," she said, forcing her voice to sound lighter than she felt.

"Here goes."

Light flickered, and a fuzzy square on the screen resolved itself into a rectangle as Macy focused the projector. Then came the familiar black and white leader: 8 . . . 7 . . . 6 . . . 5 . . .

After a moment of black screen, a title frame came up. It showed the seal that was obviously from a federal government agency. It had the eagle with a shield on its breast, like on the back of a dollar bill. But instead of the stars and stripes, the shield had a starburst pattern. Instead of the arrows and olive branch, the eagle's claw held a flask in its right and a little atomic symbol in its left. Around the seal was the text, "Agency For Scientific Investigation." There was a Latin motto, *"Nam et ipsa scientia potestas est."* Except for the fourth word, she had no idea what it meant.

After a moment, white text covered the screen. It invoked the National Security Act and at least three Executive Orders to inform the watcher that showing the following film to anyone without such-and-such a security clearance was punishable by a twenty-to-life prison sentence and several million dollars in fines.

Macy whistled, "This has got the FBI copyright warning beat all to hell."

After the dire warnings, the black-and-white film broke into hokey documentary music. Another logo appeared at the top of the screen, this one a stylized flame and the words, "Prometheus Research Institute."

Mom worked for these people?

In smaller, barely legible text under the logo, "Copyright MCMLXVI."

1966?

The main title read, "Employee Orientation Series III: Case History 867. Chemical vs. Surgical Intervention."

"I have a bad feeling about this," Macy said.

". . . in number three of this series—" said the narrator in a sudden burst of volume from the projector. Macy adjusted the volume and said, "Sorry."

Allison kept her eyes focused on the screen. On it she saw pictures of sixties teenagers, people no older than she was now. The scenes, at the moment, were just background to the narration. But Allison had already noticed disturbing things. The film showed the teenagers in an institutional environment. She got the impression of a cross between juvenile detention and a mental hospital. All the windows had chicken wire on them, and the exterior shots all had very tall chain-link fences in the background.

She almost had to force herself to pay attention to the generic narrator's voice.

". . . showed you exactly what these children are, and what they are not. The second demonstrated the current means of testing and our statistical methods. This film concentrates on methods of psychiatric intervention to alter the results of these tests. We concentrate on one case in particular to demonstrate how the interaction of psychology, physiology, and parapsychology are resulting in unprecedented inroads into—"

"What's this guy talking about?" Macy asked.

"Quiet!" Allison snapped, eyes fixed on the screen.

The film now showed a split screen with images of two teenage boys, or the same teenage boy twice. "Meet Ross and Bob, they are one of very few sets of identical twins to have been involved in the project, and their contribution to comparative studies has been invaluable."

The film went into describing Ross and Bob. As the narrator calmly went about his business, explaining telepathic double-blind testing with Zener cards, Allison began to get steadily more disturbed. The narration described statistical results the kids had with a human subject—more hits than chance—a mechanical device—no more hits than chance—and each other—close to five times better than chance. Allison listened, and heard nothing in the narrator's voice that related to these twins as human beings.

Ross and Bob weren't names; they were labels for test subjects.

It got worse.

"Over the period of testing, both subjects became increasingly less cooperative. In some cases they both became violent and disruptive. It was decided that some means of psychiatric intervention was called for . . ."

It was the passive voice of the narrator that chilled her, a voice that denied responsibility for what was being shown to her. To Allison, what was happening to Ross and Bob wasn't a psychological problem. They were being kept isolated at this Prometheus Institute for months, and they were climbing the walls. The film showed clips of them shouting at the lab assistants and doctors, breaking chairs. In one wrenching scene, Ross ripped his shirt off and began slamming himself into the wall of the testing room, crying. Allison could hear him say, "I just want to go home. Just want to go home."

I just want to go home, too.

"The decision was eventually made that the more violent of the two, Ross, would undergo a surgical remedy, and his brother would be given a tranquilizing regimen—"

It wasn't until the film showed Ross going into an operating theater, and the narrator began describing the procedure, that she realized that they were giving Ross a lobotomy.

She tried to look away as the film showed a surgeon take out an implement like a long, hooked knitting needle. She couldn't turn away as the doctor inserted the wicked-looking thing. Her eyes just watered.

Allison could only cry through the rest of the movie. She could barely hear the narrator say how Ross' test scores on subsequent Zener tests—no longer any better than chance—showed how his telepathic ability had been localized somewhere in the frontal lobe of the brain.

All Allison could really concentrate on was a teenage boy who seemed to have lost his entire personality. He had to be told to stand or to sit. He said practically nothing, the lab techs had to coax words out of him. His eyes didn't follow other people's movement, but just stared forward, blinking occasionally.

There was more to the film, almost fifteen minutes more; drug trials; the effects of depressants and hallucinogens; and the capping atrocity, a *post mortem* examination of both twins' brains.

Though the narrator didn't say so, Allison knew that even if one of the twins died naturally, to do the comparison they had to kill the other.

When the film was over, and the film was flapping slowly to itself, all Allison could think of was that this was case history 867. Over eight hundred Rosses and Bobs. It had been thirty years since. How many *more* case histories were there?

CHAPTER
FOURTEEN

26 OCTOBER   **EUCLID HEIGHTS, OHIO**

5:35 PM   **TUESDAY**

"You have to go to the cops, girl." Macy sat in the driver's seat, her sister's car idling.

Allison looked up at the gray stone facade of Euclid Heights City Hall. Her heart was racing, and there was the taste of panic in her mouth. "Macy, these are Federal Agents. What if they can get to the cops?"

"You don't have a choice." Macy shoved the ASI film canister across the seat at her. "These goons have taken over your house, and what they're doing certainly ain't legal." She patted the film. "And you got this."

"What if they ask why they're after me and Mom?"

"Tell them the truth—"

Allison shook her head. Tears were blurring her vision. "I don't want another reason for reporters to be after me."

"I said *tell* them, not *show* them. You can tell them that these refugees from the *X Files* are after you without letting them know you're a candidate for the show yourself."

Allison sighed. She really didn't know what else to do. She hoped that Detective Teidleman was in. She opened the passenger door, taking the film canister. "Come with me, Macy?"

Macy shut down the car and slipped out the driver's side. There was a slight chill in the air, and the streets were empty of traffic for the moment. Macy looked almost as shaken as Allison felt, as if watching the movie had somehow made Allison's story more real to her.

Allison knew that it had for her—

The people who had done the things on that film were capable of doing just about anything.

The two of them crossed the sidewalk and walked up the stairs side by side. The doors to City Hall gaped open ahead of them, beyond a dim corridor painted institution green. Macy's running shoes squeaked on the floor when they walked inside.

"Now where are the cops?" Macy asked.

The two of them walked inside and looked around until they found an old directory on one of the walls. Half a dozen white letters had fallen from the black felt, but it told them what floor held the Euclid Heights police. "Basement. Figures."

Allison sucked in a breath and tried to build up her own resolve to go through with this. She knew that Macy was right. This was the sane course of action. The problem was that she seemed to be trapped in an insane situation.

Just yesterday she had put someone in the hospital. She wondered how willing the cops, even Detective Teidleman, would be to help her against some government agency. Maybe they'd be just as glad to hand her over and avoid the problem.

Don't think like that. It's paranoid.

Macy led her along the corridor and down a set of stairs that led to a glass-fronted lobby that faced the parking lot behind City Hall. Outside, ranks of patrol cars faced the entrance, closing in what would otherwise be a wide-open lobby.

The two of them walked up to a desk where one officer sat, jotting something down on a clipboard. The man looked up—Allison was struck by how young he looked—and asked, "Can I help you with something?"

Macy shoved her forward and Allison caught herself up against the desk. "Y–yes. I'd like to speak to Detective Teidleman, please?"

"I can see if he's available. What is this about?"

"I–I— Just tell him it's Allison Boyle."

There was a look of recognition in the policeman's eyes, and it made her feel small and dirty. She tried to tell herself that it was nothing, that every cop in Euclid Heights must have heard the details of what happened to her by now. But she still felt violated by the cop's look.

At least that probably meant that she'd get to talk to Detective Teidleman.

"Wait over there," The man pointed over to a hard-looking bench that sat under a bulletin board plastered with pictures of missing children.

Allison walked over and sat. Macy stood and rubbed her shoulder. "It'll be all right, girl."

"Uh-huh . . ." Allison couldn't help but think of those men in her house, closing on the garage. It was like some perverse dream, and she half-expected that, if she got help from the police, all signs of what happened would be gone from the house.

The officer picked up a phone and started talking to someone. There was a brief whispered exchange. All Allison could hear was her own name a few times, and once her mother's name. The officer nodded a few times, set the phone on the desk, and stepped around and opened a door that led behind into the police station.

"Miss Boyle, would you come here?" The way he said it frightened Allison. She wanted to run away. But she thought of Mom, and how she would be letting her down if she panicked. Macy was right, this was the only sane, rational thing to do.

Allison stood up, walked up to the door, and went through. When Macy tried to follow her, the cop blocked her path. "I'm sorry, but you're not allowed back here."

"Say what? Now listen here—"

Allison grabbed Macy's arm. "I'll be all right."

"I said I was going to see you through—"

"Wait by the car, I'll be out soon."

"Uh-huh."

"Macy, it's all right."

Macy backed away, looking displeased. The cop took the opportunity to steer Allison into the police station. He took her past a number of desks. Before she had any opportunity to look around for Detective Teidleman, she was ushered into a small room furnished only with a table and a trio of chairs.

"Have a seat, someone will be with you in a moment."

"Wait, I want to see Detective Teidl—" The door was closed on her before she got the sentence out.

"What?" She grabbed the doorknob tried to open the door. The knob wouldn't move. He had locked her in here. *"Hey!"*

She felt an involuntary impulse, as if her mind was filtering through the mechanics of the lock in front of her, it felt like a spun-sugar clockwork that one push would twist and shatter. She reined in the impulse to push out with everything she could. These were the *police,* they were supposed to help.

Breaking open a door also wouldn't make the best impression.

She turned around and looked at the room. There were a trio of windows opposite the door. They were made of many rectangular panes of chicken-wire glass. There was an ashtray on the table and it gave the room the smell of a used cigarette. The walls were a dingy institution green, and up in one corner a small video camera stared at her.

When she saw the camera, she slowly let go of the doorknob and did as the officer had told her. She sat down. She took the chair at the end of the table so she could keep an eye on the door, the windows, and the camera.

She could tell just by looking that the windows weren't made to open.

When she sat, she tried to adjust the chair and discovered that the chair, and the table, were bolted to the floor. It was starting to feel less and less like this had been a good idea.

They kept her waiting, which made Allison notice that they didn't have a clock on the wall. This had to be the place where they interviewed suspects. But why was she here? They weren't planning to arrest her, were they?

The door opened, and Allison was disappointed to see that it wasn't Detective Teidleman. Instead, it was the black woman who had accompanied him when he came to her house.

The woman extended her hand, "Hello, Allison. My name's Jean Harrison. I want to help you."

Allison didn't take Jean's hand. She didn't like the way the woman talked. She sounded like a teacher who only knew your name because it was on the attendance sheet. "Why am I locked in here? Am I suspected of something?"

Jean sat down. "No, no. But because of the situation, the police believe you may be a material witness. Now I'm not a police officer, I work for the county. I'm here because you're a minor."

Allison almost laughed. "Material witness. I was there with Chuck. Of course I'm a material witness—"

"Why did you come here, Allison?"

Allison sucked in a breath. *They knew.* The police knew what had happened at her house. She didn't know whether to be scared or reassured. "It's Mom," Allison began, and she felt her voice catch.

Jean tried to sound reassuring. "I know, Allison. It's all right now. Do you know where she is?"

Something in the way she said that made Allison suspicious. She sucked in a breath and said, "No, all I know is she was supposed to come home, and these men are at my house."

Jean took Allison's hand and said, "I know this whole situation is frightening, but it isn't your fault."

Allison grabbed her hand away and asked, "*What* isn't my fault? There are strangers breaking into my house—"

The look of sympathy on Jean's face was almost too much to bear. Allison stood up. "What's going on?"

"Those men were FBI agents," Jean said. "They were there looking for your mother."

Allison's mouth hung open. She tried to say something, but the words wouldn't come. She was suddenly back in the same surreal nightmare she had escaped in the garage. She slowly sank into her chair, feeling the pulse throb in her temples.

Eventually, she whispered, "What are you talking about?"

"Your mother's a fugitive, Allison. She has been since the early seventies. She sabotaged a chemical plant in 1972—"

"This is some bizarre mistake—"

"The plant made napalm. I'm sure she thought she was fighting the war. But two security guards died in the explosion."

"No. You're wrong . . ." Even so, there was a seed of doubt there, planted by the pictures she'd seen in her mother's album. It was almost believable—

It was a lie. It had to be.

"Allison, it's true. Your mother disappeared from her

office with a substantial amount of her company's escrow accounts in her possession. There were airline tickets and packed bags in her house—"

"You don't understand." *That isn't what this is about.* Allison almost showed her what it was about. She almost lifted the ashtray off the table just to show that this wasn't about something her mom did decades ago.

But she didn't.

She didn't trust Jean.

"I know this hurts, but you have to be strong. Now there are some agents here who want to talk to you."

The panic must have shown in her face because Jean tried to reassure her. "Don't worry. I'll be here the whole time."

Allison nodded. She had to get out of here.

"I need something to drink," she whispered, trying to sound as weak and defeated as possible.

"Sure," Jean nodded. "I can go down and get you a Coke if you want."

"Thanks."

"Then we'll have that talk?"

"Sure . . ."

It seemed an agonizingly long time before Jean got up and left her alone. The moment the door shut, Allison's mind began racing—literally, it felt like. It was as if the essence of her mind was sweeping through the walls and doors around her while she tried to appear meek and motionless to the camera.

The only escape route was the windows, and she felt the malleable clay of her mind envelop the quartet of panes nearest her. She tried to solidify that mental clay around the wooden lattice that held the panes in place. She didn't have time to experiment with methodology; as soon as she felt firm in her grip on the cross-shaped lattice, she began pushing.

It felt as if she was slamming her head into the window. The wood seemed to groan in time to her pulse. Then, suddenly, the resistance was gone with a sound like a rifleshot—the sudden shock making her lose contact with her teeking senses. She turned around, opening eyes she didn't realize she'd screwed shut, and saw a new, gaping hole in the unopenable window.

The camera was a moot point now, all she could do was run.

As she dove out the window, and onto the asphalt of the parking lot, she could almost imagine she heard Agent Jackson's voice cursing from beyond the closed door of the room.

She rounded City Hall, convinced every cop in the city was after her. She thanked God that Macy was still parked in front, waiting.

Allison yanked open the passenger door and before Macy could finish saying, "What, girl?" Allison was yelling, "Drive!"

Macy was peeling away before the door was shut.

26 October Euclid Heights, Ohio

7:00 pm Tuesday

"I don't believe you ran from the cops, girl."

"I know," Allison sat, legs folded, forehead resting in her hands. After City Hall, the two of them had gone to Macy's house and had taken over the basement.

"I just hope that they don't trace the plates on my sister's car. I'll never be able to cop a ride again."

Allison just nodded. She was still too much in shock to say much of anything.

The room around them wasn't like the box-filled netherworld under Allison's house. It was a furnished rec room—wood paneling, a pool table, a bar, and, in one corner, a Commodore 64 computer that had been left behind by the march of progress.

It did share a characteristic with Allison's basement. Most of Macy's rec room had been taken over by storage. The pool table was buried under boxes of clothes. Behind the bar were stacks of magazines, predominantly *National Geographic*. Even the computer table was swamped by electronic debris, including an old Atari game system— maybe even Pong.

Allison's head was just as cluttered.

Macy sat on a folding chair she'd retrieved from under

the pool table while Allison sat on a barstool that'd been cleared of a 1982 run of *National Geographic*. Macy was hefting a cue ball.

"How come now?" Macy asked.

Allison shook her head and sighed. "Fred and Barney must have known what I did to Chuck before I did."

"Weren't using your name on the news last I checked."

"Can't be too hard to find out."

"You know what it sounds like? Sounds like these guys were watching you already."

Allison hugged herself. "That's *really* paranoid." But wasn't that just what Mom had been worried about? Maybe she knew about these guys—

No, no "maybe" about it. She had that film, she knew what these people were about, and knew what they were capable of doing. On one point Jean Harrison must be right. Mom had been a fugitive for a long time, but not because of some stupid Vietnam demonstration, and not from the FBI.

Macy echoed Allison's thoughts. "From what you're telling me, your mom was about to split town with you, and it sounds like she knew a lot more about this psychic network than you did."

Allison nodded.

Macy began ticking off points with her fingers, still holding up the cue ball. "Your mom was a parashrink, right? You think she might have worked for these Fed Flintstones?"

Allison nodded and hugged herself tighter. She didn't want to believe it, but it was too obvious to deny it—much as she wanted to. "She must have quit." *Must have.* "Run and hid from them—a fugitive just like that woman said." It suddenly struck Allison. She stood up, shaking her head. *"Oh, my."* Her voice was barely a whisper as the realization began to hit her full force.

"What is it, girl? You look like you just saw a ghost."

Allison shook her head, and felt tears streaming down her cheeks. *Forgive me, Mom. I just didn't know why.* "That's it, Macy. That's why she left. To protect *me*."

"I don't get you."

"She knew that I might have this talent. It was in my genes or something. That's why she left Dad."

"Huh?"

"It wasn't Dad she was escaping from. It was these ASI people."

Macy nodded. "Okay. I'll buy that. But why didn't he escape with you?"

Something drooped inside her. "I don't know."

"Your dad, on the phone, he knew that you might be psychically challenged—"

If they know she's a teek . . .

"Your dad sounds as if he knows as much as your mom about 'them,' these ASI geeks—"

"Yeah." As Allison spoke, her skin crawled with the thought of those men watching her. *How long,* she thought. How long had dark men in gray vans patiently recorded reel after reel of her life? Somewhere, in little gray rooms, men with little gray souls were editing her life, weighing the pieces, so that they'd only bother their bosses with the good parts.

Little gray men who found the problems of this naive little girl terribly amusing.

The thought didn't bring tears. Her heart sank a little deeper, but it burned.

Where was her mother?

These "Fed Flintstones" might have conned the cops into thinking that Mom had disappeared, leaving Allison to the wolves. Allison knew Mom better than that. Mom wouldn't abandon her. And she certainly wouldn't skip town, leaving her car in the hands of the ASI.

No, these men had her.

But what could she do about it?

"Can you catch something?"

"Huh?"

Macy held a cue ball in one hand and had the yellow notepad in the other. She'd been rummaging in Allison's paper sack while Allison had been nursing a growing rage.

"You got some rules here: You can't teek different objects in different directions, etc. The smaller it is, the harder it is for me—you—to teek it. You can't teek liquids."

Macy looked up from the pad. "So what if I toss this cue ball at you?"

It was so completely off the subject that Allison just shrugged.

"Catch."

Macy's toss caught her off-guard, but Allison tried to snag the cue ball with her teek. But in motion the cue ball slipped out of her mental fingers as if it were made of quicksilver. She had to catch it with her hands. It seemed that she couldn't get a grip on something in motion—

Did that make sense? Allison remembered in physics class how Mr. Franklin made such an issue of the fact that *everything* is moving. Things can only be at rest relative to each other. It wasn't the motion that was the problem, Allison thought. It was the fact that her teek sense was a step behind the real world. She couldn't shift her attention fast enough to follow a ball moving relative to her.

Allison tossed the cue ball back. "Try again."

Macy tossed it and, instead of trying to wrap her mental web around the cue ball, she thought at a chunk of space near the end of the cue ball's path. Instead of trying to think this teek around something, she tried to think it into a solid lump. A block of wax, or Jell-O. She had the force wrapped so tightly within her head that she expected the cue ball to bounce off it. Instead, the sensation was like having a ball bearing splash into a blob of molasses—

Her brain was that molasses, and the impact caused a familiar twinge beneath her temples. She felt her teek blob shake with the impact, and she realized her eyes were closed.

When she opened her eyes, there was the cue ball, hanging in midair about a foot from her chest.

She had, indeed, "caught it."

"Toss some more," Allison said.

Macy obliged. Pool balls splashed into her little teek net to freeze in midair. The feeling inside her skull was the same dizzy vertigo she got when she shook her head from side to side too fast.

Allison was surprised to see that the impact vibration she felt in her mind—that caused the dizzying sensation—was reflected in the balls she had already caught. She watched the cue ball, now the center of a frozen solar system, and saw it shake every time she caught a new ball.

Experimentally, Allison waved her hand between the balls. She felt no resistance. *So is this like before, and I can include and exclude matter at will?*

Allison thought of the teek glob also enveloping her hand, and her hand was stuck. She tried a few experimental tugs, and the whole complex of frozen balls seemed to vibrate themselves, following the tug of her hand. *Like they're all connected.*

The feeling she got from her hand was oddly numbing, as if it had fallen asleep.

Allison let her hand go, and began dropping the balls out of the matrix, one by one, catching them, and tossing them back to Macy.

"Allie, you're a miracle worker. If I wasn't standing here—"

"I hardly believe it myself."

"You should do Letterman."

Allison sighed, remembering some of Mom's books. "There's a guy who says he'll give a check for some thousands of dollars to someone who can prove they can do something paranormal."

"Your chance for the big time."

Allison thought for a long time and finally said, "No. This all is the province of the *National Enquirer*. No one will believe it."

"Come on, I'm looking here with my own eyes—"

"And how come no one's picked up Amazing Whoever's check? David Copperfield can make the Statue of Liberty disappear. Cue balls aren't very impressive."

Macy shrugged.

"Besides, I've been on TV enough for my whole lifetime. No TV, no news." Allison thought of the local news, more little gray men recording her life and editing for the juicy parts. And that brought her thinking back to Fred and Barney.

And Mom.

Where are you, Mom? What happened?

"What am I going to do, Macy?"

"No news and no cops. Who's left?"

Allison lowered her head. "There's Dad. Like you said, he sounded as if he knows something about these guys."

"How do we get a hold of him? The last time you saw him was twelve years ago—"

"Can I use your phone?"

Macy got up and fished around the pile of electronic waste by the Commodore 64. She came out with a black rotary telephone. She picked it up and listened. "I'm amazed. Chardine isn't using it."

Macy handed the phone over. The cord knocked over a stack of old Atari cartridges. Allison took it and dialed information.

"What city, please?"

"Los Angeles."

Within moments Allison had Macy writing down a number for John Charvat in LA.

"Charvat?" Macy asked when Allison hung up. "I thought your dad's name was Boyle."

"So did I. But Boyle's my mother's maiden name."

"Where'd 'Charvat' come from?"

"The return address on that Express envelope I told you about." Allison sucked in a breath and began dialing.

"LA?" Macy said. "My dad's going to kill me for this month's phone bill."

After too many rings, the phone was answered by a familiar voice. "Hello—"

"Dad?" Allison gasped. It was the same voice she'd heard Mom talking to.

"—Charvat. I can't come to the phone right now. Please leave your name and number—"

"An answering machine." Allison could hear the disappointment ringing in her own voice.

The machine beeped.

Allison was prepared to leave a message, giving Dad Macy's number and pleading for him to return the call. But something, an ugly foreboding, stopped her.

She slowly hung up, without leaving a message.

"What's the matter?" Macy asked.

"I don't—" Allison realized that she knew what was wrong. If these ASI people were in her house, they had the envelope with those tickets, and they had John Charvat's address. "I think they have my dad, too."

Macy shook her head. "This is too weird. Are you sure?"

"I'm not sure of anything. I should have *thought*. That UPS envelope is still sitting on my coffee table. All they have to do is look at the return address. They got Mom, of *course* they got Dad—"

Macy shook her head. "Too bad about the tickets. If Fred and Barney had just waited another day, you'd be on your way to St. Louis by now."

"Yeah." Allison's heart sank a little deeper. There was

really nothing left she could do, but turn herself over to someone. The police, the ASI, the news. They had taken her father before she even had a chance to meet him.

"Hold the phone," Allison said.

Macy looked down at the black rotary phone in her hand and said, "I am."

Allison said, "Dad was a lot more paranoid about these ASI people than Mom was."

"So? Do him any good?"

"That's just it. How much you want to bet he was en route to meet us before he ever sent that letter?"

"Then they don't have him?"

Allison shrugged. "I don't know. But I don't think he'd sit around at home, waiting for them to show up."

"That doesn't mean we know where he is."

"Yeah." Allison said, crestfallen. "We need to find out what happened to Mom . . ."

"What are you thinking, girl?"

26 OCTOBER EUCLID HEIGHTS, OHIO

7:30 PM TUESDAY

The feeling in the Boyle house was quiet and tense. Barney and Fred talked to each other in low tones in the dining room. Fred spent half the time talking to Barney, and the other half talking on his folding non-phone to the two cars he had combing the suburb for Allison Boyle.

Occasionally he would curse the fiasco at the Euclid Heights City Hall. Everyone present knew him well enough not to mention anything about it.

Jane and George were out of earshot, in the living room, tending to a now-comatose Elroy. "What's wrong with him?" George whispered.

"You keep asking that. I don't know."

"You're the one who has the doctorate in this. You're the one who went to med school. I was a bloody physicist. I'm out of my depth here."

Jane looked back at the pair in the dining room. "I think everyone here is. This was supposed to be a milk run."

"Yeah, right."

"If it makes you feel better, I'm sure Elroy's problem isn't physical."

"It doesn't."

Fred walked into the living room, trailing Barney. "Well?" he asked.

"No change," Jane said.

"Damn. We're crippled without our spotter, and it will take hours to fly one in from Dallas."

"What happened to the little bugger, anyway?" Barney asked.

"The best we can figure is that Elroy suffered from some mental form of flash blindness. As if he stared at the sun too long—though it doesn't explain the other symptoms—"

"You're comparing this girl to the *sun*?" Fred asked.

"Comparatively," George said. "The energies that form the mental waveform Elroy perceives are measured in fractions of a microwatt. The energy Allison Boyle has to liberate to move gross physical objects is orders of magnitude greater. He stared into it with no preparation."

Fred shook his head, "You should keep a tighter rein on the kid—"

"*God damn it!* If you hadn't tried to strong-arm the girl, she wouldn't have panicked. If *you* kept a tighter rein on your pet Neanderthal there—"

Barney balled a fist. "Why you cocksucking—"

Everyone was interrupted by the sound of a feline howl from outside. Fred glanced toward the dining room window as George said, "What—"

"Get the hypo," Fred told him, and started running toward the back door.

26 October   Euclid Heights, Ohio

7:40 pm   Tuesday

The sky had gone dark by the time they'd reached Allison's block. They stood on the street behind Allison's duplex. On this side of the block, rows of four-story apartment buildings faced them. Macy was following Allison's lead, but she hesitated when Allison began walking down one of the driveways.

"I don't like this," Macy said, "It's crazy—especially when I don't have the car."

Allison turned to face her. "You didn't have to come."

"Like hell I didn't. My best friend is going to get herself shot or something—can I sit by and—"

"Okay."

"I still don't like this."

Allison shrugged and continued down the driveway. The parking area in back of these apartments bordered against the backyards of the houses on Allison's street. Allison stopped in front of a vine-choked chain-link fence. Between the vines and the bushes on the other side, she could see the peak of her garage sticking up above the fence.

She had just been here, only six hours ago. It already felt like six days.

Macy walked up next to her. "You spent all afternoon scaring me with these people."

"I should let them keep hold of Mom?"

"How do you know she's there? Just because you escaped from the cops don't mean—"

"I have to do something."

Macy shook her head. Their conversation had evolved into whispers now that they were at the fence. "They'll be watching for you."

"Hey," Allison whispered back. "I'm the amazing Allison, remember?"

Allison took hold of the fence and hauled herself upward. The entire fence shook with her weight, waving foliage. The rusty fence cut into her hand and the vines made purchase for her feet vague and slippery. She'd barely gotten her feet off the ground when Macy whispered up at her, "Hey, amazing Allison, why don't you do it the easy way?"

Huh?

Then it hit her. She could levitate Babs, cue balls, and Jeeps. Why couldn't she levitate herself?

Allison summoned her mental sense, this time she could feel it pound behind her eyes, and the motion seemed more sluggish. She was getting tired. She slipped her mental fingers around herself.

A bizarre sensation gripped her, a double-layered feedback that felt like the tactile equivalent of the sound fingernails made scraping across a blackboard. She pulled herself up, and nearly passed out with vertigo as her normal and telekinetic senses tried to resolve their respective input and tied her brain in a throbbing knot.

She flew, but with a sense of shivering dizziness that made her want to throw up. All sense of gravity had left, making her feel like she was falling an immense distance even though she was moving upward. Her horizon flipped over a few times, causing her to panic. She headed toward what she thought was the ground, and hit, hard.

The entire surface of her skin had fallen asleep.

She held herself there, shaking, head pounding, for a long time before she realized that she was hugging the rear wall of her garage, and she was rotated ninety degrees from the ground. She slowly let the teek go, and she rolled gently onto the pile of dead leaves that, earlier, had held the twelve-year-old kid whose leg she'd riddled with nails.

After half a minute or so, Macy jumped down from the top of the fence. "Are you all right?" Macy whispered.

Allison groaned. Her whole head felt like a blood blister on the verge of busting open. "Now I know why only gurus do that." She sat up, rubbing her head. "You'd need to meditate six hours a day just to be able to handle it."

"Good news is you didn't wake up the Flintstones. Still up to this?"

"I have to." Allison got unsteadily to her feet. Her inner ear still seemed unsure what direction the ground was in. "But let's hold on for a little while."

They stood there for ten minutes or so while Allison took deep breaths and tried to recover. The fatigue caused by her teeking everything around was deceptive. It wasn't related to physical exertion. It was more like the sense of brain-deadening mental exhaustion she got after spending all night studying for a trigonometry test.

It would be very easy right now for her to trigger a very bad migraine.

That's it, she thought. *After I get Mom out of here, I don't teek a thing until I get a good night's sleep.*

After a few minutes Allison felt decent enough to go on.

It was an alien sensation for Allison, sneaking up on her own house. It enhanced the surreal feeling that had been growing since the weekend. It fed the paranoid thought that the things she sensed peeking at her from the shadows weren't simply residents of her mind, but were really there, snickering and meaning her harm.

The weather conspired with the feeling. Black clouds roiled across the sky like an avalanche of soiled cotton. Every few seconds a biting wind would whip dead leaves into a whirlwind around her feet.

The house remained quiet, shades drawn against advancing night.

Allison felt a sense of dread when she saw that there were no lights on Mr. Luvov's half of the building.

Mom's Taurus was still parked in the driveway, about ten feet away from the rear of the house. Allison paused next to it and looked at Macy.

"Wait here," Allison whispered.

"Wait a sec—"

"Keep watch, okay?"

Macy sighed and said, "Okay. Watch yourself."

Allison nodded and crept along the driveway. From the street, Allison's half of the house was on the right, the side with the driveway. She passed under the dining room windows and risked a peek.

The shades were drawn here, too.

To get a peek inside, she chinned herself up to the window, her foot lodged in the cracks of the brick foundation. The sound of talking came from the living room. Allison was sure. The only place she could see in was through a small gap in the dining room drapes, and that was half-obscured by a potted plant. It provided a great view of someone's back.

She eased herself down and tried to plan.

This will be tougher than I thought.

She needed to see these people, where they were in the house, before she would have any idea where they were keeping Mom.

There were two other views she could get on the living room. There was a half-window high on the driveway wall that didn't have shades or drapes on it. However, there was no way for her to reach it without a ladder, or trying to teek herself by her own bootstraps.

Then there were the porch windows.

She didn't want to go on the porch. She would feel much too exposed out there. She also suspected that someone would be sitting in the van parked out front.

Allison sighed. It was either the dining room windows, or give up. She supposed that she might teek some of the drapes out of the way. If she did it slowly, maybe no one would notice.

When she was ready to chin herself up again, she heard the loudest and most horrendous yowl she had ever heard in her life. She let go of the windowsill in panic, stumbling to the ground.

When she was on her hands and knees, something black and furry butted into her face and meowed again.

Allison had never fully appreciated how loud Rhett could be.

"Allie!" Macy called in a harsh stage whisper, back by the Taurus.

Allison backed up, hissing at Rhett, *"Shut up, you stupid cat."*

Rhett was having none of that. He was very unhappy. He wanted food, he wanted in, and he was intent on telling the whole neighborhood about it. He opened his mouth and announced his displeasure in a loud puff of fish-breath, right in Allison's face.

Allison heard the door slam in front of the house.

"Oh, God!"

Allison scooped up her cat—who started purring immediately—and ran back toward the Taurus. She'd nearly reached Macy when she heard a voice say, "Hold it right there, Miss Boyle."

Allison turned around, slowly. She stood right next to the passenger door of the Taurus. There was Fred, standing at the back door of her house, holding his hands spread, attempting to look innocent.

"Please, Miss Boyle?" he said.

Rhett curled up in her arms and closed his eyes.

"Where's my mother?" Allison yelled at the man.

Only the slightest darkening clouded Fred's features. It was brief, and his face still held a smiling openness that the circumstances didn't warrant. "Why don't you come inside, where it's warm. I'll explain everything."

There was an older man with white hair walking up the driveway now. Allison glanced at the nose of the Taurus. Macy was crouched down, between the front of the Taurus and Mr. Luvov's pickup truck, apparently unseen by Fred or the man walking up the driveway.

Macy noticed Allison's glance and began making twisting motions with her hand.

What?

Macy pointed at the Taurus and made the twisting motion again.

Allison looked up and yelled at Fred, "What do you want with me?"

"We want to help you—" Fred took a step forward, hands open. "You have a talent. We can show you how to use it."

"Where's my mother?"

The cloud slipped over Fred's features again. He took another step forward and smiled broadly. "She's safe, Allison. We can take you to her. Right now if you like. We just don't want anybody to get hurt."

Allison knew, in her heart, that she was looking at a man who found it very easy to lie.

Macy was still making the twisting motions.

What was she getting at?

Allison looked at the Taurus again, and finally saw that the keys were in the ignition.

"Don't move, girlie," came a twangy voice from right behind her.

Barney had circled around the garage without Allison noticing. Allison looked around and saw him holding a nasty-looking gun. It was pointed right at her.

"Damn it, Barney." Fred sounded angry. Allison looked back and saw him drop his hands and start walking toward the Taurus. "Guns are supposed to be a last resort."

"After Elroy, you want to take chances? After that poor bastard Charlie?"

Fred looked down the driveway, where the third man was jogging up to meet them. "Do you have it, George?" Fred's voice sounded weary.

George patted a black case he was carrying, "Finally."

Allison felt the taste of copper in her mouth. What were they going to do with her? She looked at Barney. The gun was locked on her. She began to reach out with mental fingers.

After the attempted levitation, the effort almost made her pass out. It felt like she was peeling ragged bloody chunks from inside her skull to wrap around Barney's gun. She locked the teek around the metal parts of the gun. Her head throbbed and pain fogged her vision. She fought the pain, to lock down everything she could, as hard as she could manage. She tried to feel every single molecule of that gun embedded in her teek matrix.

"She's doing something!" Barney said.

"Grab her!" Fred yelled.

Allison didn't see Fred and George react because she'd closed her eyes. Slammed them shut, because what she did *hurt*.

She felt feedback through her teek sense. She could feel Barney try and pull the trigger, as if the trigger was now part of her own body. But the trigger was locked, stationary to the rest of the gun, with a force equal to that required to lift a Jeep Cherokee. The gun was locked in place and, with all the effort she could muster, Allison yanked the gun away.

There was a cracking noise.

Barney yelled, "Shit. Shit. Shit. Shit. *My hand!*"

Allison opened her eyes and her vision cleared enough to see George coming toward her. He was fumbling something out of the black case. It looked like another gun. Allison still felt her teek holding Barney's gun, so she threw it at George.

George was still fumbling with his case when something black and metallic flew out of the sky and slammed into his stomach. He folded over it and it carried him across the driveway and spilled him, groaning, into the neighboring backyard.

Allison had to let go of Barney's gun, and that cleared her normal vision enough for her to see that George hadn't been pulling a weapon out of the case. It was some sort of high-pressure hypodermic air gun. It, and cylinders filled with amber fluid, spilled over the lawn around him.

Behind her, Allison heard the Taurus start up. She spun around to see Macy behind the wheel, yelling, "Get in, fool!"

Allison yanked the car door open, and felt Fred's hand on her shoulder. "Not so fast, Miss Boyle."

With a manic feline hiss, Rhett sank his teeth into Fred's thumb. The man jerked his hand away long enough for Allison to dive in next to Macy. The car was zooming backward before Allison could get the door shut.

As the car rocketed backward, out of the driveway, Fred ran after them. He shouted things that were incomprehensible through the haze of her headache. Barney ran behind Fred, cradling a bleeding hand. Behind them all, George struggled to get to his feet.

"Eeeyah," Macy yelled as she skidded the Taurus on to the street. "You know how to make an exit, girl."

As they spun out at the end of the driveway, past a gray van, Allison could swear she'd seen a face looking out her living room window.

The kid?

She wasn't given time to think about it. Macy drove like a wild woman. The Taurus turfed three lawns and jumped the curb twice as she pulled halfway around the block, up Euclid Heights Boulevard, back toward the high school.

At that point, their rocketing escape ground to a halt as Macy merged with infuriatingly slow traffic left over from rush hour. Rhett mewed insistently, and Allison only heard him through a head wrapped in cotton and a million miles away.

Macy yelled at the cars to move, but the light up ahead wasn't helping matters any.

"Sorry, Macy," Allison said weakly. "Bad idea."

Macy shook her head. "Done's done. Just hope that we ain't in as much trouble as I think we are." The traffic inched forward and Macy mumbled, "All the chase scenes I've seen never went *this* slow." The light ahead turned green, and Macy blared the horn.

Allison winced. "Don't do that. There's a cop right there at the intersection."

"I'd almost welcome being arrested. I'd feel safer— No, you bastard! Don't turn left! *Move!*"

The Taurus managed to get to the head of the line as the yellow light faded. "Some cop," Macy said. "Fool pulls an illegal left and porky does diddly."

They sat and waited at the intersection as the cop led a procession of cars across their path.

"Damn," Macy said.

"What?" Allison's eyes were half-closed from fatigue and the sudden light from opening them drove a spike into her forebrain.

"Flintstones at six o'clock."

Allison looked behind them, and about seven or eight cars back, she could see the ASI van. She couldn't see inside from the streetlight glare off the windshield. But the van was hard to miss. "I see them," Allison said.

"More to the point, *they* see *us*. I wanted to lose them." Macy started looking around. "Allie, you see porky anywhere?"

"Huh?" Allison turned away from the gray van in time to see Macy pull out into the intersection against the light. Horns blared from around them as she took a left through a gap in the opposing traffic.

"My God, Macy. *What are you doing?*"

"Losing men with guns." The Taurus now was heading away from most of Euclid Heights, and toward East Cleveland.

They had gone two blocks and were about a block away from East Cleveland, when Allison heard a chorus of horns back at the intersection. The van had followed their illegal left. As she kept looking back, Allison asked, "What now?"

"Like I know, girl?"

Allison could tell when they drove into East Cleveland, even without looking at the signs. The streetlights turned from white mercury to a dirty-yellow sodium and the road suddenly became a patchwork of chuckholes filled and chuckholes-to-be. The houses they passed were almost the same ones that were in Euclid Heights, but they'd become shabby and ill-used with too many families and too little maintenance. It was a neighborhood that would've frightened Allison, if she hadn't had other worries right now.

The Taurus rumbled over the patchwork asphalt for three blocks, Macy turning at random. Now that they wove through East Cleveland, they'd lost most of the traffic between them and the van, so it wasn't too surprising when the Flintstones turned on to the road behind them only three or four car-lengths back.

"Think of something," Macy said.

What? I can barely think. My head's a blood pudding. Allison watched out the back, staring at the van for long agonizing minutes. *I need to stop them.*

Allison got an inspiration and started rummaging in the Taurus for Mom's parking money. She found a handful of quarters, about five dollars' worth.

"What're you doing?" Macy asked.

"When they stop, be ready to get out of here quick."

I can't do this. Not now. I need to sleep.

Only once more, she promised herself.

She poured a protesting Rhett into the back seat and lowered the passenger window. The sudden inflow of cold air woke her up and seemed to sharpen some of the duller edges of her mind. She could think, but it also meant that her headache switched from hammers to scalpels.

As Macy drove, Allison lined up a row of quarters on top of the windowsill. As she placed each one, she grabbed it with her teek. Each effort was harder than the last, pounding into her head until she couldn't tell if the rushing in her ears was the wind or her own pulse.

Twenty quarters, locked into a line with her teek.

Allison's world thrummed with white noise, a scouring wind that abraded the flesh from inside her skull. But through that noise, she could see—see things with a razor-fine accuracy that lacerated her eyes with sheer wealth of details. She could see the dates on the individual quarters, not only see them, but feel them with the bizarre mental feedback of her teek sense. She could see the veins on the dead leaves that blew between the cars. She saw the rust spots on the van's bumper, and the scratches on its license plate.

Again, Allison had the heady feeling that what she was really doing was looking *inside* herself, and discovering the entire universe.

The line of quarters she controlled flew out behind the

Taurus, in formation. As they did, time seemed to slow down. Allison hardly felt the car's motion at all. They were frozen in this tableau. Hunter never quite catching. Hunted never quite escaping. An archetype that belonged in some special section of Hell.

Nothing moved for Allison.

Nothing but the flying line of quarters. The quarters, a score of tiny silver moons, flew down to float about six inches off the asphalt right behind the Taurus' real bumper. There, for a moment, they froze—the picture complete.

Then, with an effort of will that Allison wasn't aware she was capable of, she pumped every ounce of teek she had into those quarters. She thought of the Cherokee, and the effort that had taken, and she put all of *that* into it.

The effort made Allison yell, or realize that she had been yelling all this time. Whether in triumph, fear, or pain, she didn't know.

As she watched, the world snapped back to real-time. The silver moons became chromed bullets. The quarters shot toward the van with such force that they tore the air in their wake. With her teek she could feel the air rip with the coins' passage as if cracked by twenty supersonic whips.

Then the quarters left the realm of Allison's teek and reentered the world of physics.

The coins tore past the underside of the van, exploding all four tires in a flurry of shredded rubber. The van collapsed into the asphalt like a wounded beast, sparks flying from its rims.

The quarters didn't stop with the van. Tires blew from parked cars. Windshields shattered. Splinters erupted from a tree. And, far down the block, a stop sign rang like a gong as a hole blasted through the bottom of its S.

Allison was gripping the back of her seat so hard that her fingers were white and cold.

"My God." As she said it, the white noise crashed over her, breaking up, and leaving in its wake only the black aching hollow of fatigue. She closed her eyes and couldn't open them again.

CHAPTER
FIFTEEN

She stood in the school auditorium, on stage, stripped naked. The landing of the fire stairs had been transplanted to center stage, the scene washed by a pulsing red light that hurt her eyes.

As she tried to cover herself, Fred and Barney came on stage dressed as reporters. Barney held the camera on her, while Fred shoved a microphone in Chuck's face trying to get an interview. Fred wasn't having much luck. No matter how reasonable his questions were, all Chuck could do was hold his bleeding crotch and scream.

Mr. Counter walked on stage in a pair of swim trunks, wiping himself off with a bloody towel. "Miss Boyle," he said. "I am afraid that you aren't taking this class seriously."

Mr. Counter grabbed her wrists and pulled them away from her body. Barney filmed all of it while muttering over and over, "Shit. Shit. Shit. Shit. My hand. Shit."

"Your lines," came a whisper from offstage.

"Not seriously at all." Mr. Counter said, pulling her close enough to smell the blood on his towel. "We have to talk about your grades."

All Allison could think was, *The play's not supposed to go like this.*

The whisper returned, sounding like an off-kilter long-distance connection. *"Melissa's line is, 'Oh, Randolph, I've waited four years for this moment!'"*

Everything froze.

The scene flickered and Allison had a lucid moment when she realized she was dreaming. Then she heard Chuck's voice, still screaming, but screaming words—

"*I'm dead!*" he yelled at her. "*I'm dead! Mom's dead! Everyone's dead, sweetcakes.*"

Allison looked up into Mr. Counter's bloody face, and saw Chuck there. "Just you and me, kid."

She screamed herself awake.

Allison woke up to light, bright sunlight, streaming across her face. She tried to turn over and found herself strapped down.

She opened her eyes in a panic, light stabbing through her brain, and saw that she'd tangled her hand in the Taurus' shoulder belt. She closed her eyes and realized how much of her hurt. Her head was a dull empty hole. She had cramps in her neck and back, and her legs had fallen asleep. She opened her eyes again, slowly, shading them with her hand.

Where was she?

Allison looked around the car. *Where was Macy?*

The Taurus sat near the entrance to a parking lot. She looked down at the entrance, and saw four lanes of highway backed by a forested median of autumnal golds and reds. A blue sign faced her saying, "rest stop."

At the other end of the parking lot, near the exit, was a small brick structure with two doors, "men" and "women." There was only one other car in the lot, a dirty-green Ford pickup. Allison looked around and saw a hefty couple at one of a half-dozen picnic tables, eating out of McDonald's bags. She supposed that they belonged to the pickup.

The sight made her incredibly hungry.

Allison opened up the passenger door and got out of the Taurus, wobbling on her sleeping legs.

A two-trailer semi blared by on the highway.

She glanced at the clock on the dash of the Taurus and it said 7:45. *I slept for twelve hours.*

Allison hugged herself and said, "Macy, where are you?"

As if in response, Allison saw Macy leave the women's half of the rest rooms. She caught sight of Allison and waved. She'd changed clothes and it made her look older, or, at least, tougher. Macy wore a motorcycle jacket, sunglasses, and cowboy boots. She resembled an adolescent Grace Jones doing a *Terminator* impression.

"Morning, sleepyhead."

Allison looked at Macy and said, "Is it a stupid question to ask where we are?"

"A few exits east of Columbus."

"Columbus?" Allison felt the strength go out of her knees. She gripped the car for support. "Why'd you drive— how'd you get—*where's my cat?"*

"Calm down, girl." Macy draped an arm around her. "We got a whole day ahead of us—and you need to eat."

Allison looked up at Macy, about to say something, but Macy was right. She was ravenous.

They found a Denny's ten miles down from the rest stop, right after a sign reading, "Wheeling—70 miles."

"See, girl?" Macy said, after watching Allison decimate three cheeseburgers, a plate of scrambled eggs, three strips of bacon, and a side of hash browns. "When you crapped out, I didn't see what else I could do."

"I understand. Are you going to eat that?"

Macy pushed over her uneaten home fries. "Flintstones wouldn't need to be geniuses to find me. Could I go to the cops after stealing your mom's car? After what happened to you there? No, girl."

"So where're we going?"

"We're going to see your dad. At least there's some chance he's got some handle on what's going on."

Allison swallowed. It felt too much like she was abandoning Mom. She was afraid of what she had seen in Agent Jackson's eyes when he'd said that her mom was safe. She was afraid of her dream. Of what Chuck had said . . .

"Where, Macy?"

"You tell me. You said you had it narrowed down to two locations."

Allison nodded. The thing was, so would the ASI. They had the tickets, the whole bizarre itinerary. Mom knew where they were going to meet. Dad had told her, Allison had overheard. . . .

Where I first called you a "baby-killer."

That was a Vietnam thing, wasn't it? There was that picture in the album. Mom leading some sort of demonstration, the Capitol in the background.

Why not, they didn't have anything better to go on.

"Washington D.C.," Allison said. "That's the place."

"Whatever you say."

Allison shook her head. "You don't have to do this. I didn't mean to drag you into—"

"Stop that. This is partly my fault. *I* swiped the car."

"It was my stupid idea that put us there."

"Like I'd let you go in there alone? I got better people to be pissed at."

"Okay." Allison finished the last home fry. She looked at the meal she had just devoured and thought she should be on the verge of puking. She didn't. Emotionally, she felt like roadkill, but her body felt the same weird sense of well-being that she'd had the morning after the headache that trashed her room.

It's bad enough my mind is of debatable sanity. Don't tell me my body is going nuts, too. I shouldn't be feeling like this after Mom . . .

She wouldn't let herself finish the thought. "What happened to Rhett?"

"Don't worry about your cat. When I stopped at home to get my traveling gear, I gave him to Chardine to take care of."

"Chardine?"

"Hey, I bad-mouth my sister sometimes, but Chardine's solid. If she promises something, she'll do it. Besides, she's going to get her car all to herself for a few weeks it seems like, so she owes me." Macy gave an unconvincing grin.

"Did you tell her where you're going?"

Macy shook her head. "I slipped in and out, told Chardine I was running away again." Macy lowered her voice an octave and said, " 'As long as y'all don't get in no trouble with some boy—protect yourself, girl.' " A dead-on imitation of Macy's older sister.

"I grabbed stuff," Macy said. "Deposited cat. Stole Darnel's jacket, and I was out of there. We were in Columbus before midnight."

"Thanks, a lot."

Macy nodded. "But—"

"But?"

"This food and the gas we're using tapped out my cash as well as all the change I found in the car. Got any money?"

Allison thought back. "Everything I had, money, ID, was in my backpack." She thought hard and then said, "The police still have it."

"We better think of *something*. Or this magical mystery tour will stall out somewhere in West Virginia."

Allison nodded.

Across from the Denny's was a truck stop that was a combination motel, restaurant, gift shop, and highway whatall. Allison and Macy walked through it, trying to figure what they could do for money. It was closing on eight-thirty, and the restaurant was doing boom business with the breakfast crowd. Off the corridor, between the restaurant and the gift shop, was a darkened room from which emerged a chorus of electronic computer noises.

Allison walked in.

It was a large arcade room, the walls lined with aging video games.

Macy followed and asked, "What you have in mind?"

Allison looked at the coin slot of a decrepit *Centipede* game. It said, "Tokens Only."

"You see the change machine around here anywhere?" Allison asked.

"Right there, next to *Spy Hunter*."

Allison walked in that direction. The room was dark and smelled of cigarette smoke. She noted three other people in the room. A trucker type was playing *Pole Position* and crashing often enough to make Allison nervous about his driving skills. Two nattering little kids were playing at the *Gauntlet* game. As Allison passed, the game's digitized voice said, "Elf needs food, badly." The game sounded tired.

She passed a rickety *Star Wars* game, *Tempest,* and a phosphor-burned *Donkey Kong* game that grunted as she passed.

"Any games from *this* century?" Macy commented.

As Allison reached the change machine next to the *Spy Hunter* game, she whispered to Macy, "You up to breaking the law?"

Macy gave her a stare and whispered, "I've already stolen a car, fool."

Allison walked up to the machine, and began fumbling through her pockets as if getting a bill to feed the machine. "Stand in front of that window," Allison whispered very quietly. "And be prepared to run for your life."

Macy obliged by leaning up against the mirror that was set in the wall next to the door reading, "manager's office." As Allison fumbled in her pockets, she tried to think of the best way to do this.

The change machine was a huge floor-standing console, covered with brown pebbled vinyl. The sign said that the machine only gave tokens—five for a dollar bill, thirty for a five. There was one of those special circular locks on the front of the main panel. The kind that took a cylindrical key.

She felt inside the machine with her teek sense, amazingly easy now that she'd had twelve hours sleep and a meal inside her. Her mental fingers slipped over interior structure that she could barely picture. It felt like she was fingering a gossamer lattice, the work of some other-worldly insects.

Allison could recognize the token repository. The bin of metal tokens felt like a web of Styrofoam shells to her ephemeral teek fingers. Then she felt the more solid structure of a box where the bills seemed to go. She locked her mind around it, as solidly as she could.

Now, should I do this gradually, or should I just yank it and get this over with?

After a moment's deliberation, Allison decided that the slow and steady method would raise the entire machine rather than pull the strongbox free. So, she yanked.

The machine groaned, shook, and then the metal top flowered out with an explosion of sparks and little yellow tokens. The metal strongbox smashed through the acoustical tile in the ceiling. Allison heard a wire snap above her, and the ceiling began to sag.

Allison took a step back even though she was expecting

the explosion. Tokens clattered around her, scattering to all corners of the game room. Despite the chaos, she still had control of the strongbox. She brought it back through another tile in the ceiling, right before the manager's door yanked open.

The manager, a hefty woman with bottle-blonde hair, baggy sweater, and a name-tag saying "Hello, my name is Nancy" screamed, *"What in the FUCK is going on out here?"*

"It exploded!" Macy said as Allison caught the descending strongbox.

Fragmented tile fell from the ceiling. The munchkins at the *Gauntlet* game discovered the tokens and started gathering them up like manna from heaven. The manager, Nancy, stood frozen in shock when she got a good look at her change machine. The machine had shorted, belching smoke from a hole with curled edges resembling the top of a surreal sardine can.

Allison ran out of there before anyone could realize exactly what she was carrying. She was storming out the gift shop exit by the time she heard someone say, "Stop those girls."

Macy drove the Taurus out of the parking lot as about half a dozen people ran out the front of the truck stop. They made it back onto the Interstate without any sign of pursuit.

They were passing into West Virginia when Macy finally said, "Okay, what's the problem?"

Allison looked up from the strongbox. She had just counted two hundred and thirty-five dollars—less one tank of gas—back into it. "What do you mean?"

"We've been driving near two hours and all you do is sigh and leaf through the money."

Allison sighed.

"Stop that!" Macy said.

"I just feel bad about stealing this money."

"Oh, great. What else were we going to do? You want to give it back?"

Allison shook her head. "I just wish I'd thought of something else. It's not just the money—how much was that machine worth, Macy? A few thousand dollars? I trashed it."

"Sheesh, Allie. Of all the things to guilt trip yourself over. Look, they'll call the company and say that their blankity-blank machine blew up and nearly shredded a customer. If it isn't under warranty, the insurance'll cover it."

"Whatever." Allison looked down at the money again. "What I really feel bad about is the fact that I enjoyed it."

"Say what?"

"It was *fun.* I used this power I have to wreck someone's property, and I was enjoying myself."

"Ah."

"I thought I was better than that."

"Oh, jeez, Allie. Give that up. Everyone gets off on senseless destruction." Macy took a hand off the wheel and squeezed Allison's shoulder. "Don't worry unless you go outta your way to get your jollies like that."

"Okay."

Macy picked up the strongbox and tossed it into the back seat. "And stop staring at that. You got other problems." Macy steered with one hand as she continued rummaging in the back seat.

"What're you doing now?"

"Here," Macy said. "Play with this." She tossed Babs Bunny into Allison's lap.

"Where'd this come from?" Allison picked Babs up, not knowing whether to be happy or embarrassed.

"When I stopped home, I picked up your paper bag."

"Thanks," Allison said and, somewhat self-consciously, hugged her stuffed rabbit.

27 OCTOBER   US-48, MARYLAND

1:30 PM   WEDNESDAY

As the miles slid by, Allison thought about Mom.

She still had no idea what was really going on here, or who the ASI people were. They seemed to be some part of the government she had never heard of. And, God, that

film. Just thinking about that made her stomach turn to
water. She kept seeing that doctor inserting a needle into
that Ross boy's—

That was a violation worse than anything Charles Wilson
could ever have conceived of.

That was the Prometheus Research Institute, and Mom
worked *for those people. She knew, Dad knew . . .*

What happened to Mom? In her dream Chuck had
said—

Don't think that!

No, Mom wasn't dead. Mom couldn't be dead. She
couldn't be dead over something that was Allison's—

Allison slammed her fist into her thigh. *Don't think like
that. It can't help.* This wasn't anything she had asked for.
It wasn't her fault. She wouldn't have even concealed her
headaches if she'd known where they'd lead.

While Allison tied her brain into a knot, the radio blared.
Something from Nine Inch Nails:

"I'd rather die

"Than give you control—"

"Cheery music, Macy," Allison muttered.

Maryland shot by them, outside the Taurus' windows.
They'd been dodging this year's crop of orange barrels for
close to two hours. Lunch had been in Pennsylvania. In the
parking lot of a Roy Rogers they had debated getting on
the Pennsylvania Turnpike, and decided against it. They
were probably going to be in Washington in time for
dinner.

"You going to complain about *all* my music, girl?"

"I haven't said a word since the Nirvana tape." She'd
been thinking about other things.

Macy punched eject and yawned.

"Tired?" Allison asked, trying not to let her mental state
infect her voice.

"Yes, damn it. Want to take over?"

"I don't have a license."

"You don't even have a temp?"

"I've only been sixteen for a month."

Macy muttered something about being a year older than
all her friends and rummaged in her huge handbag. Arm
bag or body bag would be a better name size-wise. With

one hand she began pulling out tapes. "Pearl Jam, Nirvana again, Chili Peppers—U2, you can't object to U2?"

Allison shrugged. "Go ahead."

The cassette began in mid-song. *"Still haven't found what I'm looking for."*

Allison looked out at the passing farmland. There had to be something else she could do to occupy her mind. She couldn't dwell on things she had no power over.

After a bit of pondering, she fished her battered yellow pad from the paper bag on the back seat. Thinking about her teek would be more productive than anything else she could do at the moment.

Once she found it, she focused her attention on her yellow pad. There were some egg stains on it now, but it still cataloged her "Teek Rules."

"Teek Rule #1: You can't teek different objects in different directions. Teek embeds things in its own reference frame, then it moves the frame. Within the frame the objects remain stationary relative to each other unless acted on by an outside force.

"Teek Rule #2: The smaller it is, the harder it is for me to teek it.

"Teek Rule #3: You can't teek liquids. The denser (more viscous?) the better."

Allison concentrated on her recent experiences and tried to think of coherent things to add to her list, things that would help her understand this power of hers.

Much of the previous day, especially with Fred, Barney, and company, had taken on a nightmarish quality. She felt that she might go back to Cleveland and find out that none of this had really happened.

I wish.

She told herself to think things through, starting from when she'd stopped taking her notes. The Cherokee, what did that show?

It showed her that it took a lot of painful concentration to focus all this teek.

"#4: Max. lift aprox. three(?) tons."

Allison wished she had her physics textbook so that she might have some idea of the forces involved in that. What she did remember from physics was the fact that she only had half her ability listed there. If she assumed that she was working off of some finite energy—and her entire range of experimentation was devoted to putting such limits on her power—then she needed to factor in time. Couldn't figure out energy just from the force, she needed to know how far it moved over how long a time. She added, *"aprox. one foot in five seconds."* She felt she might be remembering wrong, since one thing teek did was warp her sense of time.

Which made her think of another rule, *"#5: Teek is also a sense."*

She could feel around with her teek without necessarily grabbing anything. Allison thought it was a sense akin to touch, much the same way that smell was related to taste. The teek sense was much more ephemeral, and that same quality allowed her mental fingers to slip through matter. Teek didn't feel the surface of things so much as their substance.

What was so disorienting was the fact that her teek sense also seemed dimly cross-wired into her sense of vision. Teek sharpened the focus of her vision—when the pain of overuse didn't blur everything—and gave her the surreal sense of seeing *around* objects. At the peak of concentration the sense of teek could turn the universe inside out.

"#6: If I grab an object passing through the teek frame, the frame will try to make the object stationary to itself— soak up the object's kinetic energy."

Allison had been picturing, off and on, her teek grasp as a gigantic lump of ectoplasmic clay. Throwing something— like a cue ball—at a lump of clay will cause it to stick in the mass, unless it travels fast enough to blow a hole through the lump.

"#7: The smaller (lighter?) the object is, the faster I can move it."

Allison remembered the quarters she had shot through the tires of Fred and Barney's van. Her memory of the episode had the feverish-sharp quality of a Dali painting. Every memory was clear and in focus, and in spite of that— perhaps *because* of that—not quite real.

The fact remained, however, that she'd made twenty quarters break the sound barrier. At least it *felt* like they'd broken the sound barrier, she could still feel the shock wave. Though, oddly, she couldn't remember hearing it.

Allison thought of her physics textbook and the only equation she could remember from it. $F=ma$. Force equals mass times acceleration. Apparently that explained rule number seven. Same force and lower mass meant higher acceleration.

Allison wished she could remember the equations of motion, then she might be able to put an approximate number on that force. *No, I'd still be stuck because I have no idea what the speed of sound is.*

She began to see how her "rules" went together. She connected different parts of the seven rules together with boxes and lines. Rule number seven, the smaller the faster, connected to rule four, her maximum lift and approximate power. Both of those were really one rule—she only had a finite amount of energy to dump into a teeked object.

Rule six, about grabbing objects moving through her teek field, connected back to rule number one to define the nature of the teek field itself. Her teek field was a single object, and everything connected to it acted as a single object.

The remaining rules all went together. Teek was a sense, and the limitations she had found about density, viscosity, and size all seemed more to be limits on her teek sense's ability to perceive than with any physical laws.

What was she missing in describing this thing?

Allison noted that she had nothing on the sheet that had anything to do with range. For all she knew she could knock hats off of people in China. However, she doubted that. Her notes showed that her teek seemed very well-behaved for something that was supposed to be the province of ghosts, mystics, and the *National Enquirer*.

Well, range was easy enough to determine.

Allison reached back and rummaged through her paper bag. There was still some interesting stuff in it. She pulled out a can of cream of mushroom soup.

She'd always hated mushrooms.

"Macy?"

"Huh?"

"Could you pull over to the breakdown lane for a moment?"

"There's a rest stop in three miles—"

"Not that. I want to test something."

Macy shrugged and pulled the Taurus over to the shoulder of the road.

"Keep going until the odometer rolls over."

"Okay." After a second, the Taurus rolled to a stop. "Going to tell me what you up to?"

"I just want to see what my range is."

Allison rolled down the window and, with her teek, hung the can over the guardrail, right next to the mile marker. She barely needed to concentrate to do it.

"You done?"

Allison closed the window, shut her eyes, and tried to think only of levitating the soup can. "Drive, and when I tell you, check the odometer and tell me how far we've gone."

The Taurus pulled back into traffic and Allison kept her mind snugly wrapped around the can. As she made an effort to hold the can where it was, the sense she got was— well—uncanny. She felt an immediate sense of the can growing heavier. As they moved away from it, the feeling was as if some invisible hand was pushing against her, trying to make the can rupture her teek field by sheer weight. Much too soon it was taking a real effort for Allison to keep the thing airborne. The can's weight was a pressure straight through her forehead, increasing at an accelerating rate. Within moments she was putting as much effort into keeping the can of soup airborne as she had into levitating a Jeep four-by-four.

"Now," Allison told Macy. Then, with a great feeling of relief, let go of the demon can. She opened her eyes half-expecting to hear the crashing impact as a three-ton can of soup slammed into the highway behind them. She looked back, but saw no cascades of dehydrated cream of mushroom soup. She could barely *see* the can at this distance.

"Ah," said Macy, "about one and a half tenths?"

About eight hundred feet.

Over that much distance it had taken as much effort to

hold up a single can of soup as it did to hold up a Jeep
Cherokee at about two yards.

*Want to bet that the effort goes up with the square of
the distance?*

Allison marked that as rule number eight.

According to the signs, they were eighty miles west of
Washington, D.C. when Macy saw the cop.

"Porky at six o'clock."

"How fast are we going?"

Macy looked at her. "I am *not* speeding in a stolen car."

"Just asking."

"Sorry." Macy shook her head. "We should have done
something about the plates."

Allison looked behind them and saw a state patrol car
following them a few car lengths back. The sight made her
mouth turn dry. She thought of the change machine she'd
wrecked this morning. The strongbox was still there, sitting
in the back seat. She grabbed Babs from the footwell and
squeezed her.

"Maybe he isn't after us?" Allison said with a hope she
didn't really feel.

Macy shook her head. "Something lit him on to us. He's
been back there for five miles."

As if in response, the flashers lit on the cop car.

"Damn it!" Macy slammed her hands on the steering
wheel. "I ain't going to no redneck jail."

"Pull over," Allison said, clutching her rabbit. "See what
he wants."

"He *wants* to arrest us—"

"Maybe our taillight's out or something. Pull over."

"Then what?"

"One step at a time," Allison said. "One step at a time."

Macy looked pained, but she rolled the Taurus on to the
shoulder. "If that hillbilly cop makes one racist comment—"

"Shh."

They sat in the Taurus and waited. The cop car pulled
in behind them, flashers going. Allison noted that there was
only one cop in the car, and he had picked a very desolate

stretch of road to stop them. It made Allison's natural paranoia work overtime.

The red lights on the car flashed like her pulse, and the afternoon sun etched the scene like dilute acid. They were stopped amidst low, empty hills. Next to them, across a field of brown grass, a line of high-tension towers marched toward the horizon like an army of skeletal robots.

Allison realized, that without even thinking about it, she had reached out with her teek sense. Its otherworldly dimensions were already contaminating her vision.

The cop stepped out of the police car. Even as Allison saw the cop, her teek sense strayed to his car, almost by itself.

The cop was a grim-looking man with rusty hair and mustache. He looked like an evil Ron Howard. Allison hoped the caution with which he approached the Taurus was just a matter of rote, and not because he thought them dangerous.

He walked up and tapped on Macy's window.

Macy rolled down the window and the cop said, "Can I see your driver's license and registration, please?"

"Ah, Allie?" Macy said, all her bravado gone. Allison opened the glove compartment and fished out the registration. With her teek sense still groping about the police car, actually feeling things with her fingers seemed odd, as if everything was covered with a microscopic layer of grease.

Macy hadn't moved to get her wallet and Allison had to elbow her to get her to move.

Allison handed the registration papers to the cop. "It's my mom's car, we're taking it to—" Allison almost said Washington, "—Baltimore for her."

The cop took the papers expressionlessly and clipped them to his board. "Your name is?"

Allison almost lied, but it was her mom's name on the registration. "Allison Boyle. What's the problem, Officer?" Allison was trying to sound innocent, but with her mind groping about twenty feet behind them, she was going to settle for coherent.

With the cop there in front of them, Allison couldn't risk looking behind them with her eyes. So she had to feel around the cop's patrol car blindly, using only her teek.

She really wished she knew how to drive.

"Miss, you have to take the license out of the wallet."

Was this thing the parking brake? Was this the gearshift? Or was it an automatic?

Macy fumbled with her wallet. Allison watched with one part of her mind as the other part used her teek to play with the controls of the officer's car. They were on the right shoulder of the highway. There wasn't a guardrail here, just a ditch that fell off from the gravel shoulder. On the other side of the ditch was a chain-link fence topped by barbed wire that was to keep people away from the high-tension sentinels.

"Okay, ladies. I'm afraid I'm going to have to ask you both to get out of the car."

Allison's teek hit something and the siren went *"WHOOP."*

The cop spun to face his car and Allison decided that this was the signal for her to do something. She used her teek to pump what she hoped was the right pedal.

The engine on the cop car revved, and the cop started running toward it. Allison looked back and saw that she hadn't achieved what she'd had in mind, whatever that had been. The cop car was bolting for the rear of the Taurus.

Desperately, Allison let go of the gas pedal and tried to grab the steering wheel with her teek. It tried to slip out of her grasp, but the lesson with the cue ball had taught her to lead her intended target. Once she had hold of the wheel with her mind, it grabbed talons into her brain and tried to tear itself free.

With her eyes she saw the police car on a collision course with the Taurus. Its wipers were going, the lights were flashing, and the hood was bouncing up and down, gaping like a hungry mouth.

Allison, in the brief contact she had with the steering wheel, pulled it all the way to the car's right.

The effect on the car was dramatic. The cop car was pulled off the right side of the road. When its front right tire left the gravel shoulder, the whole nose of the vehicle canted rightward, and the entire car flipped over into the ditch.

Macy used the distraction to floor the Taurus out of there.

Allison let go of the car, the familiar mental fatigue warping her mind. The state trooper stood there, frozen on the shoulder, perhaps not yet even aware that they had driven away.

Macy pulled the Taurus off at the next exit they came to. "We got to change the plates on this car."

Allison sat, numbed. All she could think of was the car flipping over. That hadn't been what she'd been trying to do. She wasn't sure any more *what* she'd been trying to do. What if it had hit their own car, or the policeman, or it had rolled into traffic? What if the cop had a partner, or a prisoner in back of the car?

She was chilled by what she'd almost done.

"Allie!"

"What?"

Macy looked scared. "Don't leave me like that, girl. Not in the middle of all this. You got to help me change the plates."

Allison nodded weakly. If they weren't fugitives before, they certainly were now—as soon as that state trooper got word back. Their names, descriptions, the car they were driving—

And all Allison really wanted to do was talk to her mother, see her father, understand *why.* . . .

"Here we go," Macy said. They were pulling into some-place called Hancock, and Macy had found a Long John Silver's parking lot on its periphery. "That white Saturn, it just pulled in."

Macy pulled into the space next to it, on the far side from the restaurant. She got out and looked around. "Come on," she said back into the car.

Allison stepped out of the car and realized that she was still clutching Babs. *When do I start sucking my thumb?* She left Babs on the passenger seat of the Taurus.

She walked around and saw that the Saturn had Georgia plates.

"Are there any tools in this thing?" Macy asked, popping the trunk in the Taurus.

Allison stood lookout, while Macy found a first-aid kit that had a pair of blunt kindergarten-type scissors. Somehow Macy managed to use them as a screwdriver to work the plates free.

Allison was glad that Macy hadn't asked her to teek the plates off. She was having difficulty concentrating right now. Her mind needed a rest.

Her life needed a rest.

She wanted everything to end, to be over with, one way or another. Everything felt as if it was crumbling, first her school, then her past, then her family. . . .

Now she felt like she was fraying at the edges herself. The person who had stolen two hundred dollars and had rolled a Maryland state patrol car wasn't the Allison she knew. Allison the telekinetic, Allison the fugitive, these were people she didn't know, people she didn't think she liked.

The process of swapping the plates proceeded in fits and starts. They had to hide what they were doing whenever a car entered the parking lot. The repeated panic as they stopped and started was almost as fatiguing as her teek.

When they were done, Macy resumed their drive south, away from US-48.

As they drove, Allison tortured herself by cataloging the ranks of people who'd been bludgeoned by her talent. Chuck was the first, and the most grievously wounded— whether he deserved it or not. Then there was Macy, who was as much a fugitive as Allison was, whose only real crime was being her friend. Then there was Mom—

Please, don't start thinking that again.

There was even poor Mr. Luvov.

As Allison thought herself into a deeper depression, Macy took secondary roads in an effort to get them out of Maryland. The road map she'd been using had been pitifully low on detail, one small sheet of paper for the entire country. Once they'd left the interstate system they were in terra incognita.

Macy's navigation was something along the lines of "aim east and hope."

They passed through too many towns that ate up too

much time and not enough miles. The sun set and the darkening sky narrowed their world into the slice carved out by their headlights.

It was nearly midnight when they rejoined the interstate system.

"Oh, Christ, how'd we get on I-81?"

"Huh, is that good or bad?"

"Get the map out and tell me."

Allison got out the map and folded it so she could see Maryland. "I can't find—"

"Oh, shit—Never mind."

"What?" Allison looked up.

"We just passed a sign saying Lynchburg in fifty."

"Lynchburg?"

"Yeah, wrong part of the wrong state. Sort of explains the mountains, though. Boy, did we get lost."

At twelve-fifteen they pulled into the outskirts of Lynchburg, Virginia.

CHAPTER
SIXTEEN

12:05 am   Thursday

The private plane that landed at Cuyahoga County Airport was out of place. Most of the planes on the tarmac were conventional-looking, prop-driven planes. The Gulfstream Starship, with its canards, swept wings, and rear-mounted propeller, looked like an alien invader.

In a sense it was.

When the plane landed, four men boarded it, the entire security complement of Fred Jackson's field team. The scientists, and Elroy, were on their way back to Dallas on a medically-equipped Learjet.

The Gulfstream turned around and began the takeoff procedure without even bothering to refuel.

Inside the plane, Fred Jackson and his team were greeted by an old man in a white suit. The man rested thick hands on a black cane. The wispy hair he had left was snow white. A thin smile showed under a white mustache, and gray eyes burned at Fred over a pair of rectangular bifocals.

"I am somewhat disappointed in this performance," the old man said.

Fred Jackson was the only man who found his seat without looking disturbed. "Mr. Stone," Fred said with an acquiescent nod.

"Fred," Stone nodded in turn to each man, "Barney, Rocky, Dino. As I've said, I find this performance disappointing."

Barney cradled a cast on his wrist. "Fuck, you ain't the only one—"

Stone glared at Barney. "Barney, you will kindly shut that sewer you call a mouth. Your accident began this shoddy performance—and has placed Prometheus at risk."

"But," Barney said.

"Science needs another human control subject, do you wish to be it?"

Barney shut up.

Stone shook his head, "I am disappointed in you, Fred. Very clumsy."

"The whole situation was unexpected, and unprecedented," Fred said.

Stone shook his head as the cabin lurched toward take-off. "The Agency for Scientific Investigation was not supposed to be an active cover. It was supposed to be for intelligence only. An interface for the local authorities. After twenty years, you may have soiled it for us."

The cabin was silent as the Gulfstream taxied for the takeoff. After a moment, Fred Jackson said, "I take full responsibility for that."

Stone nodded. "That goes without saying."

The Gulfstream took off, and after the plane began banking east, Stone spoke again. "I want you to understand something, gentlemen. At this point we have only two options. We can capture this girl, who may be the most powerful asset we've yet come across, or we neutralize the threat to Prometheus."

"Sir?"

"Because of your fumbling, and because of Boyle's previous connection to Prometheus, we cannot allow this girl to reveal anything publicly. If capture turns out not to be an option . . ."

Barney smiled. Fred nodded.

"Now, gentlemen, we are going to Washington, D.C.," Stone said. "The Maryland state police reported an—incident—with our subject's car."

28 OCTOBER   LYNCHBURG, VIRGINIA

12:40 AM   THURSDAY

"What a pit," Macy said as she opened the door.

Allison silently agreed as she followed her friend into the

motel room. The furniture had been scarred by cigarettes and water rings. The mylar wallpaper was coated by a scummy white patina. The two black vinyl chairs were giving way at the seams, exposing foam rubber viscera. The fiberglass tile stapled to the ceiling was dotted with brown rust stains that made Allison think of blood.

There was only one bed.

"*Oh* . . . I wanna smack that guy," Macy said, tossing two backpacks in the corner. "I said for the two of us. And this cost us the last of—"

Allison shrugged. "It's a queen-size bed—"

"I look like a queen? That ain't the point."

"It's got a coin vibrator thingie—"

Macy gave her a withering look. "You're not being funny, girl."

Allison sat down in one of the wounded chairs. "Sorry."

"Dibs on the shower." Macy yawned. "Check the blue backpack, I snagged some clothes from home that might fit you."

Allison nodded weakly. She felt tired, used up. *I feel like we've gone across the whole country. One day on the road. One day.*

So much can change.

What the hell was she doing in Virginia? What was she accomplishing by running to Dad? Could her absent father, a person she barely remembered, really help her with what was happening? After all, where the hell had *he* been for the past decade? He was a cipher. He knew enough to have called Mom. But he had never once tried to contact his daughter.

Why did she think he would help her? Even if he could.

Why should she think anyone would help her?

Everyone out there had their neat little lives. No one out there would want to be bothered.

She turned on the motel's TV and was greeted by the latest terrorism over the Middle East.

She sank back into the chair, too weary to change the channel.

How had she ever written anything like *Restless Nights*? She felt like she had lost the part of her that was Melissa and Randolph.

I'm not like this, Allison kept telling herself. *I don't think like this.*

The world wasn't satisfied with what it had wrought. It— *CNN Headline News* in particular—wanted to hurt her more. Allison was half asleep when she caught sight of her own face. Her high school picture had the hypnotizing effect of a serpent's gaze. As she watched, the reporter's voice sank its venomous fangs into her mind.

"—victim of the attempted rape. Both she and her mother have been missing from their Euclid Heights residence since late yesterday. Euclid Heights police insist that they are treating the event as a case of self-defense, despite the death last night of the alleged rapist Charles Wilson—"

Chuck died?

Something tiny and evil laughed just at the edge of her mind. Her brain froze into an icy lump of horror deeper than anything she had felt before. It went beyond even what she'd felt when Chuck had leveled the gun at her, beyond what she'd felt when he'd reached for the belt of his pants. She couldn't move, couldn't breathe, and she felt her heart compress into a tiny ball bearing.

Worse than the terror was the tiny voice that was glad the bastard was dead. Waves of self-loathing and revulsion swamped her like the outflow from a frozen sewer.

Somehow, without realizing it, she had done something to the TV. Blue smoke wisped from the back, and the picture tube was now a blind gray eye webbed with spidery black cracks.

The door to the bathroom opened and Macy stepped out wrapped in a battered red robe. "All yours."

Allison stood up and silently walked into the bathroom, locking the door behind her.

I killed him, Allison thought.

She began to sweat profusely in the humid bathroom. She didn't bother removing her denim jacket. She still felt chilled. Next to her, the shower emptied into a tub, and as she watched, the faucet turned and the tub began to fill with hot water.

"Hey, Allie?" came Macy's voice, muffled, from outside.

Allison looked at herself in the fogged mirror. She couldn't stand the sight. She began weeping.

There was nothing she could do now. Nothing to make any of it better. She had *killed* someone. That could never be erased.

Her body shook with racking, silent sobs that sucked all the air from her lungs.

She wanted to melt. Disappear and make all the hurting stop. Dissolve into a puddle and evaporate. Vanish into a place where her thoughts didn't matter. She looked up at the mirror and felt her teek wrap around it. Her odd perceptions reversed and re-reversed until it felt like it was the universe watching *her* from inside. She cringed.

The mirror tried to rotate against its frame, and pressed itself until it shattered against its bonds. It spun then, slowly, like a spiral galaxy of icy shards. Allison let go and the shards collapsed against the sink, spraying fragments across the bathroom.

"Allie?" Macy must have been right outside the door.

Allison picked up the largest shard and clutched the mirrored dagger in her right hand. Then she stepped, fully clothed, into the still-filling tub. The water was scalding, but the chill inside her wouldn't allow her to feel it. She sank down into the tub and looked at the shard of mirror.

The mirror was fogged white, with a few beads of blood on the edges where it had cut into her palm.

Melting into nothing would be such a relief. No more hurting. No more people would be hurt.

The door rattled and tried to open. Then it began pounding.

Allison drew the mirror across her left wrist, drawing a thin red line of blood. It barely hurt at all.

She looked at the cut, waiting for the blood to spurt, to flow away. The cut barely oozed. She'd barely cut the skin, not nearly deep enough. She sucked in a shuddering breath and pressed the shard against her wrist.

Hard this time.

She wondered why she couldn't do this to frogs in biology class.

Allison closed her eyes.

I'm sorry, Mom, I know I promised.

The door of the bathroom burst open.

"Oh, God, *Allie!*" Macy ran across the mirror-spiked

bathroom floor, sliding with bleeding feet, and half-fell, half-dove into the bathtub to grab Allison's arms. *"Don't!"*

Allison looked at her panicked friend. Macy held both of her wrists, and the hands were shaking. Allison looked at the twin red stripes on her left wrist, and for the first time she heard her own sobbing.

"He's dead," Allison said. "He's dead and I killed him." She dropped the shard of mirror into the tub.

"Damn it, Allie. Don't even *think* like this."

"It's all so rotten." Allison slipped farther into the hot water. Wet denim pulled her like a lead weight. Macy fell into the tub in her effort to hold Allison upright. Macy gasped when she hit the water and reached out with a hand to slap the cold water on full.

"Please, girl, come back here, huh? Please?" Macy had landed, sitting between Allison's legs, back to the tile wall, and knees over the rim of the tub. She put an arm around Allison's shoulders and hugged Allison toward her. "You can't leave me, hear? *Hear?* You can't die on me."

Macy began to rock back and forth, crying.

"I'm sorry." Allison sobbed into the damp robe on Macy's shoulder. "I didn't want to hurt you. Hurt anyone."

"You're my best friend. You can't—"

"I'm sorry."

They rocked back and forth until the tub began to overflow.

An unreal haze shrouded over the remainder of that night. Repeatedly, Allison felt as if she was trapped inside one of her nightmares.

Allison did what she could to clean herself up in the shower while Macy sat on the toilet and tended to her lacerated feet. Even with the shower door closed, Allison winced every time she heard a piece of glass hit the waste basket. She couldn't help picturing Macy pulling the shards out of her bare feet.

That was where, in fact, most of the blood messing the bathroom had come from. The two slashes on Allison's arm hadn't amounted to much of anything. They could have come from one of her cats.

She wondered who was feeding them.

Allison turned off the shower and got out. Macy handed her a towel. The only clean, dry one left. "Be careful, I tried to get up all the glass but—"

"Macy?"

"What?" Macy's eyes were red from crying, and the robe she wore was streaked with blood.

"Forgive me?" Allison asked.

Macy stared at her.

"Macy," Allison said. "You're my best friend in the world, and I promise that I'll never, *ever* put you through something like that again."

Macy looked as if her well of belief was almost tapped dry. "Promise?"

Allison nodded.

"Even if things get worse?"

"Yes."

"Even if someone else dies?"

Allison was brought up short by that one. Macy stood, winced, and grabbed Allison's naked shoulders.

"You *promise* me, girl. If you're my friend, you gonna promise right now that you'll never raise a hand to hurt yourself again! I don't give a shit what happens."

"I—"

Macy shook her. *"Promise!"*

"Promise," Allison said.

"Say it all!"

"I promise I won't hurt myself."

"Ever."

"Ever."

"Even if people die."

"Even if—" Allison swallowed hard. "—someone dies."

Macy looked at her with red puffy eyes. "Even if *I* die."

"Macy—"

"Say it!"

Macy's face was indistinct behind the blur of her tears. "Even," Allison said. "Even if *you* die."

Macy hugged her. "Oh, God, Allie. You scared me so fucking bad."

"I scared myself," Allison whispered, patting Macy on the back. "It's all right now."

"Really?" Macy let her go.

Allison sighed. "No. But with you here, it's better. And I made a promise." She wrapped the towel around herself and walked out of the bathroom.

"Allie, it isn't your fault about Chuck."

Allison stood in the door, saying nothing.

"It ain't evil to be glad he didn't get you."

Allison didn't have an answer for that.

The school cafeteria was dark and almost empty. Seated around her table were Fred, Barney, and Dino. Also seated were Mr. Counter, Mom, Dad in his mothball-smelling uniform, and the reporter from CNN. Everybody was grinning at her.

She looked down to see if she had her clothes.

She had, but they were damp. In fact, she was soaking wet.

Mr. Franklin walked out of the shadows wearing a surgical gown. On the white coat were flecks of red that could be rust stains—or blood.

He shook his head at Allison as if he was disappointed. "I've been told, my dear Miss Boyle, that you were only taking physics to avoid the dissections in biology."

Allison tried to speak and found herself frozen.

Mr. Franklin ran his hand through slate-gray hair. His habitual gesture left thin trails of blood. "I'm hurt, Allison. You're an intelligent girl. You should know that squeamishness has no place in the physical sciences."

"But—"

"No buts, young girl." He took off his glasses and smeared blood on them with the corner of his lab coat. "I am simply going to have to explain things for the whole class, again—"

Allison realized that it wasn't a normal cafeteria table everyone was seated at. It was one of the black-topped lab tables, the ones with the built-in sink and the spigots for the gas lines.

A blackboard had come from somewhere, and Mr. Franklin wrote on it, *"Rule #1: The universe does not care."*

"Class?"

"The universe doesn't care," said everyone around the

table. Everyone except Barney, who was mumbling about his hand.

Mr. Franklin nodded. "You see, everything is very simple. Action, reaction, forces, acceleration. No morality in the equations. No right or wrong. No human emotions mucking the works. Physics is not for the squeamish." Mr. Franklin looked down at the table. And Allison followed his gaze to the white-draped figure on top of it.

"Today's lesson," Mr. Franklin said, grabbing the edge of the sheet. "The effects of telekinesis on the human body." He drew the sheet away.

Chuck was there, cut open, laid out on a gigantic dissection tray.

Allison felt bile rise in her throat as Mr. Franklin reached for a surgical instrument that resembled a knitting needle. The world went grainy and black and white, and she realized that she was watching the documentary again, and she was seated in Mr. Counter's classroom.

Mr. Franklin inserted the needle behind the orbit of Chuck's eye and began rummaging around.

"I didn't sign up for no damn lobotomy, sweetcakes."

Allison turned and saw Chuck manning the projector.

CHAPTER SEVENTEEN

"Allie, wake up."

"Ah—what?" Allison blinked her eyes open and squinted against the sunlight streaming in the window. She faced Macy's back as her friend looked out the window.

"Get dressed, girl. I think we have a problem."

Allison nodded and followed Macy's direction because she was still too sleepy to argue. She untangled herself from the bedspread and pulled on a random assortment of clothing from the bag Macy had brought for her. By the time she'd pulled on a pair of black stretch pants that were a little too tight and a little too long, she was awake enough to ask, "What problem?"

"See for yourself."

Allison pulled on a red-yellow-green African sweater over a bra too generous for her and walked up next to Macy. The window looked over the rear parking lot, and the Taurus. The view also now included a single sheriff's patrol car that was parked behind the Taurus, blocking it in.

"The cop rolled by and stopped. He looked at our car, got on the radio, and walked over to the manager's office."

"Oh, no," Allison said.

Macy shook her head. "Get your shit together."

Allison pulled on her boots and her denim jacket. Even though the jacket had been on top of the heater all night, the wool lining was still damp. She picked up Babs and shoved the rabbit in the backpack Macy had given her. She followed it with her yellow notepad, and the ASI film can. The only other thing she had was the tattered-looking grocery bag, which was beginning to smell.

"Okay," Allison said. "What about the car?"

"It's a cop magnet. We'll leave it."

Macy picked up her backpack and opened the door. Allison followed her out. They had barely taken a few steps into the parking lot when the cop and the day manager walked out of the front office. The manager was fumbling with a large key ring.

The cop looked up and said, "Hey."

That was their cue to run.

The two of them raced out of the parking lot, kicking up gravel. Macy should have outdistanced her easily—Macy was on the track team—but Macy was already limping before they reached the edge of the lot. Allison thought of her friend's wounded feet and cringed inside.

They hit the edge of the lot and had to push through knee-high grass. The grass slashed at Allison's exposed skin and grabbed at the loose parts of her borrowed clothes. She threw a frantic glance behind them and saw the sheriff, deputy, or whoever running after them, and gaining.

Allison wished they'd been spotted by a more stereotypical southern cop type, one with the mirrored sunglasses and the sagging beer belly, one who wouldn't run worth anything. But no, this guy looked like he ran marathons for fun. Allison was already panting with breath hot enough to sear her throat, and she didn't think the cop was breaking a sweat.

The cop had already halved the distance between them.

They weren't going to outrun this guy. Or, at least Allison wasn't. Allison hung back to let Macy precede her to the top of the hill. When Allison reached the crest of the overgrown hill, she stopped and turned to face the cop. He had reached the edge of the lot.

She hoped Macy had the sense to keep running, even with her damaged feet.

Allison had to do something. It was that or give up. But what could she do without hurting him?

She stayed at the top of the hill and raised her hands.

The cop stopped running at her so fast. He started maneuvering more carefully through the grass. He held out his hands as if to say, "See, I'm not such a bad guy."

Of course he wasn't. That was the problem. This guy had absolutely nothing to do with her, Mom, or the ASI people. But she doubted that the Virginia state police would put up much of a fight if someone from the federal government came to remove a fugitive from another state.

Allison was paralyzed for a moment, thinking of some nonlethal way to resist.

As he climbed, he asked, "You're Allison Boyle, right?"

Allison nodded.

"You know, running's never solved anything." He spoke with a slow, almost hypnotic drawl.

What could she do without hurting him?

The cop kept talking as he advanced. Her frozen stature seemed to encourage him. She wondered where Macy was. Was she somewhere watching this, or was she still running?

"That's your mom's car?" He was halfway up the hill now, and Allison was beginning to panic.

Think!

"Where is your mom? People are looking for her, too."

Allison felt tears soaking her cheeks. *Not now. I can't break down now. If I don't think of something it's all over—*

Maybe she *wanted* it to be over.

The cop closed. The cop was being reassuring. Telling her to stop running before she did something seriously wrong—

She looked at his gun belt. She hadn't thought of that before, because of what she'd done to Chuck. The thought brought awful memories. But that had been an instinctive act, something that had never been in her control. Allison thought that the cop was moving slow enough, and she had enough control, to do something that was merely immobilizing.

The cop was within six feet of her when she thought her teek around the gun belt and thought it, gently and firmly, down.

The cop kept talking for a few seconds, only looking vaguely uncomfortable. He tried to pull the belt up, but it kept riding down his legs. He had to stop walking. "What the—?"

The man had the thighs of a marathon runner, and that's where the belt stopped. It had wedged itself there—incidentally trapping the fingers of the cop's right hand underneath it. The cop was frozen there, an uncomprehending look on his face as he began fumbling with the buckle with his free hand.

"Officer?" Allison said.

The man looked up at her, and she could see the terrible embarrassment in his face.

"I'm really sorry about this," Allison said. She still had her teek wrapped around the belt. With it she gently pushed the belt backward. With his legs wrapped together and only one hand free, he had no real way to regain his balance. He tipped over, covering his face with his left arm. He hit the ground and started rolling down the shallow slope.

Allison ran away to a chorus of curses overlaid by rustling foliage.

Midway into the woods she heard the cop's voice, in the distance, talking to the day manager. "Don't laugh, just help me out of this thing."

28 OCTOBER　　I-95, VIRGINIA

6:25 PM　THURSDAY

"We'll never get there this way," Allison said.

Macy dragged her feet along the shoulder of Interstate 95, holding up her thumb at northbound traffic. "What else can we do?"

Allison shook her head and trudged along with her friend, watching for police cars. They had made it to Richmond, which was almost the right direction. They had managed that in three rides. However, since the sun began setting, people seemed to ignore them. The two of them had been following the shoulder for what felt like hours.

Mileage-wise, according to the markers by the side of the

road, they had made a little over six miles by walking. It was too cold for a southern October, and blackened skies were dampening them with a misting rain. This last walk had been long enough that Allison was almost hoping for a police car. At least—with the wreckage they'd been leaving in their wake—a police car would *stop* for them. They'd be dry then, maybe get something to eat.

They went on a little longer, with no cars stopping for them, and Macy halted and sat down on the guardrail.

"Are you all right?" Allison asked.

Macy nodded, but the way she winced told Allison otherwise.

"Take off your shoes," Allison told her.

Macy looked as if she was about to object, but then she began to gingerly undo the laces on her Nikes. She did it so gingerly that Allison bent over to help. But Macy shook her head. "Don't touch."

The shoe slid slowly off of Macy's foot and Allison nearly gagged. The sole of her blue sock was purple with stained blood.

"Oh, God, Macy. You can't walk on these."

Macy was looking at her sock, as if she didn't expect quite so much blood. "Girl, without a car, what choice have I got?"

The sock peeled off, wanting to stick to Macy's foot. The sole was plastered by gore-stained toilet paper that had been an improvised dressing. The paper came off in brown clumps. "We have to wrap that in a real bandage."

There were half a dozen slashes on the one foot, two or three on the other. Allison thanked God that none of them looked infected yet.

"There's a towel from the hotel in my bag," Macy said.

As Allison fished out the white towel in the misting rain, she thought wistfully of the first-aid kit in the Taurus' trunk. The car might as well be back in Cleveland now. They had gone so far only to be stranded on the side of some Virginia highway.

Allison did her best to tear the towel into bandages and bind Macy's feet. Being stranded here was so damn frustrating, all they needed was one person going to DC. It was where this stupid interstate *went*.

Allison finished the makeshift bindings, and Macy pulled some clean socks over the bundle. She had to fully unlace her sneakers to get them back on. Macy stood up and wobbled a bit. Allison pushed her back down. "Walking on the shoulder is pointless. We're either going to get a ride or we aren't, and we've got another day to get there. So sit, okay?"

"But—"

"The ten miles we might make before your feet die isn't going to make a difference."

"Your show, girl. I just felt better moving."

"Did your feet?"

Macy shrugged. "So it didn't make sense."

After another half hour of worsening rain, Allison managed to flag down a car. It pulled on to the shoulder, rolling to a stop about a hundred feet beyond. The light had faded to the point that Allison could barely make out the vehicle until it started backing toward them.

The sight quickly dampened Allison's enthusiasm over finally getting a ride.

The car was a boxy old Plymouth with multicolored fenders and a coat hanger holding the lockless trunk shut. One taillight shone white through cracked plastic. It had a Georgia license plate.

As it rolled to a stop, a man pulled himself out of the passenger side window and sat on top of the door. He was shirtless, tattooed, and had shoulder-length hair that was slicked back and glistening in the rain.

"Hey, now. It looks like you girls could use some assistance."

Macy had to be more desperate for a ride at this point, because she stood up unsteadily and said, "Yeah, we're going to D.C."

Thank you, Macy. Are you looking at the same guy?

"Sad, Nate, ain't it? Pretty young things stranded like this?"

The car stopped. From inside came a bass, "Yep."

The man jumped the rest of the way out of the car. He wore ragged jeans and combat boots. Tattoos snaked his body. Dragons and skulls and bloody knives stretched across the muscles of his arms and chest. He smiled. Most of his teeth were stained black.

Macy stepped back as if she realized that opening her mouth had been a big mistake.

"Lucky for you, girls." he said. "Me'n Nate are going to DC, too." He giggled a little. The smell of beer drifted to Allison, even through the rain.

"Ah, thanks anyway," Allison said. "But I think—"

"Don't turn down our hospitality," he said. "You'll hurt Nate's feelings."

The driver's door on the Plymouth opened and the most obese man Allison had ever seen stepped out. Nate had hair and a beard that didn't look as if it had been cut, combed, or cleaned in Allison's lifetime. He didn't wear a shirt either, and cascading flesh made him look like a tattooed avalanche. Nate was smiling.

In his hand he held a revolver.

Oh, God.

"Well, if you don't want the ride." The thin man shrugged. "You still owe us something for stopping, right, Nate?"

"Yep."

The black-toothed man, the one who kept talking, was approaching her. Allison couldn't think straight. *The gun*— She looked at the gun. If she could just teek it away.

"Give up some sweetness for daddy." The black-toothed man grabbed her. The world slowed, tumbling inside out. Too many things to do, think about, at once. She struggled to escape the man's grasp—and her teek was over by the gun. Macy was running toward them, and Nate was moving the gun. This guy's hand was under her sweater.

Allison tried to grab the gun with her teek as she grabbed the man's crotch with her hands.

"Bitch!" he yelled as she squeezed.

Nate fired.

Something rammed into her teek field so hard that it felt as if the bullet had entered her own brain. Her teek had only managed to grab the barrel of the revolver. She'd hadn't time to grab the whole thing as she had Barney's gun.

When Nate fired, the bullet had entered her field. Like

when Macy tossed a cue ball, her teek tried to catch the
invader. But the bullet's energy tore the field to shreds. It
felt as if chunks were being ripped from her brain.

The bullet lost most of its kinetic energy, destroying her
teek's tenuous hold. Allison felt the lead slug slow to a
near stop inside the barrel. She felt the split second where
all the exhaust gases from the cartridge had nowhere to go.

She felt it when the gun exploded.

Nate screamed, an inhuman sound, like a pig squealing.
He was on fire, his massive beard had been ignited by the
back blast from the plugged revolver. The explosion had
torn his hand and arm into bloody rags.

Allison stared at Nate, and the other man clubbed the
side of her head with his fist. She fell back on the ground,
dizzy. The man was turning to look at his flaming partner
when Macy came out of nowhere and slammed him in the
side of the head with a rock the size of a loaf of bread.

As he collapsed to his knees, Macy grabbed Allison's
arm and yelled, "The car!"

Allison grabbed her backpack and stumbled after Macy.

Nate was rolling across the ground, putting out his beard,
while the nameless man held his head and vomited between
his knees.

The car was idling. Macy pushed her into the passenger
seat, got behind the wheel, and made the transmission
shudder with grinding noises as she pulled away from their
two assailants.

28 OCTOBER   ASHLAND, VIRGINIA

7:15 PM   THURSDAY

"Yeah," Allison said into the pay phone. "They're on I-
95 northbound, in the breakdown lane."

"And where are you calling from?"

Allison hung up on the 911 operator.

"Done?" Macy asked. She was sitting on the hood of the
'73 Plymouth Duster, which was idling in the parking lot
of a defunct Shell station that sat right off of I-95. The

station was boarded up, but the pay phone by the edge of the lot still worked.

Allison nodded.

Macy slid off the hood and winced when her feet touched the ground. The rain had gotten worse, soaking everything, but it didn't quite soak up the smell from the car.

Allison looked in the car and made a face.

Macy stopped by the driver's door and said, "You ain't going to freak out again. It ain't like we could've avoided—"

Allison shook her head. "No, that's not it—"

"Then what?"

"If we're going to *drive* this thing, I want to shovel out some of the garbage."

"I know what you mean."

She reached in and shut off the engine. The ignition required the use of a screwdriver. That made Allison feel a little better. This car had been stolen long before it had fallen into their hands.

It took them half an hour to shovel out the pit of the car. It was a mess of fast food containers, some boxes still containing things indescribable. A few old pizza boxes were so disgusting that Allison used her teek to avoid actually touching them. There was an endless supply of beer cans, liquor bottles, and cigarette boxes.

That was the innocuous garbage.

Under the back seat they found a sawed-off twelve gauge shotgun and a machete.

"We can't throw this out," Macy said. "Some kid will find it and blow his head off."

"Give me that," Allison said.

Macy handed her the shotgun. Allison looked around the empty Shell lot until she found a grate to the storm sewer. The grate was heavy and iron, and the gun's barrel fit into one of the slots.

"What you doing, girl?"

"Need something to give me leverage." Allison wrapped her teek around the stock of the shotgun and pulled down. The barrels of the gun pressed against the sides of the grate. The gun froze there for a moment until, finally, something gave and the stock slammed to the ground. The barrel clattered down into the storm sewer. There was a resonant clang as the end of the barrel hit something below.

There was the throb of a near-migraine behind her temples, and Allison decided that this was going to be it for her teek for a while.

She put the twisted stock of the now dysfunctional weapon on top of the pile of garbage they were making.

"Wasn't that a little dangerous?" Macy said.

"Didn't point it at anyone." Allison returned to emptying the car.

Things got uglier. They found bags of white crystal and well-used glass pipes. They unearthed a cigar box with charred tinfoil, a dirty spoon, a Zippo lighter, rubber hose and a hypodermic needle that had traces of blood on it.

"Ugh," Macy said. "These guys were crawling."

The trunk held a cardboard box that Macy tossed without even looking inside. Allison took a peek, saw the cover on the top magazine, and wished she hadn't.

God, I'm sorry about Chuck—but not these guys.

She wanted to wash her hands.

The last thing they opened was the glove compartment. It was the now familiar mess of little baggies and cigarette papers. No maps, or car registration. There was enough room in there that Allison thought that had been where Nate's revolver had come from. Also inside was another cigar box.

"What do you think?" Macy asked. "More of their drugstore?"

"I don't want to know."

"Hey, can't hurt to—" Macy had opened the box and was gaping into it.

"What?"

Macy looked up and back down at the box. She started talking a few times, gave up, and turned the box around so Allison could see the contents.

Inside, with a pile of baggies, was a roll of twenties held together by a grease-stained red rubber band.

CHAPTER
EIGHTEEN

With Macy speeding they made it to the Beltway before two-thirty. They'd only paused to fill the Duster's gas tank and have a massive order filled at a Taco Bell drive-through. Macy insisted on ordering a dozen burritos and Mexi-Melts. "I ain't stopping now but for gas. The cops *must* be after this car for reasons that have nothing to do with us."

Now that they'd reached Washington, D.C. all they had to do was find a motel where they could hole up. The flight Dad would expect her and Mom to be on wouldn't arrive until late Friday afternoon.

That was if Allison was right about what her parents' plans had been. And if the ASI hadn't found Dad. And if the cops didn't stop them.

And if the car lived.

That was the most pressing problem at the moment. The Duster wasn't a well car. It made sounds that set Allison's teeth on edge every time Macy shifted gears—and it wasn't only because Macy was unfamiliar with the manual trans-mission. The car vibrated too much, and tried to shake itself apart whenever its speed closed on sixty-five.

Every once in a while the smell of something burning—clutch, oil, or brakes—would waft from the front of the car. Fortunately their Taco Bell order covered most of the smell.

They were a half hour into urban traffic before Allison

had finished counting the money. "Six hundred and fifty dollars," Allison said.

"Whoa," Macy said. "Those creeps could've afforded a better car."

Allison shrugged. "They could've afforded a better life." She put the cigar box back in the glove compartment.

"You okay?"

Allison looked out the window. The rain had dissolved into a gray mist that turned the streetlights into cloudy haze. It was a perfect match to the cloudy gray she felt inside. "I'm numb. I don't think I've got any feelings left."

"You don't feel bad about those two creeps, do you?"

"No. That's the problem."

"I don't understand you, girl."

Allison leaned back and closed her eyes. "I don't feel *anything*. I've used myself up."

"Come on, cheer up. We've made it—"

"Does that solve anything? Will it, really?"

Macy was silent.

"The police will still be out there, and so will those ASI people. Mom's still missing. What can my dad do about them?"

"I don't know, girl. But after all this, he better do *something*."

What *would* he do? Allison wondered. She had grabbed for her father because he was the only thing she had to cling to. She had subconsciously built her father up into a savior. The enormity of recent events was making her question her judgment. What could one man do, even a man who knew exactly what was going on?

And, whatever her father's capabilities, there was still one unchanging fact: this was a man who had neither seen her nor made contact with her in twelve years. He had been absent for more than a decade, two thirds of Allison's life.

She wondered what he would think of his daughter. Would he be proud, frightened, or appalled? Did he care about her? Or like the ASI, did he only care about what she could do? What was *his* relationship to ASI? Why, why, why . . . ?

The line of questions marched mutely off into the darkness.

Why couldn't the world just stay simple?

Dad, we're going to show up as fugitives several times over, your daughter's a murderess, and your ex-wife is missing, and I doubt you're expecting Macy at all. . . .

Dad was in for a shock.

"All right?" Macy asked.

Allison nodded and closed her eyes. "I just had the sensation that my whole life was just on the tip of my tongue."

"As long as it isn't flashing before your eyes. Any Mexi-Melts left?"

Allison fished in the Taco Bell sack and said, "Just hot sauce packets and one damp burrito."

"You want it?"

Allison held the limp burrito and made a face. She passed it to Macy.

Macy took it and, in between bites, said, "I am going to be so happy when we ditch this car." Macy yawned and took another bite of the burrito. "I've got white lines running down the center of my eyeballs."

"Thanks, Macy."

"Huh, for what?"

"Everything."

Macy polished off the burrito and hugged her with her free arm. "No prob, girl. No prob."

Macy returned both hands to the wheel as they took an exit off of the Beltway. "Now, all we got to do is find a motel."

29 OCTOBER   ARLINGTON, VIRGINIA

5:30 AM   FRIDAY

John Charvat woke at 5:30. The first thing he did was check the gun on the night table. Then he turned on the light. The hotel room was empty but for him. Gun in hand, he made a careful check of the room before he went into the shower, looking out the window, checking the closet, and making sure the security chain was on the door.

Only then did he strip off the briefs he was wearing and walk into the bathroom, still carrying the gun.

Once the water began to run, the doorknob on the front door started to silently jiggle back and forth. After a few moments the door drifted open. When the door pulled the security chain taut, a pair of bolt cutters slipped in and effortlessly snipped the chain.

When John stepped out of the shower, he had a towel around his waist and a gun in his hand. Two of the three men waiting for him had guns already aimed at his midsection. The third man said, "It has been a long time, Shaggy. Now would you please put down the gun?"

John froze for a minute, blinking.

"Please, there's been quite enough unnecessary bloodshed already."

John placed the gun on an end table and stood there, dripping.

"Thank you, Shaggy."

"I don't work for you anymore, Stone. You can call me John."

Stone leaned forward on his cane and said, "I have two guns pointed at you. I think I can call you anything that strikes my fancy."

John stayed silent, one hand holding his towel. Stone waved to a free chair. "Please, sit down. There's no reason for this to be unpleasant. You know Fred. He was a field agent when you were with us, and the man to my right is Dino."

John looked into Dino's thick glasses, shook his head, and muttered, "Figures." John glanced back at the door to the hotel room.

"Don't make the mistake of thinking you're too valuable to shoot, Shag," Dino said.

"Dino's correct," Stone said. "Please, *sit.*" A hardness crept into Stone's voice with that one word.

John sat. "How did you find me?"

"Does it matter?" Stone made a dismissive gesture with the cane. "You were found because I wanted you found. First, as the security chief who somehow overlooked Carolyn Boyle's child. Second, as the child's father."

John's intake of breath was audible.

Stone smiled. "Yes, we uncovered that. Like dominos, really." He held up an open hand, fingers spread. "The first deception falls—" He closed his index finger. "—the remainder fall in short order." Stone's fingers collapsed into a fist. "You did an admirable job of covering Allison's existence. Falsifying your common address with Carol Boyle. Engineering a six-month leave for her pregnancy. Your personal handling of the surveillance after she ran out on her job." The skin on Stone's hand whitened, and his fist vibrated slightly. *"I trusted you,"* Stone said in a harsh whisper.

"What do you want from me?" John said in a voice only slightly above Stone's whisper.

Stone unclenched his fist. "In the end I can understand all that." He looked up and smiled. "You were protecting your child. Any father worth the air he breathes would do anything to protect his child. Isn't that right, Fred? Dino?"

The two gunmen nodded. Dino a little uncertainly.

"Prometheus is my child, *John*. Do *you* understand *that*?"

John looked at Stone and repeated, "What do you want?"

"Because of your daughter's talent, she's potentially a great asset to the Institute. She might be the most powerful voluntary telekinetic we've ever seen. The last thing science wants to do is harm her in any way." Stone paused.

"But?" John asked.

"But," Stone said, "—and this is largely your fault, John—she presents a potential threat to Prometheus that is just as great. Maybe greater. I cannot allow that potential to be fulfilled."

"I won't let you hurt her."

"A valiant sentiment, but please consider your options. You have two." Stone held up a finger. "One, you will help us bring in your daughter with a minimum of collateral damage." Stone held up a second finger. "Two, Fred and Dino shoot you, and I concentrate on protecting *my* child."

"You said you didn't want to hurt her."

"John, I would have the President shot if he threatened Prometheus." Stone leaned back and smiled. "Think it over. We have time."

29 October   washington, D.C.

1:15 pm   Friday

Once Allison woke, she spent over two hours on the phone to various airlines. She sat on one of the motel's twin beds, surrounded by phone books. She spent most of that time leaning against the headboard, staring at a TV showing CNN with the sound off, listening to elevator music every time she was put on hold.

Again and again she had to say, no, she didn't want to buy a ticket. She just wanted to know if they had a flight from Atlanta arriving around seven o'clock today. Fishing out any information with the few facts she had was a major production. To add to it, every single operator insisted on offering alternate flights.

Macy had already gotten up, showered, and had gone on a food run by the time Allison had finally gotten the right flight, the right airline, and the right airport.

Macy sat on the twin bed across from Allison. When Allison hung up, Macy offered her a chocolate doughnut. "What's the good word?"

"Washington National Airport, 7:05," Allison said, biting into the doughnut and collapsing back onto the bed.

"Good, we have time to figure out how to get there."

Allison sighed.

"Now what's the problem?"

What isn't? "What if I'm wrong? What if my dad never shows?"

"Kinda late to worry about that."

"But . . ." Allison's head swarmed with doubts. She just wanted it to be over with, one way or another. Waiting was beginning to eat at her.

Macy tapped her shoulder and said, "It's an airport, Allie. If no one shows, we just get the next available ticket to anywhere."

"Anywhere? Like?"

"Well, maybe Canada is out of these ASI creeps' jurisdiction."

After a moment's consideration, Allison nodded. There

certainly should be enough of Nate and Company's cash left to buy a ticket to a hub, maybe Toronto. "Good thought," she said. She hoped it wouldn't come to that. It already felt like she had abandoned Mom. That would feel like she was abandoning both Mom *and* Dad.

"So," Macy asked, "since we ditched the drugmobile, how do we get there?"

It didn't take too long for them to find Washington, D.C.'s public transportation system. By six, Allison and Macy were riding under the streets of Washington on the Metro subway system.

The D.C. subways were clean, efficient, and did nothing to help Allison's state of mind. The sheer depth of the subway system was oppressive. They had to descend an escalator down a concrete tube that was close to five stories deep. From the bottom, Allison couldn't see the entrance. And the stops themselves were antiseptic concrete spaces the size of an aircraft hangar. The unpainted concrete, and the security cameras everywhere, made Allison feel that she'd stepped into a movie set in some totalitarian dystopia.

The cameras were the most oppressive detail, especially for someone who had reason to be paranoid. Allison was briefly relieved when they emerged from the underground and entered the airport.

The feeling didn't last. After the sterile blankness of the subway, the terminal was a blaring assault. As soon as they walked into the main building Allison felt a press of humanity more claustrophobic than the tons of earth pressing down on the Metro system.

Macy walked up and stared at one of the computer screens that dotted the terminal entrance. Allison stayed close by, staring out at the people surrounding them. The police she saw scattered about made her nervous. So did the men with dark suits and briefcases. So did the raggedy-denim man at the ticket counter trying to get a steel-frame backpack checked.

What scared Allison more than the people was the way they affected her. She was looking at a mass of normal people, people with lives, children, homes, maybe even cats—and she couldn't look at any of them without viewing them as a threat.

"Your flight's on time," Macy said, making her jump. Macy patted her shoulder. "Come on, the gate's this way."

Macy walked off into the terminal building, past gift shops and fast food places whose prices were much too high. Allison noticed that her friend was limping. "How're your feet?"

"Good enough to get me there."

They passed through the metal detectors and X-ray without incident, despite the fact that it brought her much closer to airport security than she was comfortable with. By the time they reached the gate, Macy's limp was pronounced. Allison was glad for her when they finally sat down to wait.

They sat in silence for a while. The gate they were at was nearly empty. The flight wasn't due for another forty minutes or so. "Will you recognize him?" Macy asked.

"I don't know." Allison sighed. "I think so."

Macy nodded. "Kinda funny, you're running to your dad, and I'm running away from mine."

Allison looked at Macy over her shoulder. "What do you mean?"

Macy fumbled with the straps on her backpack. "Never mind."

Allison shivered. She had never met Macy's dad, but every time Macy had referred to the man, it was about him being angry at something. "Dad's going to cream me," or words to that effect. Allison suddenly hoped that all her comments were exaggeration.

"First time I had the guts to get this far," Macy said.

Allison found it hard thinking of Macy having a shortage of guts. "You never said anything."

"What's to say? Dad throws fits. It's not like he's put anyone in the hospital."

Allison put her arm around Macy and hugged her. *Here we are, Allison Boyle's dysfunction parade.*

"What you going to do, Allie? When this is over?"

Allison shook her head. "I don't know, I really don't. I've had problems thinking six hours ahead."

"I don't think I'm going back."

"What are we going to do with the rest of our screwed-up lives?"

"Hey," Macy said, "at least you got something. That teek of yours, you could live on that."

"I don't know that I want to."

"You could get that check from that Amazing whoever guy you told me about."

Allison signed. "Being a scientific curiosity? I have nightmares about dissection trays." *Dissection trays and knitting needles.*

"What do you *want* to do with your life, then?"

Allison said, "I still want to be a writer." *However, what I end up writing after all this is over may be something different from what I intended.* "What about you?"

"Don't laugh."

Allison shook her head.

"I want to be a singer—"

"Oh, shit." Allison said in a harsh whisper.

"It wasn't that funn—"

"No. Look Two gates over."

Macy looked and gave a little gasp. Right there, leaning against a wall with an unobstructed view of their gate, was Barney and another, unfamiliar-looking man. She recognized Barney from his ponytail and the cast on his right hand.

"Do they see us?"

"I don't know," Allison whispered back. Allison and Macy were seated, huddled together, back by the edge of a window. The two men didn't seem to be paying much attention to the gate. Allison couldn't tell if they had seen them or not.

"How long have they been there?"

"I don't know."

Dad, where are you?

"Girl, I think we in trouble."

Behind them the window began to vibrate with a subsonic hum, as if someone was warming up God's own TV set. Allison looked over Macy's shoulder and out onto the tarmac. An American Airlines DC-10 was taxiing up to the gate. The flight was early.

Dad, you were supposed to meet us, weren't you? Please,

Dad, if you don't show, I don't know what I'm going to do—

"They saw us, Allie. The bastard smiled right at me."

"Oh, God. Why don't they do anything?"

"Maybe they don't want to cause a scene in the terminal."

The PA made an indecipherable announcement with an airport accent that would have been at home in Cleveland. It was probably announcing the arrival of the Atlanta flight.

In response, Barney's companion folded the paper he was reading.

Why don't you do something? She thought at them. *You got Mom, and Barney is smiling and nodding at us like we're old friends.*

"Allie, I really don't like this."

"They're not going to do anything yet. They're waiting for something."

"I don't think we should wait around for it, too."

The PA made another fuzzy announcement, something about old people and folks with young children.

"I want to see my dad," Allison said in a harsh whisper.

"Girl, I hate to say this, but with the Doublemint twins here, they probably *have* your dad."

No, I am not going to believe that—

The door to the walkway opened, and people began exiting. They pooled between them and their two observers. Macy stood up. "Come on, here's our chance to get out of here."

"Macy—"

Macy grabbed her arm and yanked her upright. Allison raised her hand as if to slap Macy, or push her away, or something. . . .

"*God damn it, Macy!* I've come here for my father. I am not—"

Macy tugged. "Allie."

Allison just stared across the streaming crowd.

"Oh, my God."

Macy let got of her arm. "Allie?"

"*Is that him?*" Allison whispered.

Across the aisle of exiting passengers, Allison saw a new face watching them intently. His hair had bleached a little lighter, and he'd grown a mustache. But his eyes were the same.

"Dad?" Allison mouthed the word without actually saying it.

Dad was standing on the same side of the gate, a little to the left and behind Barney and his friend. All of them were watching Allison and Macy.

For what?

Who cares?

"You see him?" Macy whispered at her.

Allison nodded and started toward the trio.

"Girl?" Macy exclaimed, grabbing at her arm. Allison shook it off and waded into the crowd exiting the plane, working her way across. People bumped into her and cursed. When she was about halfway through the crowd, Macy caught up with her and grabbed her shoulder. "What the hell you doing? That guy shot a gun at you!"

They stopped and the off-loading crowd flowed around them. "But—" Allison began to say. She looked helplessly at her dad, and noticed that half the people at that gate had folded their papers and were watching the two of them expectantly.

Allison swallowed.

"Oh, Dad, no."

Allison turned to Macy, and someone grabbed her arm from behind. "Hello, Miss Boyle."

Allison turned her head and saw Fred Jackson. One hand was holding her arm, the other hand was in his pocket. Fred began ushering her toward Barney and her dad while shielding her from the departing passengers with his body.

"Allie—" Macy began to yell, but the shout was cut off.

Allison began to turn to see what happened to Macy, but Fred held her tightly. Allison was about to scream something, anything to get attention. But Fred had something in his pocket, and he was pressing it against her side. "Please cooperate," he said.

Allison thought he was pressing a gun into her side— *How'd they get a gun in here?*—but then there was a barely audible hiss and an insectlike sting in her side.

Oh, no.

I'm.

In.
Trouble. . . .
Whatever it was, the effect was immediate. The world
seemed to grind to a halt. Allison was wrapped in a not-
unpleasant floating sensation. She felt bloated with helium,
and Fred was tugging her along by one of her tie ropes.

A big parade it was, and her four captors seemed to take
on the likeness of their cartoon namesakes. When she
looked at Barney's friend, she said, much too loudly, "Why,
Bam-Bam, of course!"

They were *all* just big balloons, and it was the homecoming parade.

The parade was riding down Maple, toward the school,
and she was the center of attention. The crowds lining the
street were staring at her, her and the floats accompanying
her. The crowd looked terrified. Allison saw Macy and Mr.
Counter staring at her. Mr. Geraldi and his trunk-clad swim
team were trying to escape down a side street. Mr. Franklin
tried to comfort David Greenbaum's mom, who was
screaming hysterically. Allison looked around, dumbfounded, at the homecoming crowd and tried to figure out
what was wrong.

Somehow the Euclid Heights Homecoming had blended
in with Allison's memories of the Macy's Thanksgiving Day
Parade. Inflated Flintstones were bobbing around her. The
Barney balloon grabbed at her. She seemed to float down
the street, surrounded by a cartoon entourage.

It began to seep into her mind that she was drugged, and
what she was seeing wasn't quite one of her nightmares.

In fact, that gun Barney was waving might be quite real.
Barney waved his weapon—disarmingly small in a gigantic
vinyl inflated hand. Allison looked up into Barney's face
and only saw two little black circles drawn on a flat car-
toony surface where his eyes should be.

"I guess I'm not going to be homecoming queen," Allison mumbled. No one seemed to hear her.

Euclid High was empty. Allison walked through the halls
looking for people, and found the rooms vacant. The school
seemed to've been deserted for years. She wandered the
halls, brushing away cobwebs, scattering mice. At first she

thought it was nighttime. Then she saw that the windows were boarded up. There was bright blaring daylight outside.

As she wandered through hallways of chipped plaster, rusty lockers, and collapsing ceilings, Allison hugged herself. This was the worst dream of them all. She felt the stifling heat, the dust on her skin. She breathed in a cobweb and felt it tickle the back of her throat.

She stared at the disintegrating hallway and told herself, "It's only a dream."

"Yes, it is," came a familiar voice from behind her.

Allison spun around and saw, standing there, Chuck.

She wanted to scream, but her voice caught on the cobwebs in her throat.

Chuck held up his hands, both uninjured. "Peace, sweetcakes, I mean you no harm. Besides, you said yourself, this is a dream. What can I do?"

"You can—" the words caught in Allison's throat again. She began to cry.

Chuck ran a hand through his hair. He looked exactly as he always had in school. Checked shirt, blue jeans, boots. "Look, stop cryin', will ya? This ain't easy for me."

Allison looked up at Chuck and saw an expression on his face somewhere between disgust and embarrassment.

"Look," Chuck said, "we've both done nasty by each other. Can we call it even for a few minutes so that I can talk to you? Fuck, that's all I ever wanted."

"Bullshit," Allison whispered. She wiped the tears from her cheeks.

Chuck shook his head. "Look, I won't touch you. Let's have a seat." Chuck opened one of the few intact doors left in the abandoned school and motioned at her to enter. Allison inched around him, warily, and found herself in what remained of Mr. Counter's history classroom.

They sat facing each other for a long time before Allison asked, "What do you want?"

"I'm dead, what could I possibly want?" Chuck's voice dripped sarcasm.

"What are you? A ghost, a spirit, part of my subconscious?"

Chuck sighed. "I ain't quite sure, sweetcakes. No one gave me an instruction manual. All I can say is I'm what's left of good ol' Charlie Wilson." Chuck shook his head. "All I know is that that knockout drug they gave you gives me a chance."

"For what? Revenge?"

"Oh, Jesus," Chuck looked up at the sky. "A chance to talk. *Before* they hit you with their anti-mindwarp crap. I hardly need to go booga booga at you, do I? You almost offed yourself—"

"How do you know—"

"This is *your* head we're in. You leave a lot of stuff just lying around here." Chuck opened up a drawer in Mr. Counter's desk and pulled out a yellowed test paper and tossed it to Allison. Allison recognized it as part of *Restless Nights,* as corrected by Mr. Counter.

Allison looked at it and back up at Chuck. "So, what do you want?"

"I told ya, this ain't easy—" Chuck paced up and down behind the desk and finally punched the blackboard, cracking it.

Allison jumped.

"Fuck it all, I'm here to apologize—there, I said it—I know how much of an asshole I was—am—okay? I deserved everything." Chuck started for the door.

"Wait." Allison said.

"Damn," Chuck said. "Okay, what now?"

"Why?"

"Why—fuck it all to hell, you want to know why? Can't I just—"

Allison stared at him, dumbfounded. He must have taken it as a "No."

"Look, sweetcakes, we're stuck together."

"Huh?"

Chuck sighed. "What happened, you know, blood flying and all that— You doing that mindwarp shit. It tied us together."

Allison still stared, and Chuck tapped his forehead and then, gently, tapped hers. She flinched.

"If we don't call it quits and even the scorecard, we're going to live through that shit over and over for all of whatever. Kind of screw what we all got to do."

"I see." Allison whispered.

"Ah, no, you don't, sweetcakes. But I do." Chuck pulled a chair over across from Allison and sat with his arms folded over the back. "We got to be on speaking terms, sweetcakes. See," Chuck smiled. "you might need me someday."

Allison shrank back. "Never."

"Yeah, right." Chuck stood up. For a moment he was silent, then he looked around with a pained expression. "Fuck it, you have no idea how badly you've screwed things."

"I can deal with it myself."

"Shit you say. You're about to get your chance." Chuck had become translucent. He was looking at her through hands that were rapidly fading. "Say hi to Dad for me," Chuck said before he disappeared completely.

She was left alone in Mr. Counter's classroom. The scene didn't change until she woke up.

What did he mean "anti-mindwarp crap?"

CHAPTER NINETEEN

Allison woke up with a seat belt restraining her, and for a moment she thought she was back in her mom's Taurus outside Columbus. As the fog receded from her mind, she began remembering fragments of last night.

Chuck was right, I screwed things up.

She tried to remember where she was, but she had no idea. Her cheek was resting against a flat surface. It vibrated gently against her skin. She opened her eyes and found herself looking out a thick glass porthole. On the other side, blackness.

Where am I?

A small part of her mind tried to reach out with her teek—and her sense felt as if it had slammed against the side of her skull. The sudden pain made her gasp. The shock felt as if she'd sprained her ankle, but only discovered the fact when she'd put her weight on it.

Her head was stuffed with cotton, and for the first time since she'd discovered her teek, she was trapped in her own skull. The sudden sense of claustrophobia that caused was worse than waking up in a prison cell.

She hugged herself and turned her head away from the darkness outside the window. The rest of the cabin was darkened, but there was enough light to see she was in an airplane cabin. Allison guessed that it was a small business jet, not that she would know.

"Macy?"

Allison felt panic grip her.

A comforting hand rested on her arm and Allison nearly screamed. The panic caught in her throat when she saw who it was in the seat next to her.

"She's asleep—"

"Dad?" Allison's voice was strangled and small.

The man hesitated a second before he nodded, as if her voice was an accusation he didn't necessarily want to admit to. Allison realized it was.

"I'm sorry for—" he began.

"I trusted you!" Allison hissed, whispering. "I have no idea why. You were supposed to fix everything!" Tears began welling in Allison's eyes. "Why, Dad? I ran across five states to find you, and you're with these ASI nitwits who've ruined my life."

"I didn't have a choice—"

"So when do they start drilling into my head, Dad?" Allison couldn't remember ever feeling so angry. She had trouble talking.

"It's not like—"

"*Don't tell me what it's like!* I've seen a film of them lobotomizing some poor kid, they killed Mr. Luvov, and what . . . about . . . Mom?" She was shaking now, racked with tears and anger. She felt as if she was about to tumble headfirst into an abyss of hysteria that had no bottom.

She squeezed her arms across her stomach and rocked.

Dad put his arm around her shoulders, "Allie, I know these are bad people—but Stone threatened you if I didn't help them. . . ."

"Mom," Allie said. "Where's Mom?"

"I'm so sorry—"

The way he said it confirmed Allison's greatest fear. The sobs began, choking off any words. She curled into a ball and shook.

It seemed an eternity before she had the strength to ask, "How?"

She didn't move, so all she could see were her own knees in front of her face.

"Some stupid accident," she heard him say. She could hear a hollow anger in his voice. The hollowness echoed how she felt. "Carol panicked when she saw them, ran, fell."

She can't be dead. Allison tried to lie to herself, but she had suspected it ever since the Taurus had pulled into the driveway without Mom in it. Allison shook her head and closed her eyes, hugging her knees closer to herself. "What are they going to do to me?" Her whisper was so low that she barely heard it herself.

"Take you to the Institute with all the other kids. Study you—"

"Will they cut open my head."

Dad patted her back, "No, Allie."

"I saw this film—"

"Whatever it was, it must have been old. The kids are too valuable to Stone. It's the other people who're—" Dad trailed off, his voice carrying enough pain for Allison to realize that he felt for her mother, too.

"Who are these people?" Allison whispered.

"Mr. Stone?"

Allison shook her head. "All of them. ASI, Prometheus, this Mr. Stone guy, the Flintstones, you, Mom, me—everyone."

Dad sighed. "Are you up to hearing this?"

I've been up for this ever since I heard you call Mom. Allison nodded.

With Allison curled into a ball next to him, her dad began the first story he'd told her since she was four years old.

According to her dad, John Charvat, it had its origins at the end of World War II. Not the project itself, but the pathology that eventually led to the project. A pathology that germinated within an intelligence community that seamlessly slid from World War to Cold War and quietly went insane.

A knot of people within the government convinced themselves that the Soviets were capable of *anything*—and not simply in the moral sense. Any scientific intelligence from the Soviet Union was cloned in the U.S. under a cloak of paranoia and secrecy.

Any scientific intelligence.

Any.

The Prometheus project was begun in the late forties in response to wartime Soviet experiments in ESP and telekinesis. Evidence for such Soviet projects was spotty at best, and the results of the experiments were even spottier. And while the mainstream American intelligence community was paranoid of a Soviet lead in technical areas concerning bombs, tanks, and missiles, in one small corner of the CIA the worries were psionics, mind over matter, astral projection, telepathy.

In the black secrecy of the Cold War, a small cadre of men with this agenda could divert huge amounts of resources without challenge. Their agenda became Prometheus.

The project was supposed to do the Russians one better. Through the early fifties, the CIA funded the Prometheus Research Institute, which in turn funded several thousand experiments in universities across the United States. The experiments funded by PRI were fairly straightforward. Most of the tests were only slight refinements of tests developed by Dr. J. B. Rhine in the thirties. The major refinements were ones of scale. Every result, along with the identities of the test subjects, were sent back to PRI to be collated. The data pool eventually contained nearly a million college students.

None of this was terribly unusual.

What was unusual was what PRI did with those results.

After the experiments, thousands of people were contacted by PRI. High scorers on particular tests were encouraged to marry people who were high scorers on similar tests. The incentives sometimes amounted to thousands of dollars, cars, and even houses—often with the major part of the dowry withheld until a child was produced from the union.

The project was expensive, amoral, and—in terms of pairing off Rhine test high scorers at least—very successful. The Prometheus Institute was soon cataloging thousands of second-generation Rhine kids across the country.

It the mid-sixties, PRI began to see results.

The film Allison had seen had come from this era, when

the PRI had begun "taking in" second-generation Rhine kids to examine the results of the project.

The PRI experiment had *worked*. Psi effects followed the Rhine kids like a plague of locusts; precognition, apparitions, spontaneous combustion . . . and poltergeists. At the very least, the new generation scored as high as their parents did on the Rhine tests. At best, the kids could erupt into activity that had never before been available to scientific scrutiny. Out of the thousands of second-generation kids out there, PRI took nearly two thousand back to the institute for in-depth study.

Allison had seen a movie of that kind of "in-depth study."

Unfortunately, most of the second generation, while finally giving them a base to build a physiological model of psi, were erratic talents. In fact, the more powerful, it seemed, the less reliable the ability was. The poltergeists were a classic example; universally they were the most powerful kids in terms of energy expenditure—but they were limited to a brief flash of uncontrolled power during puberty, and then the power would shortly burn itself out.

The pattern was typical. A brief—and sometimes fatal—eruption of uncontrolled paranormal activity during adolescence, followed by a descent into quiescence.

While this was happening, the CIA itself was having problems.

The sixties weren't a great time for the Agency, especially its small covert subsidiary the ASI. The seventies were even worse. The public began to hear about things like LSD experiments on prisoners and military personnel. The CIA steadily tried to divorce itself from the "weird stuff." The public exposure of something like Prometheus would be a disaster, and not only for the experiments. There were thousands of families out there, created by PRI's bribery, that were terribly unstable. Most of the unions fell apart after the second kid. Many did so violently.

The typical burnout of the second-generation kids did not encourage support from the more mainstream intelligence community. In fact, the surviving second-generation Rhine kids were paranormally quiet for the most part by the time they reached adulthood. By the early seventies, PRI had run out of teenagers to study.

Gradually, the CIA weaned Prometheus away from government funding, until the organization stood by itself. By the end of the seventies, PRI became, publicly, a legitimate pharmaceutical concern specializing in neurochemistry.

But . . .

PRI was run by old intelligence men who, in turn, recruited intelligence people. There was a corporate psychology at PRI that was cut from the CIA out of whole cloth. In fact, the people who ran PRI had come from the most extreme portions of the intelligence community, and had shifted into the private sector because the CIA could no longer tolerate them.

Privatizing PRI did little except remove it from what little restraint the CIA had forced upon it. In fact, Prometheus became more entrenched, more paranoid, more secretive about the *real* work.

Prometheus, freed from the CIA, needed the funding to take the experiment the next logical step. They found their money in the pockets of Howard Stone.

Stone was a rich man. Texas rich. Oil, cattle, rail: name it and Stone owned a large piece of it. Stone was also a die-hard commie-hating patriot who had—among other things—attempted to fund a private invasion of Cuba at least three times during the late sixties. Stone was also slightly off his cork about the Bermuda Triangle, the Illuminati, UFOs, Atlantis, and—of course—the powers of the mind.

In other words, he was the perfect candidate to fund PRI.

Billions of Stone's dollars flowed into PRI as the company tried a new tack to prevent the familial disintegration of the Rhine's previous generation. They were more subtle this time, and as effective. Often they only talked to one half of the couple. They convinced some second-generation women to undergo artificial insemination. They recruited some of the second generation to come work for PRI. Understandably, quite a few of the Rhine kids had evolved an interest in the paranormal. In a few cases, PRI still bribed.

The major problem was reconstructing a list of the second-generation kids. Locating all of them was a major effort. The funding decline during the sixties had allowed many of the second-generation kids to slip through the cracks. One of Stone's major contributions to PRI was reconstructing its private intelligence capability to find those kids.

"The ASI?" Allison asked. She had unfolded a bit in her seat and was watching her dad. It was an eerie sensation just to look at him, after so many years.

"Yes and no," Dad said. "The ASI was an agency within the CIA during the sixties and the early seventies. It was responsible for overseeing Prometheus, the LSD experiments, a lot of covert ops in Vietnam—it was all but disbanded after the war."

"But—"

"It's a convenient cover for PRI's operations arm. While the ASI technically exists in Washington, it's so layered in secrecy and national security that any local inquiries by either police or private citizens are simply shunted away."

"So the Flintstones aren't the real ASI?"

Dad looked away for a moment and replied, "Nothing is real in this business."

The silence was filled with the vibrating thrum of the plane's engines. Allison wiped the tears off of her face. She felt less on the edge of a hysterical breakdown. But her head still hurt, and her gut still ached.

And Mom was still dead.

She resisted the urge to start crying again. Instead, she looked at Dad and asked, "What about us?"

Dad turned to look at her. "Us?"

"You, me, Mom—Where do we fit in this?" Allison sucked in a breath. "Am I someone's *experiment*?"

Dad smiled, "That's the ironic thing, Allie. You aren't. Carol and I loved each other, despite the strange home life PRI inflicted on us." Dad reached out and squeezed her shoulder. "Don't ever think you're the result of some 'experiment.' You were born because Carol wanted a child, and she never stopped believing that you were the best thing that ever happened to her."

Dad let go.

"Tell me about it," Allison said.

*   *   *

Dad told her that he had met Mom at PRI. By the time Carol had joined the lab staff at PRI, Dad had been working as head of PRI security for three years. Dad had come out of the ASI in Vietnam, Mom out of Duke University. Within a year Carol wanted marriage, and a family.

The problem was that PRI had strict rules against inter-employee relationships. Mom and Dad had to develop theirs in secret. Because of Dad's control of the PRI security apparatus, they could do so. Unlike most PRI employees, Mom and Dad could have a private life—even to the extent of secretly living together.

Dad said that Mom had never really known how much active intervention it took on his part to keep the relationship secret. And, even with his control of the records, marriage was out of the question. In the end the two of them agreed on a dangerous compromise, Carol would have her family, but without marriage.

"It was stupid, all the secrecy. One of us should have just quit."

"Why didn't you?" Allie asked. She couldn't help picturing herself in that situation if Dad and Mom had never separated. Would she have to sneak to school out the back door?

"Too proud, too stubborn, both of us. Another irony, clinging like that, since we both ended up despising our jobs."

No wonder, Allison thought. That kind of deception, for four years, it had to take some sort of toll.

"Dad, why did you and Mom break up?"

"Lies catch up with you, honey. Not just what we were hiding from PRI, but what we hid from each other. Or what I hid from her—" Dad's voice trailed off.

"What is it?"

"I never told her I was one of the second-generation children. I convinced myself that it was a security matter. But as the years passed, and Carol became disenchanted with what PRI was doing, I just couldn't tell her that I was, in your words, 'someone's experiment.'" Dad shook his head. "We separated because of that, and because Carol discovered that we were *both* second generation."

"That's why I'm . . ."

"Yes. Carol didn't want that. She wanted you to have a normal life. I did my best to help both of you by fogging records, and by falsifying the surveillance on Carol the year after she left. I did all I could to keep Prometheus from knowing about your existence. I stayed long after I grew to hate the place, to cover your tracks."

Dad closed his eyes and shook his head. Allison thought she could see light reflecting off his cheek.

"What is it?" Allison asked. "What's wrong?"

"I'm sorry. That's why you never heard from your dad, why you never got any visits, why I missed twelve birthdays, twelve Christmases—I couldn't control the surveillance on myself. If I had ever done any of that, I could have led them right to you."

Allison reached over and squeezed his hand and said, "I forgive you, Dad."

CHAPTER
TWENTY

Elroy lay in bed and watched the walls breathe.

He was in one of the Institute's hospital beds. Occasionally he would overhear doctors talk about activity in his temporal lobe, or limbic system, or talk about the serotonin levels in his brain. . . .

All of it was so much wind.

Wind that made the walls breathe.

At the moment the walls breathed with a pulsing blue light that vibrated in response to the humming air conditioner. Sometimes the walls were a pale green, sometimes yellow, but right now they were blue. Above him, he watched the acoustic tiles advance and recede, distorting the fluorescent light fixtures. Elroy found it rhythmic and calming and not at all unusual.

After seeing God, the world had changed. . . .

For a moment, Elroy didn't know why he had been awakened. There had to be a reason. That was the central revelation, that *everything* had a purpose. *She sees the fall of the sparrow,* as his mother said.

Then he saw the angel of fire standing next to his bed. She was a red-haired creature of immaculate beauty, wrapped in the cloak of her swirling mind—but Elroy could see the blackened dead parts of that soul.

"Get thee behind me Satan," he quoted his mother.

"Cut the crap, Billy," said the angel, a frown crossing her beatific face. "I need to talk to you."

"My name in heaven is Elroy—"

"You're back at the Institute, Billy. You can cut with the code names."

"Elroy," he said to the angel. "It was traced on my forehead by the finger of God. Like the mark of Cain on your own."

"No wonder the doctors are worried about you," the angel muttered to herself. "Call yourself whatever you want. You should know why I'm here."

"You are here to tempt me into the lake of fire."

"You're starting to piss me off, Billy—"

"Elroy."

"Whatever." The angel strode around the bed. In her wake the colors changed into a ruddy red, and the walls behind her melted and flowed as well as breathed. "Just tell me about this girl."

"She is come again."

"Cut the theology. Is she a threat to me?"

Elroy looked at the angel of fire and said, "She will cast you into the bottomless pit for a thousand years."

"You're a nutcase, Billy. They're going to lock *you* up."

"Elroy."

The angel of fire made a disgusted noise and slammed the door on her way out.

Jessica Mason stormed out of Billy Jackson's room in a foul mood. She had pulled a lot of people's favors, especially staff favors that shouldn't be squandered, to get to visit Billy. She should have stayed. A little work and she might have been able to worm something from him, but she was too unnerved by him.

Jessica didn't like being unnerved.

Elroy was not Billy, that Jessica was certain of. There was precious little of the silent little nebbish Billy Jackson left in Elroy's demeanor. When she looked into Elroy's eyes, it was almost easy to believe that the kid had seen God.

When she left the ward building, three people were waiting for her on the sidewalk. All of them were male, and with the exception of twenty-year-old Sean, all were younger than she was. Thad, the youngest and most intelligent of the three, spoke up when she left the building.

"What's the news, Jess?"

Jessica shook her head. "Billy's fried beyond recognition."

"Should I try reading him?" asked Oscar, the last of the trio. He was a black eighteen year old whose eyes never stopped moving.

Jessica shook her head. "Even if you could read past the normal interference, whatever his surface thoughts are, they're mush. And I don't want to risk you on whatever bad trip he's on."

Sean nodded slowly, his brows knotted in thought. Many of his gestures and mannerisms made people think he was mildly retarded. Even though he was slow, and lacked any creativity, as far as Jessica was concerned, he wasn't terribly stupid. Besides, at six feet ten and nearly three hundred pounds, his assets weren't predominantly mental. "What did Billy say?" he asked.

The predawn darkness had lightened enough for the Institute's floodlights to begin switching off. A light next to them shut off just as Sean spoke. It made Jessica nervous.

She didn't like being nervous.

"He thinks she's the Second Coming. Apparently he saw God."

Oscar whistled.

"That isn't uncommon," Thad said. "The godhead is a common theme both with schizophrenia and with hallucinogenic drugs. There's a considerable overlap with psi activity."

"Thank you, Professor," Oscar said.

"So Billy goes schitz," Jessica said. "That doesn't tell us much about this girl they're bringing in."

"Actually," Thad disagreed, "it speaks volumes."

All eyes turned to Thad in expectation of an explanation. Thad swelled a little under the scrutiny as he spoke. "This is a lay understanding, but with Billy we had a passive uncontrolled ability—Class I, primarily sensory. External events triggered the chemistry in his brain that allowed him to see people's auras."

"You're getting obtuse, Thad," Oscar said.

Thad ignored Oscar. "Technically, external psi events put

Billy into a state of hallucination. Like mescaline or LSD—
don't look at me like that, you're taking the same classes
I am, I just pay attention . . .''

Jessica did attend the same classes, and she got what
Thad was saying. Psi was like a highly specific tab of LSD
as far as Billy was concerned. Then Billy had seen something overwhelming enough to put him into a permanent
overdose.

Whoever this girl was, she might not be the Second Coming, but she was trouble.

30 OCTOBER   NAVARRO COUNTY, TEXAS

7:25 AM   SATURDAY

Allison spent the rest of the flight staring out the window
and trying to think of how she could have done something differently.

She had failed Mom, she'd failed Dad, she'd failed Macy,
and she'd failed herself. She felt wrung out and wretched,
worse for the swath of destruction she'd left behind her
to no purpose. Three days of running into the hands of
the enemy . . .

And Macy shouldn't even be here. This had nothing to
do with her.

The plane had been flying away from the sunrise all
through the night. The dawn finally caught them as they
made an approach to land. Watching through the window,
Allison saw no city—only rolling acres of nothing below
them.

As the plane banked, she saw a narrow ribbon of access
road slide into view across tawny scrubland. As the plane
made the final approach, Allison finally saw the Institute.
Their destination was a surreal landscape of buildings
carved out of red dawn light and mile-long shadows. Allison saw what looked to be two major fences surrounding
the complex. The outer one was a double line carved miles
out into the badlands, the inner one hugged most of the
buildings in the center of the complex.

The place was huge. It reminded Allison of a military base of some sort. *Perhaps at one time it was.*

It had its own airfield and runway, resting in the no-man's-land between the two fences. There was a single runway, half a dozen taxiways leading to half a dozen hangars. The control tower for it was the tallest structure in sight.

As the plane descended, Allison caught a glimpse of what looked like tract housing between the fences. She lost sight of that behind the central complex as the plane landed. The central area, which sped by Allison's window now that they were on the ground, could have been any slightly dreary suburban office park, if it weren't for the twenty-foot fence surrounding it.

The pilot came over the PA and said, *"Welcome home."* *Welcome home, indeed.*

Despite Allison's violent objections, they separated her from Dad and Macy when they landed. They pulled her off the plane first, and when she started fighting, they threatened to drug her again. She quieted because whatever they'd given her was *still* interfering with her teek.

Macy was still asleep in one of the seats, and Allison was sure she'd been drugged as well.

She was escorted by Fred and a man with thick glasses he called Dino. They walked her off the tarmac and to a waiting golf cart. They deposited her inside, and stood aside as the cart sped off.

The cart was driven by a uniformed security guard, and in back was a young woman in a white coat. She held a clipboard, and when she looked at Allison, her smile was almost sincere.

"Hello, Allison. Welcome to Prometheus—"

With those words, the world around her seemed to rapidly go insane. Allison nodded absently as the woman spoke. "We know transitions are difficult, so I've been assigned as your orientation officer. If you have any difficulties, special requests, or you just need to talk to someone, that's what I'm here for."

The golf cart sped up to a gate in the inner fence. The fence was plastered with warnings about electrification. Barbed razor wire curled in over the top, arcing inward for at least a yard. Every dozen feet a camera was mounted on a post extending above the fence, panning the interior.

"We do our best to make the students comfortable."

Guards with automatic rifles scrutinized them before they let them through. The woman blithely talked on, as if this was something normal. Allison was gripped by the urge to run screaming into the desert.

The golf cart trundled in through the gate. "Curfew is from ten at night to seven in the morning except when there's an announcement otherwise. Any security area will be well marked, but if you're unsure, ask a member of the staff. The cafeteria serves breakfast from seven-thirty to ten, lunch from eleven to . . ."

Allison couldn't pay attention, her eyes were on the armed guards, the cameras, the signs on certain buildings that said, "Absolutely no admittance."

There are people with guns here. They've killed my mother. I'm a prisoner and she's talking as if this was college admissions.

The incongruity was beginning to get to her. She felt an urge to ask about financial aid. Just the thought almost sent her into giddy laughter that would have been too close to hysterical sobs.

I'm losing my mind.

"You'll have the weekend to get your bearings. If you wish to attend services tomorrow, we have a nondenominational service—"

The woman went on, and on, and on. . . . Schedules, services, medical access, and classes. This place *was* a college. Though, interspersed with their instruction, Allison would be scheduled for examinations by the science staff.

The golf cart finally stopped at something resembling a pre-graffiti housing project. The woman led her into the building and showed her to her room. As far as Allison could tell, the place was a dorm.

Higher education in Hell, Allison thought as the door shut behind her, leaving her alone in the room.

The room did a dorm—or a prison cell—one better by having only one bed and its own separate bathroom. It bore some resemblance to a tiny hotel room, or a private room in a hospital emptied of the medical equipment.

A feeling of shocked numbness, a feeling that had been growing for days, froze her to a spot in front of the door. She didn't want to take a step into the room, as if taking that step would be some sort of acceptance of what had happened.

She was also afraid to move. She could feel the jaws of some giant trap that hovered outside the periphery of her vision. If she took a single step, the jaws would snap shut on her, tearing her in half.

When she finally had the courage to move, it was to try the door behind her. The door was unlocked and opened soundlessly into the hall. Somehow, that was the scariest part of all of this. The pretense . . .

Allison closed the door and stepped into her room.

Her captors were well organized. In her room she found the backpack Macy had loaned her—*where did they take Macy?* Inside, she found Babs and the ill-fitting clothes that Macy had swiped for her. Notably missing was the film can.

Taking the film seemed hypocritical to her, as if removing it could deny the events it portrayed.

The backpack was on the bed. In the lockerlike closet, she found the duffel bag that Mom had packed for her. Seeing that, it was hard not to break down again. Allison refused. Instead, she zipped the backpack open and began putting clothes away. She organized things, and tried not to think about the implication that she was stuck here.

There was a digital clock mounted permanently on the wall. Occasionally it would emit an irritating beep to alert her to a scrolling message. At the moment it was to alert her that the cafeteria was open for lunch.

The fact that there was no way to shut the thing off was the most concrete indication that she wasn't a free person.

The beep had interrupted her in the middle of reading the orientation packet they had left in her room. Her eyes kept misting over at the details, but the text felt like a collage cut from brochures advertising resort hotels, Ivy League universities, and high-class drug treatment programs.

The threats to shoot anyone who leaves were buried deeply in the subtext. File under, "unmatched security."

The clock buzzed again, and Allison looked at it.

A new message was swimming through the liquid crystal beneath the time, *"Participation in fewer than two meals a day is indication of medical or psychological difficulty. If you are in need of assistance, please dial ext . . ."*

"Do you have a camera in here?" she asked the little device. It didn't answer, but it stopped scrolling. *And when I was nine, I wanted a big brother.*

Her irritation was somewhat mollified by the fact that she *was* hungry. She still wanted to yell at the thing that *of course* she had psychological problems after what she'd been through.

She didn't, because if there were cameras, there might be microphones.

Allison looked up at the empty room and muttered, "But I'm taking a shower first, and I don't care who's watching."

Showering and putting on her own clothes lent a bizarre sense of normalcy to her situation. The illusion of freedom her captors lent her contributed to the feeling. There was little question in Allison's mind that the effect was intentional. She had no idea how many kids were here, but it wouldn't be good for PRI if the majority of them felt like prisoners.

Even if they were.

In her orientation packet was a map of the complex as well as a laminated ID card with her high school picture on it. The card had a blue border on it, a blue that matched about half of the places on the map. Instructions in the packet told her to wear the ID clipped to her at all times, present it on demand, and stay within the areas designated by it.

As she followed the map to the cafeteria, she noted that none of the blue areas came within a hundred yards of the perimeter fence.

Once she left the dormitory—the "girls' residence," according to the map—the sense of entering a world slightly askew returned full force. Teenagers were everywhere. People her own age, many younger, a few older, had accumulated in the courtyard outside. They sat on benches, played basketball and tennis in a large area between the residences, ran back and forth carrying books and backpacks, rode skateboards. . . .

The sight froze Allison for a moment on the steps to her building. People passed her, going in and out. She got a few stares but nothing more. There were enough people here for a new face not to be extraordinary enough to interrupt the routine.

It looks so normal, Allison thought. The residences, the library, the tennis courts all could have been lifted whole from some private prep school.

But everyone wore a laminated ID tag, the courtyard was dotted with white poles topped by either spotlights or cameras, and Allison knew that barbed wire and armed guards waited just outside the blue area, behind the carefully arranged buildings.

She glanced at her map and realized that the off-limits zones, the barbed wire, the guards, wouldn't even be visible from anywhere within the blue area.

She looked at her fellow prisoners and wondered what *they* told themselves. Was this just a special school to some of them? Did some come willingly? Most of her expectations seemed false in the face of the population before her.

She forced herself to remember her mother, and the kids on the film. She tried her teek sense, and couldn't push through the haze that the drug had made of that part of her mind. *These are evil people, and they've taken everything I had.*

A deep sense of loss gripped her as she wove through the crowd. She barely noticed when several people looked in her direction.

CHAPTER
TWENTY-ONE

Allison's feelings of being watched intensified when she entered the cafeteria building. It wasn't just the cameras, which seemed to watch every inch of the place. It was her peers.

The cafeteria echoed with conversation, but as she passed tables filled with people, the conversations would lower and she would feel their gazes burn into the back of her head. It was a waking rehearsal for one of her nightmares. She felt naked and lost, and it took an effort to avoid running back outside.

I am a wreck.

Allison picked up a tray and got in line. While she waited, she tried to order her thoughts. She couldn't just give up, not while Dad—and *especially* not while Macy—were still in the hands of the Institute. It didn't take a genius to see that they were hostages to her good behavior.

It also didn't take a genius to see that she was being tested right now. She wasn't under any illusions that she wasn't under supervision. Every once in a while, out of the corner of her eye, she would catch one of the security cameras explicitly following her.

Just the thought of being constantly watched ignited a fire in her stomach.

I'm only going along with them because I can't think of what else to do. I'm not giving up. She ran that thought through her mind a dozen times as she loaded her tray with food. The thought didn't convince. It certainly *felt* as if she'd given up.

Allison sat down at an empty table because she didn't feel like talking to anyone. Not here. She also felt a distinct lack of friendly faces out in the crowd of lunch-goers. She had to remind herself that these people weren't her captors, and were as trapped here as she was.

Despite being surrounded by hundreds of people her own age, Allison felt more deeply alone than she had at any other point in her life.

She ate mechanically, because her body told her to. She stared at the center of her tray as she ate, so she jumped when a male voice asked, "This seat taken?"

Allison bolted upright. The guy stood across the table from her, holding his own tray. He would have stood out even in a normal situation. His hair was so blond it was white, making him look like a teenage Billy Idol. He wore a black motorcycle jacket over a dirty T-shirt that showed a bullet-riddled smiley face.

To look at him, he defined the word "dubious."

"Suppose the whole table is taken?" Allison said.

He looked up and down the length of the table. His smile never wavered. "Suppose I just warm the seat a little for the tea party?"

"Suppose you bother someone else?"

"Come on, are you going to turn down the only welcome wagon you're going to get? I maybe scruffy-looking, but I do represent the voice of dissent in this place." He spoke with an accent that seemed to come from Boston, a voice oddly out of sync with his appearance. "I promise to vacate as soon as the Mad Hatter shows up."

Allison sighed and gave a slightly uncomfortable nod. When he sat, it brought home the fact that she hadn't been this close to a boy her own age since Chuck.

She repressed a shudder.

"Call me Zack, everyone else has to." He held out a hand. "Welcome behind the looking glass."

Allison debated letting his hand hang there, but she decided that being rude was pointless. The truth was, she needed all the friends she could get. She shook his hand and noticed he was wearing fingerless gloves. She also saw a tattoo braceleting his wrist. The picture was of thorns biting into the skin, drawing blood. She felt proud of herself for not yanking her hand away.

"You've got your references mixed."

"Hm?" Zack said, taking his hand away.

"The tea party and Mad Hatter are down the rabbit hole, not through the looking glass."

"So they are. I guess they aren't going to show."

A giggle ambushed her and Allison turned it into a cough. "I'm Allison," she managed to say.

"I know," Zack said. "We have a rather effective gossip mill here at the Übermensch Club."

"Übermensch Club?"

"Catchy, huh?"

Allison picked up a cheeseburger that looked like every other warmed over burger that she'd seen in every other cafeteria she'd ever been in. In between bites she said, "Actually it's perverse."

"That's the point," Zack said. "Needless to say, the powers that be—both within and without—aren't amused by the phrase. They can be touchy about terms like 'master race.'"

"What are you doing here?" Allison asked.

"Same as everyone else. I had the bad sense to choose parents involved in Prometheus' master plan—"

"No," Allison set down her burger and looked Zack in the eye. "I've just been kidnapped. I've just found out my mother's been killed. I've been forcibly separated from my father and best friend. And I'm still recovering from the junk they doped me with. . . . Why are you here talking to me?" She managed to get it all out without her voice cracking.

Zack showed little surprise, though he dispensed with his smile. "Well, for one, I'm here because the powers that be expect me to be. I try to fulfill their expectations, otherwise they start to think. Never a good idea." Zack lowered his voice. "I'm sorry about your mom and all that, but don't go telling your life story to everyone."

"Why shouldn't I? After what's happened I should, should . . ." She had lowered her voice to Zack's level and found herself choking on the words.

"I know where you're coming from, Allison. Some of us have been through as bad or worse. It's not something the staff likes us to talk about. If they decide you're disruptive, you can end up locked up in the ward with the vegetables and the schizoids."

Allison sighed. "Some dissident you are."

Zack shrugged. "I'm all this place's got. They only tolerate me because I'm number two on the food chain after the ice queen."

"You just lost me."

Zack shrugged. "Well, you know why you're here, right? Telepathy, clairvoyance, the whole *Weekly World News* shtick?"

Allison nodded.

"Without getting into the Institute's labeling system, just say they value some minds more than others. And when it comes to affecting things outside people's heads, the field amounts to me, Jessica, and a bunch of dice-rollers." Zack tilted his head to the left, over his shoulder, "You can see her holding court over there. Heir apparent of the new world order."

Allison turned to look. The table Zack indicated sat slightly apart from the others. To add to the emphasis, all the tables at that end of the cafeteria were filled, all but the separated table. Only six people sat there. The girl Zack referred to was easy to pick out, an attractive redhead with a gaze as sharp and glittering as a razor blade.

All they need is a flashing neon sign saying, "in crowd."

Allison wondered what would happen if she tried to sit down at that table. It probably wouldn't be pleasant.

"Bitch has got half this room cowed 'cause she's got Stone's ear. The other half don't matter."

"I see."

Zack shook his head. "No, you don't, but you will."

"You don't sound cowed."

"I'm number two on the psychokinetic parade, remember?"

Allison had begun to relax a little, but the mention of psychokinesis tightened her up. Zack didn't seem to notice.

"What does she do?"

"Pyrotic, that's why I call her the ice queen."

Zack seemed to wait for a reaction and Allison managed to say, "Uh huh." Inside, more than ever, she felt as if the world had gone insane. She couldn't really be having this conversation.

"You'll get classes in it, don't worry. The Institute wants smart little storm troopers. Just think of it as crippled telekinesis, all she can do is dump heat into something—you know, random molecular motion, dink, dink, dink." Zack waved his index fingers as if they were molecules bouncing off the sides of the tray with each "dink." "She just speeds up the dinking," he said.

Allison stared at him, and he slowly removed his fingers from the tray.

He gave her a weak smile. "Just had a physics exam. I'm still a little punchy."

"Crippled telekinesis?" Allison said, slowly.

"Am I overdoing the mental BS?" Zack asked. "Sorry, you just got here. I guess you need a few classes before it all makes sense—"

Allison shook her head. "She dinks. What do you do?"

"Hell, I'd show you, but they've got me on their little pharmaceutical leash. They're sort of afraid of me pulling my superman act over the barbed wire—wonder why."

"Superman—"

"Another example of crippled telekinesis. I can actually move things—or rather, *thing*."

Following Zack's conversation was like watching a film of a Ping-Pong game from which a dozen frames had been removed at random. "Levitation?" she asked, not sure she was interpreting him correctly.

"Technically it's a higher order than what Jessica can do, but since I'm just limited to moving my own body I'm second on the hit parade."

"You can levitate?"

Zack smiled at her. "Well, when I'm not on the Institute's little yellow pills—"

"How can you do it without puking?"

Zack's smile left, "Well, ah—"

"When I tried it, I thought I was going to die. It was like jumping off a cliff or something, I didn't know which way was up and . . ."

Zack was staring at her.

Allison suddenly remembered where she was. She looked around for eavesdroppers. She didn't see any.

"When *you* tried it?" Zack whispered.

Allison nodded.

"What do *you* do?" Zack asked.

Allison hesitated before answering, but she didn't see any profit in hiding the information. It wasn't as if the Institute people didn't know what she could do.

"Move stuff," Allison said.

"Move stuff? Like what?"

Allison hesitated before saying, "A Jeep Cherokee."

Zack swallowed. "How far did you push it?"

"Lifted. A foot off the ground."

Zack leaned back, causing the chains on his jacket to jingle. "Jess is going to freak when she finds out Stone has a new number one girl."

Allison shook her head. "I'm nobody's number one girl."

"Go with the flow, Allison." Zack rummaged in his pocket. "Come on, where is it?"

"Where is what?"

"CARE package. I'd be some welcome wagon without a gift. Ah, here we are." Zack pulled a tube of papers out of the inside of his jacket. "Until you get around to requisitioning stuff for your room, you should have some reading matter."

Zack handed the sheaf to Allison.

"This is more entertaining than the orientation manual, and has just as much bearing on reality."

Allison looked at what Zack had handed her. It was half a dozen copies of *The Uncanny X-Men*.

"Comic books?"

"Life is God's comic book," Zack said. "Keep you from being bored." He picked up his tray and left. Allison stared at the comics for a few minutes before resuming her lunch.

When Allison went back to her dorm, she noticed a rec room on her floor. It had a couch, a TV, a Ping-Pong table, and a dartboard. However, what captured Allison's attention was the phone on one of the end tables.

She didn't have any illusions about getting an outside

line, but they *were* keeping her father and Macy somewhere around here. She took a seat on the couch and gathered up the phone. For the moment she was alone here—except for the camera that had swung around to watch her. Allison looked up at the camera and thought about the little gray men on the other side.

There was a throbbing behind her forehead as her teek tried to fight free—

Allison tried not to let it panic her. *It's just a "pharma-cuetical leash" like Zack said.* They wouldn't do something to damage that when that was what they wanted.

Allison still felt as if her teek had been stolen from her. She looked down at the phone and picked it up. There wasn't a dial tone, which didn't surprise her. However, there was the hollow sound of an open connection.

Now what? I don't have a phone book.

"Now that I've recovered some of my wits, maybe I should talk to my orientation officer."

Allison rummaged through the orientation packet. She found a name and extension number for the woman who had welcomed her here. "Extension 0340. Dr. Zendel."

She dialed the number and glanced up at the camera locked on her. *Keep staring at me and eventually I might do something interesting.*

"Dr. Zendel," came a female voice over the phone.

"This is Allison Boyle. You told me to call if I needed anything."

"Yes, what?"

"I need to see my father."

"Well, I'll see what I can do for you. But you'll have to understand that—"

Allison felt the knot of anger flare in her stomach. "I understand that they're as much prisoners as I am, and the only reason you have to keep us separate is to intimidate me."

"Please, there's no reason to use that kind of language."

"If we're *not* prisoners, I want a taxi to Dallas, or at least an outside line."

"Your packet explains the security—"

"Bullshit!" Allison yelled into the phone. Her hands were shaking. "You tell Mr. Stone or whoever else holds

your leash that if they want Allison Boyle to conform to
this charade, they'll have to give me constant reassurance
that John Charvat and Macy Washington are unharmed.
You got that?"

"Allison—"

"We're not on a first name basis, Dr. Zendel."

"—there's no need to be upset. I can schedule a counsel-
ing session for you to help you deal with this anger."

"You'll schedule a session with my father."

"I don't know if I can. . . ."

"Does Mr. Stone want his new number one telekinetic
in a cooperative frame of mind or not?" Bringing that up
was a calculated risk. For all she knew, Zack had been
feeding her a long line of nothing. He didn't appear to be
the soul of veracity. But Allison was furious and was barely
in control of what she was saying.

But Dr. Zendel didn't take issue with it. Instead, she
said, "I'll see what I can do, Miss Boyle."

"You do that," Allison said, and hung up the phone. She
looked up and noticed a young girl, maybe ten years old,
peeking around the door to the common room. As soon as
Allison caught sight of her, the girl ducked around the door
and disappeared down the hall.

Allison looked back to the phone. *"Miss Boyle,"* she
thought, *my teek has some pull here even when they've
drugged it out of my skull.*

She looked up at the security camera in the corner of
the room and said, "And what are you looking at?"

To her surprise, the camera began panning again.

It was late in the evening before she picked up Zack's
comic books and began reading them. As she expected,
they were garish, violent, and had a continuing story line
that she was barely able to follow. She smirked at most of
the writing even though she could identify with the "perse-
cuted mutant superman" theme.

She was halfway into the first copy of *Uncanny X-Men*
when she noticed the pinholes. The whole page had been
perforated. She leafed back and saw that it was true
throughout the comic—every word balloon had been

pricked full of holes, and every hole was underneath a specific letter.

Allison scanned a word balloon at random and read only the letters that were pointed out by the tiny holes, "...v e t o u n d e r s t a n d t h..."

Zack was giving her a secret message. Instinctively, she looked up for a camera. If there was one in her room, it was hidden.

She tried to look casual as she flipped back to the first page. The note was filled with misspellings and missing vowels, but after the first few words she didn't notice that, or the lack of punctuation. She could almost hear Zack's Boston accent through the pages;

"Congrats, you found the secret code. I like smarts. Here's the deal—

"Everywhere's bugged. Don't talk in buildings. If you need to hide from a camera, use the staff bathroom. There are blind spots in courtyard, but don't trust them unless you have to.

"Head count. Out of every ten kids; one head case is in the ward; two buy into ASI prep school gig; three know better but won't make waves; and the other four narc for the staff or buy into Stone's new world order big time.

"Watch the last group. Jess the ice queen runs the lot, and she has Stone's ear. She's dangerous as hell. People she don't like tend to vanish.

"Staff'll drug you as long as they think you're a risk. They also got kids that'll see a mind lighting up. Jess and her storm troopers aren't drugged.

"If you don't take their little yellow pills, they'll shoot you up. Bad choice. Pill's got fewer side effects.

"You have to understand that Stone's a raving fruit loop. You know it when you see him. If you meet him, don't buy the dotty uncle act, he's capable of anything.

"I am the dissenter here, such as I am. If you just want to get by without rocking the boat, you better not see me again. If you feel otherwise, I'll be standing under the camera post between the tennis courts tomorrow at noon.

"Ditch the comics before the staff finds them, but don't be obvious about it. (Toilet's a no-no. they strain the sewage.)"

Allison put the comic down and tried not to shudder. There was little there that she hadn't seen herself, but having her suspicions confirmed didn't make her feel any better. The references to the "ward" gave her visions of the ASI documentary.

Worse was the implication that these people would continue drugging her.. She *hated* the thought of that. She'd been aware of her teek for less than a week, and it already seemed an essential part of her. The drug cut a ragged hole in her mind that ached as badly as any of her headaches.

Worst was that reference to Jessica "vanishing" people. Having Prometheus and ASI to worry about was bad enough. But having to worry about someone else with paranormal powers, someone who *wasn't* drugged into ineffectiveness—

Allison could understand why so many kids, according to Zack, "won't make waves." Some of them weren't even thirteen yet. . . .

She decided that she might, indeed, want to rock the boat. But only after she had a good look at the crew, and where the boat was headed.

CHAPTER
TWENTY-TWO

Allison dreamed again. All through the night she ran through the empty halls of Euclid Heights High School. She tracked clouds of dust after her, stormed through empty classrooms, tore open rusted shut lockers. All looking for a hiding place.

At first, she thought she was hiding from Chuck. But soon, as a dream panic gripped her, she realized that she was *looking* for Chuck. She had to find him—

But Chuck was nowhere to be found.

Eventually her search ended on the fire stairs where it had happened. Chuck's blood still soaked the concrete. The blood was still tacky even though the fire door was long rusted in a half-open position and a pile of dead leaves rustled in a corner.

Just as she'd lost her teek, now she'd lost Chuck.

It should have pleased her.

Instead, the loss terrified her. She collapsed on her knees and wept, allowing the leaves to blow over her body. As the leaves did, their rustling seemed to form a single whispered phrase:

"It is time, this is the only time, it is time, this is the only time . . ."

It sounded strangely like Chuck's voice. She tried to call out, but the leaves filled her mouth. The whisper was cut off then, the screeching of the fire door slamming shut against the rust.

The screeching went on forever. . . .

*   *   *

The screeching didn't cease until Allison sat up in her bed. The sound was the infernal clock attached to her wall. More infernal in that it had no snooze alarm, and it reactivated the moment she tried to lie back down again.

Her first coherent thought was, *This is the only time.*

"Only time for what?" she mumbled. Her mouth tasted like leaves.

Allison woke up further when she realized that there was a real aftertaste of leaves in her mouth. She swished her tongue around her mouth, expecting to feel the gritty sensation of munched foliage, but the only thing in her mouth was the slightly icky feel of unbrushed teeth.

It scared Allison, because the taste didn't go away. It was as real as the bed she was sitting on. She tried to convince herself that she was still dreaming. It didn't work.

Do people hallucinate tastes?

Allison supposed people did, and she was sure that when they did, it didn't represent anything pleasant.

Before she had collected her thoughts enough to get out of bed, the clock on the wall buzzed again and, simultaneously, the door to her room slid open. The noise, the door, and the sudden light nearly made her tumble out of bed in surprise. While her surprise didn't jerk her out of bed, it did startle her badly enough to yank her blanket up to her neck, causing the tangled bedding to cut off circulation to her leg.

As waves of phantom needles rippled across her sheet-tangled leg, a nurse walked into her bedroom. At least Allison assumed the woman was a nurse or some sort of orderly. The woman wore a familiar white coat, and a green-bordered name tag that Allison couldn't read in the darkness. The woman carried a tray.

Allison watched the woman, frozen more now by the invasion of privacy than by fear. The nurse placed the tray on the end table under the clock and said, "Time for your medicine, Miss Boyle."

Allison noted the use of her last name, perhaps her phone call had had more far-reaching implications.

She looked at the tray and wasn't surprised to see a small Dixie cup of water, and a smaller paper cup with a small yellow pill inside it. She considered refusing, but she remembered Zack's warning. If she didn't take the pill, they'd shoot her up.

If this promised to be a milder experience, she wasn't going to tempt fate. She glanced at the nurse. The woman wore a benign expression, no visible sign that she was here to drug someone into subservience.

Allison picked up the paper cup with the pill inside. "Do I have to take this?" she asked.

"We don't want you hurting yourself, or others, by accident. Until you've had some training."

Allison almost voiced another objection, but she knew it would be fruitless. Worse was the fact that there was some logic behind the nurse's excuse. Unchecked, she had killed Chuck without knowing what she'd been doing. These paranormal abilities could be dangerous if they weren't under control.

Allison was convinced that the nurse believed this yellow pill was for Allison's own good. She was also convinced that there were a couple of gorilla-sized orderlies waiting in the hall in case she was less than cooperative. She'd seen *One Flew Over the Cuckoo's Nest.*

Allison downed the yellow pill.

The only immediate effect that Allison noticed was the disappearance of the leaf taste in her mouth.

The nurse insisted on checking her mouth to make sure she'd really taken the pill. Allison endured it, however degrading it felt. The sooner she could get these people to trust her, the sooner she could find some sort of an opening that would get her out of this mess.

At least, that was the theory.

Allison showered, dressed, and ate a depressing cafeteria breakfast. The only light point in her morning routine was the absence of the teek-shaped hole inside her head. Her teek still refused to work, blocked by the drugs she'd been given, but at least with the pill—as opposed to the injection—the absence wasn't a constant physical sensation. She no longer felt constantly on the verge of a migraine.

She resented the fact that it made her more comfortable about the loss.

When she returned to her room it was close to nine-thirty, and the clock was buzzing again. She looked at the clock with a visceral hatred. She could feel her teek try to ram through the drugged part of her bra: It was almost a reflex action, and before she could relax the effort, it drove a spike into her forehead as bad as any she had felt before. As bad as when she had lifted the Jeep. All of it was directed at the hateful-sounding clock.

If her teek had been operational, the clock would have exploded on the far wall, shattering. As it was, the clock was unfazed. Allison had to grip the doorframe for a moment. She did her best not to show the effort she had just undergone. People were watching, people were always watching. She couldn't allow them to see anything suspicious.

The clock continued to buzz, and Allison walked up to see what it wanted.

Across the liquid crystal was scrolling a message that she had an appointment with Mr. Stone today.

"Mr. Stone?" Allison whispered. The head honcho wanted to see her. The maniac in charge of Prometheus. Allison assumed that she might meet the man eventually, but never this soon. She wasn't ready.

What was she going to say to the man who held her life in his hands?

The display told her to go to the administration complex to meet her escort. Immediately.

"I've read it! Would you stop that infernal buzzing?" Allison said into the air.

On cue, the clock ceased its cacophony, but not before she had a chance to notice that the buzz had changed tone slightly. The buzz stopped with a static crunch, as if the speaker had popped.

Allison was out of her room and halfway to the administration building before she thought that she might have done something to the speaker, even through the drugs.

The administration building was a cross-shaped, five-story structure at the edge of the student-accessible area. The mirrored windows made it look like any other anonymous office building. The only thing at odds with the archi-

tecture were the two boxes on the roofs of each of the
three wings facing the student area. The boxes appeared to
be made of armored glass, and Allison could see gunports
and armed gua·ds moving around inside.

Inside the building, next to the fountain that took up
most of the lobby, Allison was met by Dr. Zendel. The
doctor gave her a nervous smile. "I'm here to take you to
Mr. Stone's office," she said.

There wasn't the condescending manner that had tinged
her earlier speeches. Allison thought the woman had left
the program she was comfortable with.

"Lead on," Allison said.

She looks as nervous as I feel, Allison thought.

The doctor walked off down a corridor deeper into the
building. As they walked, she told Allison, "I've managed
to arrange an appointment with your father and Miss Washington. It will have to be tomorrow after classes." After a
pause, she added. "We certainly don't want you to feel
intimidated, Al—Miss Boyle."

Allison didn't respond. She kept her peace mostly out of
a spiteful impulse not to do anything to make Dr. Zendel
more comfortable.

Allison was led through a long corridor, down a set of
stairs, and through underground tunnels that must have
passed far beyond the bounds of the administration building. The corridors definitely passed out of the blue-accessible area. The second door they passed in the administration
building had been marked "green-access only."

When they reached the elevator that was their apparent
destination, they had gone from green to yellow.

Once in the elevator, Dr. Zendel had to offer her ID
card to a reader next to the elevator's keypad. That was
when Allison noticed that her card was green-bordered,
like most of the pseudo-medical staff she'd seen. Allison
interpreted the doctor's nervousness to mean that, in the
normal course of events, she wasn't allowed in this part of
the complex.

It was somewhat reassuring to see one of the staff as out
of her depth as Allison was.

Zendel didn't press any buttons. It was the elevator, or

some computer running the elevator, that decided where they were supposed to go. The doors closed, and the elevator rose. It went up two sublevels and then proceeded to rise ten stories above ground. Allison thought that put her in one of the taller structures in the part of the PRI complex that looked like an office park.

When the door opened, they were greeted by a marble wall supporting a giant chrome logo of the Prometheus Research Institute, a stylized flame logo with the initials PRI underneath.

The doctor led her off to the right, and Allison followed. The halls were expensive corporate chic, all marble, wood, deep carpet, and brushed-chrome furniture. Dr. Zendel led her up to a glass wall with another card reader. The border—subtle but unmistakably one of the security labels— was red. If Allison was reading the colors correctly, this was two security levels away from what Dr. Zendel normally had access to.

Allison noticed the doctor glance at one of the security cameras as she ran her green ID card through the reader.

The door opened with a pneumatic hiss, and Dr. Zendel looked visibly relieved.

They walked into a reception area beyond the glass, and a male receptionist said, "Mr. Stone's expecting you."

The doctor began to lead Allison down a corridor to their right, but the receptionist added, "Just Miss Boyle, Doctor."

Doctor Zendel froze for a moment, apparently unsure of what to do. Allison looked at the receptionist.

"Just down the hall, Miss," he told her.

Great, I get to face this guy alone. Nerves clutched her with a renewed strength. Even having Doctor Zendel to go through this with would be preferable to going through this alone.

It took an effort to continue down that hall.

Every few feet down the hall was marked by a painting on the wall. A sense of familiarity stopped her in front of one of the pictures. It had an Egyptian motif, golden pyramids and such against a galactic starscape. Centered in the picture was a light-shrouded human figure with an animal's head. "I've seen this," she whispered.

There were posters—if not of this particular work, then definitely by this artist—hanging in the window of a New Age bookstore not far from Euclid Heights High.

She stood there, staring at the picture until she decided that she was just delaying the inevitable. She turned and kept walking, but she kept an eye on the paintings.

The pictures were eerie. The themes were old—old beliefs, old gods—but they were rendered with modern hands. In some cases with photographic realism. Looking at some of the portraits gave her the same sense of razor's edge unreality that she got when she really concentrated on her teek.

Slipped in among the shamans and the totems were some other portraits. Portraits of people she had never seen. Little brass tags identified the portraits as Edgar Cayce, Nina Kulagina, Dr. J. B. Rhine—all people she was barely familiar with from scanning Mom's book collection.

The hallway ended at a heavy wooden door. After a moment spent deciding whether or not to knock, she sucked up her courage and pushed her way into Stone's office.

The first thought that struck Allison as she walked across the Persian carpet was, *So many books.*

She had walked into a misplaced library. The room was a square, maybe twenty-five feet on a side, with twelve-foot ceilings. And three walls were bookshelves. *All* bookshelves, except for the one gap where the door opened into the room. They were massive, glass-fronted, floor-to-ceiling bookshelves made of heavy dark wood. It was the most impressive library Allison had ever seen.

"Finally," came a voice from across the room. Allison tore her gaze away from the shelves and looked at the desk. Howard Stone, huge and enigmatic, faced her from beyond a desk.

One of the paintings she'd passed had been a scene of the Easter Island statues transplanted whole to a lunar environment. Stone reminded her of that painting. His smile was hard, cold, and only as deep as the point of a chisel.

"Sit down." He motioned to one of a pair of massive red-leather armchairs that faced his desk.

Allison sat.

The desk, and the wall behind him, didn't fit the rest of

Stone's office. Most of the office seemed out of another century. A century of wood, leather, and glass. Stone's desk was white enameled metal with chrome trim. It almost looked like a bathroom fixture.

The wall behind him, the only wall without bookshelves, was hidden behind ranks of video monitors and electronic equipment that ran floor to ceiling.

Stone stared at her across hands folded atop his cane.

"You wanted to see me," Allison said.

Stone nodded. "Since before you were ever born."

"Ah . . . right."

He caressed his cane in a way that made her uncomfortable. "I'm sure you have questions. Don't you?"

Allison looked at him, "Other than what you've done with my father and Macy? No."

"Oh, don't worry about them. They're perfectly safe. I'm sure Dr. Zendel told you you'd see them shortly— But perhaps you should let go of your old life."

"My *old*—" Allison was having trouble controlling her voice. Anger and fear were balled up in her stomach and her voice couldn't decide between shouting and crying. "It's *my* life. What gives you the right—"

"Please, I didn't mean to upset you." He made a small wave of his hand as if he was dismissing her emotions. The gesture only made her angrier. "But you should be ready to accept something new."

"What? Being the CIA's latest mental weapon?"

Stone laughed. It was a grating sound, much too loud, a sonic bludgeon.

"I don't see the joke," Allison said.

"I'm sorry," he replied. "You really have no idea what Prometheus is? Do you?"

"I think—" Allison thought of several things she could say, and rejected all of them. Finally, she said, "Why don't you tell me?"

CHAPTER
TWENTY-THREE

31 OCTOBER   NAVARRO COUNTY, TEXAS

9:45 AM   SUNDAY

"For me, it began when I saw the Apollo Moon landing on TV."

Allison wanted to interrupt, but the look in Stone's eyes had a shiny cast that made her decide against interrupting him. It was the kind of look Charles Manson would give her.

"Until then, I didn't know the meaning of my life."

"Uh huh."

Stone wasn't paying attention to her now. She had the feeling she was listening to a speech rehearsed many times, before many different audiences. Stone was physically imposing to begin with, and he took on a *presence* that made Allison shrink into the chair.

"At the end of the sixties, I was a billionaire several times over. None of it my own. My father had made my fortune, and by the time it had reached me, the money had its own life. It multiplied well enough without me. That left me a shallow, listless youth. By thirty years of age, no word or deed of any consequence could be applied to me.

"My peers didn't think so. Through the latter half of the decade I was picketed and slandered by children not much younger than I. I was part of the military-industrial complex then."

You aren't now? Allison thought. She didn't have the nerve to speak.

Stone squeezed his cane, and Allison heard his knuckles

crack. "I understood none of it. How, within a few short years, a generation so close to me had become so alien. It was as if the UFOs had landed and exchanged all the children.

"When I saw the Moon landing, I knew that was what had happened."

Stone stood up. Allison felt a quite different fear now, the fear of being locked in a room with a crazy person. Stone seemed to notice the change in her expression. It was a rote recognition, as if this was the point in the play where the audience drew back in shock. From the depth of Stone's eyes, he could be talking to an empty chair.

"Don't dismiss me yet. You, of all people, have seen glimpses of the other world."

Allison nodded because she had no idea what he'd do if she didn't.

"Imagine my thoughts upon seeing the Moon landing. I had cluttered my mind already with the teachings of gurus and mystics, disciples of this new generation I didn't understand. And until the telecast, I had no understanding."

Stone looked up at the ceiling, as if regarding the sky. "Then the realization hit me. I was seeing an event millions of miles away, and *a billion people were experiencing the same event!*" Stone held his breath in a dramatic pause, still staring at the ceiling. "Every one of them," Stone finally said, "The same thoughts. Everyone the same vision. Everyone the same collective dream. That was when I knew."

Stone waited and Allison realized that this was the point in the speech where he wanted to be prompted.

Allison gave him the minimal, "Knew what?"

Like a programmed mannequin at an amusement park, Stone launched back into his story. "The upheaval in the sixties was the first stirrings of the Change." Allison could hear the capital C. "With the Moon landing I realized that I was seeing the collective unconscious made flesh. Our primitive unconscious, our primal fears, our dreams and fantasies all becoming one with the screen."

Yes, of course, uh huh— Allison shrank a little deeper into the chair.

"That was only the first realization. More and more it

became obvious that the realm of the spirit was closing in upon us. Technology itself was unearthing the ancient shamans and bringing them to life. Physicists have delved deep into the heart of the quantum and have found the Buddha looking back."

Stone started pacing, swinging his cane around to indicate both the bookshelves and the complex beyond them. "Before Prometheus ever came to me, I knew my life's work would be to help engineer the Change. Even then I could see a great racial longing. I saw it in the children who blew their minds on LSD looking for the doorways inside. I saw it in the UFOs. Not aliens, I now knew, but travelers from *within*. I see it now, in the eyes of televangelists, the channelers, all those who believe in something, anything—"

What about Elvis? Allison thought.

"There's a longing for the next step, the New Age, the other world. It draws humanity like a salmon upstream to spawn. I saw all this, but there was no guiding force, no plan for the next stage in humanity's evolution—"

"This is where you come in. Isn't it?" Allison said it so quietly that she didn't know if Stone had heard.

"By the time I had heard of the Prometheus Research Institute, I had amassed this library in pursuing my studies." He indicated the books with his cane. "It is the most extensive of its kind."

He leaned on his cane. For the first time Allison thought he was really seeing her. "You're right. Originally this was funded by the CIA. But the CIA disassociated itself at about the time there were the first signs of Awakening. Perhaps they're afraid of the Change. Perhaps they should be." Stone shook his head. "I was a patriot with money, and eventually the Institute contacted me to help finance what the CIA no longer supported." Stone smiled a wide, unrestrained grin that scared the hell out of Allison.

"I did that, and more. I bought them out. Gave them a new direction. A true direction. I've turned Prometheus into the instrument to open the doors of the Change."

Stone stared deep into Allison's eyes. His stare was more intimate, more violating than Chuck's had ever been. Allison sank back in the chair, raped by Stone's gaze. After a long pause, he said in a gentle voice, "After all these years, and all these children— You are the first one to be fully Awakened."

Stone's eyes were intense, empty, and saw much too deep.

"Awakened?" Allison managed to say.

"Yes, I have been waiting for you, one like you. Someone who has fully linked to one of the ancient powers. In the words of my PhDs, you are our first fully operant telekinetic."

Allison straightened in her seat. "What do you want from me?"

"We are here to learn to access the other world. With one door open, we can discover the keys to others. You are but the first of a new order. With your help, there will be others."

Allison felt Stone's gaze on her and couldn't help imagining herself as the incubator for this nut's master race. "I get the picture," she whispered.

"Good." Stone walked around his metal desk and sat down again. Allison could hear the chair protest. "You are the first of many, Allison. You will help me bring the Change."

Allison swallowed and pulled herself up in her chair. *Remember your advantage,* she told herself. *Don't act afraid. In this man's sick little world, he* needs *you.*

After willing herself calm, she managed to speak in a voice whose stillness surprised her. "If you want any help from me, I have to have regular visits with my father and Macy."

He made a dismissing gesture with his hands as if it wasn't even an issue. "It is not a problem, Miss Boyle." He nodded at her, and she took that as her cue to leave.

Before she reached the door Stone added, "You were chosen, Allison. Not by me or Prometheus. Your conception is the result of the synchronicity of the other world. You are the Change willing itself to happen. Remember that."

Allison shuddered as she closed the door behind her.

She was led back by an anonymous-looking guard. Dr. Zendel seemed to have disappeared somewhere. Allison didn't think she'd miss the doctor, but anything would have been preferable to the blank-faced security goon who appeared as if he'd shoot her as soon as look at her.

Allison noticed that *his* ID tag was red. That placed him at the top of the security hill as far as Allison could determine. Blue, green, yellow, and red. Blue on the bottom. Red on the top. Allison didn't find it encouraging to think that a lot of the staff she'd seen with the students were only one step above her, security-wise.

This guard, leading her back to the blue area, held the first red ID tag she'd ever seen. She noticed that, unlike her ID card, the red-bordered one only had a photograph and the PRI flame logo, no name.

She was slightly tempted to ask this guy his name, but only slightly. He looked like a twitchy Gary Busey on a bad day. When they reached the lobby of the administration building, she was glad to be rid of the guy.

31 OCTOBER   NAVARRO COUNTY, TEXAS

12:13 PM   SUNDAY

For lunch, Allison walked through the cafeteria, grabbed a cardboard cheeseburger, and walked back toward the residences. Between the two large residences were a pair of tennis courts, a basketball court, and a small park set up with benches. The whole courtyard was walled in on three sides, on the left by the boys' residence, on the right by the girls', and ahead of her, beyond the basketball court, was a building that Allison thought was a gym.

She walked between the tennis courts and leaned up against one of the whitewashed camera poles. There wasn't any sign of Zack yet. Allison sighed.

If it weren't for her severe lack of options, she wouldn't even be thinking of meeting with him.

She turned her gaze upward and watched the cameras above her as she ate her burger. There were three cameras up there, pointing out the corners of an equilateral triangle.

None of them panned down enough to see within a dozen feet of the pole they were mounted on.

Thinking about that, she looked around the courtyard to see which cameras were watching *her*.

The cameras were in the obvious places, the upper corners of the gym wall. Looking around, Allison couldn't see anywhere that wasn't fully covered by some camera or other, at least momentarily. It was depressing.

"BOO!"

The shock almost made her spit up her cheeseburger. She jumped, turned around to slap Zack—his voice had been unmistakable—and stopped.

She was looking at Billy Idol in a pair of funny-nose glasses. Her hand froze in midair. She snorted once, and swallowed. She tried to control herself and the effort made her tremble.

"Happy Halloween," Zack said.

Allison lost it. Something about hearing Zack's upper class Boston accent—incongruous already—coming from behind a garish plastic nose and whiskers made her keel over laughing. She tried to tell herself it wasn't that funny. But, as she plopped on her butt, holding her stomach, she thought, *Maybe it is.*

After a second she managed to choke out, "Some entrance, Zack."

"Did I do something funny?"

Allison almost lost it again. But she managed to control herself this time. She managed to pull herself upright. "Please, take those things off."

Zack took off the glasses, somewhat sheepishly, and looked at them with a slightly bewildered expression. "Sorry," he said.

Allison shook her head. "No, it's all right." She actually felt a little better. It was the first laugh she'd had recently that didn't feel as if it was a symptom of her sanity slipping. "Come on, let's go for a walk. You can show me around."

Zack shrugged and started walking, and Allison fished *The Uncanny X-Men* out of her pocket and handed them to him. "Your comic books."

Zack looked at her and arched an eyebrow. "Finished them already?"

"All of them," she replied. "I'm a quick reader."

They walked around in front of the administration building. "So, are they listening to us now?"

"Truth is, I don't know." He lowered his voice. "I do know they're watching. There's a camera panning after you."

Allison shrugged. "I expected as much." More quietly: "You were right about Mr. Stone."

"You've seen him already? I'm impressed."

"So's he, apparently . . ." Allison looked across, back at the dorms. "So where's this ward?"

"*The* ward, and it isn't in the student area, of course." Zack waved off in the direction of what appeared to be a classroom building. "It's over behind me. Believe me, you don't want to screw around with that place."

"I take it that's separate from the medical facilities I was told about."

"You bet, the staff won't even admit the ward exists—"

"But you know different?"

Zack laughed. "Ever try to keep rumors from spreading around a population of telepaths?"

Allison looked around at the kids crowding the courtyard, feeling more exposed than ever. Zack seemed to notice her concern. "Hey, don't worry, you're safe from that at least. Doubly safe."

"Huh."

"Their little yellow pill? Most of the staff take 'em, too, 'cause the drug blocks the telepaths out. It's like locking the door from both sides. Besides which, you're too high up the food chain for them to read anyway."

"Come again?"

"You'll hear it all in your orientation class. But simply said, all this mental BS interferes with each other. The more power, the more interference. A 'path trying to read off you, me, or Jess would be like trying to tune in a crystal radio next to the main generator at Hoover Dam. Static city."

"Even if I'm not doing anything?"

"Yeah. You just have to stand next to someone with a lower order power and they not only can't lock on you, but they'll have trouble picking up anything."

Allison nodded. It made her feel a little better. The last thing she needed was to worry about someone running around in her head.

That made her think about Chuck.

Something must have shown on her face, because Zack put his hand on her shoulder. "Hey, are you all right, Allison?"

She shook her head. "Allie, everyone calls me Allie."

"Okay, Allie. Did I say something—"

"No, no." She wiped her eyes. "I just reminded myself of someone. I'd rather not talk about it, okay?"

"Okay."

"Now . . . why don't you tell me about Jessica?"

31 OCTOBER   NAVARRO COUNTY, TEXAS

12:45 PM   SUNDAY

"She is kinda pretty," Sean said in his slow drawl. His accent wasn't characteristic of any particular place, or, if it was, it was a place unique to him. It didn't hamper Jessica's understanding of his speech. She had known him too long. She didn't respond, since anything she might say would be lost while Sean had his concentration focused out the window.

While Sean stared out the window of the small meeting room, Jessica faced away from him, seated in one of the overstuffed chairs surrounding the oval table that dominated the room. Her gaze was focused on the page in her hands. She stared at it without seeing it.

At the moment Jessica and Sean were the only people in the room. They were here because it was one of the few blue-accessible places that she knew for a fact wasn't monitored. Since they didn't lock up the classroom building for the weekend, the small lounges for the "teachers" made convenient meeting places. This one was especially convenient since it overlooked the courtyard where all the PRI kids congregated.

"She's still talking to Zack, but a pole's in the way of

his mouth—'' Jessica heard Sean shift his weight behind her. She continued staring at the sheet of paper she held in her hands.

"Ah, he's saying, 'She's into control. She gets the guards to . . .' dunno, '. . . stuff in here.' She's asking something, I can't see."

Jessica nodded. Sean was largely deaf in both ears, from a childhood accident. It made reading lips second nature to him, and made him useful to Jessica. Such a pedestrian talent was overlooked by almost everyone in this storehouse of the miraculous. With one pair of binoculars, Sean was almost as good as a clairvoyant.

It was predictable. Zack had made a beeline to the newcomer. That was almost standard operating procedure. It was never much of a problem before. *Zack* was never much of a problem before, even though his talent was valued highly enough that Jess couldn't convince Stone to have him dealt with. Zack might be untouchable, but no one else was. And, unlike Jessica, Zack alienated both Stone and the staff. He didn't have the subtlety to use them to get anything done.

With a few well-placed words, Jessica could undo any amount of Zack's rabble-rousing with the regular students.

However, Allison Boyle was not a regular student. Jessica only had to think of the wreckage of Billy Jackson to realize that. Worse, from the conversation Sean was relating, Allison Boyle knew how special she was.

She had already talked to Stone.

Already.

Sean fed her more of their conversation, wrapped in his nameless accent. Jessica let it bleed into her mind without paying attention to the individual words. The sense of it was enough.

Allison Boyle accepted Zachary Lanagan's evil interpretation of both Jessica and Prometheus, a feeling that seemed reinforced by the means the field agents used to bring Allison in. Even if all Jessica had to go on was Billy's reaction, it was obvious that the whole episode had been badly handled, to say the least.

Worse, unlike Zack, Allison Boyle seemed ready to use the value of her power as a lever with the staff. Allison was telling Zack how she had dealt with her orientation officer, Dr. Zendel.

All of this sank in. Each sentence of the conversation below seemed to tear its own little hole in Jessica's peace of mind. Up to now she had built everything so carefully. Everything since she had come here was supposed to protect her, keep anyone from being in a position to hurt her. As long as she was in control, as long as she was too valuable, too cooperative to harm, she was safe.

What would happen to her if she wasn't the most valuable talent that Prometheus had? Zack disliked her, but there were people—people on the staff—who *hated* her.

"Jessica?" Sean placed a hand on her shoulder, breaking her out of her reflection. She jerked, a circle of gray ash collapsed from the center of the pages she was holding. A small wisp of white smoke trailed up from the pile it made on the table.

No, I can't lose control. Not of Prometheus and, God help us, not of this! *Not* now!

Jessica stared at the pile of ash for a moment, thankful that Sean knew enough not to ask if anything was wrong. She put down the paper and turned so that Sean could see her speak. "Let's go see if Oscar's read anything useful lately."

Sean nodded. He bent over to grab a wastebasket and started brushing the remains of Jessica's paperwork into the can. Her eyes focused on the paper again.

They were copies of the autopsy results on Billy Jackson.

CHAPTER
TWENTY-FOUR

01 NOVEMBER   NAVARRO COUNTY, TEXAS

7:13 AM   MONDAY

"What the hell's going on?" Allison screamed at the dust-strewn corridors of Euclid High. Her voice echoed through dark, abandoned hallways. Deep in the distance she thought she heard an echo say, "Little Miss Perfect said, 'Hell.'"

The nightmare, the same nightmare. How many times was she going to be trapped here? Mere repetition had gotten through to her. She was fully aware she was dreaming now. It did no good. She felt trapped here, mired in a frustration as solid as glue.

She walked, or she tried to walk. Single steps seemed to take aeons. Dust billowed up from her steps, and fragments of gray plaster crunched under her feet. Her hand brushed a locker. The resulting shower of rust and paint flecks itched madly.

Her mouth tasted dry, dusty.

She called out, "I know you're here, somewhere. Why are you hiding?"

The echo came back. "You're hiding. You're hiding. You're hiding."

"Help me," she shouted. Shafts of sunlight hung from cracks in the boards covering the windows. She pushed through each dust-heavy shaft as if it were a physical barrier.

The clocks here, all of them, were stopped at twelve. She was passing one now. It hung over the door to an empty, darkened classroom. She stopped there, unable to push herself any farther.

As she did, she thought the shadows in the classroom moved slightly. She peered inside and whispered, "Chuck?"

The echo came back, even softer, "Now."

The clock fell from the wall, smashing at her feet. . . .

Allison sat bolt upright in her bed, fully awake. Her pulse raced in her neck, and her skin was clammy with perspiration.

To her surprise, the demon clock on her wall wasn't sirening her wake-up call. She sat breathing deeply and cursing both Chuck and her subconscious. They were probably one and the same.

The whole right side of her body itched.

She looked at the clock and saw she had nearly fifteen minutes before the nurse came with her little yellow pill. The thought was depressing, but at least she had time to shower. She needed it.

Her mind was still wrapped up in Euclid High as she walked into the bathroom, so she didn't notice until she turned on the light.

The right side of her body, especially her arm, was covered in fragments of paint and rust. She had to stop herself from gasping.

It's not there. It's like the leaves. A hallucination.

That didn't make her feel any better. She told herself to ignore it; she couldn't start cracking now. She especially couldn't start cracking in front of any hidden cameras. Who knows what they'd do with her if they thought she was going crazy.

What if I am going crazy?

She got into the shower and tried to calm herself down. It didn't help that the rust and paint flakes stubbornly refused to wash off. When she finished her shower, that whole side of her body was flushed and red from scrubbing. And it *still* itched.

When the nurse came, at seven-thirty, just like last time. Allison expected some comment about the dirt on her arm. It felt as if it was actually starting to raise a rash. But, as she'd feared, the nurse didn't even seem to notice.

She went through the routine with the pill, and by the time the nurse left, the paint, the rust, and the itch were all gone as if they'd never existed. Just like the taste of leaves, before.

01 NOVEMBER   NAVARRO COUNTY, TEXAS

9:23 AM   MONDAY

Her first "class" was at nine-thirty. She had learned that
via yet another unsubtle invasion of privacy—as if she had
any privacy left. While she had been out getting breakfast,
someone had gone into her room, collected her notebooks
and her backpack, and arranged it all on her bed along
with a little computer-printed schedule.

Her first reaction had been a desire to throw the backpack across the room, but she was restrained by the paranoid instinct telling her that they were always watching. So
she put on a show of taking it in stride.

Inside, though, she still burned. She wanted out of this
place. She wanted Dad, she wanted Macy, and she wanted
her own life back. She told herself that she'd gladly give
her teek back to get away from these people.

However, what frightened her was the possibility that
was a lie. She wanted her teek, and she was afraid that
they might offer it back—take her off this drug—and ask
something in return she shouldn't give.

That was what was preoccupying her as she sat in a lecture
room in Prometheus' classroom building. Everyone else
seemed to just accept things here. Even Zack took this captiv-
ity, and the desires of their captors, as given, unalterable.

The "students" who filed into the hall didn't look like
prisoners. They didn't act like prisoners. She couldn't help
but wonder how many in this room were dragged here by
force. If many were, the acceptance they showed did not
encourage her.

It would be easier if I just gave up.

The thought, after everything that had happened, especially after what happened to Mom, made her ashamed of
herself. Thinking about Mom now, knowing that there
wasn't anything she could do—

The instructor interrupted her thoughts. She wiped her
eyes and glanced at the printout. She wasn't even sure what
class she was in, she had just gone to a room number. The
sheet told her that this was "Standard Orientation."

Below her the instructor was saying, ". . . every first

Monday. All new students are required to attend each monthly lecture their first year here."

It was hard for her to conceive of a more depressing thought than the idea of her "first year," at this place.

"Some of you are new arrivals, and some of you have been here for a few months. I want to remind you all to pay attention, since what we cover here in this orientation lecture is fundamental to your ability to understand and do well here at Prometheus. Everything I'll say bears repetition, and you should pay attention even if you've heard it before—am I right, Mr. Harris?"

Someone in the first row turned around to face the front. "Yes, ah, right, Dr. Lawrence."

Allison wiped her eyes and watched Dr. Lawrence. It was just like any other class she'd ever attended, except this one felt as if it might be a matter of life or death. She paid attention.

As Zack had told her, Orientation told her more about PRI's classification system, and it told her why she was so valuable to these people. PRI divided psychic abilities into three broad classifications.

Class I was defined as purely sensory in nature, and was statistically the most common talent among the kids here. According to Dr. Lawrence, almost all of these talents could be considered variants of telepathy. Even things like psychometry—the reading of "psychic impressions" on objects—and precognition, were telepathic in nature. The telepathic talent seemed to operate on some quantum level where commonsense ideas of time and location meant very little. Images from the past or future meant contact with a past or future mind, and the mind was a nonlocalized event, a wavelike entity that extended beyond the physical body.

Much of it went over Allison's head. Dr. Lawrence often apologized for all the scientific jargon, but he went on using it anyway.

Class II was defined as nonphysical interference in the physical world. That contradictory definition applied to the much rarer talents that affected probability in some predictable fashion. The operation of these talents was obscure and not well understood, and Dr. Lawrence didn't do a good job of explaining it. Allison gathered that this group included the dice-rollers she had heard about. From the explanation, the Class IIs did not directly affect the motion of the dice to make a number come up, they altered the probability of a number coming up. Dr. Lawrence said that Class IIs directly altered the probabilistic wave equations of quantum mechanics—whatever that meant.

Allison was a Class III because she dealt directly with physical matter and energy. Class III grouped the only talents that dealt with the gross manipulation of macroscopic objects. It was the rarest talent of all, amounting to two people in all of PRI. Three people including Allison. Fortunately, Dr. Lawrence didn't point her out to the rest of the class.

There were countless subtleties to PRI's classification system. There were Class I talents that didn't fit into a subclass of telepathy. And when Dr. Lawrence began talking about tests and comparisons, Allison was uncomfortably aware of the film she had seen.

Those twins had been here, and they had died here. She became conscious of the things Dr. Lawrence *wasn't* talking about. Like *how* they had come to find what certain drugs did, or *how* they had located the hot spots of activity in the brain.

"By now all of you, even those of you who have recently arrived—" This time Dr. Lawrence did look at her. It was the first time he'd acknowledged her presence as anything other than just another captive student. "—have some idea of where you are in this classification system. I would like to remind you that this is merely a catalog, and not a measure of worth. All these talents are incredibly valuable when reproducible, and all our researches indicate that they come from a common source in the brain. The same neurochemistry is involved in all of these, and as we progress with our genetic sequencing, it appears that a common cluster of genes is responsible as well."

He walked out in front of the podium to look at all of them, but at Allison in particular. "As we teach you about your own powers, you're teaching us how they work. And all of you who show *any* ability have the potential to show them all. Think about that whenever you feel unduly burdened in one of your classes. Someday one of you may give us the key to unlock all of this in all of you. . . ."

The bell rang. Dr. Lawrence looked up at the clock and said, "Class dismissed."

01 NOVEMBER   NAVARRO COUNTY, TEXAS

1:15 PM   MONDAY

The phrase, "all of this in all of you," had run through Allison's head most of the day. What if PRI could manage that? What if there was some magic neurotransmitter that could give everyone with the right genes the ability to read minds, or levitate—

Or to teek a quarter at the speed of a bullet?

No wonder so many kids seemed to accept this. They were being offered a huge incentive. "Stick with us and one day you'll work miracles." Allison now understood that there were more than the obvious reasons that she, and Zack, and Jessica were valuable to PRI. They were proof that such power was possible. PRI could encourage their students by telling them that, one day, *they* could do that.

The rest of her morning had been filled with classes that wouldn't be out of place at Euclid High. In fact, they gave her some of the same classes. Someone, somewhere, must have gotten hold of her class schedule. That served to make her just that much more paranoid, and made her feel even more alone and exposed.

And all that was nothing compared to what she was undergoing right now. She'd known that, eventually, they would insist on some sort of physical examination. But she wasn't prepared for it. After everything else, the little computer-written line on her schedule, "1:30 PM Medical Appointment—Room M-1005," terrified her.

Now, at fifteen after, after barely eating lunch and ignoring Zack in the cafeteria, she sat in a cold waiting room clutching the little slip of paper.

The waiting room was uncomfortably similar to every other hospital waiting room she had ever been in. The chairs were cheap metal tubing and plastic, the floor slick linoleum tile, and the walls were cream-colored and covered with standard public health posters. Somehow the ordinariness of this place made it worse. Her mind kept drifting back to the last time she was in a hospital, right after Chuck had attacked her.

Worse, when she didn't think about that, she thought about the film, and long needles. She thought of walking away several times. But what good would it do? She was trapped, and they were more than capable of forcing her to cooperate, and cooperation was the only real lever she had with these people.

The last line on her paper was, "6:00 PM Family Visit—Room A-3307." That kept her going, and it trapped her. She was going to see Dad and Macy, but if she began fighting now, they could easily take that away. She had made a bargain with Stone, cooperation in exchange for Dad and Macy.

She was ashamed by the wish that she wasn't bound by such a deal, and by the wish that she didn't care about the hostages they held for her benefit.

"Allison Boyle?" called the nurse, like every other nurse in every other waiting room.

They try so hard to keep this all normal, Allison thought, *and all they manage is to make everything more bizarre.*

They tried to make it comfortable, they even had a woman doctor do the examination. It didn't help. Allison still had to undress, and even with the hospital gown they gave her, she still felt naked throughout the whole endless process.

They took her blood, her urine, her saliva. They poked and prodded every crevice in her body. They laid her on a slab, strapped her head in a vise so it couldn't move, and rolled her into a huge machine they called a nuclear magnetic resonance imager. They taped electrodes to her chest, her arms, and her forehead, and recorded a lot of wavy lines.

Allison gritted her teeth and endured it all, even though it seemed a more thorough rape than Chuck ever could have managed. The only high point to all of it was when they commented that they would be testing her telekinetic abilities sometime tomorrow.

After that, the thought that they would take her off their little teek-nullifying drug, even for a little while, made the rest of their examinations tolerable.

CHAPTER
TWENTY-FIVE

01 NOVEMBER   NAVARRO COUNTY, TEXAS

5:43 PM   MONDAY

"Christ, man, when are you going to do something?" Allison's friend, Macy, paced through the living room making a point of walking in front of the television.

John Charvat wasn't watching the TV anyway. He was seated in one of two chairs that occupied the living room of one of the Institute's prefab houses. He wondered if housing Macy with him was a security decision, some sort of subtle psychological move on Stone's part, or if it was simply a matter of efficiency. There had always been something of a housing shortage here, and many employees lived "off campus" so to speak—even though security would prefer it otherwise.

Not much had changed here. From his point of view that was a good thing.

"Are you even listening to me?" Macy said. "Has it sunk in to that buzz-cut head of yours that we're prisoners here?"

Yes, and that every word you're saying is being recorded. John allowed himself a furtive glance upward at a vent in the wall above the television. There would be one of four security cameras that covered almost every square foot of this house. He had made a point to sit with his paper, and his crosswords, right in plain view.

"There's little I can do, Macy. We're fifty miles from the nearest city, twenty from the nearest interstate. Nothing gets in or out of this place without Stone's blessing." John kept writing with the marker in his hand. His notes were cryptic and strayed out of bounds of the crossword puzzle. He kept the writing tilted on his knee out of view from both Macy and the camera.

"That's your daughter they're keeping prisoner—and you're sitting there with a damn crossword puzzle."

"What do you want me to do? Plan some daring escape? How?" John marked a bold line on the paper that represented the main fence line dividing the tract housing from the airstrip.

"You worked here—"

John nodded. "Then accept that I know how unlikely escaping this place is." John knew exactly how unlikely. On his little map he had marked all the observation towers in the Institute's private little suburb, in the past two days he'd managed to refamiliarize himself with the setup. There were only a few places where the terrain offered some cover from the cameras. He had come up with a very circuitous route to the airfield.

Even with the constant surveillance, John felt perfectly safe saying his next thought aloud. "Even if you and I got out of here, Allison's still in there, behind three layers of security. How would you get her out?" *How will I get her out?*

Macy shook her head and said, "Damn." She dropped into the other chair, rubbing her arms and—to John it seemed—trying not to cry. "It's so rotten, just sitting here, not being able—"

"I know."

"If we could just pretend that we're getting out of here. Even if we're fooling ourselves, I'd feel better."

John nodded. He looked at his little map. *Am I fooling myself just to make myself feel better? I haven't flown anything since 'Nam, and how* am *I going to get Allison out of that place?*

John folded the paper and reached over to attempt to comfort Macy—

Just then, without warning, the door burst open.

John's first thought was, *They don't need us anymore.*

His second thought, as three of the Prometheus security goons marched into the center of the living room, was, *They saw the map.*

Macy stared at them, as if she'd been expecting them. "So? What now?"

A more innocuous-looking woman followed the guards into the living room. John noticed that the name tag read "Dr. Zendel." Unfamiliar name, after his time. Even so, looking at her, John had her pegged as Psych—

"If you'd please come with us, Mr. Charvat, we have a meeting scheduled."

John stood up, paper folded in his hand. "With whom?"

"Miss Boyle," Dr. Zendel said, with a hint of annoyance.

Macy jumped up and said, *"Allie?"*

John felt just as excited as Macy. Not just because they were letting them see his daughter. Stone had no reason at all to keep him and Macy happy, which meant that this was happening to keep Allison cooperative. The fact Stone was allowing this meeting—in fact, Dr. Zendel's whole attitude—meant that something significant was happening with "Miss Boyle."

01 NOVEMBER   NAVARRO COUNTY, TEXAS

6:02 PM   MONDAY

"Dad!" Allison cried when he walked through the door. She ran up and hugged him. He stopped in the doorway, as if surprised at her reaction. She must have surprised him, since she'd surprised herself.

Allison recognized the man who had opened the door for Dad. He was the evil-looking Gary Busey type who'd escorted her from Stone's office. "One hour," he told them. The door shut after him.

Allison let go of her dad and looked at the door, "Hey, what about Macy?"

"Don't worry. She's all right."

"But I'm supposed to see *both* of you."

Dad walked over and sat down on the couch. The room was an institutional attempt at a living room, including a recliner and a coffee table. But the large mirror facing the couch was somewhat out of place.

"From what they said," he told her, "which wasn't much, you'll get to see her tomorrow."

Allison shook her head in disgust. "What? Are they afraid I'll try and escape with both of you? You have any idea how many of their armed goons are in this building—"

"Actually, yes, I do."

Allison turned and looked at Dad. He looked trapped. Allison was confounded by equal waves of sympathy and irritation at this man she hardly knew.

She sat down next to him. "I don't know anything about you, you know."

"I'm sorry about that. I'm afraid you don't have the greatest father."

Allison took his hand. "Why don't you tell me about him?"

He chuckled. "To be honest, it isn't very interesting—"

Allison didn't believe that, and her look must have told her father so.

He sighed. "For a while I had the normal family setup— at least normal when I was growing up—two parents, a brother, and my granddad all on a little farm in upstate New York. Lived there until I was eighteen, when I was drafted."

Dad went to Vietnam in 1966. It didn't take long before he was transferred into special operations run by ASI. He was promoted and placed in charge of special psychological operations over North Vietnam.

"What was it you did?"

"Mostly air-dropped things. Pamphlets, drugs, odd little boxes built by the CIA—"

"No, I mean you were one of PRI's kids, weren't you? That was why they recruited you, right?"

"Oh, yes . . ."

Dad told her that, by the time he entered the Army, the ASI had developed a number of blood tests that could screen out probable psychics. They had a laundry list of indicator hormones and neurotransmitters, and they were able to slip the tests into otherwise normal physicals. In Vietnam they managed to screen out over a thousand people that way. Many of the talents were unstable, liable to burn out while the person was still a teenager. Most of the people ASI recruited were eighteen, and half were still "usable."

Dad's talent was what Prometheus called a Class II. He

was a dice-roller. Or, as his friends in the Army called him, he was a lucky charm.

"It was a side effect of my talent that most of my tour was boring. Most of the time we were never even shot at. There was one time we were hit by a SAM, but the missile never went off, it just sheared the tip off of one wing."

ASI had him pilot thirty or forty missions into North Vietnam, until the blood tests suggested his talents were flaring out. Shortly after he was grounded, he slipped in an Officer's Club and fractured his leg. He spent the rest of his military career in a hospital.

"By then, I'd put in my time and the Army discharged me."

Unfortunately for Dad, things had changed while he was away. His brother and grandfather had died in a fire that had swept through the farmhouse. His parents dealt with it as best they could, but the stress ended in their divorce, and the sale of the farm.

"My grandparents?" Allison asked.

Dad smiled. It was a sad smile, but the first real one he'd given her. "Oh, they're still kicking. Your granddad opened a farm supply store back home. He's still running it, and a few others as well. He refuses to retire. Your grandmother went back to school, moved to Washington, D.C. I think it might have been a reaction to my being drafted, but she became an antiwar activist. She actually met your mom before I did. She was working for Amnesty International last I heard—but I don't keep in touch much."

It was incredible hearing about his half of her family. It was incredible just having an extended family.

"I'd like to meet them someday."

Dad reached out and squeezed her hand. "I hope you can."

"Your brother," Allison asked. "How old was he?"

"Sixteen."

"Do you think . . . ?" Allison couldn't finish the question. But she could see in her dad's eyes that he knew what she was asking. These talents PRI bred, they could be dangerous. Dad had said that the more powerful the talents of the second generation were, the less reliable they were.

"That he could have been the cause of the fire? I wish I knew."

"Why did you keep working for them?" Allison asked.

Dad sighed. "No grand reason. I did it because they hired me and they paid well. There isn't much work for ex-spooks."

"So you ended up running security here?"

"Eventually—"

Dad was interrupted by the door opening. "Your hour is up," said Mr. Busey, as Allison had begun thinking of the guard.

"But," she began to object. The time had gone much too fast for her. There was so much else she wanted to talk about, even when she excluded the things she couldn't say while PRI was monitoring their conversation.

"Shh, Allie," Dad said as he stood up. "I'll see you in a couple of days. They don't want you to think they're keeping me from you." There was a little smile in the way he said that, as if he was hoarding some secret victory between them.

"Yeah, right," Allison responded, realizing that Dad was aware of how much Stone valued her. He might even know that she was the one who'd forced the meeting.

"Hey, this will work out somehow." Dad's voice made it an empty sentiment, but something in his eyes said, "We'll get them." She wondered if she was imagining it.

"Believe it or not, I do love you." He squeezed her hand as he said "love" and let it drop as he left.

Allison looked at her hand. There were things she needed to talk to Dad about. Things she couldn't talk about in front of microphones.

But what if those things weren't what she was talking about? She kept staring at her hand, thought of Zack's comic books, and began developing the germ of an idea.

"This will work out somehow," she whispered.

01 NOVEMBER   NAVARRO COUNTY, TEXAS

8:15 PM   MONDAY

George sat at one end of the table in the briefing room, Stone sat at the other. At the moment, George was shaking his head, an expression of disbelief on his face.

Stone held up his hand to silence a scientist who was speaking. "Is there something wrong, George?"

George let out a humorless chuckle. "Wrong? If I understand right, you killed Elroy to cut open his brain. What the hell could be wrong?"

The scientist who had been addressing the room said, "There were chemical and structural studies that we couldn't do with the NMR—"

"Christ, Simpson thinks I'm objecting on a practical basis," George whispered.

"We can talk about your problems later," Stone said to George. Then he turned to Simpson and said, "Please, continue."

Simpson nodded, glancing at George before he went on. He pressed a button on the remote in his hand; in response, an image was projected on the wall of the room. The image was a magnified view of a tangled mass of nerve cells. "This shows what I've been describing about Billy Jackson—Elroy. Pay particular attention to the density of the interconnections here." He pressed the remote again. "And here. These are from sites we know are related to Class I activity. And for your reference—" The image changed again to show a picture formed of a series of vertical gray bars, each crossed by random black stripes of varied intensity. Three sites had been highlighted by red boxes. "This is Billy Jackson's genetic profile. The marker sites we relate to Class I, II, and III activity are indicated."

Simpson walked in front of the projection and pointed to the one box that enclosed a number of black bars. "Obviously, from Billy Jackson's profile even the nonbiologists here can see this is the Class I site. The other markers are absent." He indicated the other red boxes, which enclosed empty spots on two other bars.

"Now, back to the anomaly—" He pressed his remote. The image changed to a view of neurons again, similar to the first but slightly different. "This is from the only site—so far—that we can associate with Class III activity. These branchings should not be there. And the biochemical tests bear out the fact that Billy Jackson had developed into a latent Class III."

Stone shook his head. "Is this something we could have missed earlier?"

"Emphatically not. Biochemically, at least, Billy Jackson changed after he went into the field. For the first time we have a brain and neurochemistry different from the genetic profile."

"I assume you've double-checked everything?"

Simpson nodded.

"So what about the girl?" Stone asked.

"We've only got preliminary tests from the blood the field team extracted. We'll have better data after this afternoon's tests are fully processed."

"Fine," Stone said, "you've hedged. Now what do we know?"

"She just has the Class III genetic markers, which we could have predicted. But the chemical markers—" he paused.

"Yes?"

"This is preliminary, you understand."

Stone nodded.

"She has all the markers we associate with Class I *and* Class II activity."

One of the seated scientists shook her head. "Great! You've just shot down all the work we've done in genetic sequencing."

"No," George said. He was still shaking his head, and he said wearily, "He hasn't. Your great Change, Stone, isn't it?"

"It's why I called this briefing." Stone gave George a cold smile. "You should be happy that, for once here, physics has led the life sciences."

The scientist who'd complained about genetics spoke. "Would someone explain this to me?"

Stone looked at George, "You are the physicist, and you did bring the girl in."

The color drained from George's face as he stood. He gave a curt nod to Simpson, almost a dismissive gesture, and began to address the assembled scientists. "Most of you are here, at PRI, because you are practical scientists. My realm has been theory, trying to explain the data you people keep handing me. Collectively, we in physics have tried to provide the Institute with a coherent description of the nonlocal mind, a quantum description of the events you record here. A description of the mind as a wave function."

George walked in front of the projected neurons. He did not look like a man used to talking before an audience. His eyes tried to hide in the shadows of the projected image.

"Our best effort so far has been predicting the interference of one mind with another, especially how some talents will cancel others. But it is characteristic of waves that interference need not be destructive, damping the wave. There is a possibility, which we've predicted, that there could be constructive interference."

There was an excited babble in the room which persisted until Stone cleared his throat. George loosened his tie as the crowd grew silent. Stone said quietly, "Layman's terms, for the psychologists."

There was one nervous chuckle in the room. It wasn't from George.

He walked over to a lab cart where a pair of small devices sat. "Mr. Stone wanted a demonstration. I have here a pair of signal generators." He switched on one of the devices, and a low, numbing tone filled the room. "You're listening to a rather low-amplitude sound wave." He turned on the other. Another low sound filled the room, and the combined noise was barely audible. "Two sounds are now being piped in from opposite ends of the room, through the PA system. In a perfectly controlled environment you would be hearing nothing now, because both waves are exactly ninety degrees out of phase. The interference is destructive, the waves are destroying each other, in the way that psi talents cancel each other out."

George adjusted the dial on one device, "Note that I am not changing the *amplitude*—the 'volume'—of the waves—"

Even so, the low bass sound became louder and louder until it hurt the fillings in the listeners' teeth and vibrated the floor beneath them. The sound was becoming intolerable just at the point Stone said, "Enough." He had to raise his voice.

George flipped the switch on one of the boxes. The

sound level dropped down to the original soft bass tone. "That was constructive interference."

01 NOVEMBER   NAVARRO COUNTY, TEXAS

11:05 PM   MONDAY

Allison sat on the roof of the girls' dormitory. The area was fenced in well short of the roof's edge, but she could still have a view of the area beyond where she was supposed to go. At the moment, she was staring off in the direction of the landing strip, invisible now except for the lights along its edge.

She had been sitting here and thinking for hours.

"Allison Boyle, I presume." The voice was female, and it came from behind her. Allison turned to face the speaker, though she had an idea of who it was.

"Jessica Mason," Allison said.

It was. Her red hair was unmistakable, even in the ill-lit gloom up here. Something about Jessica, her expression, her body language, something subliminal, put Allison on edge.

"I'm here to offer a belated welcome to the Institute." She smiled at Allison, but it was a frightening smile. It was a smile someone might make while inflicting, or receiving, great pain.

Allison nodded and said, "Thank you." It was the only appropriate thing she could think of.

Jessica walked to the fence surrounding the small courtyard on the roof. Light from below painted chain-link shadows on Jessica's face. "I see you're already pushing the boundaries, Allison."

"Huh?" Allison stood up.

"It's an hour after curfew. What if security found out?"

It was Allison's turn for a grim smile. "I'm quite sure they know exactly where I am at all times."

Jessica looked at her, and her smile disappeared. "You're taking liberties. That's dangerous."

Allison folded her arms and resisted an urge to back

away. Fear had run her life for so long now that it seemed that she had little left. "What do you want?" she asked.

"I want to know what *you* want, Allison."

The tone of voice, her forced familiarity, reminded Allison of Chuck. The thought should have scared her, or at least heightened the paranoid anxiety that had gripped her ever since PRI had brought her here. Instead, Allison felt her resolve strengthen. She looked Jessica in the eyes and tried to discover something in there.

"I want to be left alone." *I want my life back.*

Jessica stared back with an intensity that seemed to deaden any expression she had. "Is that all? I hope it is."

An odd breeze brushed Allison's cheek. A wind warmer than the cooling scrubland surrounding Prometheus, a breath of air from much earlier in the day. Then it was gone. Jessica looked away as the breeze passed, and Allison remembered what Zack had said. Jessica was not under any chemical restraints.

"You've talked to Zachary Lanagan."

Zachary Lanagan? In another context, Allison might have found the name amusing.

Jessica was still talking, pacing in a slow circle around her. "He's given you some distorted notions of who I am."

"So who are you?" Allison asked.

"Do you know what this place really is? Do you know what it means?" Jessica kept pacing around her. The words sounded as if they were written by Howard Stone, but the tone was much different. There was no trace of idealism or mysticism, however twisted, around Jessica. Her speech was matter-of-fact, basic, practical. "Prometheus is designed to make superhumans. Everything here is designed to create people who do what we do, better than we do, freed of all the accidents of biology." Jessica stopped pacing. "You know what it means when they succeed?"

"Stone's Change?"

Jessica laughed. "Stone wants a Messiah. He wants his little factory to churn out a hundred thousand Christs. . . . There's going to be a change all right. But it's going to be a less than spiritual one." She turned around and looked at Allison again. "When they open that door, unleash that power, we are going to inherit this planet."

This time Allison did take a step back. "What are you talking about?"

"Inevitability. The question is not if we'll take control, but who will be in charge when it happens."

"That's insane," Allison said. Her voice had faded to a whisper.

Jessica smiled coldly. "Why? Even with what's here, in this compound today, a competent leader could take over a small government completely. One coercer here, a few dice-rollers at the polls, enough telepaths providing enough information to control the legislature. And then there are the Class IIIs like you and me. . . ."

Allison stepped back again, and Jessica took a step forward. "The human body is such a delicate instrument." Jessica smiled when she said that.

"You can't be serious about all this?"

"Don't be naive," Jessica snapped. "Whatever Stone says, it's why we're here. PRI thinks they'll be in control when the floodgates open. But it will be *me*."

"I see."

"I don't think you do. You've come in here, and you've taken some obvious security in the value Prometheus places on your talents. But I've spent six years here, preparing. If I wanted to, my people could take this place. Do you believe me?"

Allison was speechless. All she could do was stand there and look at Jessica. Belatedly, the fear finally came. It was no longer the paranoid fear of PRI, but fear of just how little control they might have over what they were unleashing. Slowly, she nodded.

"You want to be left alone. I'll leave you alone. But I want you to believe this. I've earned what I have, and God help anyone who threatens it. Anyone. And never once think your value to Prometheus protects you from that." Jessica turned and left Allison alone on the roof.

Beyond the airstrip, the Texas wilderness looked lonelier than ever.

CHAPTER
TWENTY-SIX

Allison sat up in her bed. The taste of dust was in her mouth, and the memory of the abandoned corridors of Euclid Heights High was fresh in her mind. Three nights in a row. It was starting to scare her. It was as if Chuck had locked himself into some dim corner of her mind and waited for the moment when her defenses were at their lowest to torment her.

That thought woke her up the rest of the way. She sat in her bed and ran her tongue over the hallucinatory grit in her mouth. Maybe that was exactly what was happening, why she heard the whispers about time, why she noticed all those clocks.

As if to confirm the suspicion, the taste of dust disappeared, as if she had already swallowed their little yellow pill. She shuddered. *If I'm right, that means I really* am *in some sort of contact with Chuck, and these are more than just nightmares.*

It was an ugly thought, but she could almost hear Chuck's voice saying, "Bingo, sweetcakes."

She hugged herself and whispered, "Stop calling me that."

Allison tried to shower the feelings away. She didn't want to believe that Chuck was still there, in her head. It was fine to think such things in a dream, but it was very bad when the idea began to make sense in the real world—

If there was still such a thing as the real world.

But it made a perverted sort of sense. Chuck's nocturnal visits could have been a product of her own mind, but if they were, why did they cease when they put her on the yellow pill? She could even remember, before he had faded away, about him mentioning something about "anti-mindwarp crap." Could that be the same thing as Zack's "pharmaceutical leash?"

She even began wondering how Chuck could know something like that before she did.

Why was she looking for him in the dream?

Zack said that those drugs did more than disable her teek, they interfered with everything. Maybe even some psychic process in her own head. Maybe the reason Chuck faded away that last time was because that's when the anti-psychic drug kicked in for the first time.

As she toweled herself off, she knew what Chuck was trying to say with these nightmares.

It is time. This is the only time.

She stood in front of the sink and looked at the faucet. And, like a limb numb from lack of use, she could feel her teek reach out. The sense was much fuzzier than she was used to, and much fainter. It was as if she was drunk and much too far away. But her teek was there, and it brushed through the metallic lattice that was the substance of the faucet.

She tried to tie it to part of the faucet, and it was like groping through ethereal mud. The effort built a pressure behind her forehead that felt as if it must burst through the skin.

Her own hand reached for the faucet, her fingers touching it lightly as she felt her teek move it, letting the water into the sink.

Allison smiled.

That was it. The drug only lasted so long. By this time in the morning, the dose they had given her was beginning to wear off. That was what Chuck was saying. Suddenly, Allison felt as if freedom might really be within her reach.

She let her teek sink back into her head. They were going to be testing her today, and she was going to see Macy. The closer she came to escaping this place, the less she could afford to let the little gray men behind the cameras realize what she was thinking.

But it was very hard not to smile as she brushed her teeth.

When the nurse gave her the little yellow pill, Allison's teek clamped onto it with a throbbing death grip. As the nurse checked her mouth, Allison held the pill in an agonizing stasis, hovering in her throat, feeling as if it would strangle her. When the nurse left, she pulled it back into her mouth.

When she dressed, she spit it into her hand as she pulled a shirt over her head, the cameras none the wiser.

02 November   Navarro County, Texas

9:35 am   Tuesday

George slept at his desk, his head resting on his arms. The office was dark, the only light a dusky rose glow seeping in from the closed louvers on the windows. Jane stood in the doorway, quietly watching him.

After a few minutes, she knocked on the open door.

George grunted and stirred, slowly pushing himself upright in his chair. He blinked up at Jane, glanced at the windows, and then at the clock on his desk.

"Long night?" she asked.

George ran his hands through his white hair. "When my first thought is 'am or pm?'" He stretched and grunted. "Yeah, long night."

Jane walked over to the windows and opened the blinds. George shaded his eyes and turned away. "You lit some sort of fire under Stone's ass last night, you know that?"

"Yeah," George said. "I know."

Jane turned around, facing George's back. "Mind telling me what's going on?"

George waved a hand in a helpless gesture. "Didn't you know?"

"I wasn't at the meeting—"

"About Elroy, I mean."

Jane folded her arms. "What about him?"

"They found Stone's Holy Grail. Apparently what pushed Elroy over the edge also induced some latent Class III biochemistry, including some changes to the gross structures of the brain."

"That's great. No wonder Stone's—" Jane's expression faded as she walked around the desk to face George. "You're talking about more than a simple NMR map, aren't you?"

George nodded. He looked up at her and said, "Aren't you the one who keeps telling me that I knew what I was getting into with all of this?"

Jane nodded and sat at the end of the desk. "Yeah, that was me, wasn't it?" She exhaled and shook her head.

George turned in his chair and started tapping at a computer keyboard. "I've been trying to come up with some workable model for what happened. I've given lip service to constructive interference, but saying that is a long way from coming up with a working model."

"Constructive interference?" Jane's voice sounded uncertain.

George nodded, apparently unaware that Jane was facing away from him. "The wave model we've been using does well in predicting Class I behavior, but it's incomplete. We've always assumed that the sensitivity of the purely mental forms carries all the way through the spectrum. But there's some underlying unity there, and with the power of the Class III, there's a chance that the waveform's more robust, that constructive interference might not destroy the basis of the talent—"

Jane turned around and held up a hand. "Stop for air. You've lost me."

George did take a breath, a deep one.

"Now," Jane said. "Can you talk down to the biologist for a moment?"

George nodded. "Yes. It *is* simple, really, if I can ever get the math to work out. Each talent is like a wave on the ocean. What defines what it does is the shape of the wave. It extends in several dimensions, but just picture it in two dimensions—wavelength and amplitude. Two waves meet, and you have a new wave, one plus the other, which

has a different wavelength, and a different amplitude. Can
you picture that?"

Jane nodded.

"Destructive interference happens when the two waves
damp each other's effects, flattening out the wave. Constructive interference reinforces parts of the wave, increasing the amplitude. Unfortunately, I think our models are
confused."

"Why?"

"Because all Class I interference seems destructive, because talents seem to screen each other out. A telepath
cannot read a Class III brain, and so on. But I've begun to
think that's because telepathy might just be too sensitive
to *any* alteration in the waveform. Other talents, especially
Class IIIs, may be much more robust, maintaining their
characteristics throughout all sorts of interference."

"I think I follow you. But why is this important?"

"Because of what happened to Elroy. There's feedback,
and when two talents interact, there may be a change in
the biology." George looked up from the computer.
"That's the theory anyway."

02 NOVEMBER   NAVARRO COUNTY, TEXAS

1:45 PM   TUESDAY

Allison lay on a table with growing impatience as a doctor attached wires to her forehead, her arms, and just about
everywhere else. They were going to test her teek, and
despite the indignity of being strapped down and told to
perform on demand, she wanted to let loose her newly
freed talent. It wanted to be used. She felt the same curiosity about the limits of her teek, the same need to find the
limits that had prompted all of her experiments.

She was also curious about what exactly they wanted her
to do. The room they'd placed her in was cramped with
examination equipment. The green-tagged lab technicians
barely had room to maneuver around her.

"Now just listen to the instructions over the speaker,"

the tech to the left told her as he attached the wires from her body to boxes lined against the walls. "If you feel any discomfort, say so and we can abort the test."

Come on, let's get started. . . .

The tech to her right had rolled up her sleeve and was swabbing her arm. "When we set up the drip, there may be a slight feeling of euphoria. That's normal."

Allison nodded, though inside she felt the first twinges of fear. If this was to counterbalance the effects of the yellow pill they'd been feeding her, what would it do to her when she wasn't drugged at all? Their little pill was still safely in her pocket, gathering lint.

She felt the pressure of the intravenous needle as it slid into the vein in her arm. Instead of a bag, the tube leading to the needle led off to another machine. The tech taped it in place.

"There we are," he said. "You'll be ready in about five minutes." He looked across her at the tech with the wires, and they nodded at each other. They both walked out of the room, leaving her to stare across at a blank wall made of acoustical tile.

Great, what if I have to go to the bathroom?

At least now she had some idea why they said she shouldn't eat or drink anything today. She lay there for long minutes, until it felt like the table had dropped away from beneath her, leaving her floating.

"Hello, Miss Boyle," came a voice from an invisible speaker. *"Please relax, while I explain the testing apparatus."*

"Relax," Allison muttered to herself, "I'm flying."

In front of her, the wall she faced began withdrawing into the ceiling. Behind it was a glass partition that appeared a foot thick. The window looked out on blackness. As the man spoke to her, spotlights began to come on in the room beyond.

"The machine you see was built for industrial use, so you needn't worry about damaging it."

The thing spotlit in the next room *looked* industrial. Four threaded columns emerged from a square metal base that was four feet on a side. The columns were taller than Allison was, and each was thicker than her arm. At the top of the machine, the columns screwed into a metal plate, and between the base and that plate, each column supported an arm that angled in toward the center of the framework. The four arms all reached in to hold one side of a silvery metal plate. The plate was a foot square and mounted so that it faced her.

"This machine was originally designed for testing alloy samples to destruction. We've modified it to measure the stresses on the sample. Each of those arms can measure forces in three dimensions up to . . ."

There was a partially imagined whisper in her ear, "Hiya, sweetcakes."

Allison blinked and turned her head, which wasn't a good idea. The stuff dripping into her arm was making her light-headed.

"Miss me?"

Allison closed her eyes to make Chuck's voice go away. But instead, she was greeted by the Euclid High School now familiar from her nightmares. The sight was as vivid as the room where she was strapped to a table. The vision was even more surreal because the voice from the speaker was leaking in here.

"—tension and compression as well as movement in space. The sample we want you to work with is a plain carbon steel—"

Even as she heard the speaker's voice, she could taste the dead air and cobwebs in the abandoned science wing. In her mind she walked down a corridor lit only by dagger shafts of sunlight prying through the cracks in the window boards.

Somehow she could still be strapped to a table somewhere at Prometheus, and be *here* kicking dust, garbage, and old leaves. She was tempted to open her eyes and end the vision—

Chuck's voice came from one of the labs she passed. "Sense of euphoria, huh?"

Allison turned to see Chuck leaning in the doorway of Mr. Franklin's classroom. "It is the drug," Allison said.

"Bingo," Chuck said. He waved her into the lab, "Come in here before that guy stops droning."

Allison could still hear the voice from outside. *"—monitoring pulse rate, electrical activity in the brain—"*

She cautiously followed Chuck into the lab. The room was swathed in darkness and cobwebs, and things skittered around in the corners. The blackboard had collapsed at an angle. On the floor, between it and the teacher's desk, was a mummified corpse. Allison stopped, staring at it.

"Oh, jeez," Chuck said, "That guy'd be harmless even if he was real." He kicked the body with a steel-toed boot and was rewarded with a billowing cloud of dust.

Allison winced. "Did you choose this place?"

Chuck looked at her and shook his head. "You think I like being trapped here?" He shoved the body out of the way with his boot and said, "At least they ain't warm and squishy."

"They?"

"Come on, take a seat. We ain't got but a few minutes before you're supposed to perform."

There was one unbroken seat available. When she sat, she saw that Chuck had some of Mr. Franklin's physics apparatus. He had a slide projector out, pointed at the blank spot on the wall where the blackboard had fallen away.

"First off," Chuck said, "you got to get off of that pill. But you knew that."

Allison nodded, she had already figured out how.

"Things you don't know— I was one of Stone's kids. Telepathy, saw in other folks' heads."

"My God."

"Believe me, sweetcakes, He had nothing to do with it. Was thing numero uno that fucked up my excuse for a life." He paced in front of the slide projector, framing his face in the light. Chuck looked a little odd, as if he was a double exposure, something that was more a projection than actually there.

"You're fading," Allison said.

"You noticed," Chuck said. "I said we don't have time, and it's taking what I got left to talk while you're conscious." The shadow on the wall behind him began graying out. He looked at his hand and said, "Fuck. Quickly, three things—

"One, you got to get out of here *now*. I still occasionally hear things on the melon pipeline. All hell's going to break out soon, once that redhead figures out Stone's found his Change."

Allison stood. "What do you mean?"

Chuck held up his hand, she could see though it now. "No time. The more I keep up with this, the less it's me. And I got two more things. This place, the High School, it isn't imaginary."

She was still standing, and as she watched, Chuck seemed to loose his individuality. He wasn't just fading, but he was taking on the same gray cast as the rest of the school around them. His voice even seemed to be losing its character.

"What do you mean?" Allison said.

"It's all the same thing," said the ghost Chuck. "Telepathy, telekinesis, precognition . . . It's all from the same place. This *is* Euclid Heights High in a decade or so."

"How?"

He shook his head. "No time. I'm losing it—" Quickly, he arranged dusty glassware on the table. He fiddled with an electronic device connected to a threadbare speaker. He pointed the speaker at the glassware. "This is your idea I found, but I need to pull your attention to it before the shit hits the fan."

He flipped the switches on the device, and the room was filled by an irritating high-frequency hum. He angled the speaker slightly, and dust billowed up from the desk. Motes scrambled in the beam from the slide projector, seemingly passing through Chuck's body as if he wasn't fully there anymore.

Chuck began tuning the dial on the box. Allison saw his mouth moving, as if in explanation, but she couldn't hear his words over the rising tone from the device. The sound was painful, like an ice pick in her ear.

Then, suddenly the glassware in front of the speaker shattered.

Chuck turned off the device, and the sound faded. He said something inaudible.

"I can't hear you," Allison whispered. At first she thought the noise had deafened her. But she heard her own voice perfectly well, and from another world, she heard the voice from another speaker. "*—await the final checks while the technicians calibrate their equipment. Then we can begin the tests—*"

Chuck looked at her. He had lost almost all definition, becoming little more than a shadow, a thickening in the air. One of his hands brushed the control to the slide projector. A slide fell into place, replacing the white glow with a picture of a suspension bridge. The photo had caught the central span in the midst of bucking like a bronco.

Allison knew the picture. She had seen a film of it in Mr. Franklin's physics class, in this same room. It was the Tacoma Narrows Bridge in Puget Sound. She remembered watching the bridge shake itself apart in what the film's narrator described as a "mild gale."

"What are you trying to say?"

Chuck wasn't there to answer. It seemed like he had dissolved underneath the projection.

"*. . . we're ready, Miss Boyle.*"

Allison opened her eyes and rejoined the real world. After that waking dream, it was a bizarre feeling to realize she was still strapped down here. Allison was confused, torn between wondering what had happened with Chuck and puzzling out what he'd been trying to say to her. The floating feeling had gripped her with redoubled force, and parts of her body seemed impossibly far away.

The man behind the speaker was telling her to use her teek to try and pull the metal plate from the framework. Allison stared at the massive machine, and groped out with her teek—

She had expected some resistance, but the effects of the "pharmaceutical leash" had all but vanished. Her sense flowered out almost instantaneously, flipping her world inside out with dizzying rapidity. If they hadn't strapped her to the table, she would have fallen off.

If anything, the stuff they had dripping in her arm—the stuff that made the real world float and seem far away—made her teek sense sharper. She could feel more of the matter around her. She could feel the individual grains making up the cinder blocks in the next room, like solidified foam. The metal of the testing machine was honeycombed with small crystalline structures. She could feel wires, and screws, bolts, washers. . . .

When she closed her eyes, she felt as if she knew this machine better than she knew anything else in her life.

Allison smiled, Chuck and Euclid Heights High forgotten for the moment. Her heart was racing with the rush of her teek. She clamped her senses around the small test plate with a feeling of exultation. She'd rip it free of its moorings, show them what they were dealing with—

She pumped all of herself into the effort, when she'd done as much as she'd done to the Jeep, she was barely aware of the twinge it caused in her temples.

The plate barely seemed to move at all.

She tried again, in another direction. Still, the plate was held fast by the massive armatures. Frustration slammed her like a fist. These Prometheus people were pulling some cruel hoax on her, only pretending they'd freed her teek. She tried again and again, and it was like pounding her head into the cinder-block walls.

"Good, good. Now if you could try some other mode of movement—"

They were playing games with her. They had drugged her so they could laugh at her expense. The drug only made it worse. It hadn't just freed her teek sense. It seemed to have freed every single emotion she had.

"—Miss Boyle? Are you all right? We can stop now if you—"

Allison ignored the voice. She'd had enough of this. She was gripped with anger and frustration; some of it was directed at Prometheus, but the vast majority of her raw emotion was focused on that square metal plate that hung, mockingly immobile, in front of her.

A mild gale could take down the Tacoma Narrows Bridge, why can't I teek free a chunk of metal?

With that thought, she dislodged the idea that Chuck had been trying to prod free.

Vibration.

It wasn't the force of the wind that had taken the bridge down, it was the frequency. The wind matched the natural frequency of the bridge, each vibration increasing the amplitude of the shaking. . . .

That she could do.

As soon as the idea came to her, she had her teek begin throttling the metal plate. With the shaking of the plate, she felt, with her sharpened teek, the sympathetic vibrations in the machine holding the plate in place. She began a fast, rhythmic shaking. In a way it was just like pushing someone on a swing. You just had to keep pushing a little bit, at the right time, when the swing was moving away from you, and the arc would keep getting longer and longer. That was what she did. She shook the plate with the vibrations of the machine, reinforcing the shaking, the violence of the shaking becoming a little worse with each jolt.

"Miss Boyle, what are you . . . ?"

The voice was interrupted by a noise. The noise was a rumbling, almost subsonic hum that Allison could feel through the table. She could open her eyes now, because what she was doing was becoming easier the more pronounced the shaking became. It was now very easy to feel when to push her teek.

The rumbling became worse. Looking through the window, the machine's vibration was visible. Allison could see dust dancing across the surfaces of the machine, and the details seemed blurred, as if it was all slightly out of focus.

As she watched, the resonant hum was overpowered by a gunshotlike snap as part of the framework failed catastrophically. A bolt flew from the machine and into the glass partition. The window starred, fracturing her view of one of the massive screw columns toppling away from the machine. The framework collapsed with a sound like a car crash.

Allison heard the speaker say, *"Oh, shit."* Even though she knew she wasn't thinking quite straight, Allison smiled.

02 November   Navarro County, Texas

3:23 pm   Tuesday

Jessica sat on one of the benches in the courtyard and felt the world slipping away from her. The character of the staff had changed; she couldn't get hold of people, they wouldn't talk to her. Jessica knew that it was Allison. Mr. Stone and Prometheus had found a new toy, and suddenly they didn't see her as that important.

Most significant was the fact she sat alone in the courtyard while most of PRI's population were in classes, or being tested in the medical building. She should have been in the medical building herself, undergoing her own weekly ritual of tests. Jessica had never much liked that part of PRI's regimen, but it had given her an opportunity to feel her power. She tried not to think that the tests gave her some sense of worth.

And the Prometheus scientists had bumped her tests for Allison Boyle's, leaving Jessica sitting alone in a hot, dry courtyard. She had called on everyone she knew in science when she discovered the rescheduling, and no one would respond to her. All she could reach was voice mail.

She was glad that the staff was too rushed to schedule anything in place of her tests; no one needed to see her this strung out. It was an effort to keep her talent reined in. Every time she saw a guard across the courtyard, she felt an urge to unleash everything. . . .

The 3:30 bell sounded and people began filling the courtyard, passing between buildings. For the first time in a long while, she looked out at the mass of people, PRI's students, and wondered how many were truly her allies. How many would follow her when the time came?

The question had a note of urgency to it, now that she felt that the time was coming. With Allison here, the only way Prometheus' implicit promise to her was ever going to be fulfilled was for her to take it herself.

Oscar and Thad were pushing their way through the crowd toward her. She stood up when she saw them.

Thad was frowning, and that was never a good sign.

"Jessica," Thad said as soon as they were in earshot, "we need to talk."

"What is it?"

"Billy Jackson's apotheosis—" Thad said.

"Stone's Change," Oscar added.

Jessica looked at them both and saw in their expressions something as inevitable as an oncoming train. The two of them stood there, perhaps wanting to be taken somewhere

where they wouldn't be overheard. To Jessica, the secrecy didn't seem to matter anymore.

"What do you mean, Stone's Change?"

Oscar looked around at the students streaming around them.

"What do you mean," Jessica repeated harshly, "Stone's Change?"

Thad spoke. "The rumors are all over the place, but Oscar managed to read from a primary source."

Oscar nodded. "Dr. French, genetics. She was at a meeting last night. Apparently Billy was affected by Allison—"

"Christ," Jessica said, "I could see that."

"No," Thad said. "Oscar means physiology, not psychology. That was the reason for the postmortem you were concerned about."

No. Not now.

Oscar nodded, "Billy was a latent Class III when he came back."

They kept talking to her. She'd been right, the secrecy didn't matter. The rumors had already leaked from the staff, the students around her already knew that something unprecedented was going on. Something that trivialized all of Jessica's effort since arriving here. What was she, if now they could ignite a given talent in anyone's skull?

She was just another cipher, a null, a lab rat.

Nothing had changed since her father had died. She was still only someone's toy. Stone's toy. All her dreams were nothing more than something else to keep her in line. What were they going to do to her now? Now that she knew she was worthless to them. . . .

"Jess?" Thad said.

She ignored him. She walked toward the medical building, through the mass of students. Inside that building was Allison Boyle, the person who'd made worthless everything Jessica was.

CHAPTER
TWENTY-SEVEN

They'd left Allison strapped to the table for a long time after their tests concluded. Long enough for the fluid in the tube going into her arm to change to clear, and for her to recover a bit from the drug. The giddy high was replaced by a dull ache behind her temples.

She'd had ample time to curse herself for a lack of caution. Tearing apart their machinery was not going to help things. She was supposed to cooperate and gain their trust, make it easier when she decided to escape from here— Though, if Chuck was right, she didn't have time for the subtle approach.

Of all the people to have the psychic hotline to.

She looked at the tube going into her arm. The fluid inside the transparent plastic was clear. She was waiting to feel her teek being drugged away again. Her senses were wrapped around the needle in her arm. She could yank out the needle, or the tube from the machine, but that would only be a delaying tactic. If she was going to do something, it had to be something they wouldn't notice.

She had to block the stuff flowing into her arm. She couldn't crimp the IV tube with her teek, that required moving two surfaces in different directions. She could move a whole segment of the tube up, down or sideways, but that wouldn't block the flow.

It took her a moment to realize that she could also rotate the tube. She slid her teek up the tube, feeling along its length. The plastic felt as if it was woven of silken fibers finer than hair. She felt back until she had reached inside the machine itself, then she rotated a length of tubing a few times, counterclockwise.

Even though she could barely sense the fluid with her teek, she could tell when it stopped flowing inside the tube. It suddenly became that much harder to sense. She held the tube like that, until they came to unstrap her.

Without that to worry about, all she'd had to think about was escape, and Chuck. When they did come for her, the techs were apologetic for making her wait so long.

"Sorry to leave you here for so long, there were some technical problems we had to deal with."

Is that so? Then what happened to the man on the speaker?

To her immense relief, the first thing they did was remove the needle from her arm.

She noticed they removed the wires a little more gingerly than they'd applied them, giving her a little more respect. *Could they be afraid of me?*

Of course they were afraid. Even if they thought she was drugged, she had a history of leaving destruction in her wake. It'd already killed one person, and she had torn apart a piece of industrial strength testing equipment in front of these people. If she wasn't so preoccupied, it'd frighten *her.*

"Be careful standing, Miss Boyle," said one of the techs as he unstrapped her. "You may feel somewhat disoriented."

The fact was, she didn't feel disoriented at all. Her head felt clearer than ever, especially now that she wasn't teeking that damn tube. The tech must be expecting some residual effects from the drug that'd supposedly been feeding into her arm.

Allison tried to feel as drunk and as mushy-headed as she had when she disembarked from the plane, and she got to her feet unsteadily.

"We'll take you to your room. You can rest until your six o'clock meeting."

Does everyone here know my schedule?

Allison leaned on the tech, because that's what he seemed to expect. And he led her out of the testing area, followed by the other one. As they left, Allison noticed that many of the scientists that'd been hovering around the area seemed to have left as well. Apparently they'd seen all the interesting bits and had better things to do now.

The testing area had been below ground level. The techs took her up in an elevator. Allison wasn't thinking about where she was being led, so she didn't notice Jessica until they had walked her into the lobby of the medical building.

The techs walked her toward the glass doors that led out to the student courtyard. Allison glanced around and noticed Jessica watching them from one corner of the lobby. Jessica glared at them, and Allison straightened up, because she now noticed something that the techs seemed to have overlooked. The guards here were unconscious.

When Allison straightened up, the tech who'd been supporting her seemed to realize something was wrong. He noticed the guard by the front door, and started walking toward him, leaving the other tech by Allison.

Allison looked up for the omnipresent security cameras. When she saw one, she saw a haze of white smoke hovering around it.

Oh, no!

The tech who'd gone to examine the guard never reached him. The tech broke out into a sweat and collapsed halfway there. "What are you doing?" Allison said, looking at Jessica. She felt a hard edge of panic slicing into her.

"I'm not letting you take everything away from me," Jessica said. Her voice was cold and emotionless. It scared Allison more than Chuck had.

The remaining tech was edging away from her.

Allison backed away from Jessica. "They aren't going to let you get away with this, they'll drug you, or worse!"

Jessica shook her head, "With you alive, I've already lost Prometheus."

"You can't—"

"Can't what?"

Ten feet away, Allison heard a weight hit the floor. She turned and saw the last tech slump.

"I can't *what*?" Jessica said. "Who'll stop me?"

Good question. Everyone here was unconscious, and the cameras were blinded. How would anyone know that something was going on here? "One of their spotters must have seen you doing all this." Allison waved her arm across the lobby.

Jessica shook her head. "They took their best spotter in with you, trying to force an apotheosis on him. They took him out on a stretcher. Him and every scientist in this building went to the Ward about ten minutes ago."

Allison felt out desperately with her teek as she kept backing toward the doors of the lobby. Jessica slowly walked toward her.

"There are other guards in this building," Allison said. "One of them must have heard something—"

Jessica shook her head. "If they have, it's too late. With you gone, I'll have everything back. They won't dare harm me if they don't have another Class III to fall back on."

Allison had almost reached the doors to the lobby, but she had to stop because of the heat the doors were emitting. She turned and saw that the glass seemed to be glowing slightly.

Allison looked up at the sprinklers.

"The water's shut off," Jessica said. "The smoke detectors and the fire alarms are melted. It was the first thing I did."

The carpet around Allison was turning black. The char stopped about fifteen feet away from her. *Why isn't she attacking me directly, like she did the guards and the lab techs?*

At the moment it didn't matter. She had to get out of here.

Allison grabbed the door with her teek as small jets of flame began shooting from the carpet around her. She pushed the door open as hard as she could. . . .

Several things happened at once.

The stressed door flew open against a warped frame, and the stressed glass shattered. A wind blew in from the outside, sucked in by the burning carpet. The small flames exploded toward the ceiling fanned by the sudden wind. Someone outside the building screamed, *"Fire!"*

Jessica yelled, "No!" as Allison dived out the broken door.

The transition from total isolation to chaotic mob was

almost instantaneous. She stumbled out into the courtyard, and was absorbed into a converging mass of PRI's students.

She turned and saw the front of the lobby engulfed by a wall of flame. As she watched, more glass shattered, and she saw Jessica emerge from the flames, apparently unscathed. Jessica glared at the crowd around the front of the lobby. A pair of kids emerged from the crowd and started toward her. Everyone else kept their distance, halting their approach toward the burning building.

Jessica looked the crowd over, and her gaze locked on Allison. She seemed about to say something, but she was interrupted by a sound like an air rifle. Allison saw a large dart sprout from Jessica's neck.

An expression of surprise crossed Jessica's face before she collapsed. One of the approaching kids caught her as she fell.

Allison backed away from the scene, into the crowd, as Prometheus guards converged on the front of the medical building.

She tried to kill me. The thought wouldn't go away; it kept repeating itself, over and over.

"My God, what about the people in the building?"

The guards erupted from the crowd, surrounding Jessica and the two kids. From somewhere, Allison finally heard an alarm going off.

02 NOVEMBER   NAVARRO COUNTY, TEXAS

5:53 PM   TUESDAY

Allison never got that rest before her six o'clock meeting. The guards hustled her into a tiny meeting room, and people shot questions at her for two hours. They acted as if she was the one who'd gone nuts, not Jessica. As if all of this was, somehow, her fault.

She went over what happened at least three times. Each time she neglected to mention the fact she wasn't drugged anymore. She was gambling that they didn't know, and couldn't tell. Allison was also using her supposedly drugged state as an excuse to give them slow and muddled answers.

Chuck was right; she had to get out of this place. Some of the people questioning her, the scientists mostly, seemed to be trying to *defend* Jessica, to find some excuse for her actions. The security people questioning her weren't any better. The incident gave them leave to be paranoid about everyone.

The scientists tried to blame her for Jessica's outburst, and security put her in the same Class III category—as a threat. Allison considered herself lucky that they released her to go to her meeting with Macy.

Even then, the anonymous Gary Busey type escorted her the whole way, even through the blue student areas where she was supposed to have free range.

Security is going to be a nightmare after this, Allison thought. *Even if I keep from being drugged, even with my teek, they're going to be watching me under a microscope.*

I'm going to need help.

The guard left her in the familiar, institutional living room. She hoped that she'd be able to get her plan across to Macy in the hour they'd be given. Zack had given her the idea how to communicate under everyone's nose—but when she had the idea, she believed she was going to have time, that she'd have more than the one visit.

Macy was smart, she'd pick up on what Allison was doing. She'd have to. Otherwise Allison would be completely alone in this.

They let Allison stew for a few minutes before they opened the door and let Macy in. Macy stood in the doorway for a few moments, looking at her, before she said, "Hey, girl. How you doing?"

Allison stood up and hugged her. "I'm doing all right. God, I've missed you."

"Same here," Macy said. "No offense, but your dad ain't the greatest company."

They separated, and Macy wobbled a bit. Allison took her arm and asked, "Are you all right?"

Macy shrugged. "They've given me stuff for my feet, got me a little twirly. Stitched up my feet—" She sighed when they both collapsed on the couch. "Boy, did we screw up, didn't we?"

Here goes nothing. Allison took Macy's hand in both of hers. "Do we have to dwell on it? You know we'll get through this. These people are just trying to understand what I can do. I'm just glad you're here to see me, so we can talk."

With each sentence, Allison squeezed Macy's hand, emphasizing a specific word. It was fairly simple, *"Do . . . You . . . Understand . . . Me . . . ?"*

At first, Macy looked at Allison as if she thought her friend was nuts, but then a confused expression crossed her face, as if she could tell Allison was doing something and was trying to figure out what.

Allison kept going, trying to weave the important words into sentences that didn't sound contrived. "They chose to hand—" *squeeze—* "us an opportunity to talk—" *squeeze—* "to each other. Even if they—" *squeeze—* "forced us into this, can't—" *squeeze—* "we try to see—" *squeeze—* "a more reasonable way through it . . . ?"

Hand talk, they can't see it. Understand?

Allison felt as if she talked for twenty minutes, saying aloud what her captors wanted to hear, desperately trying to emphasize what she wanted Macy to hear. But, eventually, after an eternity, Macy squeezed her hand back.

Yes.

02 NOVEMBER   NAVARRO COUNTY, TEXAS

8:41 PM   TUESDAY

After her meeting with Macy, Allison spent her time looking for Zack. The powers-that-be had allowed things to slip back to a normalcy that felt even more false and surreal than usual. The only evidence of Jessica's outburst were sheets of plywood covering the entrance of the medical building, and a slight smell of smoke hovering over the courtyard.

There were still kids around, walking in the floodlit

courtyard. But everyone was quiet, their conversation muted. It was as if everyone Allison passed had suffered some private tragedy that they couldn't bring themselves to talk about.

The area of the courtyard next to the medical building was deserted. No signs warned anyone away from the scene, everyone seemed to be avoiding it automatically. It seemed as if some unspoken fate would descend on someone who showed too much of an interest in what had happened.

Allison didn't want to draw attention to herself, so she avoided the area along with everyone else.

She finally found Zack in the gym between the dorms.

The gym was a large open area, surrounded by an indoor track. Half the lights in here were out, and it seemed Zack was the only person here this late. He was running along the track, alternately passing from light to dark, visible to invisible.

Allison watched him make a circuit of the track. He seemed to run effortlessly. His face was lost in concentration. He didn't even appear to notice her watching. It was the first fully serious expression she'd seen on his face. He wore shorts and a tank top. What she saw made her think that skinny wasn't the right word to describe him. He was thin, but she couldn't think of anyone that well-muscled as skinny.

The bracelet on his wrist wasn't his only tattoo. A tiger rode his right bicep, the image seeming to take a feline stretch every time Zack swung his arm. Allison caught sight of another tattoo on his back. She could only catch a glimpse of green when his collar flapped. She wondered what it was.

"Hey," Zack said as he rounded the corner in front of her for the second time.

Allison didn't know why, but she suddenly felt embarrassed for watching him. She did her best to ignore the feeling. She stepped under a light as Zack slowed to a walk. "I need to talk to you," she said.

"You need to talk to me?" Zack asked, still walking. Allison paced him around the track. "What the hell happened between you and the ice queen today, Allie?"

Allison shrugged. "As far as I'm concerned, it's Jessica's problem. The PRI people can deal with it."

Zack stopped talking. "Allie, that's not just cold, it's wrong— "

Allison shook her head. "I didn't expect her to get sympathy from you."

"Damn it. She is one of us, trapped here as much as everyone else. And it isn't just her the techs are going to deal with. If they get paranoid about the psychokinetics, we're all three in trouble."

Allison grabbed Zack's arm. "Like I said, it's Jessica's problem. It's Prometheus' problem. And I need to talk to you."

Zack nodded. "Okay, let me get a towel."

They walked out into the courtyard, away from the buildings. Zack wiped his face with a towel and said, "So talk."

From his voice, Allison could tell he was disturbed. There was little of the wiseass tone he'd had before. For a few moments Allison wondered if she could trust him. But who else did she have? There was no time to coordinate with Dad and Macy. They were as much on their own as she was. She needed help to get to them, and Zack was the only person she had.

She noticed cameras following them, and she turned away from them and whispered, "If you could get out of here, would you?"

"Fuck, yeah, Allie. What do you think—" Zack stopped wiping his face and let his towel drop to his side. He lowered his voice to match her own. "You aren't being hypothetical."

Allison shook her head.

"If this is about Jessica, the medics will handle her."

Allison made a disgusted sound. "Some dissident. I want out of this place. They have no right to imprison anyone here. The only thing Jessica's making me do is try this *now*."

"Do you know what you're dealing with?"

"I need your help, Zack."

Zack looked at her, "I don't know what kind of help I can give you while I'm drugged."

Allison looked at him and said, "I need someone who knows this place. Even if you're drugged, I'm not."

"What?"

Zack stared at her and she reached into her pocket. Shaded from the cameras, she opened her cupped hand slightly so he could see a single lint-covered pill on her palm.

Zack stared and said, "Fuck, put that away."

Allison did so.

"So you ain't drugged?"

Allison shook her head. "If they didn't have two hostages—and I could figure out how you're supposed to levitate—I'd be gone by now."

Zack whistled, "How'd you avoid swallowing their little pill? They're pretty thorough."

"I can move a Jeep, something that size isn't much of a problem."

"You mean you swallowed it?"

"Halfway anyway."

Zack grimaced. "I take it you have some sort of plan?"

Allison nodded. "We get my dad to their airstrip."

"Okay, how?"

"That's open . . ."

Zack looked at her.

Allison's whisper became lower and harsher. "I'm sorry, but I don't have the time. If I'm getting out of here, it's got to be before they have the time to really think about what happened with Jessica. I'm committed to this. Tomorrow. Do I have your help or not?"

"You know you're borrowing trouble. Just having me around is probably going to cause enough interference to scramble anything telekinetic you do."

Allison hadn't thought of that. She tried an experimental feeling out with her teek, and it was like trying to drag her sense though clay. But, like she'd said, she was committed. "I need to know where I'm going, Zack."

Zack stared at her a long time before he said, "Hell, it'd seriously fuck with my self-image if I refused."

Allison held out her hand and said, "Tomorrow, then?"

Zack took her hand and said, "Tomorrow, then, beautiful." Zack did something then that she never expected. Instead of shaking her hand, he kissed it lightly on the back.

He walked away. Around her the wind picked up, carrying a warmth she felt mostly in her cheeks.

02 NOVEMBER   **NAVARRO COUNTY, TEXAS**

11:28 PM   **TUESDAY**

When Jessica awoke from her sedation, the fire was locked in her skull. She tried to reach out, to *feel,* from her bed, but that part of her mind was senseless, mute. She couldn't feel the tiny motes that made up the matter around her, and that meant that all the burning went on inside her.

They hadn't drugged her for years, not since they had told her that she was their most valuable talent here. Today had proved them liars. Jessica Mason didn't matter at all to these people, to Stone. Even what she could do, the one thing that raised her above everything else, that was expendable.

And they had taken that from her.

Jessica sat up in her bed, in her darkened room. She stared at the door across from the foot of her bed, knowing it was locked. She knew it was locked because her father had always locked the door after he hurt her.

He had always locked the door, and in the morning he apologized and tried to explain himself.

They would have to come for her eventually, if only to dose her again. Their injection into her mind couldn't last forever. And she knew that Howard Stone would want to talk to her, to apologize and try to explain himself.

She had always believed that, if they didn't love her, at least she mattered to them, that at least her well-being meant something. She had managed to convince herself that she was important.

She was wrong. She was just Jessica Mason, and no one gave a shit about her. If she screamed in the night, no one would come running. If anyone said they cared about her, it was because they wanted something from her. If she died, no one would weep over her grave. . . .

To hell with all of them.

They had to come for her eventually. Their injection couldn't last forever. When they came for her, she knew what she would do.

Stone's would be the last apology she would ever have to hear.

CHAPTER
TWENTY-EIGHT

03 NOVEMBER   NAVARRO COUNTY, TEXAS

6:30 AM   WEDNESDAY

" . . . *All hell's going to break out soon, once that redhead figures out Stone's found his Change.*"

"*What do you mean?*"

"*This place, the high school, it isn't imaginary.*"

"*What do you mean?*"

"*It's all the same thing. Telepathy, telekinesis, precognition—it's all from the same place. This is Euclid Heights High in a decade or so.*"

Allison sat up in her bed, drenched in a cold sweat. It wasn't even a dream of Chuck this time, it was more of a dream of a memory of Chuck, or what he had said.

What he had said. It scared her. It scared her that what she had dreamed might be real. What could cause that to happen to Euclid High, what could cause the bodies?

I can't think about that now. I have to think about getting out of here. . . .

Allison took a shower, trying to plan ahead, hoping that Zack was correct about where the Ward was.

7:00 AM

John Charvat was awake and staring out the eastern windows of one of the prefab houses hugging the residential sector of Prometheus. The window faced ranks of similar houses marching off toward the chain-link perimeter. The dawn was rose-colored; John watched out the window as the light began painting his shadow on the far wall.

There were two bedrooms in this house, the door to one of them was still closed. He turned away from the window and walked up to that door, knocking softly. There was a murmured response that sounded half asleep.

John nodded to himself and walked into the bathroom.

He closed the bathroom door, opened the shower stall door, and turned the hot water on full. With the shower stall open, the bathroom began immediately filling with humid fog. John stared at the mirror over the sink as his face dissolved into gray. He made no move to undress.

When the mirror was completely fogged over, he stepped on the lid of the toilet. His fingers slipped on condensation as he fumbled with a vent over the toilet. He moved carefully, making very little sound.

Pulling the grate off the vent, he revealed the camera beyond. Its lens was as fogged and white as the mirror. He lowered the grate and placed it on the sink. Then he reached for the roll of toilet paper.

He took a single sheet and separated one ply of the tissue. Very gently he draped the single thin tissue over the fogged lens. He smiled to himself again, stepped off of the toilet, and began the work of opening the window.

7:15 AM

Jessica's wait was rewarded. She had barely felt some return of her numbed senses when her door opened. Three orderlies and a doctor came in with little of the social pretense that seemed second nature at PRI. No one approached her until they had all entered and had positioned themselves.

Jessica didn't move, she simply glared at them.

The doctor held an air-powered hypodermic in his hand and he was looking at her warily. "I hope you'll make this easy for all of us, Miss Mason."

"You're early," Jessica said.

He stared at her blankly, then glanced back at the rest of the orderlies.

"Seven-thirty is when you're supposed to dope people." Jessica looked at him.

He shook his head and replied, "We want this to cause as little disruption as possible to the other students."

You would have done me in my sleep, if I had slept.

"I want to see Mr. Stone," Jessica demanded.

No one had made a move for her yet. That was good. They were afraid of her. But she could barely feel with her extra senses. She could do these people no damage, no matter how much they feared her, no matter how much she wanted to. From the way she felt, she needed at least another hour before she would be fully recovered from last night.

"We need to do this if you're to see him," the doctor said.

Jessica nodded. "When do I see him, then?"

He looked back to one of the orderlies, and Jessica noticed that the man wasn't an orderly after all. He was security, a familiar looking guy in a suit and with a bald-eagle pin on his tie. Fred, the field agent who'd brought her in. Maybe he felt some proprietary interest in her. Fred finally spoke. "Stone wants to see her ASAP, so as soon as she's ready to go."

While he talked, Jessica felt with her crippled senses. Her mind groped through a buzzing particulate world filled with tiny vibrating motes. The air was a swarm of gnats, and the structure of the hypo was a network of tiny snakes, each viper buzzing, and twisting in a tiny confined space. To this view, the world was vast, and her mind swept through it at impossible speeds. The bouncing rotating insects followed her point of view like a cloud filled mostly with nothingness.

It was a pedestrian exercise, simply opening her mind to the impressions of the matter around her. But with the drug still damping her power, the effort set her heart racing and brought the taste of copper to her mouth. She felt sweat dripping down her back, her cheeks, between her breasts. It was a superhuman effort to keep from closing her eyes in concentration. She managed, by force of will, to stay motionless, sitting in the same position she'd been in since they'd entered her room.

"So," said the doctor, "can I please have your arm?"

Jessica nodded and slowly raised her arm. As she did, her mind fell into the vial that fueled the air hypo. The few ccs of liquid made up a thick universe as vast as Jupiter. Compared to the gnats of gas molecules, or the short vipers of polymer chains, the drug was made of minnows and leviathans. It was the leviathans that mattered. The minnows were water and salty ions. The whales floating in this Jovian world were complex neurotransmitters, each engineered to fill spaces in Jessica's synapses.

Sweat stung her eyes as she fed the leviathans the minuscule amount of energy she could muster in her drugged state. The monster molecules spun and bent. There was barely enough energy in Jessica's burst to raise the temperature of the liquid, even so small a volume. But all of it was pumped into the minuscule fraction of the liquid that was the active drug.

The leviathans spun themselves past the breaking point, some slammed into the minnows, absorbing the small ones and becoming something else. Others flew into each other and disintegrated into a cloud of smaller beings. Some spontaneously exploded.

By the time the hypodermic reached her arm, most of the leviathans had died.

7:20 AM

George walked into his office carrying a large cardboard box. He slammed the door shut behind him with his foot. The office was plunged into gloom, the only light a few ruddy trickles from the louvered windows. He made no move to turn on the lights.

He tossed the box on top of his desk, knocking his phone askew. He ignored the phone and grabbed an oversized wastebasket from beside his desk. The wastebasket had a shredder built into the top of it.

He set it down next to a filing cabinet.

The phone began beeping at him. George fished in his pockets for a few minutes before he found a key ring. His hands shook as he unlocked the cabinet. Once it was unlocked, he slid the bottom drawer open. The drawer was filled with multicolored file folders hanging on rails.

George began pulling out the files' contents, feeding them into the shredder. Pages of notes, long passages of mathematical equations, many handwritten, all were sucked into the shredder. At least twice, George fed pages too fast, and he had to unjam the machine.

When the basket filled, he dumped the contents in the corner of his office, and began on the next drawer. Sometime in the middle of the third drawer, long after the phone had given up on attracting his attention, there was a knock on the office door.

George froze, a personal memo trembling in his hand.

The knock came again, more insistent this time. George looked down at the shredder and backed away from it, dropping the memo. He kept backing away until he was next to his desk. He had to step over the phone.

He faced the door as the knock became an insistent pounding.

"Y–yes?" he said quietly.

His visitor took that as the cue to enter. The door swung inward, flooding the office with light from the hall beyond. George blinked at Barney. Barney was shaking his head. Unlike George, Barney's clothes were neat, he'd shaved, and he appeared as if he'd gotten at least some sleep in the past forty-eight hours.

George bent down and picked up the phone at his feet. "What do you want?"

Barney was still shaking his head. "Never play poker, George," he said in his Western twang. Barney reached over and turned on the light switch with his cast, flooding the room with more light.

"I don't know what you're talking about."

"Don't fuck with me. You're not good enough to fuck with me." Barney looked around the office, which showed all its disarray in the unkind light. "You're panicking, George."

George laughed, almost a hysterical giggle. "Panic? That's what this is?"

Barney shook his head. "I can't let you rabbit on us."

George shook his head. "You're perfect, you know that? They couldn't have done better if they engineered you for your job."

Barney took a step into the room and closed the door behind him. "I think you should calm down before you do something regrettable."

George kept shaking his head, waving the phone in his hand. "You never had any morality for this place to corrupt, did you?"

"Cut the sentimentalist bullshit, George." Barney reached into his jacket with his left hand and removed a gun, an automatic with a silencer attached. Instinctively, George backed up. "Fred gave me a job. If something becomes a security risk, I have to deal with it."

George laughed again, "Christ. You're enjoying this, aren't you? There aren't any other security people here because they might spoil your fun." Barney leveled the silenced gun at George, but he couldn't stop laughing. "Go ahead, shoot. It'd be the capping insanity."

Barney kept the gun level. "I never liked you." He took another step toward George. "What the fuck did you think you were doing?"

"Coming to my senses. Elroy—" George caught his breath. "I mean Billy. Billy was one thing. That was accidental, and maybe he'd gone beyond hope. But we went and forced another kid to go though the exact same thing. We placed a sensitive too close to that girl when she lit up. We deliberately drove another kid insane."

"I'm touched. That doesn't answer my question. How were you intending to get out of here?"

"I wasn't."

Barney stopped approaching and stared.

"That surprises you?"

"If you weren't about to bolt, what the hell are you—"

"You don't understand guilt, do you? This isn't something I can run from. The blood's on my hands."

Barney kept staring at him.

"You see, all that's really left for me is to erase whatever contribution I've made to this insanity. My work, my notes . . ." George gestured toward the corner of the office, where the pile of shredded documents were piled.

Barney stepped back and looked where George had indicated. "I don't see what—"

Barney was interrupted by George swinging the base of the phone into his face. The gun, in Barney's off hand, discharged with a muffled report, and both men fell to the ground.

George brought the phone down twice more on the back of Barney's skull. The gun didn't go off again. He dropped the phone and rolled over on his back.

Beneath him, shreds of paper began to absorb a spreading red stain.

7:35 AM

Allison waited for Zack in the courtyard between the dorms, her attention divided between the cameras and the residence building. She was alone out here: the only people she'd seen had been a few boys who'd slipped into the gym.

Standing here made her feel exposed and conspicuous. Their security had to be paying extra attention to her, after yesterday. In a way she counted on that attention. If all of Prometheus' attention was directed inward, at their potentially dangerous kids, that meant they might overlook the fringes of their security—like Dad and Macy.

She just had to pray that Macy had gotten her message to Dad, and that they managed to slip away to the airstrip.

Early sunlight washed over the courtyard, and the air felt hot and dry. It felt too much like the air in the medical building yesterday. Allison found herself looking around for Jessica more than once. She had to tell herself that it was an irrational fear. Jessica was drugged and under guard somewhere. What Allison had to worry about was Prometheus Security—the little gray men behind the cameras, the men with the guns. . . .

More people began emptying out of the buildings around her, and she began worrying about Zack. About the time when she seriously began to think he might not show up,

Zack came out of the boys' residence. He looked flushed, and his eyes showed lack of sleep. He walked right up to her and pulled her arm. "Come on."

Allison followed, away from the courtyard and the half dozen other early birds. Zack led her to a corner of the academic building, away from everyone, and stopped. "If we're lucky," he said, "this is a blind spot."

"Good. How much time do you think we have before security is on to us?"

"You really haven't planned this out, have you?" Zack shook his head. "Minimum, they're after us already. Maximum, two hours when we don't show up for a class."

Allison looked around. "We better assume we have some time."

"So what now?"

"We need to give them something bigger than us to worry about."

"Like?"

"Can you get us to the Ward without setting security on us?"

Zack smiled. "That I think I can do. It isn't really that far into the restricted area—but let's get inside first." He nodded toward the entrance to the classroom building.

"Why?"

"I need a faculty washroom." Allison stared at him and he laughed. "I know, should have thought of it before I left—but, considering that our mutual interference isn't going to let you telekinese that pill out of me, I've decided to resort to more primitive methods."

Allison found herself making a face when she realized what he meant.

"Come on," Zack said, taking her arm. "They'll be less suspicious if it looks like we're making out or something."

7:45 AM

John stopped working at the window in response to a knocking at the bathroom door. Macy's voice came from beyond. "Hey in there, I need to use the bathroom."

John glanced briefly at the vent he'd doctored. He waited until Macy pounded again. "Hey in there."

After another pointed delay, John said, "I'm in the shower." His voice carried a feigned irritation that didn't show in his expression.

"Come *on,* this is an emergency. I've been waiting fifteen minutes."

Another pointed pause.

"Hello?" Macy said.

John let out a sigh that again didn't match his expression. "Let me grab a towel." He stood up and reached in to the still running shower and shut off the water. The fog in the bathroom began to dissipate immediately with the breeze from the now open window. John was still fully dressed, and he made no move for a towel.

"Okay," John said. "The door's open."

Macy opened the door, rushing in and slamming it behind her. "Hey!" John said, "you could wait for me to get out of here—" He glanced again at the blinded camera.

"I said it was an emergency," Macy replied as she went to the window. She looked at it and glanced at John. John nodded at her.

The window Macy faced had taken John nearly half an hour to open. The effort showed. The only tool he'd had to work with was a pair of nail clippers. With them, he'd unscrewed four small metal contacts from the window sash, pulling them and their connecting wires out from their mounts. Now, buried in those mounts were lengths of wire that John had earlier stolen from a lamp cord.

The ends of the four lengths of lamp cord led up to similar contacts in the window frame, preventing the circuit from being broken by having the window open.

Beyond the window was a screen. It was operable, but instead of sliding it open, John had laboriously cut a hole though it with the clippers.

Macy looked over his handiwork for a few moments, then she slowly pulled herself though the window. John waited a few moments for her to clear the space under the window, and then he followed.

Once his feet touched the ground outside, he reached through the screen and very gingerly pulled the window shut again behind them. He'd anchored the wires firmly around the mounting screws, none came loose. Even so, when the window slid home, he exhaled with visible relief.

"Safe?" Macy whispered.

John nodded and said, "For the moment. There's no visual surveillance beyond the roads and the immediate area around the security fences." After a long pause, he said. "What does she think she's doing?"

"Escaping, like us."

John shook his head. "Macy, I *ran* the security for this place. I know where everything is, and *I* don't know how she thinks she's getting out of the middle of the complex."

Macy shook her head. "We slipped out of the house easy enough—"

"We slipped out of an employee's residence. The security on the students is much tighter." John looked off down a rank of backyards that marched off to a tall chain-link fence. "We also haven't managed to slip anywhere yet."

Macy followed his gaze. "Now what?"

"Get close to the airstrip without being seen." John started moving across the backyards, keeping an eye on the windows. He whispered, mostly to himself, "Allie, please, God, know what you're doing."

7:50 AM

Zack led her through the classroom building, and Allison couldn't help noticing the cameras that peppered every intersection. She told herself that it wasn't time to be nervous yet, she hadn't stepped out of the area that she was allowed to be in. She hadn't done anything that would set security on her. Not yet.

Zack led her up three flights of stairs and to a men's room door. To her chagrin, Zack pushed her through the door. She experienced a brief wave of fear. She shook herself loose from Zack and said in a shaky voice, "Don't do that."

Zack backed in the direction of the stalls. "What?"

Allison folded her arms across her chest and said, "Never yank me through another door."

"Sorry. Look, wait there. I'm pretty sure that security doesn't have this place monitored."

Allison waited there, standing just on the inside of the men's room door. She had to tell herself a number of times that Zack was not Chuck. The only things they had in common were age and gender.

Allison had to cover her face when Zack started retching.

Another way to get off their drug, Allison thought. *Not something you'd want to do every day.*

Allison wanted to think about something else, so she tried to feel out with her teek, experimentally, to find out how badly Zack's presence was interfering with it. To her relief, she found that Zack's presence wasn't damping her ability at the moment.

That made her feel better. Just using the sense was a liberating feeling. Waferlike tiles separated by ephemeral grout, porcelain that felt like some iced pastry, and—

To Allison's surprise, there was a blind spot to her teek sense. There was a roughly spherical patch almost ten feet in diameter blocking out part of the bathroom. Allison had to open her eyes and allow her other senses to leak in before she realized that the blind spot was centered on Zack.

So that's how it works, Allison thought. She felt she could understand what Zack was talking about now as far as interference went. She couldn't affect anything in that little dead area around Zack, and if she actually stood within that dead area, she would find her teek slogging through the same clay as it did last night. Having a visual picture made it much easier to understand.

And that must be why Jessica never attacked me directly, for all that she was trying to kill me.

Zack finished retching in the stall and stumbled out accompanied by a flushing sound. He went over to the sinks, muttering, "That's not as easy as it looks."

He turned the faucet and began cupping water into his mouth and spitting it back into the sink. He didn't bother taking off his gloves to do so.

"Are you all right?" Allison asked.

Zack nodded into the sink. "I hope that made a difference. I'd hate to do that for nothing." He straightened up and looked into the mirror, wiping his mouth.

Allison looked at the stall. "Why didn't you try this before?"

Zack looked at her, and his smart-ass smile was back. "Aesthetic considerations aside, first, I have no idea if the drug'll wear off in time to do any good. Unlike you, my talent's all or nothing. I can't 'sort of' levitate. Any metal fog and I'm grounded. Second, doing that is *real* unsubtle. I figure I have one shot before they figure it out."

Allison nodded, but she saw something else in Zack's expression. She thought that there was at least one more reason he hadn't experimented before; he was scared, and he didn't want to make the attempt alone. He'd probably been ready to try this for a long time, but all he'd needed was someone to push him.

"Okay," Allison said, "you're going to lead us to the Ward now."

Zack nodded. "I just have to think about how we slip out of the student area." He stood looking thoughtful for a moment. "How badly does my presence interfere with what you do?"

"If you're ten feet away from me or whatever I'm trying to do."

"Hm . . . So tilting a camera isn't a problem for you?"

"You have something in mind?"

"We don't even have to leave the building until we're into the green area."

CHAPTER
TWENTY-NINE

Jessica felt ill.

The whole set of goons had accompanied her to the glass-walled reception area to await Mr. Stone's pleasure. During the wait, waves of nausea and dizziness enfolded her. She'd broken down what they'd drugged her with, but it still had an effect on her body.

She doubted that the orderlies would care how she felt, even if she told them. They were there to keep her under control. She doubted Fred was here with her well-being in mind.

To hell with all of them, Jessica thought as she gritted her teeth against a rushing headache.

It seemed that the reception area had been in stasis for hours before the receptionist told them that Mr. Stone was ready.

Finally ready to meet his wayward child. She couldn't manage even an ironic smile at the thought. Her anger was too great. When she stood and checked the large chromed clockface above the desk, to see how long she'd been waiting for him, the clock told her that it had only been twenty minutes.

It had seemed much longer, and the distortion she felt in her time sense only deepened the emotions she felt.

Fred, the security man, led the way down the art-plastered hallway. The orderlies followed, stationed behind her. She kept her gaze fixed on the back of Fred's neck. Paranormal sensations leaked into her awareness. She felt the ebb and flow of particles within his flesh, something like she'd imagine plankton in a swirling ocean current might look.

The headache and the nausea weren't dimming her abilities in the least. Her senses seemed to hone themselves on the pain. At that thought, she did manage a nearly invisible smile.

Fred turned and held up his hand outside Mr. Stone's door. "Wait here a moment." She hated the reassuring tone in his voice. It was only there when he talked to her.

He opened the massive door and slipped inside, leaving Jessica out here with the orderlies. The door shut slowly enough that Jessica could hear the beginning of an argument.

". . . Mr. Stone, I don't think it's a good idea to—"

The door cut off Fred's voice, and the soundproofing was good enough that Jessica couldn't even tell that anyone continued speaking, much less tell what they said after that.

However, she could guess. Stone liked to see kids alone, especially when he had some grand point to make. He liked captive audiences, and he didn't like divided attention. Of course, Fred wouldn't like the idea of leaving him alone with her, even if she were drugged.

Fred was right.

But, in the end, Fred wasn't in charge. He opened the door a few minutes later, a disgusted expression on his face. He waved Jessica inside.

She walked in, and the door closed behind her, shutting her up alone with Mr. Stone.

8:05 AM

Allison and Zack didn't talk once they left the bathroom. Zack had explained everything to her before they left the one area he was certain wasn't bugged. Allison could feel her heart racing as they wove their way through the classroom building.

The corridors were still mostly empty, though they now passed the occasional office where teachers were preparing for classes. At one point they even passed one of the PRI faculty in the hall. The man greeted them in passing, and

it took all of Allison's self-control to return a "good morning" that didn't sound like a panicked gasp.

They were still in the blue area, the place where they
presumably had open access. Zack had said that even if
they were paying special attention to her movements, she
would have to fall out of view for an extended time before
security started worrying. Allison hoped that when security
panicked, they'd have no idea where she was—and by the
time they had an idea, they'd have other problems.

That was the theory anyway.

But what kept running through her mind was the fiasco
she had started when she had gone home to try and save
Mom. She hadn't had the best of luck with impulsive
schemes like this.

Great time for second thoughts, Allison chided herself. *If
I'm really lucky, Dad and Macy are already at the airstrip.*

She could start doubting herself, but she couldn't very
well turn back now. No matter what happened, she had to
stick this out to the end.

Together they made it to the stairwell Zack had told her
about. It was one of the few interior transitions between
security levels that didn't have a permanent human ob-
server stationed at it. Up the stairs were more classrooms,
but down the stairs led to a green area that Zack said was
storage and maintenance.

When they entered the stairwell, Allison felt a brief surge
of panic, the same as when Zack had pulled her into the
bathroom. She saw the concrete steps and froze. She stood
there hyperventilating for a second, and when Zack
touched her, she almost screamed aloud.

Zack looked concerned, but he didn't say anything,
which meant he was still worried about microphones. Allison had to keep telling herself that this was a different
stairway, and Zack was a different person—but only the
conscious part of her mind seemed to agree with her. The
rest of her body seemed to insist on having a panic attack.

She kept breathing deeply, waiting for the spike of a
migraine, and waved Zack aside. What she was supposed
to do next needed him to be more than ten feet away
from her.

It took Zack a few moments to move; he seemed unwilling to leave her. The delay made Allison want to scream, but he finally did move, freeing her teek.

Feeling out into the stairwell drained the emotion, as if the act distanced her from the place. Feeling the insides of everything—the cinder block, the metal railing, the concrete stairs—seemed to lessen the impact of the object. To her teek, the solid surface everything displayed was illusory.

After a few minutes, Allison had forgotten her distress and was concentrating, eyes closed, on groping for a camera that was out of view down the stairs.

Zack had told her two important things about this stairwell. First, the landing just inside the door, where they stood, was a blind spot. The other side of the solid fire door was covered by a camera, but on this side they had to go half a flight in one direction or the other for a camera to see them.

Second, the cameras in here activated and panned based on motion sensors, which made sense in a little-traveled area. This meant that the cameras slept until activated, and if they were disabled before then, the guards monitoring them wouldn't know something was wrong until they actually checked the cameras.

Of course, most people couldn't get close enough to disable a camera without activating it. Allison didn't have that restriction on her. She found it below her with her teek.

It was far enough away that sensing it took some concentration. That aside, however, it was easy to distinguish from the matter around it. She could feel the thin skin of the metal box, and the ephemeral electronics that skin protected, the skeletal armature mounting it to the cinder-block wall, and, most importantly, the threads of the camera's wiring snaking through the armature and into the wall.

It wasn't far enough away that pulling those wires free cost her any real mental effort.

She opened her eyes once she was confident that the camera below them was blind. "Come on," she mouthed to Zack, and she started down. Zack followed closely as she stepped over the chain marking the separation of the blue and green areas.

The chain was deceptively innocuous. The only sign that

it marked anything significant was the fact that a placard hung from it reading, "absolutely no admittance."

Once they crossed that line, their margin for error had diminished to nothing. If any Prometheus guards came across them now, they would almost certainly face the same fate as Jessica had. *Please, Dad, Macy, be there. . . .*

When they reached the landing below, the camera, blinded and inert, let them pass. All she had to do was get them both past three more cameras, and they would be outside again.

8:10 AM

Jessica sat wordlessly, staring at Mr. Stone. He had gone into a reprise of his vision for the new age of mankind, and how they were on the cusp of a Change greater than any one of them. Jessica didn't really listen. All she could think of was how he loved to hear himself talk.

Stone walked back and forth in front of his desk, pausing to lean on his cane whenever he wanted to emphasize a point. She watched him, and suddenly she really noticed how his distant expression reminded her of her father.

"I understand how you might be hurt," Stone said. "But just because we've found another Class III, it doesn't mean we value you less. Everyone here is an integral part of the whole."

Behind Stone, a small wisp of white smoke emerged from the phone and the intercom.

Stone was oblivious to it. He kept talking. "You can't abandon our work here, not after how far we've come. I can't understand how you can turn away from us when we're on the cusp of a great awakening."

"You don't understand anything," Jessica whispered coldly.

Stone stopped and looked at her. It was the first time he had looked directly at her since he started speaking. "What do you mean?"

Jessica stood, realizing as she did that when he leaned on the cane, she was as tall as he was. She could look him in the eye. It was surprising, as if the impression of size that Stone gave was as much a fraud as everything else about him.

"I'm not one of your disposable children."

For the first time since she had met him, Howard Stone looked surprised. Then he looked angry. "None of my children are disposable—"

"Tell that to the wrecks you keep in the Ward. Tell that to the kid the docs fried yesterday. Tell that to Billy Jackson."

Stone resumed pacing. He worked his way around the desk. "The sacrifices are necessary if we're to the control the Change."

"You mean if *you're* to control the Change."

Stone stood on the other side of the desk, leaning on his cane. He had regained a little of his composure. "I was the one to see the Change coming."

"Who better," Jessica said. Stone nodded. He must have been deaf to the irony in her voice. Jessica felt her stomach churning, and perspiration made her clothes stick to her body. Her temper finally boiled over into her voice. *"Bullshit!"*

Stone's expression lost its carefully regained composure. "There's no need for that kind of—"

"You arrogant hypocrite." Jessica walked up to the other side of the desk. "You think you can dispense power and take it away as if you were some sort of god? You think you're the chosen one? You think you're the prophet of the age?"

"I think our conversation is over." Stone reached over and pressed a button on the intercom. The button clicked, but nothing happened. He pressed it repeatedly.

"Solder is designed to have a low melting point," Jessica said.

Stone looked up at her. His face had gone ashen. "What do you mean?"

"Electronics don't take well to abrupt rises in temperature."

"You? You're supposed to be—"

"Pharmaceuticals can be cooked, too."

He stared at her. For once he was speechless.

"You gave me all I had. For that little taste of power you gave me, I would have done anything for you. Did you ever understand that? Could you? If you'd only asked, I would have burned a city to the ground—"

"Jessica . . ." His voice sounded a little choked.

"Do you know now how much I hate you for trying to take that away?"

Stone slumped in his chair, shaking his head. He was flushed and sweating. "Please . . ."

"You're not going to get your Change. You're not going to buy your way into messiahhood." Jessica leaned over the desk. "And the only taste you'll have of this power you've been hunting is what you're feeling right now."

Stone loosened his tie. Behind his glasses, his eyes appeared unfocused. "What are you talking about?"

"Do you think every manifestation has to be blatant? You've taught me a lot since I ignited my father's clothes."

Stone stared at her, blinking slowly. His breathing was becoming deep and ragged.

"Your blood doesn't need to boil, Stone. All it needs is to have its temperature rise a dozen degrees or so." Jessica smiled. "I can feel your heart pumping. I can sense the liquid rushing like a periodic avalanche. And with each pump, I'm dumping a little more energy into it. I've been doing it a few minutes already—"

Stone's eyelids drooped. "Stop it," he muttered. His cane clattered to the floor as he sagged into the chair.

Jessica walked around the desk and leaned over him. "I want you to know one thing."

He shook his head weakly. "Stop," he repeated. His face was now flushed beet red.

"Your dream is going to burn," she said.

8:15 AM

George's lower body was awash with blood from the hole in his gut, his face was pasty white and lined with pain. His left arm clutched across his abdomen as if it had been welded there, and his movements had a jerky, random quality.

It had taken him nearly half an hour to drag himself the ten feet to his desk, and another fifteen minutes to pull himself into his chair. The path he'd taken, all fifteen feet, was blazed by his own blood and trails of shredded documents.

Occasionally he'd wince and jerk his head. Or he'd gasp and catch his breath as if someone was kicking him. But most of the time, as he typed at the keyboard of his computer, he wore a sickly grin.

In all that time, no one had come. In that time, Barney never moved. Barney stayed where he had fallen, face-first into a pile of shredded paper, his left arm draped across the shredder, the remains of the phone scattered by his head. Barney's gun now lay on the desk in front of George.

He'd been typing one-handed at the keyboard for nearly fifteen minutes before he heard a pounding on the door. On the screen, a question flashed at him, "Format Drive N: (Y/N)?"

George reached for Barney's gun with his right hand. He pried his left hand away from his gut and pressed the "Y" on the keyboard. He leveled the gun at the door.

The screen responded with, "All Data on Drive N: will be erased. ARE YOU SURE? (Y/N)?"

From outside, George heard someone shout, "This is PRI Security. Whoever is in there, step away from the computer."

With a shaking hand George pressed "Y" again, smearing blood across the keyboard.

The door flew open and three guards stormed into his office. "Drop the gun," one of them ordered. "Step away from the computer."

George said, "Fuck you."

The room erupted in about fifteen seconds of gunfire. The monitor exploded, splinters erupted from the desk, and half a dozen bullets slammed into George's upper body. When it was over, George slumped out of the chair, sliding to the ground. He hadn't returned fire once.

One of the guards looked around at the shredded documents, the blood, and the two corpses, and said, "What a fucking mess."

8:20 AM

"What are we waiting for?" Macy asked.

She and John had made their way down to a sun-dried

drainage ditch. John had led them to just within sight of the airstrip and stopped. He lay on the sloping edge of the ditch, flattening himself as much as possible.

"We're only going to get one chance at this," John said. "We're going to need Allie's diversion. Or, at the least, a gap in their patrols."

Macy nodded without looking at John. She was staring down the ditch, to where it ended. About a hundred feet away was the fence surrounding the airstrip. Below the fence, the ditch ended in a six-foot-high concrete wall. The wall was pierced by a corrugated metal pipe about four feet in diameter.

"What about the drainpipe? We wouldn't have to go through the front door."

"You do see the camera up there, don't you?" John asked.

Macy nodded, but kept looking down in that direction. "Yeah, but it keeps on panning."

John turned his head to look where Macy was looking. Above the pipe's outflow, mounted on a post on the far side of the fence, a camera did slowly pan across the ditch. The way it was angled, they weren't swept by it, a few dozen more feet in and they would be.

"What are you getting at?" he asked.

"Does anything cover the drain?"

"Not really, but—"

"So within about ten feet of the wall, the camera can't see you."

"Yes."

"How fast can you run?"

John stared at her as she slipped over the side of the ditch and crouched on the flat, concrete-lined bottom. "Come on," Macy urged him. "I know I can make that distance before the camera pans back."

John inched down the edge of the ditch a little. "What about your feet?"

"Shut up about my damn feet." She scowled. "If we make it down there, can we get through?"

"There should be a grating blocking the drain."

"Something we can get past?"

"Possibly."

"Good, I'm tired of waiting." Macy turned away from

him, touched the ground in front of her with her hands. The camera ahead panned across the ditch, and once it had passed, she dashed toward the concrete wall at the end of the ditch.

8:25 AM

Allison and Zack had made their way through the basement of the classroom building, leaving a trail of disabled cameras in their wake. The basement was a dark maze of boxes and shelves. The combination of dark dust and cobwebs reminded Allison too much of her nightmares. When they finally reached the opposite end of the basement, Allison was glad to be out of it.

The stairway they took led back up into the classroom building. On the ground floor there was a short hall and two doors leading off from the stairwell. One led back inside the building, and the other looked outside, onto a part of the Prometheus complex that Allison had never seen before.

They both inched up toward the door, and Allison kept an eye out for the ubiquitous surveillance cameras. Beyond the chicken-wire glass in the door, Allison saw a cluster of buildings. The buildings were almost interchangeable with those in every office park she had ever seen.

If she hadn't lost her sense of direction—which would have been all too possible in the maze of the basement— the student area was all behind them now.

Zack nodded toward the door, at the buildings beyond the glass. "There it is," he whispered. It was the first time he had spoken since they'd slipped out of the bathroom. The sound scared her, and made her think of microphones in the walls.

She told herself to calm down. Her plan, such as it was, assumed that security would be closing in on them by now. Disabling the cameras was only a delaying move. She knew it was likely that, by the time they got to their destination, security would know exactly where they were. They certainly would shortly afterward.

What Allison hoped was that, by then, security would be worried about other things.

Allison looked out the window, trying to see what Zack was talking about. Behind the classroom building was a small courtyard. There were a few benches and plants, but it all had the sparse look of an area that no one really used.

"Where?" she finally whispered back.

"Ahead and to the left," Zack said. "That building to our immediate left is a wing off the medical building. See the walkway?"

Allison nodded. Now that Zack had pointed it out, Allison could see that the neighboring building was the same place they'd tested her, and the place where Jessica had gone nuts. She was just seeing it from a different angle. From the second floor emerged a walkway that led to another building farther back.

"The Ward's at the other end of that walkway."

The building that Zack talked about didn't look that different from any of the other buildings. If she didn't know better, Allison might have thought it was another classroom building. It was all the same anonymous concrete and glass.

She still couldn't see where the cameras were, though she knew that there had to be at least one covering the courtyard in front of them. She was about to ask Zack about it, when she heard a door close above them.

They both looked back toward the stairs. Footsteps echoed down the stairwell toward them. They came at a near running pace.

"Shit," Zack said. "I think the gig's up."

Allison darted up toward the stairs, out of Zack's disruptive sphere of influence, and felt out with her teek. She didn't feel up the stairs, where the sounds came from. Instead she felt out through the door back into the building. If security was closing on them, that was where they *should* be coming from.

They were there, on either side of the door. She could feel bone like a petrified spiderweb, fibrous muscle, and the crystalline solidity of the weapons they carried. Four or five men, waiting to push through and grab them. Allison's heart began pounding in her ears.

"Move," she told Zack in a harsh whisper. As she did, she

wrapped her teek around the door. She had to delay them, if only for a few seconds. Her mind slipped through the skin of the door and found the mechanical skeleton of the latch holding the door shut. To her teek the inside of the door, next to the doorframe, was a tightly fitted collection of levers attached to a single tongue of metal that held the door in place.

Allison found the lever that led to the handle on the opposite side of the door and, with all the force her teek could muster, pushed it in a direction it wasn't designed to go. The sound of warped metal echoed through the stairwell, and to her teek sense, the tightly-fitted machinery of the lock had turned into an immobile lump of metal.

"Move," she repeated as she turned to run after Zack.

The footsteps above them were closing, and as she turned, she could hear the guards on the other side of the broken door trying to force it open against its frozen lock.

Zack was already in the courtyard by the time Allison reached the door. She ran through it before it shut completely.

Somewhere, a siren began to wail.

As she ran to keep up with Zack, she remembered what had happened to Jessica. Somewhere, above them—and in a moment, behind them—there'd be a sniper with a tranquilizer gun.

Her teek's response to the thought was automatic. She wrapped herself, and the dead spot containing Zack, with her teek. The effort of covering such a wide area was a pressure behind her eyes. She had done it before she had fully emerged from the door, and before she could reconsider the effectiveness of spreading herself so thin, she felt something dart through the skin of her teek field.

Like when Macy had tossed a cue ball at her, Allison could feel an object splash into the field, and her brain felt the ripples as the field soaked up the energy. It hadn't been going as fast as a bullet, but it was fast enough to be painful.

Another invader tried to slice through her overextended field, tearing through her mind like a ghostly mosquito. Then another. And another.

The impacts became painful, another blow to her skull trying to prevent her concentration. She had to screw her eyes shut and run following her teek sense alone. She could follow Zack that way, he was a fuzzy blind blotch right in front of her, a ragged hole in her teek that otherwise blanketed them like a twenty-foot-diameter umbrella. The sheer wealth of sensory feedback was nearly as bad a blow as the needles firing into her teek. She could feel the whole universe wrapped around her.

Except for that hole where Zack was. She could feel nothing inside it. Worse, as they ran, the angle of the shots began to shift to focus ahead of her, toward him. Not only was it farther away and harder for her to teek, but if a dart punched through into the dead area—

The snipers confirmed her worst fears. She felt a rapid succession of three shots. The first shot slammed into her awareness above her. Even with her eyes closed, she could feel it plunge in and stop, hovering a few inches above her, as if it had plunged into a vat of molasses. It was another hard mote of matter hovering around her, like the others she'd stopped as they ran.

The second plunged between her and Zack. It was farther away, and the impact felt even worse, more like a bullet than a compressed air dart. This one took even longer to stop, descending to eye level before stopping between them. As it slowed, the dart briefly brushed into the dead area around Zack. Even though it was on the fringes of the area, it was as if the dart ceased to exist to her teek, and she didn't feel it again until it tumbled to the ground at her feet.

She was running over the lost dart when the third one pierced her teek about fifteen feet in front of her. The impact knocked the breath from her, even though it was primarily mental. If the last impact had been like a bullet, this one was like a small cannonball. It blew through the grip of her teek, and shot through the dead area around Zack.

Then, suddenly, she had run into the blind area and lost the sense of her teek. She collided with Zack, and they both tumbled to the ground next to the Ward building. The sirens seemed louder than ever.

CHAPTER
THIRTY

Macy's limping sprint ended with a dive into the drainage pipe, just as the camera began sweeping the ditch as part of the return pan. She didn't land well, sliding into the pipe on her shoulder, and John winced as he watched her dive in.

John leaned forward and called in a harsh stage whisper, "Are you all right?"

In response, Macy waved at him from her spot on the ground. She scrambled to her feet, crouched in the pipe and out of view of the camera. She duckwalked backward, nearly falling with her unsteady gait, and waved John forward.

John slid off the slope where he'd been presenting as low a profile as possible, and, in imitation of Macy, crouched in the bottom of the drainage ditch. He wiped his palms on his jeans as he locked his eyes upon the camera.

Macy kept gesturing frantically.

John waited, breathing deeply and wiping his hands. Then, as the camera panned past the ditch in front of him, he ran. He didn't limp, as Macy had, but he was older and couldn't match her for speed. He kept his gaze on the camera.

By the halfway point, John's cheeks were puffed with effort, his face was flushed, and the camera was already on its return pan. He sucked in his breath and accelerated.

Macy crouched in the pipe waving him forward and mouthing encouragement to him.

When the camera began to pan over the ditch, John was fifteen feet away from the mouth of the pipe. John dived forward, toward the cover of the concrete wall ahead of him. He hit and rolled on the concrete floor of the ditch, tearing his clothes and abrading the right side of his body.

He scrambled to the concrete wall next to the pipe, and leaned against it. Macy came to the mouth of the pipe and whispered, "You made it."

John nodded and wiped his forehead. His hand came away smeared with equal parts blood and sweat. "I'm not in shape to do things like this anymore."

"You beat the camera?"

John nodded again, still catching his breath. "Pretty sure I dived out of sight in time. Let's get into the pipe." He began pushing himself up the wall.

Macy put a hand on his shoulder, "Maybe you should give yourself a minute to rest. You trashed yourself pretty good."

"I don't think we have a minute," John said.

As if in response to John's words, a distant klaxon began sounding. Both of them froze in response to the bleating siren. "For us?" Macy said, the emotion leaking out of her voice.

"I don't think so," John said. "That may be Allie's diversion." He pushed himself up and entered the pipe. "We'd better move."

8:35 AM

Agent Fred Jackson stood outside Stone's office, talking into a pseudo-cellular phone. The sound of a security alarm from outside leaked through the walls.

The orderlies didn't look comfortable, and Fred—the one security person there—looked angry. He paced between the orderlies and the door, shaking his head as he shouted into the phone. "What do you mean, dead? Are you sure? How in the hell did this happen? When? What's the damage?"

As he talked, a trio of guards ran up the corridor toward him and the orderlies. The orderlies edged over to the walls, next to a painting of Annubis, to let the newcomers pass. The guards had their weapons drawn.

"Wait a minute," Fred said into the phone. He stopped pacing, pressed the phone to his chest, and snapped at the three guards, "And what the hell are you all about?"

They stopped in front of him and the lead one said, "There's been a serious security breach—"

Fred nodded. "Christ, I know that. I hear the damn alarm. I'm talking to the cleanup team now."

The three of them looked at each other with blank expressions.

"Shoot-out between security and one of our scientists. Security breach in the mainframe, right?"

The trio still looked confused.

"Right?" Fred repeated. This time it didn't sound as if he was asking a rhetorical question.

The lead guard shook his head. "I don't know about that. We're here because there's an active loose in a secure area—and Mr. Stone isn't responding to any calls."

"Shitfire." Fred backed up and pounded on the doors to Mr. Stone's office. The sound was muffled by the thick wood of the door. "Stone's in a meeting. Who got loose, where?"

"Allison Boyle, a Class III, near Medical. We have to talk to Mr. Stone, sir."

Fred nodded, and his knocking took on a desperate character.

"Who's Mr. Stone having a meeting with?" one of the other guards asked.

Fred stopped knocking, shaking his head. "Oh, fuck." He drew a gun from a shoulder holster.

"Sir?" said the lead guard.

"I told him," Fred muttered. To the others he said, "Jessica Mason is in there with Mr. Stone. She's another Class III." He looked back at the door. "We've already had problems with her." He backed away from the door and waved one of the new guards forward with the gun.

The orderlies backed down the hall as the security team followed Fred's lead and flanked the door.

One of the guards opened the door and stepped inside,

covering the room with his gun. After a moment he said, "My God."

The others slipped in after him. Fred yelled at the orderlies, "Someone get a medic in here."

Inside Stone's office, a grayish haze hung from the ceiling. One of the guards bent over behind the desk feeling around Stone's neck for a pulse. The guard was shaking his head.

Fred led the guards around the other side of the table. Video monitors and other piles of electronic equipment had been tossed onto the floor. A large section of the wall behind the desk, where the equipment had been mounted, was bare. A six-foot-long section of drywall had fallen from the wall and had broken apart on the dead pile of electronics.

One guard picked up a section of the drywall about a foot square. A hole was burned through it, about the diameter of the guard's little finger. The rest of the drywall was perforated by similar holes.

"How could this happen without setting off the smoke alarms or the sprinklers?" one of the guards asked.

"She disabled them," Fred said. He kicked the warped plastic case of a smoke detector as he approached the hole in the wall.

The hole went completely through the wall. A section of the rear wall, about six feet tall and four feet wide, was missing except for the metal studs that used to hold the drywall. Those studs all showed signs of being exposed to great heat. The surface of the galvanized metal was dark and had a rainbow sheen, especially around the fasteners where the drywall had been attached.

Beyond the wall was a darkened office, empty.

"Fuck it," Fred said. He put away his gun and pulled out his phone. He pressed a button and said, "We have a situation here."

8:40 AM

Allison opened her eyes when she hit the ground. They'd fallen under the walkway between the medical building and the Ward. The door to the Ward was about ten feet away. Zack scrambled out from underneath her, grabbing her arm. They started moving again just in time to avoid being hit by another dart.

He pushed through the door into the Ward. As soon as they were through the door, Allison could breathe again. "Are you all right?" Allison asked.

Zack reached up and pulled a small dart from his jacket and handed it to her. "I guess it didn't make it through the leather." He kept looking out the door and said, "That's a lot of darts."

Allison saw what Zack meant. Ten feet from the door, where the two of them had collided, a semicircle of darts lay on the ground where they'd been dropped by her teek. "Yeah," Allison responded.

"Here comes the cavalry," Zack announced.

Allison looked up from the ground and saw a quartet of guards making their way across the courtyard. They were halfway toward them already. "Run." Allison yelled.

She wanted to barricade the door, but these weren't like the fire doors she'd jimmied closed with her teek. These doors were mostly glass. She turned and started down the hall, and this time she pulled Zack after her.

"You're the guide," Allison shouted at him, "Where do they keep the kids in here?"

"I don't know."

"You don't know?"

"It's not like I've ever been in here."

Behind them, Allison heard the door to the courtyard fly open. She pushed Zack ahead of her, down an intersecting corridor, around the corner from their pursuers.

The corridors here were bare cinder block, and the ceiling snaked with an assortment of pipes. They passed brown-painted doors that were featureless except for white stenciled numbers on their faces. Behind some of them, Allison could hear the hum of machinery.

"We need to get upstairs," she said.

Zack nodded. Getting to the kids was part of the plan, and right now it looked like the kids, and everything else, were upstairs.

Allison had no idea how valid her plan was at this point.

It was falling apart just like every other initiative she had taken so far. Security wasn't supposed to be after them yet. How were they supposed to get out of this, even if they launched a decent distraction?

Dad and Macy were probably already in the hands of Prometheus.

Somewhere, in the back of her head, she heard a lone dissenting thought. *Think like that and you're going to die, sweetcakes.* With the thought came a horrid sick feeling that she didn't know whose thought it was.

She and Zack turned down a dogleg in the corridor which ended in a stairwell. At the corner was a freight elevator, and sitting in front of it were a pair of wheeled carts carrying between them about a dozen cylinders of compressed gas.

How serious am I about getting out of here? Allison thought as Zack passed the cylinders. She thought about her mother and had the answer to her question.

They both took the turn, and she could hear the security people running after them. When they turned, Allison stopped running and gasped, "Keep going, I'll meet you upstairs."

Allison could see an objection rising in Zack's face, and she shouted at him, *"Move!"*

He moved, though he didn't look pleased about it.

As soon as he had gotten beyond ten feet, and her teek began working again, she gripped the top valves of the canisters and began twisting them off. They broke off with the sound of sheering metal and escaping gas.

She didn't see their pursuers, but she could hear them in the corridor around the corner from her. She heard their running feet come to a halt as the fourth valve clattered to the ground. She heard someone down there blurt out, *"Shit."*

Allison began backing toward the stairs as her teek gripped the top of canister number five.

"Allison! Allison Boyle!" someone yelled from around the corner. "Give yourself up. You don't want to do this."

The top of the fifth canister spun free with a hiss. Allison kept backing toward the stairs. She yelled at the people around the corner, "You better move back from there."

"You can't get away with this. Give yourself up before more people get hurt."

More people get hurt? No one's been hurt yet.

Allison pushed the stairway door open behind her. Before she stepped through, she took out the dart that'd been caught in Zack's leather jacket. She tossed it into the hallway behind her.

"Back out of that hallway," Allison said, "and no one will get hurt." She stepped into the stairwell and pulled the door shut. When the door was shut, she grabbed the dart with her teek, lifting it off the ground and pointing it down the hall toward the canisters.

She stared down the hall through a tiny rectangular window, her view segmented by chicken wire. Her mind wrapped around the tiny dart with a numbing grip. The effort throbbed in her skull in time to her pulse.

"Give yourself up," came the voice, distant and small through the metal door. Allison was barely aware of the noise as she aimed the dart down the hall. *All that oxygen,* she thought, *one spark* . . .

"Give yourself up," the voice kept talking. "This is going to be your only chance. Security's been told to use lethal force to protect the complex."

On one level Allison was aware of the words, but on another her world was a fixed tableau, the dart floating in the corridor, the emptying canisters, and the trajectory between them. Her mind was tensed like a spring behind the dart, and when she felt-saw motion, her teek let the dart go before she was ready.

The motion was one of her pursuers rounding the corner. The man had a gun out. The dart shot down the corridor, faster than it was designed to go. Allison had been startled into throwing the dart, and the man had moved between it and the canisters.

Allison had planned to strike the dart off the canisters, and spark an impassable fireball. Instead, the dart slammed into the abdomen of the guard. It struck like a bullet. The guard's stomach erupted in a flower of blood as he doubled over.

Allison backed away from the window as the man collapsed. He fell into the carts, knocking canisters every-

where. The gun fell from his fingers. Allison tried to grab
the gun with her teek, but everything was going too quickly.
The gun struck the ground and discharged—

The corridor erupted in an orange fireball around the
man, and Allison ran, tears streaming down her cheeks.

8:45 AM

Jessica had spent all night planning the destruction of
Stone's dream, the dream that had betrayed her. Finishing
Stone wasn't enough, she knew that. Stone had been the
brain behind the machine called Prometheus, but PRI had
existed before Stone, and could conceivably exist after
Stone.

To Jessica, that possibility was now intolerable. Prometheus now saw her power as a threat, not an asset. Jessica
knew extremely well what that meant; she had seen it too
often. Threats to Prometheus ended in the Ward at best;
at worst, they were destroyed. Jessica knew, because she
had once helped identify such threats for Prometheus.

Stone had taken that control from her, and if she couldn't
control this thing called Prometheus, she had to destroy it.
If she didn't finish it, then Prometheus—in whatever incar-
nation—would surely destroy her.

She also knew, very well, what the heart of Prometheus
was. It wasn't the dormitories where the kids were kept.
For the most part the kids were expendable to Prometheus.
It wasn't in the classrooms, which were only a tool to keep
the kids in line—like the cafeteria, the gym, and everything
else that helped to shore up the facade that somehow the
kids' imprisonment was voluntary.

No, the heart of Prometheus was research. The testing,
the examinations, the processing of medical data that was
supposed to eventually lead to Stone's Change.

When she made her way back to the medical building, she
didn't make the mistake she had made yesterday. She
did not walk out into the open where a sniper with a dart
could put her down. She had left through the hole she'd
burned into Stone's wall, and had walked downstairs to the

underground tunnels that connected most of the Prometheus complex.

As she had walked, and as the degenerate drugs in her veins ate at her gut and her brain, she let her power slide behind the walls of the corridors. Inside the walls, synthetic insulation slid off of wires. Bare wires shorted out, charring their outlines in the wall, showering sparks from light fixtures, burning out security cameras.

As she had walked through the corridors to the medical building, everything electric died behind her. Twice, guards had tried to stop her progress. Once they were armed with darts, once with firearms. In both cases, a sudden influx of heat had ruptured their weapons. In the first instance, the liquid tranquilizer vaporized within the darts, wrapping the guards in a searing anesthetic cloud. In the second, the ammunition had exploded within the clips, tearing the guards' hands apart.

Both sets of guards had been easily finished off by cauterizing the major arteries in their necks.

There were doors locked in her path, but their components were metal, and their low specific heat easily succumbed to Jessica's will. Heat warped the locks holding the doors shut, until the door's skin glowed red through charred and bubbling paint. After that, they were easily forced open. No door delayed her more than fifteen seconds.

When she pushed her way into the basement of the medical building, she was driving the technicians ahead of her. Her warped and steaming door opened onto a forest of empty cubicles. To her left was a glass wall behind which sat the researchers' mainframe in air-conditioned comfort; to her right, three or four of Prometheus' researchers were pushing through an exit, away from her.

Jessica smiled, even though it felt as if the entire surface of her skin burned. Sweat stung her eyes, her muscles were cramped, and a migraine flowered behind her eyes. She was dimly aware that there was a possibility that her manipulation of their drug might have poisoned her. But she was past caring. If anything, her talent seemed more powerful than ever.

Her awareness expanded past the suspended ceiling, into

the pipes feeding the sprinkler system. The effort was almost reflexive now. Even in a point of view that rendered physical objects into an endless matrix of motes, she could still tell the copper pipe from the solder that held it together. The solder was a layer of motes that responded much more quickly to her power, so quickly that the solder went fluid, its motes escaping the binding of its matrix, long before the energy could escape into the nearby water.

For each pipe she did, the water pressure separated the pipe for her, draining the sprinkler system. Behind her, water began leaking around the squares of the suspended ceiling.

She walked into the room and turned toward the mainframe. This was the heart of Prometheus—research, information, the data they'd pried loose from the skulls of the kids they controlled. She stared into the white room. Inside were a number of white cabinets about as tall as she was. In the center of the room was Prometheus' Cray, sitting like a chunky top hat central to the room.

Jessica focused on the Cray.

Inside it, behind one of the panels, insulation began to slide off of wires, connections began to discolor, and semiconductors cracked, releasing white smoke.

All over the Prometheus complex, networked computers began to crash. When she was certain the computers were dead, and the air-conditioned room behind the glass was hazed with smoke, Jessica turned to follow the fleeing technicians upstairs.

8:50 AM

Allison caught up with Zack at the third floor landing. As she climbed up the stairs, she watched him strain against the door, trying to pull it open. He grunted acknowledgment to her when she was up next to him.

After another pull, Zack said, "Maybe we should drop this idea? I think we've already confused the hell out of them."

Allison shook her head. She could still see the man engulfed by the fire, and that wasn't helping her ability to plan their escape. "What's on the other side of the door?"

"Look for yourself," Zack said. "But you've got to get the door open. They've buttoned up the stairwell tight."

Allison bent over in front of Zack and looked out the rectangular window. The corridor here was the same shape as the one downstairs, but the walls were whitewashed, and the floor was carpeted. As downstairs, an elevator sat at the corner where the corridor doglegged out of her view.

Also, there was a new feature: a round mirror set at a forty-five-degree angle in the corner.

"Look in the mirror," Zack said. "What you can see is set up like a mental hospital or a prison. I think that's it."

Allison could see what Zack meant. The mirrored corridor ended in a wall that had a large featureless door. Set in the wall next to the door, was another chicken-wire window, behind which she could see an orderly moving around. This was it, or at least part of it. Behind that door were the kids Prometheus decided to lock up—

Was it right to go through with this? Allison thought of what the guard had said, *"Lethal force."* If she went through with this, she'd be putting those kids in danger.

Security made up her mind for her. She heard a door above them slam open, and she heard something small clatter down the stairs. Her eyes, nose, and mouth began burning.

"Tear gas," Zack said, pulling his shirt collar up over his nose.

"Away from the door," Allison hissed, trying not to inhale. She placed her hands over her mouth and closed her eyes. "Give me room."

She felt it when Zack had backed his interference away from her. She reached her teek through the door, finding the metal tongue holding the door shut. It didn't want to move, but she yanked it back inside the door with all the strength she could muster. The metal snapped, igniting a burning pain inside her skull to match the pain in her eyes.

She stumbled out the door for fifteen feet or so before she felt safe opening her eyes. The air still burned them, and everything was blurred. Zack, who sounded as if he was coughing up part of his lungs, slammed the door behind him as he followed.

Allison felt dizzy and realized she was still holding her

breath. She gasped, and when she started breathing, her coughing rivaled Zack's.

Tear gas? Allison thought. *Lethal force? They're terrified of us.* A small part of her mind, which sounded like Chuck, said *Why shouldn't they be?*

Allison began to realize just how irrevocable this all was. Even if she wanted to surrender, there was no way she could disarm herself. Right now, she was supposed to be drugged, so Prometheus security wouldn't even be able to trust *that* anymore. To these men, she would always be a threat. . . .

"Move," Zack gasped in a hoarse voice.

Allison nodded and whispered back, "Stay behind me." Her own voice sounded raw. "Watch my back."

Allison headed down the dogleg and toward the door to the secure part of the Ward. The door itself was emblazoned with all sorts of security warnings, "Yellow Access Only."

The orderly had seen them coming, and he was aiming some sort of weapon at them through the glass. There was a speaker mounted next to the window and it activated in a burst of static. "Now, why don't you just stay there and wait for the guards. We don't want anyone to be hurt here."

The gun he held wasn't a tranquilizer gun, Allison could see that. It was a real firearm, something designed to kill people. The orderly was red-faced and sweating. He looked terrified. However, his possession of that weapon made her lose whatever sympathy she had for him.

She wrapped her teek around the gun, a familiar sensation by now, and yanked it out of his hands. Unlike Barney, his grip was neither firm nor steady enough for the maneuver to injure him. He simply said, "Oh, fuck," as the gun flew out of his hands to slam into the glass shield separating him from Allison. The window turned opaque with cracks as it bowed out around the gun.

Allison kept pulling the gun, and the window made a sound like someone grinding sand into concrete. The window continued deforming in a convex bulge toward her. The only thing keeping the window an intact sheet was the chicken wire embedded in it.

Then the window stopped resisting her pull on the gun, and the window flowered out around the bulge, spraying fragments of safety glass everywhere. Allison let the gun go and it skittered on the ground behind her. Through the hole in the window, the orderly stared at her, aghast.

"Get out of here," Allison told him, her voice raw with gas and anger.

The man ran.

8:55 AM

"We should wait for her," Sean said. He faced Oscar and Thad in the nearly empty classroom building. "She'll know what to do."

Thad looked out the window of the lounge. His voice was heavy with irony. "I'm sure she would, Sean."

Oscar shook his head slowly. "The security here is panicked—"

"I can see that when I look out the window," Thad said. "Tell me something I don't know."

"What did you say, Thad?" Sean asked. The others ignored him.

"There's no need to act like an asshole, Thad."

"Sorry," Thad said. He continued looking at the window. The courtyard was normally filled with students at this hour, and the classroom building was normally a hive of activity. But the sirens seemed to empty the grounds, as if it was an air raid. Occasionally a group of guards would run across the compound, toward the medical building. "I would like some specific information."

"I was going to tell you. What I picked up seemed to be at least two students loose in the medical complex."

Thad cursed and turned around. "That does seem to be where everyone's running. Could it be people from the Ward?"

Oscar shrugged, "Do they have Class IIIs in the Ward?"

"It *is* her."

A disturbed expression crossed Sean's face. "Does this mean Jessica isn't coming today?"

Oscar looked downcast and Thad nodded. "I'm sorry, Sean, it seems that way." Under his breath, so Sean wouldn't read his lip movement, he added, "You poor love-struck bastard."

"Now what?" Oscar said.

"She isn't coming," Sean said, his odd accent growing thicker as he spoke.

Thad paced. "We have a lot of problems. From guilt by association all the way down to the fact that Prometheus security is probably going to make life here rather unpleasant after an incident like this."

Oscar nodded. "Don't I know it. But what the hell can we do about it?"

"We can get while the getting's good."

Oscar stared at him.

Sean shook his head. "Get what?"

"Security's in chaos right now," Thad said. "I don't think electronic surveillance away from the medical center counts for much at the moment." He reached out and grabbed Oscar's arm. "And with our telepath here, we can avoid the human guards."

"Just like that?" Oscar asked.

Thad shrugged. "We have an opportunity here. We take it or we don't." He tilted his head toward the dormitories. "We aren't likely to get a better one."

"You want us to leave?" Sean asked.

Thad looked up at the large man and said, "You don't have to come."

"You'd abandon Sean here?" Oscar said, distaste coating his voice.

"If he chooses to stay and wait for Jess, we aren't abandoning him."

"You're a cold bastard."

Thad shrugged. "I'm a pragmatist. I want him to come—I've always wanted to try our good luck charm in Vegas—but the time to leave is *now*. I'm not going to spend the time fighting about who's going."

Sean looked downcast. "Jess isn't coming, is she, Oscar?"

Oscar sighed, reached up, and put a hand on Sean's shoulder. "I'm afraid not, buddy."

Sean stared at Thad with moist eyes and said, "Let's go."

CHAPTER
THIRTY-ONE

03 NOVEMBER   NAVARRO COUNTY, TEXAS

9:00 AM   WEDNESDAY

Fred led a security detail, following Jessica Mason. It took them nearly half an hour to reach the mainframe in the basement of the research building. It wasn't because Jessica was hard to follow. The swath of destruction she wrought through the corridors of Prometheus blazed an unmistakable trail. What ate up time was the caution Fred enforced on the three-men team he'd appropriated.

Even Fred seemed to chafe against the restraint he placed on the team, but the need for such restraint was graphic and undeniable. The corridors they followed were illuminated by charred calligraphy, marking the location of every wire that had been buried within the walls. Twice they came upon guards who had been less cautious than they were, piles of corpses with burned hands and livid necks.

At the second pile of corpses, Fred had told his team, "Our only chance against this is surprise. We have to use overwhelming force before the target is aware of us."

The team had nodded in unison.

When they reached the mainframe, a choking white haze had migrated from the computer room to flood the entire basement. With the reduction in visibility, the team had to slow even further.

Fred shot questions into the pseudo-phone that connected him to what was left of Prometheus Security. After a few moments of heated debate over the phone, he called his team together at the opposite end of the computer room.

"Here is the news," Fred told his team. "We're authorized to use all necessary force to secure this situation. The sabotage here has taken down the whole network, including surveillance, but we have the rogue elements contained in the medical complex. Both buildings are surrounded and contained." He nodded at all of them. "Since the target is not leaving the building, we're going to do slow sweeps, by the numbers. If you see the target, you take it out."

Fred's team nodded.

Then one of them opened the exit and covered the stairwell beyond. Carefully, one by one, the team slipped up the stairs, after the target.

9:05 AM

The Ward made Allison sick. Ten minutes of throwing open doors told her that no distraction would come from here. Even Zack was left speechless. What Allison expected—and from Zack's reaction, what he had expected—was to find something akin to political prisoners. The forced normalcy of Prometheus elsewhere led her to expect to find regular kids here, dissenting, maybe disturbed like the twins she had seen in the film, perhaps even violent—

But not like what they found.

The doors, all of them, had shutters over the windows in them. Each door was stenciled with a case number, no names. Each of them had electronic locks that Allison had to force with her teek. Each of them opened on the same scene.

The rooms in the ward were large, their size necessary to contain life-support and monitoring equipment. Central to each room was the bed, and strapped on the bed was an immobile figure. Some of the kids were nearly cadaverous, some appeared to be sleeping, while some only stared at the ceiling when Allison pushed the doors open.

The two of them slammed open door after door, only to see the same thing. Boys, girls, catatonic, fed through tubes, breathing through tubes. It was like an intensive care ward, but Allison had the awful suspicion that none of these kids had anything wrong with them—at least not before they'd come here.

Only one of them spoke to her. When Allison opened the seventh door, the boy on the bed actually focused on her for a few seconds. "I know you," he whispered. "Pretty . . . Pretty . . ."

Allison raced to his side, but he had degraded into mumbling something incomprehensible. She looked at the kid's face, which had a wild expression on it, and felt an incredible feeling of hopelessness.

She looked up at Zack, who stood in the doorway staring at the babbling kid, and said, "It's like all they are to them is a life-support system for a brain."

Allison shuddered.

"Let's get out of here," Zack said. "We can't do any good here."

She didn't want to leave, but she looked down and saw that the kid wasn't even aware of her presence anymore. She didn't realize she was holding the kid's hand until she let it go.

After that, she let Zack lead her through the halls. "I'm sorry," Allison said to him.

"This isn't your fault," Zack said.

"Yes, it was *my* idea." Allison grimaced. She felt disgusted and naïve. "I was expecting some sort of prison revolt. Just open the doors and these kids would, would . . ." Her voice was choked off by a sob. It had been a stupid romantic notion, and now she and Zack were trapped here because of it.

She had stopped moving, and Zack put his arm around her to lead her along. For once the touch didn't feel uncomfortable. "Come on, Allie, you had no idea of the shape these kids were in." Zack sucked in a breath. "I certainly didn't."

They stopped in front of another secure door. Next to it was another glassed-in office, but this time there wasn't an orderly. "Hold on," Zack said. "I'll open this one."

Allison nodded as Zack slipped into the little guard office. It was obvious now that this security setup, unlike a prison or a mental hospital, was more interested in keeping people out than keeping them in. If she had given herself at least one more day to think, she would have realized how pointless ducking into the Ward would be.

"How do we get out of this?" she asked. All the initiative had drained out of her, she had no idea what to do next.

"We're doing pretty well with improv," Zack said from inside the little glassed-in office. "Good news, from the monitors in here, their security system seems to be down."

"Could that just be the office there?" Allison said, walking up to the glass and staring at Zack through the chicken wire.

"The camera down the hall, is the light on, is it moving?"

Allison glanced down the hall at the camera that should have been panning down the hall. It was frozen and its little LED indicators were dark. "It seems dead."

"Luck's on our side. No guards since the tear gas. That's why. No clue where in the building we are." Zack looked around the little office and picked up a little Styrofoam cup and sniffed it. "I guess they evacuated people quick."

"We don't have time." Allison said. "They know what floor we're on at the least."

Zack looked up at her.

"The orderly was the last to see us, and they must have flooded all the stairwells with gas—"

Zack frowned. "And shut off the elevators. They're trying to contain us, drive us somewhere." He flipped a switch to buzz open the door in front of them. Allison pulled it open and held it for him as he made his way out of the office.

"There's one direction I bet they haven't surrounded," Zack said.

Allison got his meaning immediately. "You think you can?"

Zack shrugged. "Worth a try when we get to a window."

"You're sure you've recovered from—"

"Who knows. Let's move." Zack pushed through the door.

If Zack could manage it, without getting shot, it was probably the only chance they had for getting to the airstrip. At least Zack's shot. Allison couldn't see herself teeking herself airborne and surviving. She could still vividly remember the feeling of dizziness and vertigo right before she slammed into the garage.

But it had to be possible, if Zack could do it.

What happened when she tried to levitate herself? She gripped herself with her teek and . . .

Realization struck her. Allison muttered, "I'm a fool." She slipped out the door after Zack. As she did, she called after him, "Hey, I've figured out the problem . . ." She trailed off.

Zack stood in the center of the corridor, staring down toward where the walkway connected the Ward to the medical building. The scene was empty of people, but Zack was backing toward her, away from the walkway.

Allison realized that she was hearing more than one siren now. Additional wails were raised against the klaxons that had accompanied them ever since they'd left the classroom building. These new sirens were closer, more piercing, and coming from beyond the walkway.

"Do you smell smoke?" Zack asked.

9:10 AM

Jessica Mason walked through the research building, leaving flames in her wake. No more guards stepped into her path, the building had been evacuated ahead of her. She was only accompanied by the sound of fire alarms and the crackle of the flames themselves.

Pain also accompanied her. There wasn't only the searing within her skull. Now every muscle in her body was torn by cramps that felt as if they severed her limbs. She was sweating and racked with fever, yet somehow she managed to continue walking.

She felt disconnected, watching from some tiny flare of identity inside herself. The pain didn't seem to reach her anymore. Instead, the pain seemed to feed the power.

Jessica really wasn't thinking anymore. The destruction was supposed to be a release for her anger, but instead, every time she destroyed something it seemed to heighten her fury at Stone, at Prometheus, at everything.

She'd balled herself up into her anger, and now she simply lashed out at everything around her. All the craft, all the subtlety, all the control, had eroded away. She no longer disabled the sprinklers, she simply fed the heat of her anger into random objects as she passed.

Couches erupted into black synthetic smoke. Bottles of chemicals exploded into corrosive clouds. Electronic equipment melted and sparked. Carpeting melted and charred in her path. By the time she reached the second floor of the building, her attacks were completely reasonless and random.

Then she turned a corner and saw him. Zachary Lanagan. They stared at each other through the walkway. Both of them frozen in recognition.

He backed away, and Jessica stepped forward. Seeing him—the person who had derided her, mocked her attempts to control what was happening, someone who held in disdain everything she had just lost—it fed the rage within her.

Jessica pushed everything she had at him, every flare of emotion fed into her power. She willed a holocaust and sensed . . .

Nothing.

The damn interference.

Suddenly, now that her anger again had a focus, her mind began to sharpen. To work again through the pain. She felt part of the world again. Heat blew against her from behind, where parts of the medical lab burned. White smoke scoured her nose and throat with the scent of charred foam rubber. Her skin was flushed, the sweat stinging where her flesh had been seared. Between her and Zack, the air in the walkway rippled in the morning light, casting shadows like water.

Above all were the twinned sensations in her heart, the feverish agony and the insatiable anger.

Zack might have sensed something, because he scrambled back from her. Someone was behind him—

Her.

There she was, the avatar of everything Jessica had lost.

Her replacement. Allison Boyle. Allison called something down the walkway to her, "Wait! We aren't the enemy."

Jessica laughed; the sound was strangled and tasted of soot. *Everyone* was her enemy.

She couldn't get past the interference, but the fire could. *Damn them both,* Jessica thought as she focused her mind above the two of them, around them.

"We can get out of this together," Allison was saying. Jessica tuned out the voice and closed her eyes, concentrating on the upper surface of the ceiling suspended above their heads. "Please, we can get past all of them."

It was hard to do at this distance, especially with tiles that weren't supposed to burn, but she could feel the tiles themselves begin to char, then smolder, sucking oxygen through the crawl space between the tiles and the ceiling. The temperature rose, the flames feeding themselves now with little help from her power, above the smoke detectors and the sprinklers, immune.

"We can help each other—"

Jessica could sense what was about to happen, so she opened her eyes. She didn't look at Allison, or Zack. She looked at the ceiling above them. She smiled as she saw the wisps of white smoke drifting down between the metal framework. Then the smoke was sucked back into the ceiling, one or two tiles were actually blown upward, in toward the ceiling, as the fire tried to feed its voracious appetite for oxygen.

And then the ceiling exploded.

9:15 AM

It happened too quickly for Allison to absorb it all at once. From out of nowhere came Jessica Mason. One minute Allison was trying to talk to her, the next, Zack was yelling, *"Allie, look out!"*

With those words, Allison felt him shove her toward the walkway. Allison stumbled forward, falling to the carpet, as the world erupted around her. It was as if Hell itself

opened above them. The air was sucked out of her lungs
as a burning wind blew her to the ground.

Burning debris fell on her back, and Allison rolled away,
out from under it. She scrambled away until she could think
clearly enough to realize that she wasn't on fire herself.
Then she looked back the way she had come.

There was nothing back there but a solid wall of smoke,
roiling toward her. Behind it, all she could see were flickering orange highlights that hissed and spat at her.

"Zack!" Her voice was hoarse, and sucking in the smoke
made her gag. *"Zack!"* she yelled between coughs.

Only the spitting flames responded to her. The smoke
stung her eyes, blurring her vision. She pushed herself to
her knees and looked around, but everything had turned
an even gray. The walkway was filled with opaque smoke.
Allison was beginning to feel dizzy.

Air, I need air, or I'm going to drop right here.

She felt out next to her with her teek, locking it into the
nearly insubstantial matter of the window. Then she pushed
it away from her.

She heard a crack as the window was freed of its frame,
and smoke began pouring out the hole in the walkway. She
could breathe a little now. Allison blew out another window and started standing up.

"Zack!" Her eyes were still watering. She kept telling
herself that he was on the other side of that holocaust and
couldn't hear her.

With the two windows open, the air cleared around her,
enough so that breathing didn't cause her chest to ache.
She tried to teek a third window, and felt into a dull dead
sphere of interference.

She almost thought it was Zack, but it was coming from
the wrong side of the walkway. It was suddenly difficult for
her to breathe for reasons that had nothing to do with
the smoke. She stood, shaking, and faced the direction of
the interference.

Jessica had to be stopped, and Allison knew of only one
way to stop her. She dove through the smoke at the interference. Even though she couldn't see through the smoke, she
was able to aim at the center of her teek's dead zone. Then
she passed the threshold, and her teek was blind to her—

And she knew that Jessica's pyrokinesis would be just as dead, as long as they were this close to each other.

Allison slammed into Jessica's midsection in a flying tackle. Jessica hadn't been expecting it. She folded over and fell to the ground in a heap under Allison. Allison scrambled for Jessica's hands, to pin her—

"Bitch," Jessica hissed at her through soot-blackened lips. Allison felt nails rake her face. She managed to grab hold of one hand in the scrambled tangle of limbs, but Jessica pounded on her, clawed at her with her other hand.

"Stop it." The smoke blurred Allison's eyes as she fought for control.

She may have stopped Jessica from burning anything more, but she was sprawled on top of someone four years older and as big as Macy.

"Stop it," Allison pleaded, "Before anyone else is hurt—"

Allison felt the breath forced from her lungs as Jessica slammed a knee up into her kidney. The pain sucked all the strength from her limbs, and Allison fell on her side.

Jessica rolled over, on top of her, wrapping her hands around Allison's neck. "But I *want* people hurt," Jessica said as she began to squeeze.

Allison scrambled madly against her, bucking, kicking, clawing at Jessica's face. But, like Chuck, Jessica was just too heavy for her to move. It felt like the world was beginning to spin, and, weirdly, the world began to lighten—

The smoke was clearing. Beyond Jessica's face, Allison could see the sky through the glass ceiling of the walkway. With the lack of air, it almost felt as if she was falling up into it, up into the sky. She knew she could give up, and things would be so much easier.

Even as the thought crossed her mind, Allison remembered her own voice saying, ". . . *even if people die.*"

She had promised Macy. Giving up wasn't an option anymore, if it ever had been. With the thought, she balled her hand into a fist and brought it up to Jessica's chin as hard as she could. The impact felt as if it broke her thumb. It did break Jessica's grip on her neck, allowing Allison to suck in deep, greedy gasps of the clearing air.

Jessica's head snapped back, and one hand went to her face. She wiped blood away from her hurt lip, her expression darkening, when the windows around them began shattering.

Allison watched in horror as blood erupted from Jessica's chest and mouth. It seemed that Jessica was already falling on top of her before she heard the first echoes of the gunshots.

Oh, God, that's what Zack meant. They were driving us here to the walkway, nothing more than an exposed glass tube that the snipers can shoot us through. The smoke was our only cover. . . .

Allison's thoughts spun in chaotic spirals as guns continued firing, and glass sprayed across the interior of the walkway. Being flat on the ground had been the only thing that had saved her.

Worst of all, Jessica was still moving. Blood was leaking everywhere, coating Allison. Jessica had been hit two or three times, and she was still moving on top of her.

Jessica reached up and put a hand on Allison's face. Allison winced, but it wasn't an attack. As gunshots played out above them, Jessica stared into Allison's eyes. She coughed a few times, spitting blood from her mouth and nose.

"Your turn, I guess," Jessica said.

Then she closed her eyes and rested her head against Allison's chest. Allison watched as her breathing came to a shuddering halt.

Allison realized that, until that point, she had never truly hated anything before.

She stayed there as the smoke continued clearing, and as the gunfire came to a halt. She stayed there, immobile, understanding what Jessica had felt. Prometheus had rained so much destruction on so many lives that even Jessica's lashing out seemed only justice.

A team of men entered the opposite end of the walkway, from the direction that Jessica had come. Leading the team was a man in a suit. His hair was slate-gray, and he wore a bald-eagle pin in his tie. He looked unmoved by the carnage in front of him. He spoke into a little phone and Allison could hear him say, "Stand down, we're securing the area. Get *some* teams out to handle the other security breaches."

Agent Fred Jackson, ASI. . . .

CHAPTER
THIRTY-TWO

When she saw Fred Jackson, Allison realized that she could feel out with her teek. The interference from Jessica was gone now. Jessica was gone now. The evaporation of the interference brought her death home to Allison more than the body lying on top of her.

"Watch your approach," Fred was telling the people behind them. "The snipers may not have cleaned the area. If you see a movement, shoot."

They didn't see her, or they didn't realize she was alive. She must look dead, covered with blood, soot, and glass, and with Jessica's corpse covering her. Allison froze every muscle, trying not to breathe.

These evil bastards wanted to *kill* her now. Even this precious talent of hers was expendable if it threatened their little project. It wasn't Stone's metaphysical Change. It wasn't the kids or the extraordinary things they could do. All that was important was Prometheus. All that was important was the damn organization, and to hell with anything that threatened it. It was a cancer; Prometheus had no goals, no purpose beyond perpetuating itself.

The destruction it caused, the people it killed, those weren't even a side issue. Allison realized that Fred would gladly kill every kid in the complex to save Prometheus. The inherent contradiction wouldn't even occur to him.

The guards closed on her, Fred in the lead. She had to do something, she couldn't hold her breath forever.

Remembering a line of quarters breaking the sound barrier, she felt out with her teek, and grabbed the fragments of safety glass the bullets had scattered on the carpet. Hundreds of solid little cubes embedded themselves into the ectoplasmic clay of her teek.

The group was spread through the walkway. Fred was ahead of all of them and almost upon her. Two others guarded the entrance they'd come through. The remaining one followed a distance behind Fred, looking everywhere Fred wasn't.

The glass rose, tilting to form a fragmentary wall between Fred and Allison. For a moment the glass hung there like a beaded curtain as she tried to reorient her teek to point down the walkway. It gave Fred time to react.

"Shit," he said, firing his gun. Allison felt a bullet slam into Jessica's body. In response, every ounce of energy she had at her command pressed those glass cubes down the walkway.

The sound of the glass striking every surface was like a short burst of rain, or a brief sizzling, like a hamburger on a grill. The effects of the glass tearing through the walkway were horrible.

Fred fell backward, scores of bloody holes torn into his face and body. The guard behind him dropped his gun and fell to his knees, clutching a spurting wound in his neck. The guards by the door slid to the ground, blood pooling around them. The wounds were worse than what Jessica had suffered, it appeared as if the glass had shattered—no, exploded—when it had hit.

Allison gasped and pushed Jessica off her. Then she scrambled back, without standing up. She kept low, all the way back to the Ward building. Back into the smoke, and cover. The floor here was damp, which meant that somewhere the sprinklers were working.

She didn't have much time to think about it, because armed guards appeared at the other end of the walkway. She could see them duck around the corner, looking up toward her. She backed farther into the smoke, trying to be invisible.

She found herself hoping that one of them would break

cover so that she'd have a shot at him, and she hated herself for the thought.

One of them rushed into the walkway, holding up a riot shield for cover. He took a station in front of one of the two wounded guards in the rear. Then they began removing the guard under cover. They were too far away for her to do anything effective, and teeking something like a quarter or a piece of glass wouldn't be effective against one of those shields.

They had her trapped against the fire behind her, and they knew it. They could swarm the walkway and overwhelm her in a few minutes. What could she do?

She looked out at them. There were now a trio of guards, huddling behind the Plexiglas shields, vaguely inhuman behind gas masks. It was like a war zone. Most of the glass had been blown out of the walkway, making it look like some half-blasted bridge in an old war movie—

Bridge.

There was no way her teek was strong enough.

However, they had reached the third guard, the one with the neck wound, and there were half a dozen of them in there, behind their shields. By the time they were in range for her to do something directly, it would be too late.

Allison wrapped her teek around the superstructure of the walkway, the end nearest her. Like the Jeep Cherokee, the metal offered her solid purchase for her teek, but actually forcing energy through her teek into something so massive—it was like tearing out hunks of her own brain. It wasn't only that she was trying to move tons of material, but she was trying to feel the resulting vibration.

She thought it would be impossible with her mind rubbed raw by all that had happened. However, in the midst of the effort-induced migraine, she felt the shift. Even though it was less than a millimeter, the fact that the object was so large, and occupied all her mental awareness, made it noticeable.

At the greatest deformation she pushed with all her ability, and let it rebound back.

The guards in the walkway had reached Fred. She was aware of them even though her eyes were closed. Everything in the walkway floated through the awareness of her teek. She felt her body curl into a ball.

She reversed the force of her teek at the point of greatest rebound. And repeated. And repeated. It was much slower than the machine they had tested her on, but somehow she fell into the pattern, the rhythm became as natural as her pulse. In fact her pulse conspired with her to match itself to the natural frequency of the walkway. Her heart, the dagger throbs in her skull, and the vibration of the walkway, all worked in time with each other.

She was dimly aware of movement in the walkway, the guards pulling what was left of Fred Jackson out of harm's way. The vibration was becoming noticeable. First it was audible as a screeching of twisted metal, then the movement of the structure reached a point where the guards could notice it. The guards stopped their advance.

The larger the vibrations' amplitude, the easier it got for Allison. The sound was now like someone repeatedly swinging a rusty door open and closed, open and closed. The walkway's movement was now measurable in centimeters, not millimeters. Allison's mind was so full of the walkway that it felt like her entire world was moving up and down in time to her pulse.

The walkway's sounds became louder, more insistent. She could hear the guards curse, and with her teek sense she could feel the mass of their bodies retreat back from where they'd come.

Allison still strained with the effort. It felt as if she was methodically slamming a hammer into her skull. The pain of it had become so regular and intense that it was numbing.

As the guards retreated, Allison slowly opened her eyes. She was on her side on the ground, sweat stinging her eyes as she stared past her knees. Seeing the walkway almost broke her concentration, even though she knew what to expect.

The walkway had been a gently arching rectangular tube connecting the second floors of both buildings. Now that arch was deforming up and down, more than six inches in the center, enough to see that something was wrong, enough to make the walkway look alive. The floor of the walkway sank and rose like the ocean.

Some of the guards sent wild shots toward her, but she still had the smoke back here for cover. She couldn't stop now or break her concentration.

For a long time—it felt like hours when it could have been only minutes—it seemed that the walkway was too well engineered. It would sway and buck that six inches, but no more—no matter how much of her teek she pumped into it. There was something in the design that was absorbing the shock she was putting into it—

Allison closed her eyes again and felt with her teek as she pushed on the walkway. In a weird way she could sense the forces inside the metal framework. It seemed as if the stresses inside the material changed the texture inside it slightly, but she could feel it with her mental fingers.

She found what she was looking for. A pair of struts inside the wall, almost directly below her. They were solid, but stressed a dozen times more than anything in the walkway. Every time her teek pulsed the walkway, the struts sucked up the excess like a shock absorber.

It took her a moment to think of how she had any hope of dealing with it. After a few moments, she shifted the focus of her teek to the structure immediately above and connected to one of the struts—only one.

She opened her eyes again. It took a few moments for an asymmetry to develop in the shaking of the walkway, a rolling side-to-side motion that was less than the up-down motion, but growing in amplitude.

With her teek, she could sense the asymmetry develop in the stresses felt by the struts below her. They were no longer equal. The one below her teeking effort was actually now under much less stress than the one next to it. Allison could feel similar effects all over the walkway. The asymmetrical deformation was multiplying stresses all over.

The structure sounded as if it was in pain. The ripples in the floor had grown in amplitude. The center of the bridge now deformed over a foot at its greatest extension, but now when the right side was raised a foot, the left was lowered by the same amount.

Allison could feel the walkway twisting itself apart just

like the Tacoma Narrows Bridge, bucking and moaning as if caught in an invisible hurricane. What remaining glass there was in the walkway's windows began to shatter, ruptured as their frames twisted out of true.

The guards stopped taking potshots at her.

Then, like the Tacoma Narrows Bridge, something gave way as the floor twisted. The left side of the span deformed downward, and with an explosive mechanical snap the floor kept going downward. Gravity peeled it away as if the floor of the walkway was shed skin.

The floor had been an integral part of the structure, and without it, the skeletal framework around the walkway began folding in on itself, tearing away from Allison's building and collapsing into the courtyard below.

When she let go of her teek, Allison passed out from exhaustion.

9:40 AM

"Am I dead?" Allison asks the empty halls of Euclid Heights High.

"No," comes an all-too-familiar voice. "I am."

She turns toward Chuck, her face burning with anger. "I thought I was rid of you."

"Not that easy, sweetcakes." He shrugs. "I just thought you'd like to know."

"Know what?" Allison asks.

Chuck waves his hand at the school around them. Allison looks, and it takes her a moment to realize that the school isn't abandoned. Kids are going to and fro, pushing past both of them, going to classes. The windows are open on a sun-filled sky.

"You did it," Chuck says.

"Did what?"

Allison regained consciousness believing that Chuck was kissing her. She pushed someone away and coughed up a few hacking breaths before she opened her eyes and saw Zack.

"What—" she tried to say, but she had to keep coughing up gobs of sooty-tasting phlegm. Even as she rolled over and coughed her throat raw, she could feel her face flushing.

"Thank God," Zack said. His Boston accent seemed even thicker now. She looked up at him. He didn't look good. He was covered with soot, his leather jacket was charred in places, and there was a nasty red burn on his right cheek. "I thought I lost you for a moment."

Allison nodded, still trying to figure things out. The coughing finally stopped, and she managed to suck in enough air to talk. "I thought you were dead." She looked up at him. "How'd you know the ceiling was about to explode?"

Zack smiled, winced, and raised a hand to his cheek without quite touching it. "I saw *Backdraft.* When a fire starts to inhale its own smoke, that's *bad.*" He slowly lowered his hand away from the wound on his cheek. "I pushed you away and tried to get out myself, through the door. I was a little late, but I made it." He winced again when he smiled. "Just."

Allison nodded. She was still concentrating on breathing the fresh air. Which made her realize that they were no longer in the medical building.

She tried to stand up, and Zack said, "Take it easy, I don't know how long you were lying there sucking up smoke."

Allison nodded and stood anyway, even though it made her feel dizzy. They were on a roof somewhere in the Prometheus complex. She turned around and felt disoriented until she saw a pillar of smoke about a thousand yards away, marking the medical building.

"Where—how—what—" Allison was dumbfounded, and a more than little wobbly. How long had she been out?

Zack stood up next to her, putting a supportive arm around her. "Where is an outbuilding sitting at the end of Prometheus' runway." Zack turned her away from the complex so she could see the tarmac, the hangars, and the control tower. "How? The air-Zack express."

Allison shook her head, "But the interference?"

Zack grinned again, this time with only the uninjured

part of his face. "There are ways around that. Ever see
Rescue 911?"

"What?"

Zack gestured at the ground where she'd woken up.
Lying on the ground was a long length of fire hose, tied
into a loop on both ends.

"They raise people into helicopters all the time. I just
dangled you out of range—landing was a bitch, though."

"Zack, you're a genius." Allison hugged him.

"The face, watch the face."

9:50 AM

Macy paced in front of the open door of the Gulfstream
Starship. She held one of the oversized tranquilizer rifles
carried by the Prometheus guards. Up until fifteen minutes
ago it had belonged to the man crumpled in a heap by the
hangar door. It had been over an hour since they had
emerged from the drainage ditch.

From that point, it only took ten minutes and three
guards for John to get them to the plane. Then it was a
matter of waiting.

Every few minutes Macy would glance over at the cock-
pit windows to watch John work on the plane. The rest of
her time was evenly divided between looking at the crumpled guard and staring at the chaos the Prometheus complex had become.

Since John had handed her a gun and told her to guard
his rear, seven guards had passed the hangar. Only one of
them showed interest in the airplane, and he stopped his
approach when he saw Macy and the rifle.

There were more escaping students than there were
guards. For the past fifteen minutes, since the echoes of the
last gunshots had faded, stealth no longer seemed a priority. The hangar opened on to the tarmac, and was in sight
of two of the major gates into the PRI complex, and both
seemed open and unguarded now. People flowed out of
them without challenge, in cars, golf carts, and on foot.

During the wait, Macy's expression grew darker and

darker. Occasionally she'd wipe her cheeks and mutter, "Allie, come on, girl," as she stared off at the smoke. Then she'd glance at the crumpled guard and begin pacing again.

It was almost ten o'clock when she raised the rifle at two figures walking toward the hangar. It took a few long moments before recognition dawned on Macy's face and she lowered the rifle. *"Allie!"*

Macy dropped the gun, ran up, and embraced Allison. When she broke off the hug, Macy looked down at the combination of blood and soot that she'd smeared on her own clothes and said, "Lord, girl, you look like hell. Are you all right?"

"I'm ambulatory," Allison said in a hoarse voice.

Macy looked over to the boy Allison was leaning against. He looked as bad or worse than Allison did. "Who's your friend?" Macy asked.

"Macy meet Zack, Zack, Macy."

"Charmed," Zack said.

"Great, I worry about your ass for hours, and you're going around picking up guys."

Zack shook his head, "Actually I picked *her* up."

Allison erupted into hoarse laughter.

"I don't get it," Macy said.

"Long story," Allison told her. "Anyway, he's coming with us."

"Hey, you can bring Rush Limbaugh as far as I'm concerned, as long as you're back." Macy put an arm around Allison's shoulder. "Now let's see if your dad can fly us out of this place."

He could.